HEARTLESS

ANNE STUART

D1553831

Impeccably Demure Press

READER LETTER

Dear Reader:

Okay, okay, I know I left you hanging at the end of SHAMELESS, and I promise I'll try not to do it again. Sorry it took me so long to get Emma and Brandon back together, but he was busy in the Highlands, healing, and she was learning to be a surgeon, and they weren't ready yet. But now they are permanently, eternally...spoiler alert...Happy Ever After, and I hope it was worth the wait.

Anne

CHAPTER 1

The pleasure of your company is requested at the baptism of Alexandra Emma Brandon Rohan, on the afternoon of March the eighteenth, in the one thousand eight hundred and forty-fifth year of Our Lord, to be held at the village church of St. Anne the Doleful in Upper Rippington, Suffolk, and to be followed by a reception at Starlings Manor immediately thereafter.

BRANDON LOWERED himself carefully into the chair. He'd learned not to throw himself into furniture as he once had—the price he paid was far too dear. He was wet and cold—he'd spent the last three hours hiking among the unforgiving crags of Ben Tarquin in the Scottish Highlands, his home for the last three years of self-imposed exile, and steam was rising from his woolens as he edged closer to the fire.

"By the smell of those wet clothes, you've been giving yon Tammas a run for his money," Noonan observed sagely, and Tammas, the springer spaniel who had traced Brandon's every step, lifted his head at the sound of his name, then dropped it down again. The dog was even more exhausted after their long hike than Brandon was. He used a gnarled walking stick to help him keep his balance with his impossibly game leg, but Tammas had to run ahead and double back, leaping with excitement, while Brandon had learned to keep a steady pace, inured to their lengthy, daily excursions.

"Give me a chance to dry out, old man," Brandon replied sourly. "I still haven't taken a swim, and the water in the burn is colder than a witch's tit. Let me just warm my bones before I subject myself to more punishment. And I might add that you're smelling none too sweet yourself."

Noonan cackled, pouring himself a deep dram of whiskey against the Scots cold. Brandon eyed the drink dispassionately. He had trained himself not to long for it, and he could even pour for someone else without his hands shaking, spend the afternoon with an open bottle and not break into a sweat. It was opium and its bitch of a sister, laudanum, that had twisted him in knots. The huge amounts of alcohol he'd consumed had only been to manage the effects of the stronger drugs, but he had no intention of ever going near any of them again.

He'd learned to work through those cravings by hiking no matter what wretched form of precipitation was coming out of the sky, and in the Highlands it was always something, followed by endless swims in the burns and lochs—sometimes breaking a thin film of ice in order to torment his body.

The results, slow but steady, were satisfying. His mother would have said positively remarkable, but his mother doted on her four children, no matter how badly they behaved, and he'd been the prize transgressor.

All this was well and good where he was. Returning to the bosom of his family, to civilization and all its temptations, would be another matter entirely.

Noonan was watching him from beneath his bushy brows, his expression wary. "So, are you going to go to the little one's christening?" he demanded suddenly. "You missed the first one, and this wee one is named after you."

Brandon's head shot up. "How did you know about that? Have you been reading my mail?"

"Of course not, me boy," Noonan said indignantly. "Your brother sent me a letter at the same time, asking me to make sure you do what he wants. It's time for you to go back home."

"This is my home," he said stubbornly. "It's not like this is Melisande and Benedick's first child. Why all the bother now?"

"It's the first girl, she's named after you, and you're her godfather."

"I never agreed to that. And it's only her middle name."

"Can't call a wee lass 'Brandon' now, can they?" Noonan snapped. His voice softened. "It's time, laddie. You can't hide away up here forever."

Brandon said nothing, staring into the fire. They were in the kitchen of the gamekeeper's cottage at Ballykeep, the estate his father had given him when he turned twenty-one—he'd refused to reside in the big house—and the peaty smell mixed with wet dog, wet wool, and whiskey was a familiar comfort.

Noonan was right, the sly old bastard, he thought wearily. There was no way he could live here forever until he'd faced his demons back home. There were ghosts back there, ghosts he had to lay. It was past time to face them and banish them once and for all. He had to make peace with Benedick at the very least, and see if he could find the answer to the half-memories that teased at him, disrupting a good night's sleep and offering no clarity in return.

He gave Noonan a grim smile. "We'll leave in three days' time."

"*We* will?" Noonan echoed in a startled gasp. "You know I don't go south of the border, me boy. It's no' good for me health." He managed a hangdog expression.

"I go, you go. They've forgotten all about you and anything you might have been involved in."

"The blasted police never forget anything," Noonan said glumly. "The only reason they haven't found me is they'd never believe a good Irishman would hide out in an uncouth, backward, benighted place like Scotland."

"It was over twenty years ago, and my family is not without influence in these matters. Either you come with me or I stay put. And what do you think the marchioness would have to say about that?"

Brandon knew perfectly well that Noonan was more afraid of Brandon's mother than a horde of policemen, and Noonan's glare left him unmoved. The old man reached out and took a drink straight from the whiskey bottle, wiping his mouth with the back of his hand. The rich

smell of the whiskey almost overcame the homely smell of food cooking, but Brandon didn't flinch.

Noonan eyed him gloomily. "Your mother isn't even going to be
there—she's still travelling in some godforsaken place with your
father."

"It doesn't matter. She'll hear you failed in your duty. She won't be
angry, of course. She'll just be very, very disappointed in you."

Noonan shuddered. "God save me."

"My brothers are intent on reforming me," Brandon said. "Charles
is convinced I should marry to redeem my reputation. He'll probably
be waiting with a special license and a bride at the ready. I need you to
protect me, Noonan."

Noonan snorted. "And you're so docile you'll go along with it
without a whimper?" He blew out a disgusted breath. "You're really
going to make me go, aren't you?"

"Same back at you, old man."

EMMA CADBURY WAS COVERED in blood. It splashed her face, her
hands, up to her elbows, and she scrubbed away at it, at her nails,
ignoring the discomfort.

The girl had died. Emma had done everything she could, and she'd
been convinced that this time she'd won the battle, but the poor girl
had died anyway. She was the third one in a week, and no matter what
Emma had done she'd slipped away, nameless in death as she had been
in life.

The smug, ill-trained coterie of men who served at Temple
Hospital had refused to look at the girl, and when things had turned
bad there'd be no one to save her. Emma scrubbed her hands more
fiercely. This had happened too many times, and she should be used to
it by now. She had yet to figure out why the women hadn't survived
when they appeared to be on their way to recovery, and she would not
forgive herself for that.

She was alone now in the small room they'd set up for her and she
stripped off her bloody clothes, down to her chemise, kicking off the

stained slippers and throwing everything into the bins, including the cap that covered her hair. Patients died. She couldn't weep for each one.

She stepped inside the cold shower bath the hospital had grudgingly provided. They could hardly let her leave the place covered in blood, and the handheld pump was easy enough to operate. The head of surgery, the stately Mr. Fenrush, had accepted her under duress, but Temple Hospital was the best in London, in the entire country, and she'd wanted to work there rather than a glorified butcher shop. Benedick Rohan, her best friend's husband, had generously seen that she did, and Mr. Fenrush's outrage had caused her a little discomfort and a fair amount of quiet amusement.

She was anathema to him on every level. There were a few female physicians, with their very proper honorific of "doctor," in other countries, but not in England. Female surgeons, ones who actually cut into flesh, beggared the imagination of all but the most broad-minded of men. Emma was content to work behind the scenes so as not to horrify English society. The fact that this particular surgeon had also been one of London's most notorious madams in her early twenties would have made it even more appalling. The revolt that had followed her appearance had been long and ugly, led by Fenrush himself, who seemed to view her as a colorful combination of the Antichrist and the Whore of Babylon with a trace of Jezebel and Satan thrown in for good measure. He was a Godly Man, or so he had informed her, but instead of praying over her he seemed more likely to cast her to the wild dogs, as Jezebel was, or into St. Matthew's fiery furnace.

Instead he had no choice but to accept her presence, to treat her with the barest minimum of decency, since Benedick Rohan, Viscount Rohan, heir to the Marquis of Taverstock, was a major benefactor of Temple Hospital. If Benedick withdrew his support, there would simply be no hospital, and at least she labored in obscurity, and the men were more than happy to take credit for her successes.

Mr. Fenrush's absolute hatred of her always struck her as extreme, but she'd run into it before, usually in similarly Godly Men. When Fenrush realized he couldn't get rid of her, he had done what he could to make her presence invisible. She entered the operating room after the chloroform had been administered and was shunted from the place before the patient woke up and discovered the horror of a female's hands upon him.

But in between, she was learning everything, and some of the supervising surgeons had eventually let her participate and then conduct the surgeries.

She generally counted herself content, which was a triumph in itself. Between the hospital and her work at the Dovecote, her best friend Melisande's charity for fallen women, she found her life filled.

A rough cough wracked her body again, and she let out a sigh of weary frustration. It had been a terrible week, and not just at Temple Hospital. She still had smoke in her lungs from the recent fire, and the foul London air wasn't making it easy to get rid of the irritation.

The Dovecote had gone up in flames. Her dearest friend's townhouse, the building that had served as a home for what were described as "the poor unfortunates,"

and what Melisande's husband had named the Gaggle, was gone. This place for the women to live and learn a new profession, a way station to a new life, was now a pile of rubble and ash.

It had been a close call. Melisande lived with her husband in Suffolk, and she'd already repurposed the dower house on the estate for her soiled doves. The last few women had left the day before the fire, thank God, or Emma would have been burying her old friends like Mollie Biscuits and Long Polly.

Instead Emma had been alone in the place when the fire broke out, trapping her, and if she weren't so familiar with the house she would never have survived. As it was, she'd managed to escape with nothing worse than a lungful of smoke and a few scratches, minor inconveniences that were slowly abating.

Now she cleared her throat as she wound her braids around her head, securing them with a few rough stabs of the metal hairpins. She didn't bother to check in the mirror someone had placed for her convenience. She knew her hair was neat, she knew what she looked like, and if she forgot, those around her reminded her.

Emma Cadbury was cursed with a beauty that no effort on her part could diminish. That beauty, that perfectly symmetrical arrangement of features, had only caused her misery, pain and disaster. She'd been forced to become a whore, and she'd spent five years servicing strangers until the woman who'd entrapped her died and Emma took her job. As the youngest madam in England she no longer had to endure the pawings of men, and she'd been gloriously, happily celibate ever since. She had every expectation that pleasant state would last the rest of her life, at least if she had anything to say about it.

Her one regret was her loss at a chance of children. She was a born nurturer, and she expended that energy on her patients, on the never-ending supply of soiled doves looking for a new life, and on her friend Melisande's babies. She'd just delivered Melisande's second in three years—not that Melisande had needed much help. She was made for having babies, sailing through pregnancies with no trace of morning sickness or unexpected tears, and her labor and deliveries were fast and efficient. Considering that her panicked, overprotective husband had lost his first two wives in pregnancy and each time he'd expressly forbidden Melisande to get pregnant, this was a Very Good Thing.

Emma threw her drab cloak over her shoulders, ready to face the cool night air. She could feel the crackle of paper in her pocket: her formal invitation to the christening of Melisande's daughter, and she was looking forward to it. Days of being coddled, the chance to check in on the doves at the Dower House near Starlings Manor, would enable her to return to the hospital rested and refreshed and ready. Ready to deal with Mr. Fenrush's haughty superiority and attempts at sabotage, to deal with the myriad of indignities heaped on her by his sycophantic followers.

In truth, she would have given a great deal to apply her impressive medical skills elsewhere. On the battlefield men wouldn't be so picky. Had she been present in the Afghan War, she might have been able to treat the injuries of Melisande's brother-in-law, Brandon, at the time they happened, instead of leaving him with a ruined face, a weak leg, and the need to disappear into alcohol and opium.

She would never have me Brandon Rohan had he not ended up in the ward of the charity hospital she'd been working in, and it had taken her a long time to recognize the connection between her best friend and the desperately wounded soldier who had no memory of his own name. She'd been foolish, letting down her guard, but then he'd disappeared, which she counted a blessing.

She had little use for men, but Brandon Rohan had been unlike any other. Broken as he was, his wry smile, the beautiful unmarred side of his face, his strong hands had made her think of things that should have shamed her. She wouldn't have called it desire—that was not for the likes of her—but she had found herself wondering what it would feel like to be in bed with him instead of servicing a wheezing old man or a vicious young rake.

She knew that pleasure in the act of copulation, much less joy, was impossible for someone like her, but she thought of him sometimes and wondered what could have happened if life had been different. Before she had fallen from grace she'd been a solidly middle-class country girl, far beneath his touch. Still, Brandon was a younger son of a marquess, and the Rohans were notorious with their refusal to follow the dictates of society. Anything could have been possible.

Not any longer.

She refused think about it. Well, hardly more than the rare occasion when her defenses were down and her spirits were in the doldrums. Even good, sweet country girls didn't marry aristocrats. She was content to know he was now safe and happy, far away in the Highlands, and no longer her concern.

She let herself out the back door into the cold, gloomy streets near the London docks. Mr. Fenrush had barred her from using the front door in case anyone suspected she might have a more active job than rolling bandages. The power wielded by Benedick, Melisande's husband, was impressive, but it would never do to overestimate the amount of tolerance in the medical establishment. There was only so much an impressive donation could buy.

Emma moved down the back streets, her head down, unworried. She carried a pig sticker with her, and most of the denizens of the area knew who she was and kept a respectful distance. She was both one of them and a step above, and she was generally left in peace. If some drunken gentleman happened to wander off the beaten path and think she was fair game, she either disabused him of the notion or one of the locals would take care of it.

It wasn't a long walk to her lodgings, for London neighborhoods were a confused mass of slums, the bourgeoisie, and the upper classes, and when you turned the corner you never knew what you might find. The shabby house in Dosset Street was clean enough, and a short walk along the docks to the hospital, and that was all she needed.

Viscount Rohan and his lady were still offended that she refused to stay in their mansion on Bury Street, but she'd been adamant. Someone had to keep an extra sharp eye on the girls of the Dovecote, and Emma's lodgings were just a short walk away from there as well. That excuse had gone up in flames, but she still had no intention of leaving her neat rooms. She'd already accepted more help than made her comfortable—on this she would hold firm.

The streets were busier than she expected. It was autumn, darkness was coming early, and she pulled her hood over her dark hair, threading her way through the crowds. This area was busiest at night, and she had no illusions as to how most people made their living. She had done more than her share of sewing people up, administering tonics, seeing to the dying. She helped anyone who came to her house, be they thieves, river pirates, whores, or runaways. Her path home led her down by the river, and the water was her guide when she didn't want to look up and show her face. She was hurrying by, trying not to identify what was floating in its malodorous waters, when someone in the throng brushed up against her.

She didn't like being touched, and she had already pulled her cloak more tightly around her when she was bumped again by the milling crowds. And then a third time, hard, and she felt herself falling, flailing, toppling into those dark, cold waters with a scream dying in her throat.

She sank like a stone as the river closed over her head, and for a moment she struggled, panicking, blinded by the murky water and the darkness. Almost immediately, though, her level head took hold, and she kicked, pushing herself upward toward the light, until she broke through, gasping for air.

No one seemed to have noticed she'd fallen, and she struck out, heading toward the dock and the slime-encrusted ladder that led to dry land, thanking God her country upbringing had included swimming. Her shoes were heavy, her skirts even more so, and the water was numbingly cold. By the time she crossed that short distance she was gasping for breath, her limbs leaden.

Her fingers slipped on the mossy wood rungs of the ladder on her first attempt, and she tried to call out for help, but her voice was only a muffled croak that barely reached the scurrying denizens of the docks. Taking a deep breath, she tried again, hauling herself upwards with an unladylike grunt.

It took all her strength to hold on to the ladder, her heavy skirts pulling at her, and she stayed very still, trying to gather her resolve. Gritting her teeth, she climbed another rung, and then another, until her sodden skirts were free of the water. She knew she should unfasten her cloak and let it go, but she was unwilling to admit even that much defeat, so she simply kept moving, gasping for breath, until someone finally noticed.

"There's a woman down there," a rough voice called, and suddenly everyone was peering down at her as she clung to the ladder, unable to move any higher. Blessed hands reached down for her, and she was hauled out of her watery grave, pulled to safety as she sprawled on the filthy streets, fighting to catch her breath.

Remembering the unimaginable filth beneath her, she managed to sit up. Her rescuers gathered around her—Becky, who ran the pastry shop, was there, and Jem from the nearby hostelry. For a moment, she thought she saw Collins, one of Mr. Fenrush's servants, but when she looked again he had disappeared into the crowd. She struggled to her feet with the help of her rescuers and managed a lopsided smile as she thanked them in a hoarse voice.

"Now you come along, dearie," said Becky. "You need some dry clothes and a warm fire.. ." The woman wrinkled her nose. "And a bath, I'm thinking. I'll help get you home."

Emma glanced around her. To her surprise she wasn't far from her rooms, and she nodded with gratitude. She could have walked it by herself, her wet skirts dragging after her, but for once she was willing to accept help. She had treated Becky several months ago for a woman's complaint and refused payment, so she could accept this much as a fair trade.

She even managed to inquire after Becky's health. By the time they reached her front door she was ready to collapse, but she refused any more assistance, gathering her sopping skirts over her arms to keep them from making too big a mess, not caring if she exposed an indecent amount of leg. It wasn't until she was safe inside her rooms on the first floor that she began to shake.

Holding onto a wall for support, she began to strip off her clothes —her cloak, dress and petticoats, her shoes, until she was just in her chemise and knickers. She leaned her head against the wall, uttered a low curse, and stripped off the rest, until she was completely naked. Her home consisted of two rooms—a parlor and a small bedroom— and she headed toward the back, immeasurably grateful that she always paid for water to be brought. There were two larger ewers, warm from being near the banked fire, and a strong carbolic soap she used to cleanse herself once more—she was a firm believer in cleanliness when it came to medicine, unlike the majority of her colleagues. Even her long hair smelled of the river, and she sighed as she leaned over the basin and scrubbed her scalp. If she lived at the mostly unoccupied Rohan house on Bury Street she could have the luxury of a warm bath —for now she had to clean herself piecemeal. When she was as clean as she could get she drew on a warm, shabby robe and sank into her one comfortable chair, too weary to even stir up the fire. At least she would have a full bath when she arrived at Starlings Manor.

She leaned her head back against the chair. She'd had the devil's own luck recently—first the fire, now this. She was well overdue for a rest. Until then, she needed a cup of strong tea, some toasted cheese, and the indulgence of the small and very expensive orange she'd bought yesterday. Then she would review her notes for the day, pack for her journey to Starlings, and fall into bed.

Where she would never, absolutely never, dream of Brandon Rohan's beautiful, ruined face.

BRANDON WAS LATE, of course. He'd underestimated just how damned uncomfortable more than a week in the saddle would be. He was stronger, better, but it had been a long time since he had ridden such a distance. His thighs were burning, his knee was in agony, his bum ached, and he wanted nothing more than a hot bath before he made himself presentable. His only consolation was that Noonan looked as disgruntled as he felt.

They had no idea he was coming. Starlings Manor was enormous—it could easily swallow up scores of guests, so prior notice wasn't a necessity, and he hadn't been certain he was actually going through with it until he approached the front gates. If there were any problems he and Noonan could sleep out under the sky—he done it often enough in the less hospitable climate of Scotland, in rain and snow, and the soft Suffolk air would be far more comfortable.

Something else was aching as well. His stomach was a hard, painful knot of nerves. He hadn't been among company, hadn't seen most of his family in three years. Would they have forgiven him?

"Maybe we ought to stop at the inn to clean up before we show up at the house," he said gruffly.

"None of your excuses, Master Brandon," Noonan said in the same rough voice he'd used to drive him over rocky trails to strengthen his knee. No matter how much Brandon had hurt, he'd endured Noonan as the old man pummeled and pounded and pulled at his crooked leg until he'd passed out from the pain, only to come to and find the old man was still torturing him. The ability to walk without much of a limp came at a steep price, but he'd willingly paid it.

He stared up the long, winding drive, and accepted there'd be no delaying his reentry into society, or at least into his family. Without another word he nudged the horse on toward his brother's house.

Starlings Manor was a well-run household—the servants had seen him coming, and by the time he and Noonan had reached the broad front steps the grooms were already there to take the reins.

And watch him dismount, Brandon thought with a trace of bitterness. Somehow, he had to climb down off a horse with grace when he was hurting just as he endured the worst of Noonan's torture.

There was no way to spare his weak leg, but for once Noonan decided to be generous, scrambling down off his horse and heading toward Brandon, taking the reins and pushing the grooms aside.

"I see to my master and no one else," Noonan said in a threatening tone that was almost unintelligible with his Irish brogue. He moved to Brandon's side, shielding him from the eyes of the stable hands, and his support was almost invisible as Brandon threw his bad leg over the horse and set it on the ground, weaker than it had been in years.

"Told you we should have taken the carriage," Noonan muttered under his breath. Brandon responded with a grunt, waited until he knew he was steady and stepped away from his mare.

Screw your courage to the sticking post, he reminded himself, turning to Shakespeare's Prince Hal for inspiration. He could face them all without betraying weakness and face them he would.

He and Noonan were halfway up the front steps when Richmond, their aging butler, came rushing up. "My Lord Brandon! Is it really you? I could scarce believe it when I saw you coming but I said to Cook, no one has that Rohan face except the Rohans."

"It's me, Richmond," he said, resisting some cynical comment about his imperfect countenance. "Time doesn't stand still for most of us, unlike you. You look younger than ever." The butler was eighty if he was a day but damned if the old man didn't smirk with appreciation. Richmond had always been susceptible to flattery, something that had been very useful to a misbehaving teenage boy.

"You've missed them, you know." Richmond said.

Sudden relief washed over Brandon. He was prepared to do his duty but putting off his trial by fire was a blessing. "I was afraid of that," he lied. "It's hard to keep track of time when you're travelling such a distance. When was the christening?"

"Why, it's happening at this very moment, Lord Brandon," Richmond said cheerfully, missing Brandon's stiff expression. "If you ride fast you might make it to the church on time."

Bollocks, Brandon thought, his momentary reprieve vanishing. "I couldn't show myself to my sister in such a state," he said, brushing at his breeches. "I've got half the dust of Scotland and England on my clothes, and Emma is worn to pieces."

Richmond jerked his head up, looking at him strangely. "Emma?"

"My horse," said Brandon. "That beautiful black mare you see over there. I've been pushing her much too hard for the last ten days."

For a moment Richmond was silent as if considering something and then he straightened. "Surely you don't think a house such as Starlings would be so ill equipped as not to have extra horses? The coachman will mount you immediately and if you give me five minutes I can get the dust out of your clothes and off your face and make you quite presentable, even with such long heathenish hair."

"Don't even think about it." Brandon hadn't cut his hair since he left for the North and it reached well past his shoulders. He indeed felt like a heathen, a wild man, and he liked it so much that he had no idea when or if he would cut it off. Right now it was in a braid down his back and he was leaving it that way, whether his stuffy brothers would be horrified or not.

Then again Benedick wasn't nearly as stuffy as he used to be—ever since Melisande had taken him in hand he'd become positively playful. The third Viscountess Rohan had brought his brother back to life. It had taken Brandon a while to see that but once he did, he blessed the woman who had only seemed to be an annoyance while he had sought out his various perverse pleasures. He wasn't looking forward to meeting her again with a clear mind—he could remember little from that time and most of it was horrifying.

Benedick might be less stuffy now, but this time his older brother had every right to lecture him, to take him to task for the things he had done. Brandon deserved every harsh word, and he would listen without protest. He owed his brother for his life, for bundling him off to Scotland when chaos had erupted, for cleaning up the horrific mess he'd left behind.

He'd been such a coward for that short, dreadful time when he'd run afoul of the Heavenly Host, the group of harmless miscreants who'd unaccountably turned evil. He'd been drinking too much, though he couldn't remember why, presumably from the pain he'd endured, and with the amount of opium he'd smoked it was lucky he'd survived. Once he'd gotten to Scotland, Brandon had sworn never to shirk his duty again, and he'd fulfilled that promise. Nothing would expiate the sins of the past, but he wouldn't stop trying. He'd already come this far—he wasn't about to start out his visit to his family by running away, no matter how desperately he wanted to.

He nodded. "Noonan can see to my coat," he said gruffly. "Just find me a mount." He debated whether to specify a calmer ride than he was used to. Damn it, there was no shame in a bad leg, particularly considering how much work he'd done to strengthen it, but he couldn't bring himself to ask. He'd always ridden the wildest horses, reveling in his mastery, but that was another lifetime.

"Merlin, Master Brandon?" Richmond suggested, and Brandon made sure not to show his relief. Merlin was a huge gelding with perfect manners—even a young girl wouldn't have trouble controlling such a gentleman. Had Richmond known? Of course he had. He'd been there in London, knew the breadth of Brandon's injuries.

He nodded his acquiescence while Noonan brushed the dust from his coat. His old friend was grumbling under his breath the whole time. "You want I should come with you, me boy?" he muttered.

"You can't take care of me forever," Brandon said, pulling away as Merlin was brought forward, already saddled. A moment later he was mounted and ready to go, and for a brief moment he wondered what would happen if he took off for the North instead of across the fields to the small chapel attached to the estate.

Pride was all he had left at this point, and he hadn't much to waste. He wasn't going to cut and run. He nodded at Noonan, and then took off into the afternoon light, heading for the chapel.

CHAPTER 2

Baby Alexandra slept through the christening in her mother's arms, her sweet, pink face serene in the sleep that always came at inconvenient times and never when her mother was exhausted. Emma's hands itched to hold her, but she remained decorously still beside the baptismal font as the old vicar droned on and on about smiting the devil and watching over this precious child. Emma doubted that she and the vicar had the same view of the devil, since he seemed to think she was Old Nick's incarnation, but she would defend this baby with her life, as well as Alexandra's brother Gabriel who now sat in the front pew, restless on a mild Saturday afternoon.

She would get a chance to hold the baby soon enough, once Alexandra awoke and started to shriek, probably the moment the vicar poured cool water on her little forehead. It would serve the disapproving old man right.

Not that he disapproved of the baby or her parents, or even any member of the notorious Rohan family—he wasn't a complete fool when it came to who provided his living. But Emma was a different matter. High spirits in an aristocrat equaled degradation in a middle-class girl, and the old man clearly knew her history.

Too damned bad. If she tried to cower away from anyone who

knew her past she would spend her entire life running away, and she'd already wasted too much time as it was.

No, she'd made herself a good life, a happy life. She had Melisande's children to dote on, she had the Dovecote, she had her work. She had far more than she ever thought she might have, and she was foolish to long for more. She shifted slightly in her too-tight shoes, the only pair she owned that weren't stained with blood or the filthy Thames, and smiled at the sleeping baby.

The sound of the heavy wooden door opening was enough to pull her attention away, and she looked up, through the mottled shadows. Everyone turned to see a tall, strong figure standing in the doorway, the bright daylight surrounding him. He looked like a fallen angel, and Emma's breath suddenly caught in her throat as he started down the aisle toward them, not rushing, moving with a kind of casual grace that belied the faintest of limps. Her skin began to prickle.

"Brandon!" Viscount Rohan called out, his voice filled with joy, his face taut with emotion. He moved swiftly down the aisle to meet the newcomer halfway and pull him into a rough embrace.

Emma instinctively ducked her head. She was wearing one of the new poke bonnets with a wide brim, and if she kept her head lowered he'd have a hard time seeing her face, and she could fade into the background. She edged behind Melisande surreptitiously, trying not to draw attention to herself.

She didn't want him to see her face, to even notice her presence. She'd let go of the ridiculous fantasy of Brandon Rohan long ago, and she was the better for it. He had been the only person on this earth who'd made her vulnerable, and she would rather abandon all pride and hide than risk her heart.

The elderly vicar had taken a step back to allow the family reunion, and the christening guests buzzed excitedly. The dark exploits of Brandon Rohan and the Heavenly Host had never been adequately covered up, and they would find a great deal to gossip about.

And then, amidst the flurry of embraces and excited laughter came the words she most dreaded. "Emma, allow me to introduce my brother-in-law Lord Brandon Rohan to you," Melisande said, socially correct when she cared to be. "Brandon, this is my very dearest friend, Mrs. Emma Cadbury."

Emma nodded her bowed head, keeping her eyes lowered. She didn't want to see the strong, muscular body that had replaced his skeletal, broken one. In truth, she didn't want to look at him at all—she was much better off with him living four hundred miles away in the Highlands of Scotland.

A large hand reached out to touch hers, and lightning sizzled through her arm. He had removed his riding gloves, and she could feel his strength in the hand that had once been thin and weak. "Mrs. Cadbury," he murmured, and she knew that voice so well. It was cool now, though, different from the faintly humorous one when he'd lain in hospital, his body ruined but his spirit intact.

The monsters of the Heavenly Host, that decadent group of so-called gentlemen, had put paid to that, until he'd ended up.. .

She wasn't going to think of that. She dipped a slight curtsey, keeping her head down. She didn't want to look at him—this was hard enough. She'd managed to forget about him—at least, almost everything about him, but if she saw him she'd be vulnerable once more, and she couldn't afford any weakness.

"Lord Rohan," she murmured, making her voice a little more raspy than normal. She didn't want to do anything to jog his memory, to look at her closely. He'd probably thought she was a figment of his imagination, the so-called Harpy who'd bullied him into taking his medicine, who'd dressed his wounds, and teased him back to life.

The woman who had saved his life the night he decided to hang himself.

"If we may continue with the baptism.. ." the vicar was saying in a disapproving voice.

"Stand with Emma," Melisande said helpfully. "She's Alexandra's other godparent."

Without a word Brandon took his place by her side, and she cast a covert glance at him from beneath lowered lids. He was much taller than she remembered, but then, she'd never stood beside him. His injuries had kept him bedridden for the short period she'd taken care of him. One look told her he was wearing his dark hair in a long, unfashionable queue, a second was that he was very much bigger than she was. Scotland had been good to him. Despite the ruin of his face and leg, the ruin of his life, he'd managed to pull himself back from the brink of utter disaster and become the man he should be. That knowledge filled her with joy, something she would celebrate more fully when she was safely alone. He was going to be fine. She'd always known it, but having the proof standing beside her almost banished her complicated emotions.

Keeping her eyes down, she observed what she could see of his body. His legs were impossibly long, and he didn't use a cane. That in itself was astonishing when she remembered the wounds she'd bandaged, but in that quiet time in the hospital she had learned one thing—he was as stubborn as she was. She wouldn't put anything past his abilities.

She could see his ungloved hand resting lightly at his side. He had beautiful hands—she'd always loved them. Long fingers, elegant and strong, and suddenly she remembered something else.

Brandon Rohan had made her feel things she'd thought she was incapable of feeling. After years in the trade, servicing men for their pleasure, she had been sure she could never bear to have a man's hands on her again.

But he had touched her, and she'd wanted more.

Now fate had thrown them together once more, and her normal courage failed her. She wouldn't panic—she simply had to get through the christening and the festivities afterwards and hope he didn't pay any attention to her. Tomorrow morning she'd come up with some excuse to head back to London rather than spend the next five days avoiding him. In truth, she had good reason to go. The sudden rise in attacks on what people thought of as "the poor unfortunates" meant she had more work, given that Mr. Fenrush and his coterie refused to waste their time with undesirables. She'd already spent two days at the large Dower House that served as the rural Dovecote, the term some wag had come up with for Melisande's home for women wishing to change their lives, and for the time being there was nothing else to do. The newcomers to Rippington, the London Gaggle, had settled in nicely, though Mollie Biscuits and

Long Polly still complained loudly. Emma would have been worried if they hadn't.

It was ridiculous to think that Brandon might recognize her. When he'd come back from the Afghan War he'd been concussed, his memory hazy, all his energy concentrated on staying alive. That time in the charity hospital would hardly have lingered, particularly once he got his memory back. Touching her would have meant nothing to him.

She managed to stand very still—her time in the operating room had taught her that particular skill, and when the moment came to pledge herself to her tiny goddaughter she stepped forward and spoke in a low voice, ignoring him.

He did the same, treating her with the courtesy of a stranger, and when Alexandra awoke screaming with the first drops of baptismal water on her tiny face he laughed, and Emma couldn't resist stealing a glance as she accepted the squalling baby from the priest.

She hadn't remembered his smile. He was a handsome man even when he was tormented, darkly brooding, lost in the hell of the Heavenly Host's domain. He was breathtaking when he smiled.

He must have caught her staring at him, for he glanced down at her, but she quickly ducked her head, turning her attention to the baby. Alexandra wasn't fond of strangers, but for some reason she seemed to like this tall, strange man who held out one strong finger for her to grasp, and her blue eyes focused on him, her tears drying up as quickly as they had come.

The service ended shortly thereafter, and Emma took a deep breath. She would have to bear the close presence of Brandon Rohan for less than a day, and she'd endured far worse. Tomorrow she would be back in the city, she reminded herself, back in her crowded rooms and her work at the hospital. Tomorrow all this would be over and if she were very careful she need never see him again.

Alexandra's nurse stepped forward to take the baby from her, and Emma had no choice but to release her, reluctantly. It was then she made the dire mistake of lifting her head, only to stare directly into Brandon Rohan's cool blue eyes, his half-ruined, half-beautiful face, and it felt as if her stomach dropped to the cold slate floor of the chapel.

She kept her own expression carefully blank, and there wasn't a spot of recognition on his face. Brandon Rohan's Harpy had disappeared into the mists of his memory, and she was nothing but a stranger to him.

It was relief that swept over her, she told herself. She would still need to be careful, but over the last three years he'd forgotten her face, her very existence, and little wonder, given the shape he'd been in. Any connection she might have had with him had vanished into the air, and she need never worry about it again. This was relief, she told herself firmly.

"Brandon, you accompany Mrs. Cadbury back to the house," Benedick said. "You don't mind, do you, Emma?"

Of course, she minded, but she couldn't think of a viable excuse. Fortunately, Brandon was equally unwilling. "Much as it would honor me, brother mine, I'm afraid I've brought my horse. Unless you've brought an extra groom, I'll have no choice but to ride."

"We'll send someone back for the horse."

"I'm a dusty mess," Brandon said.

"Emma won't mind. She's a surgeon—she spends her days in far more disgusting conditions than even you could provide."

Emma froze, afraid Benedick's casual words might jog Brandon's memory, but the man beside her didn't blink. "Well, in that case I promise not to bleed on her unless I find it absolutely necessary."

It was a joke, Emma realized belatedly, and she was supposed to laugh at it. Today of all days she didn't feel like laughing, but she forced her mouth into a polite smile. He'd forgotten her well and truly—even the reminder of her connection with hospitals hadn't jarred his memory. Surely, she could survive a ten-minute drive back to the country house without incident.

Except when he put his hand on her arm to help her up into the carriage. She'd flinched, as she always did when a man put his hands on her, but his hands were different, far worse. They were familiar. Wickedly, heartbreakingly familiar.

She had touched him, bathing the fever from his wasted body, changing his bandages, reading to him, even singing to him in her soft alto, the old Welsh lullaby her granny used to sing to her, "All through the night." She'd kissed his sweating forehead when he was suffering from delirium. She'd held his hand when he grew restless, and impossible as it seemed, she'd almost fallen in love with him. She'd kissed his mouth ...

Looking back, it was nothing more than a dream, a dream he'd already forgotten, a dream she'd best let go of, and fast.

She only had to survive an uncomfortable five minutes of polite conversation during the short drive and she would be free. She eyed him covertly as he dropped into the seat opposite her, keeping her head lowered.

The carriage started smoothly enough, and she waited for him to begin the required social dialogue. He said nothing, and the silence grew long and labored until she finally looked up, almost defiantly.

He was watching her with lazy curiosity, seemingly unmoved by the social gaffe. "They're gray," he said.

"I beg your pardon?" The most obvious topic of discussion was, of course, the weather, but it was a clear, beautiful day with a bright blue sky, not a cloud in sight.

"Your eyes, Mrs. Cadbury. They're gray."

Oh, God help her, he wasn't going to flirt with her! That would finish her entirely. She put on her coolest look, one that managed to frighten some of the younger surgeons who tried to lord it over her. "How observant," she said in a flat voice that sounded just the slightest bit more hostile than was necessary. It appeared that she hadn't taken his forgetfulness as well as she'd hoped.

"Well, considering that you seem to find my dusty boots to be of alarming fascination it required a real effort. Have you known my sister-in-law a long time?"

"Years," she said shortly, then realized she was compounding her rudeness. "We work together on her projects."

"Ah, yes, Sweet Charity. I gather that was her 'nom de guerre.' And what do they call you?"

"Mrs. Cadbury," she said repressively.

He was singularly unmoved by her attempts to thwart him. "I somehow get the feeling you disapprove of me, Mrs. Cadbury. Have tales of my sordid past reached your delicate ears?"

If anyone had a sordid past she did, and she wasn't about to pass judgment on anyone, particularly someone in Brandon's position, broken by war, victim of the depredations of the Heavenly Host. She lowered her eyes again. "I make it a practice not judge other people."

"Let he who is without sin among you cast the first stone?" Brandon said softly. "May I assume you are not without sin?"

This was worse than she'd imagined in her most devilish daydreams. He was playing with her, a woman who was a complete stranger to him. In another man she might have almost called it flirting, but there was no light in his blue eyes, in his ruined face. "No one is without sin, Lord Brandon."

The right side of his mouth quirked in amusement, the left side, the damaged side, was still. He looked so different and yet exactly the same—she would have known those brilliant blue eyes anywhere. The left side of his face had improved with the years. One eye still drooped, his mouth was frozen in a saturnine smirk, but the skin was no longer raw looking, fading instead to a textured patchwork of scars. The right side of his face was. . . beautiful. "You strike me as the exception, Mrs. Cadbury. If temptation ever came your way I'm certain you would scare it off with that forbidding expression of yours."

Forbidding expression? Never in her life had anyone told her she had such a thing. She wasn't sure whether to be offended or pleased. "In truth, Lord Brandon, I am particularly impervious to temptation."

"Never given in? Even once?"

That was one thing she could answer truthfully. It hadn't been temptation that had sent her into men's beds, it had been desperation. "Never."

He leaned back against the squabs while she sat ramrod straight. "Well, it's a rare soul that can claim that distinction. You quite put me to shame."

It was her own shame she felt. What would he think if he knew she'd once been London's youngest madam? "I don't. . ." she began, but the carriage had drawn up in front of the sprawling manor house Benedick Rohan had bought for his wife.

"You don't what?" he said, but she was already free, the door opening, and escape was at hand.

"I don't wish to keep you away from your family, Lord Brandon," she said politely, taking the groomsman's hand to step down onto the wide, curving drive. "Enjoy your visit."

BRANDON WATCHED her move away from him with dignified but impressive speed, and he frowned. His social graces were sadly rusty, but Melisande's friend seemed to have taken him in dislike. She must have heard rumors of the way he'd ruined his life three years ago – it was hardly a secret. It was no less than he deserved, but he'd worked hard to put the guilt behind him. He truly didn't want to wallow in it again.

He could simply avoid the woman. That, or see if he could change her mind about him, but that would be a very bad idea. Back before the war he'd been a charmer – he could get any pretty girl to smile, and Mrs. Cadbury was a very pretty girl, but he was much better off keeping his distance. There was no room in his life for a casual liaison, a mistress or a wife. He was still doing penance, and probably would for the rest of his life. He had been a drugged wreck of a man, participating in acts that appalled him, when he remembered. At the time he'd derived no pleasure, he'd simply gone along with it, and he wasn't through paying for all those sins.

No, Mrs. Emma Cadbury of the beautiful gray eyes and the stern expression was decidedly none of his concern. He would mend fences with his brothers and then head back to Scotland, where life was far simpler, and forget all about the woman.

Except that she wasn't forgettable. There was something about her that would haunt his dreams, a timeless feel to her, as if he'd known her before and would know her forever.

And then he laughed out loud as he climbed out of the carriage, managing the feat without favoring his aching leg. Had the sight of a beautiful woman suddenly turned him into an adolescent? The very idea of a stranger touching his non-existent heart was absurd. He was a practical man – there was no room for mooning over what he had chosen not to have. He glanced at the front entrance as he made his way carefully up the broad stairs. There was no trace of her, like some fairytale princess she'd disappeared. In a few days, he would do the same.

Two hours later the reception was in full force, a crush of people that Brandon endured with a grim smile. He'd known his time as a hermit was coming to an end, but that didn't mean he had to like it.

"Where is my esteemed brother Charles?" he murmured to his sister-in-law as she cooed over the baby in her arms. In truth, he had expected to find anything to do with children boring, but this little scrap of a thing was oddly appealing, with her red face and fierce blue eyes. "I expected to see his disapproving face glowering at me wherever I went."

"Charles has been delayed," Melisande said glumly, making no effort to defend her pompous brother-in-law. "He'll be here tomorrow."

"Excellent," he said, equally glum. Charles could make any comfortable time an exercise in gloom. That gave him a second reason to make an early escape. He glanced around the room, then gave in to temptation. After all, he'd be gone soon enough – he could indulge himself. "And where is the fascinating Mrs. Cadbury?"

Melisande didn't bother looking up from her cooing infant. "She should be here, though she tends to end up in a corner somewhere more often than not. You didn't say anything to offend her, did you?"

Brandon raised an eyebrow. "Why should I do that? She's a perfectly amiable female, if somewhat shy."

Melisande made a derisive sound and Brandon's eyes narrowed. "Why do you find that amusing?"

"The thought of Emma being shy or even particularly amiable. She simply doesn't have much use for social conventions, or men, for that matter."

He was getting drawn in, and he cursed himself for even bringing up the subject. Teasing Charity Carstairs Rohan would fix things. "Indeed?" he said in a fop-like drawl. "Is she one of those extraordinary women who prefer their own sex? And since you're her dearest friend does that mean. . .?"

"Behave yourself, Brandon!" she snapped. "I would have thought three years in Scotland would make you think before you spoke."

He laughed. "On the contrary, like Mrs. Cadbury I have a similar disregard for social conveniences. And I also prefer women. We have a great deal in common."

"She does not prefer women!" Melisande said. "At least, not in the manner you're suggesting. She simply doesn't care for men. I expect it comes from her studies. She is a surgeon, which is extraordinary, but I know the other surgeons treat her with a fair amount of disdain."

"Perhaps. A surgeon? How extraordinary. And what made her decide she wanted to cut into human flesh? Part of her dislike of the male gender, perhaps?" he said lightly.

"I have no idea. Why don't you ask her?" His sister-in-law was sounding irritated with him, and he couldn't blame her. He was irritated with himself. What happened to his plan to keep away from temptation?

"I would like to," he said, "if I could find her. That's what started our conversation, if you remember." He gave Melisande his most beguiling smile, one he seldom bothered to use. "I don't suppose you have anything other than claret punch to drink."

Melisande's gaze darkened. "You'll find a bottle of brandy in Benedick's study, if you must."

"No, my dear sister-in-law, I'm looking for something with less alcohol, rather than more." He despised having to admit it, but there was no choice. He hadn't had a drop of wine, beer, or spirits since he'd left for Scotland, and he wasn't about to start now.

Her obvious relief annoyed him, but he said nothing. "There's lemonade on the children's table."

"I'd rather not haunt the children, thank you very much. This face can be a bit daunting. Is there anything that looks less like a child's drink?"

Sweet Charity sprang into action. "I'll have Richmond bring you something immediately. It's a warm day for March."

"Could he bring me Mrs. Cadbury as well?" he said dryly.

"If you look hard enough you'll doubtless find her, unless she's trying to avoid you."

His eyes narrowed. "Why should she?"

Melisande shrugged. "No reason I can think of. Go rescue your brother from the vicar, would you? Benedick despises him, but he's forced to be polite."

"Certainly, my dear. I have no great fondness for the clergy myself. But if you see your friend you must promise to hold onto her for me." Might as well be hanged for a sheep as for a lamb.

"I wouldn't think of it," Melisande flatly.

Brandon gave her his most perfect smile, perfect for the unmarked side of his face, that was. "Someday you'll have to tell me all about your little friend," he murmured. "In the meantime, I suppose I owe my brother my support."

"You owe him a great deal more than that. And leave Emma alone. She doesn't need your kind of trouble."

"You offend me! What kind of trouble am I?"

She reached up and whispered in his ear. "Catnip."

He stared at her, nonplussed, but his sister-in-law whirled away. He glanced across the room. Benedick was trapped by the vicar and in between was a bevy of brightly clad young misses, many of whom were sneaking glances at him, both horrified and fascinated. They failed to interest him.

He would give the other side of his face to be back in Scotland, he thought, keeping his gaze impassive, or any place where people didn't stare at him and whisper.

Benedick managed to detach himself from the vicar and he was moving among the guests, the perfect host. He needed no rescuing, more's the pity. Sooner or later Brandon was going to have to abase himself, beg forgiveness for the copious and horrifying sins of the past, but for now he had better things to do.

He had to find the young woman who'd watched him so gravely. The woman with the bowed head and the gray eyes, the woman who reminded him of something, someone. He intended to find out what.

CHAPTER 3

The reception was even more crowded than she'd imagined, Emma thought, hiding her dismay as she slipped in the side door of the rooms. She knew very few of these people, and most of them would have nothing to do with her, which was just as well. She had no patience for the indolent upper classes. She only wished the Gaggle had been there, the hard-working women who'd serviced these very men and now simply wanted a better life. Melisande had invited them, of course. Her friend had never favored social conventions over generosity of spirit, but the Gaggle was more sensible. They'd sat quietly in the back of the chapel, they'd left quickly, and most of the guests hadn't even realized they were there. None of them would allow Melisande to commit the social breach of inviting them into her home, and never would.

She could have done the same, Emma thought wearily, if she hadn't been Alexandra's godmother. She moved silently through the crowds, eyes alert, a polite smile on her face. Many of the guests were as accepting as their hosts, but there were a number of them who had to be invited despite Melisande's protests, and the last thing Emma wanted to do was run afoul of them, particularly the vicar.

Emma despised him, and she made it a practice to do everything she could to avoid him. They'd been introduced once, and he'd ignored her ever since, much to her relief, but she couldn't rid herself of the notion that he watched her, presumably dreaming about placing the wanton woman in the stocks, if they even still had such things.

Well, she *had* been a wanton woman, she reminded herself. She had sold her favors for money, not that she'd ever seen much of it, and such things were not to be overlooked by a man of God, apparently. She was tempted to brush by him, whisper "Mary Magdalene" in his ear, but that would have been a very bad idea. As far as she knew Mr. Trowbridge had no sense of humor and was best avoided all together.

She was instantly aware the moment Brandon Rohan entered the room, watching him as he bent over Melisande and the baby. She watched as emotions played over Melisande's face – wariness, disapproval, and then laughter, and the unmarked side of his face lit with his own smile. She'd forgotten the power of that smile, and it struck her like a blow. She needed to leave.

She had almost made the stairs when she heard the baby's fretful cry. She hesitated for just a moment, and when she resolutely turned again she came face to face with the vicar, his hand clamping painfully around her arm.

"Excuse me, Mr. Trowbridge," she said politely, trying to free herself. *It only needed this!* "I was just on my way to help Lady Melisande. . ."

"I think that tiny baby would do well away from your wicked influence," the man said, moving in on her, somehow managing to herd her toward the French doors that led to the terrace. He was very strong for such a thin, dried-up old man, possibly even stronger than she was, and for Melisande's sake she wasn't about to make a scene.

"I beg your pardon," she said in the frosty voice that had cowed many a young surgeon. The vicar didn't cow so easily.

"And well you might," he said, moving her ahead of them, out the French door that still stood ajar, even though the pleasant spring breeze had sharpened. As he pushed her across the wide terrace toward the steps that led to the gardens, she stumbled slightly, unused to walking backwards. "Alexandra Rohan is a good Christian baby. She doesn't need a handmaiden of the devil nearby."

"Handmaiden of the devil?" Emma echoed. She wanted to laugh at the melodramatic phrase, but she sensed this was no laughing matter. "Don't be absurd, sir. I'm no danger to anyone."

He was holding her too close to him, and he smelled of sweat and dust, like dirty clothes left in a cupboard. She wrinkled her nose, wondering if she should call for help, but that would be ridiculous. A country vicar wasn't a threat. Chances were he simply wanted to chastise her for the errors of her ways. She could survive being prayed over —it wouldn't be the first time.

The terrace was deserted now. "Mr. Trowbridge," she began, trying to sound conciliatory and failing. She was growing angry, and she had an impressive temper when riled, her greatest failing. "Would you please release me? We are both guests of Viscount and Lady Rohan, and they would be most displeased to know you'd manhandled me."

He'd maneuvered her down the steps, and now he pushed her into the tall boxwood, out of sight. "I doubt he would care – he's merely indulging his flighty wife by having you here," Trowbridge said darkly. "I know your kind—degenerate and evil. You fornicate for money, you have unnatural congress with those women. . ."

He'd gone too far. "Males, females, dogs, cats, anyone who's got the price," she said, slipping into the familiar Cockney tones of the women she'd worked with. "Have a problem with that, do you, ducks?"

"Shameless," he muttered. "Shameless, foul temptation in such a pretty package."

"Well, I wouldn't be much of a temptation if I weren't pretty," she pointed out in a practical voice. Really, this was too ridiculous. She didn't want to slam her knee into his privy parts, but he might not allow her any other choice. "Let go of me, sir, or you'll regret it."

He moved even closer, and his foul breath was hot on her face. "You'll be the one to regret. . ."

"I suggest you do as the lady requests," a smooth voice interrupted them. "Or I might have to make you. May I remind you that my brother has charge of the living here, and he can easily replace you. All it would require is a word from me."

Emma could feel the color drain away from her face. Of all people, it was Brandon Rohan standing there, quite negligently, a cool expression on his half-ruined face.

To her relief Mr. Trowbridge immediately released her, and she stumbled back, almost toppling into the bushes. She hadn't realized how unnerved she'd been.

The vicar had regained his composure, giving him a pious smile. "Just a private conversation, Lord Brandon," he said. "Mrs. Cadbury misunderstood my concerns."

Brandon raised an eyebrow. "Did she, now?"

The vicar swallowed. There was a silky menace in Brandon's rich voice, and Emma suddenly remembered he'd been a soldier, a war hero in fact. There was a deadly quiet about him that was threatening, even to a pompous cleric like Mr. Trowbridge.

The man cleared his throat. "Of course, you did, didn't you, Mrs. Cadbury?" He turned to her, but there was no question in his beady eyes. He simply assumed she would cover for him. "She wouldn't think of making a fuss and embarrassing her generous benefactors."

Oh, wouldn't she? Emma thought, annoyed. But Trowbridge had known just how to prick her—the Rohans were indeed her benefactors, though she had always thought of them as friends. The man's words had forcibly reminded her just how separate and alone she really was.

She had too much experience stifling her reactions to let it show, and she met Brandon's dark expression with a cool smile. "You're very thoughtful, Lord Brandon," she said, "but there's no problem here. The vicar was merely giving me spiritual advice, but we're done now."

There was no sign of gratification in Trowbridge's face, just solemn piety. "Perhaps you misunderstood, Lord Brandon, because you've been away for so long. I must say it's good to see you looking so well. Your necessary sojourn in Scotland has agreed with you."

Brandon's cool expression didn't change. "How kind of you to keep track of my whereabouts. The Highlands of Scotland are not for everyone, but I find them quite amiable. And as you reminded me, the trip was necessary."

The words were softly spoken, but the vicar finally seemed to realize he was treading on dangerous ground. An awkward silence filled the afternoon, broken only by the buzz of conversation filtering into the garden. "I'd best leave you two—fortunately I have no need to worry about Mrs. Cadbury's reputation, such as it is. Again, my lord, I'm delighted to see you again." The vicar turned, making a hasty escape.

Emma knew she should make an excuse, follow the vicar. The last thing she wanted was a tête-à-tête with Brandon Rohan, the man who'd forgotten all about her, the man who still affected her, but for a moment she was frozen. He was looking down at her and for the first time in three years she felt alive again.

"Do I really know that man?" Brandon said in a lighter voice. "I would have thought he was one thing I wouldn't forget."

The words surprised her, but she had no intention of discussing his lack of memory. "I have no idea, my lord." She looked up, forcing herself to meet his eyes. She no longer wore her enveloping bonnet, and her face was there for him to look at. "You're very kind to come to my rescue," she added. "But Mr. Trowbridge would never cross the line —it was simply a misunderstanding."

His winter-blue eyes drifted over her, and she wondered what they saw. A woman past her first youth, pretty no matter what she did to disguise it, a woman who was shunned by society and disdained for her very existence.

But he wouldn't know that. He didn't know anything about her. As far as he knew he'd never seen her before.

"I see," he said, and she knew he didn't believe her. Brandon Rohan had come to her rescue without even knowing who she was. And he never would know, not if she could help it. The whole situation was absurd, laughable, but her sense of humor had vanished.

"I should go in," she said suddenly.

"I'll escort you."

"There's no need."

"I beg to differ," Brandon said, holding out his arm. "My sister-in-law would never forgive me if I allowed her dearest friend to wander around the gardens alone. What if someone decided to accost you?"

She looked up at him. The bright sunlight had faded, dusk was coming on, but she could still see him quite clearly. He looked so different from the dying man she'd tended in the hospital, so different from the ruined soul who'd run afoul of the Heavenly Host. The left half of his face was still a crisscross of scars and ruination, and she'd seen the almost imperceptible limp. But he was tall, towering over her own middling height, and his shoulders were broad. He radiated health and strength, so very different from the broken man she'd foolishly come to care about.

This man didn't need her care. He was healed, or as much as he could be, a man seemingly at peace with himself and the world. Except that his smiles were few and fleeting, and there was a darkness in those icy-blue eyes.

"Most people wish to avoid me," she said before she could think better of it.

"Why is that, Mrs. Cadbury?"

He remembered her name from their brief introduction, even if her face was lost in the mists of time. She managed a rueful smile. "I am not of your class, sir. I am a working woman, doing the best I can with no family to rely on."

"Indeed. You are a surgeon, my sister-in-law said. That must require nerves of steel. It's little wonder that the vicar failed to intimidate you."

He was right, though she wasn't about to tell him so. It did take a lot to frighten her. In truth, the unexpected return of Brandon Rohan was the only thing that had managed to break her hard-won calm in years.

"So you see, I'm entirely capable of returning to the house on my own," she said, and yet she didn't move. Didn't want to move.

"Maybe I need you to protect me," he said.

She laughed, as she was expected to, but his words gave her a strange start. She *had* protected him, watched over him, saved him. She would still do anything he asked of her, if only to keep him safe.

She was being absurd. She'd never seen someone less in need of saving now. "I think you'll manage very well, Lord Brandon. Melisande has told me of your service in the late war. You are, in fact, a hero. Doubtless people will wish to shake your hand, not stab you in the back."

"Yet they'd stab *you* in the back?" His voice was quizzical, and she once more cursed herself. Their long conversations so many years ago had been casual, free of social constraints. Now he seemed to pick up on every offhand remark she made.

"Of course not," she said, mentally dismissing Mr. Fenrush, the surgeon in charge, and his hostile underlings who'd probably burn her at the stake if they could. It was little wonder that, despite the vicar, this country village still managed to feel peaceful and welcoming in contrast.

"Then what did the vicar want from you?"

She thought quickly, coming up with the best lie she could think of. "In fact, he was warning me about my habit of walking to the village and back. He was afraid I might catch a stray bullet."

This guileless answer didn't appease him. "It's not hunting season."

Emma bit her lower lip in frustration. "I thought it was always hunting season."

"Clearly you're not much of a country girl," he replied.

"I am. I grew up in Devon. My family, however, were middle class, and hunting wasn't a part of their life." Unless they were hunting the devil and scouring it from their daughter's flesh.

Brandon said nothing, simply surveying her in the gathering dusk. He held out his arm for her to take, but at that moment Emma's precious courage failed her. She was exhausted from her long hours of work at the hospital, annoyed with the vicar's bullying, but most of all she was shaken to the core by the sudden reappearance of Brandon Rohan.

She hadn't allowed herself to think of him over the last three years, sternly dismissing him from her mind when he would appear. She had no such power over her dreams, and countless times she'd found herself talking with him, lying beside him, doing things with him that she knew she would hate in real life. But in dreams the touching, the tasting, the possession no longer seemed like an assault, and she would wake up damp and shaking with longing.

It was all too much. She couldn't bring herself to put her hand on his arm, to touch him in any way—it brought back too many sensations. It was cowardice, pure and simple, but she wasn't going to fight it any longer, no matter how rude or peculiar it might look.

"I believe I might retire to my rooms," she said, annoyed to hear a breathless note in her usually calm voice. "I've very tired, and I have a long trip back to London tomorrow."

He frowned. "Tomorrow? Why so soon? My sister informed me you were going to stay the week."

She felt her stomach tighten. "You were talking about me?" she blurted out, and then shut her mouth, appalled at her bad manners.

He raised an eyebrow. "Melisande likes to talk, and I have learned to simply let her choose the subject. I wasn't checking up on you, Mrs. Cadbury, if that's what you were thinking."

She didn't know whether to be relieved or disappointed. She kept her expression calm. It was one of her great strengths—to appear unmoved despite the circumstances she was thrust into. She'd learned that in her childhood, and the life that followed had given her more than enough occasions to improve that particular skill.

"Of course you weren't," she said quickly. She was reaching the end of that vaunted calm, and she had to get away from him. "Why should you? But it remains that I'm too tired to return to the celebration. Good-bye, Lord Brandon. Have a safe trip back to Scotland."

He was watching her, and there was no way she could read his expression, guess at what he was thinking. "Oh, I'm not returning to Scotland, at least not any time soon. My brother Charles is arriving tomorrow, and much as I'd prefer to avoid him I occasionally do my duty. Besides, there are far too many interesting. . .things here in the south of England."

Was he suggesting one of those interesting "things" was her, or was it her wistful longing? It didn't matter. Their paths wouldn't cross again —she lived in a very different world, thank God, and she knew how to avoid occasions that were detrimental to her peace of mind. She wouldn't, couldn't give up visiting Melisande, who was more a sister than a friend, but she would take care to come when no one else was visiting.

"Then I wish you a pleasant visit," she said hurriedly, turning to walk away.

Her hope of a quick escape was dashed as he caught her wrist, and she couldn't help her sudden wince of pain. The skinny old vicar had been rougher than she realized.

Brandon immediately released her, his thunderous look made more menacing with his half-ruined face. "Did he hurt you?" There was danger there, which startled her. The sweet, broken soldier in the hospital, the lost boy fighting addictions and evil companions in his brother's house—this was a far cry from those very different incarnations of Brandon Rohan. This man was cold, strong and dangerous.

She lied, of course. "Heavens, no. I hurt my wrist yesterday. Just being clumsy, I imagine. If you'll excuse me, Lord Brandon. . ." she said, edging away.

This time he didn't stop her. "Certainly, Mrs. Cadbury."

"I don't expect we shall see each other again," she said stiffly, pleased with herself.

"Don't you? You may have your expectations dashed."

She jerked her head up, startled by his enigmatic statement, but there was no answer she could make. "Well. . .good evening," she said hurriedly, awkwardly, and walked away from him so quickly it was close to a run. He probably thought she was extremely odd, but that was of little consequence. As long as she didn't see him again she'd be safe.

She wasn't going to consider why she thought he was dangerous. True, he looked immensely strong compared to the frail invalid she'd seen before, but he'd been a charming, gentle man back when he hadn't even known who he was. The return of his memory, even the depredations of the Heavenly Host, couldn't change someone that much, could they? But there'd been that moment of inchoate rage when he suspected that the vicar had hurt her.

She wasn't going to think about him, she told herself sternly. She would never see him again. The well-planned shrubbery closed about her, putting her out of his view, and she breathed a sigh of relief as she raced on.

CHAPTER 4

Brandon watched her run away from him, her dull gray skirts flying, her dark hair coming loose. She was moving as if the devil were at her heels, which shouldn't surprise him. To her he was a stranger, a scarred, ferocious former soldier who loomed over her, manhandled her as that bastard Trowbridge had.

She thought she'd escaped him, and if he had any sense at all he'd let it be, and he was, after all, a sensible man.

He could control his bodily urges, and the good widow up in the Highlands would take him gladly and ask for nothing but pleasure in return. He could close his eyes, pretend that her red hair was a silky black, that her eyes were cool and gray and then stormy as he ... . . .

Hell and damnation! He had no business fantasizing about his brother's mysterious houseguest in such a way. He waited another minute, long enough for his inconvenient hard-on to subside, and then started back to the house, trying to keep his gait even. His leg was killing him, but he had no intention of giving in to the pain, of showing any sign of weakness. He had something important to do, and he had learned from Noonan and the harsh Scottish weather never to accept any limitations. He quickened his pace with no sign of his inner grimace and went in search of the good Mr. Trowbridge.

Instead he found his older brother bearing down on him, and the dream of exacting punishment vanished. It was time to atone for his sins, and he squared his shoulders, waiting.

EVERYTHING WOULD HAVE GONE ACCORDING to plan, Emma thought, if she'd been able to sleep. It was such a simple, biological act that so many people took for granted, and it was constantly denied her. In her studies at Temple Hospital she'd done some research on the mysteries of sleep, and she had a fairly good understanding of why it eluded her.

She'd been so young when she'd first arrived in London. Fifteen years old, with no more than a sixpence tucked in her shoe, she'd managed a ride with a farm cart that had deposited her down by the docks just at dusk. It had seemed like the greatest good fortune when the grandmotherly woman had taken one look at her, recognized a lost soul, and brought her home to her fancy house. There had been other young girls there, laughing, chattering, brightly dressed, but they hadn't spoken to her, eyeing her with a kind of pity as they went about their toilette, and Emma, exhausted and frightened, didn't stop to wonder what kind of place she was in. She'd been given a bath and a flimsy night robe, a warm drink, then tucked into a huge, luxurious bed, where she'd immediately dropped into the last safe sleep of her life.

Only to be awakened an hour later by pawing hands and laughing voices and pain and terror as she was passed from man to man, her virgin's blood staining the soft linen sheets beneath her. She'd been drugged, she realized, and she'd been unable to fight them, unable to say a word, slowly letting the numbness take over. She'd learned to love that numbness, anything that would take her mind away from what her body was doing.

Unfortunately, understanding why she couldn't sleep didn't end the problem. She should be done with it by now, she'd told herself on numerous occasions as she'd walked the floors during those endless hours between dusk and dawn. The situation had been exacerbated by the profession she found herself in—blood and death were seldom conducive to restful sleep, even if she managed to save many of her patients.

The women were the most painful to her, slashed, strangled, maimed in horrifying ways by their customers. Emma had no illusions —she was no better than any of them. By the time she'd taken control of Mother Howe's house at the tender age of twenty, sharing in the profits and the running of the place with the other women, she'd discovered that even on nights when the house was shuttered she still couldn't sleep. Every time she closed her eyes she'd feel the hands pawing at her, the voices taunting her, feel the pain between her legs.

Some of her friends had learned to like it, but she never had. Some of her customers had been kinder than others, but she never grew accustomed to their possession of her body, the smell, the rutting noises they made. She tolerated some men, hated others, but as far as she could tell the only decent man alive in this world today was Melisande's devoted husband Benedick.

That explained why she was wide awake in his household at three in the morning when everyone else was safely asleep. What it didn't explain was why she was wanting Brandon Rohan's hand on her arm once again.

The covers were on the floor, and she kicked them out of the way with her cold, bare feet. She'd forgotten to bring slippers, and her toes were freezing. Of course, she couldn't sleep with cold feet, she reminded herself. What she needed was a warm brick and a not-too-exciting book. Those two remedies had always proven marginally successful, at least, and she knew from past visits how to acquire both things without bothering the servants. Benedick's study was always unlocked, and he had any number of boring tomes. Bricks were in the kitchen, and she was self-sufficient enough to warm one herself—she didn't need one of the harried maids to lose what little sleep they had just to wait on her.

She knew full well that laudanum would have done the trick. She had never serviced a man without the blessed, dulling effects of the drug, and more than anyone she'd understood Brandon's craving when he'd been so lost. But it was vicious stuff, one needed more and more, and it had cost more than one young woman her life. Young Meggy's death had changed everything—Emma had taken over the brothel, now floundering under the haphazard direction of Mother Howard's truculent sister, and personally thrown all the laudanum into the filthy waters of the Thames. There would be some happy fish, she thought cynically, watching it dissolve. There would be unhappy women back at the house, including herself.

They'd gotten through it, all of them working together, and even if she stayed awake for weeks on end she would never touch the stuff again. She handled it and opium often enough in the hospital, and she viewed it impassively. She knew what it could and couldn't do, how it felt, but by some unexpected grace she no longer wanted it. She avoided alcohol as well, just to be safe, but nights like this, when she hadn't slept for what seemed like centuries, she found herself wishing she could try it.

Perhaps she could deal with the precipitous reappearance of Brandon Rohan the same way she'd dealt with the laudanum. Not by drowning him in the Thames, she thought with a quiet laugh, but simply by forswearing any time with him, any thought about him. Sooner or later the cravings would cease, wouldn't they?

Cravings? What an absurd word for her strange affinity for the man. She'd worked it all out in her brain during the last three years—her quiet relationship with the broken young soldier had been untainted by the life she had led. They hadn't known anything about each other —he had forgotten everything, and she had chosen not to share. He called her Harpy, she'd called him "sir" in defiantly polite tones that belied the warmth of the connection they were forming. It had been like she was a child again, her relationship clean and simple, everything a possibility.

But it had been an illusion, a dream, and there was no way she could ever live that life again. Her world at the hospital was dark and squalid, enemies and obstruction all around her, but at least there she was helping. She simply had to keep at it and put the dream of Brandon out of her mind.

The night was silent. The sprawling country house wasn't quite full, though Melisande had assembled a respectable house party to celebrate Alexandra's christening. Emma knew most of them, and there wasn't a ramshackle member in the bunch. No one would be wandering around in the wee hours, getting up to mischief. They'd all been here before, and they'd been well behaved. She'd be fine if she slipped out of her room in the middle of the night.

Idiot, she told herself. Everyone had been here before but Brandon Rohan. There was no guarantee that *he* would be safely tucked in bed. She was a fool if she didn't consider that possibility.

But what was the likelihood? She could stay in her room, edgy and sleepless, and possibly too weary the next day to extricate herself from Melisande's loving clutches, or she could take a chance and go in search of surcease.

No, she would venture out, and she could be phlegmatic about it, a gift that had gotten her through life. If she were meant to see him one more time, then she would deal with it. What she couldn't deal with was another sleepless night.

She wrapped a shawl around her shoulders and stepped, barefoot, into the silent, empty corridor. She made her way down the side stairs kept for the family's use, making her way down two more flights to the main floor.

One of the footmen was in a chair by the stairs, sound asleep, and Emma slipped past, a smile on her face. Servants were treated very well at Starlings Manor—she had no doubt they were even encouraged to sleep while on duty in the dark of night. She moved through the halls like a ghost, down to the ground floor, and headed to the library.

The heavy door was open a crack, just a faint glow of firelight filtering out, and she hesitated a moment, suddenly unsure. It was highly unlikely Benedick would still be awake—he usually ended his evenings early, in bed with his wife by his side, but there would probably still be coals, and her feet were freezing. She pushed open the door, letting the delicious warmth surround her, and stepped inside, closing it behind her.

THERE WERE times when Brandon preferred darkness to candlelight, disappearing into the shadows, and tonight was one of them. He sat back, unseen, his feet on Benedick's desk, a cup of tea in one hand, his bad mood momentarily distracted. His leg was bothering him even more than his forced immersion into society, with the polite social questions that somehow felt like a vast intrusion into his life. There was nothing he could do about it but drink tea and try to think about something else. Sleep was an impossibility, and it wasn't just the pain that was ripping it away.

He'd planned to get the hell away from Starlings Manor as soon as he could. He was going to mend fences with his brother and sister-in-law, force himself to be polite and well-mannered, and run back to Scotland like the coward he was.

He still planned to. For some reason he wasn't quite as eager to go, and he wasn't sure if it had anything to do with Melisande's eccentric friend. Whoever heard of a woman surgeon? Her manner was odd as well, strangely hostile when he was pulling out any charm he still had buried beneath his scarred hide in an attempt at courtesy.

But he liked her eyes. Those gray, stubborn eyes that looked at him and didn't see a cripple or a supposed war hero or even the depraved soul he'd been when he became involved with the Heavenly Host, and he had little doubt that as a close friend of the family she knew all the horrific details. For a secret organization it was surprisingly notorious – a group of bored and degenerate aristocrats intent on smashing every rule of decency and honor in their quest for gratification, and he would carry the shame of his involvement for the rest of his life. His descent into the madness of opium and brandy paled by comparison – at least with those compulsions he'd only hurt himself.

No, that history would be impossible for most people to overlook, particularly someone with the clear intelligence of Emma Cadbury. Trying would be a waste of his time.

He'd been hoping to make amends to his brothers and return home within a week, but Charles wasn't here yet, and he had no intention of waiting for him. Besides, Benedick was the one he'd injured – only stuffy Charles's rigid standards of decency had been offended by Brandon's attempts at self-destruction. Charles could damned well get by without an apology.

There was nothing for him here, Brandon thought, nothing at all.

Everything was soft and easy in the south, in ways that were no good for him. He'd found his true home in the wild and windy north, the rocky crags, the foaming surf, the mountain streams, and the scouring winds. The wild beauty of the Highlands spoke to what was left of his soul, and he needed to be back there.

Not to mention the jarring results of his conversation with his long-suffering older brother.

Indeed, it had been worth more than a week on horseback to clear the air with Benedick, to finally be able to ask his forgiveness and to have his own appalling actions be gently dismissed as an aberration. He owed Benedick so much, more than he could ever begin to repay, and his need to purge his soul had been foremost in his mind for the past three years.

It turned out there was no purging necessary. Benedick had simply pulled him into his arms, then given him a swift punch in the shoulder, and with a great deal of throat clearing they were back on solid ground.

Until Benedick mentioned their brother Charles's Machiavellian plans.

"Why not marry?" Benedick had said. "You don't have to be madly in love—I promise you that part is completely exhausting and far from practical. If you can avoid such passion your life will be simpler."

Brandon had laughed at that. "You'd prefer a boring, bloodless union to your current wedded bliss?"

"Of course not. I didn't have any choice in the matter—I can't live without her. I assure you our situation is extremely uncommon—most husbands and wives lead separate lives of quiet contentment. You could do the same, and it would go a great way toward repairing your reputation."

"What if I don't wish for my reputation to be repaired?" he'd shot back.

"Have you thought about our parents' feelings in the matter?" Benedick said gently, and the guilt had begun to roil inside Brandon once more. Of course his parents would want his name unclouded, not because they cared much for social standing but because they hated to see him at any kind of a disadvantage.

"I should marry for our parents?"

"Of course not. A solid marriage will help you return to society, give you children, which, I promise you, are a joy behind comprehension. And I'm sure Charles would never pick an unsatisfactory partner for you."

"He's already picked one?" Brandon had said, alarm sweeping his body.

Benedick shrugged. "You know Charles and his habit of arranging everyone's lives to his satisfaction. I wouldn't be surprised if he arrived with a future bride for you in tow. In fact, I would have thought he'd be here already."

And that was when he'd decided to leave, abandoning the temptation of the mysterious Mrs. Cadbury. She would have to remain an enigma.

Stretching, he leaned back in the leather chair, loosening the tie that held his long hair back. His tea was growing cold, the fire had died back into coals, and he should make his way up to bed. It was far better than the narrow cot he used for sleeping up in Scotland, but it looked cold and empty to him, and he hadn't been able to make himself strip off his clothes and lie down. He knew from experience there was no way to get comfortable with his knee like this, and he leaned over and rubbed it absently. Sooner or later his eyes would grow heavy, sooner or later he'd limp his way to bed.

And then he froze. She was coming. He couldn't hear anything—he'd been deaf in one ear since he'd been wounded, and if his head wasn't turned in the right direction someone could sneak up on him, proving that even if he was otherwise sound of body he'd still be no good as a soldier. He was basically useless, and he'd accepted that. It was just punishment for his crimes.

Even so, he was sure who was approaching the library in the dead of night. He knew with an absolute certainty that it was the woman who'd been preying on his mind since he first saw her.

Perhaps the mysterious Mrs. Emma Cadbury was simply another trick of fate, something to tempt him that he couldn't touch. He had no right to be around any woman, and he knew it, but. for some reason he really, really wanted to touch her.

He didn't move, not even when the door was pushed open and she stepped inside.

The only light in the room was the glow of the fire. It was so dark he couldn't see her clearly—just the outline of her body in. . . Damn it, she was only wearing her night rail, with a warm shawl wrapped around her. It didn't disguise the curves that he'd somehow known were lurking behind her drab and baggy clothes, and he cursed mentally. He was already having enough trouble keeping his mind dutifully chaste.

She went straight to the fire, kneeling in front of it, and the coals illuminated her face. Her hair was down around her shoulders, a cascade of dark curls that were a far cry from the severe, tightly braided coiffure she'd sported earlier. He'd seen she was beautiful beneath her frumpy armor, but she was more than that, she was absolutely breathtaking, and she clearly didn't want anyone to know.

He'd never known a woman who didn't use her looks and her femininity to her best advantage, and this one was more blessed than anyone he could remember. She looked pensive, staring into the fire. She wasn't a girl—she might very well be as old as he was, even older. It didn't matter. She'd be exquisite at any age. She sat back on her heels and surveyed the wall of leather-bound books. She still hadn't sensed he was in the shadows, watching her, which surprised him. He'd known she was near before he'd even seen her.

He didn't dare move from his place in the darkness, his legs propped on Benedick's desk. He was content just to watch her, the way she moved, the shifting emotions on her face, as she made herself comfortable, when suddenly that lovely body stiffened, and she slowly turned her head until she was looking directly at him as he lounged, unnoticed.

"Do you make a habit of spying on women?" she said in a cool voice, the same cool voice she'd used off and on with him the entire day. She had no reason for hostility, and it made him even more curious.

He didn't bother taking his feet off the desk—for one thing it was relieving the pressure and pain in his knee, for another he didn't want to appear discomfited by her presence. "I was here first," he pointed out. "You invaded my privacy. I'm hardly the one to blame." Which was untrue—a gentleman would have immediately made himself known, but he no longer had any interest in being a gentleman. That ship had sailed many years ago.

He could see it quite clearly in her mesmerizing eyes. The fight-or-flight response was something he'd grown used to in the army, had felt it himself on numerous occasions, but he'd never been smart enough to run. Too much pride, he supposed.

Emma Cadbury looked as if she suffered from the same defect of character. He didn't bother looking away, giving his curiosity full reign. "Have we met before?" he said suddenly.

She didn't move. "I cannot imagine any occasion in which we might have done," she said in her clipped voice.

He tilted his head to one side, surveying her. "No, I can't imagine it either. You're not precisely forgettable, you know. There's just something about you that feels familiar. Even your name strikes a bell."

Her face tightened so slightly that someone with duller eyesight might not have noticed, but that was one thing that hadn't changed despite all the damage his body had suffered. "You're mistaken." Her voice was as tight as her expression. "I'm an old friend of your sister-in-law, but I seldom attend social gatherings. The only reason I'm here this time is because I'm Alexandra's godmother. As you saw with Mr. Trowbridge I'm not particularly welcome in society, and I prefer to keep to myself." There was just the faintest flush on her high cheekbones, and he wondered if it came from the fire or her own words.

"Why?" he said softly.

He'd managed to startle her. "Why what?"

He swung his legs off the desk and set them on the floor, managing to keep a grimace of pain off his face. "Why aren't you welcome in society, why did the vicar feel he could accost you like that?"

She rose with that almost unnatural grace, clearly sensing he was more a danger with his feet on the floor. "Because, Lord Brandon, I was a whore."

CHAPTER 5

Emma wasn't certain what she expected from Brandon Rohan. Immediate contempt was the most likely response, or an insulting demand for sexual favors. In truth, she was hoping for one or the other, something that would wipe any lingering emotions forever. All he had to do was look at her with disdain and she'd be done.

Brandon Rohan simply raised an eyebrow. "I don't actually use my title," he said casually.

She did her best not to gape at him, too startled to say anything more. Then she rallied. "Why not? Why don't you use the advantages you've been given?"

The faint twist of his mouth could almost be called a smile. "Why don't you use your beauty—it's just as valuable a commodity, perhaps more so than a courtesy title. Oh, that's right, you did, but apparently you don't any longer, which begs the question, why did you offer up that particular bit of information?"

He still wasn't looking at her with any sort of distaste, merely bland curiosity. It unnerved her, when he already set her off balance. "Someone would have told you, sooner or later," she muttered, feeling graceless and not caring.

"I'd be forced to hit them if they did," he said. "And I'm afraid telling me makes no difference—I'll still have to hit them, and that complicates things, since I've been expressly forbidden to pound on the vicar, due to his position and his scrawny appearance. However, I expect my brother would forgive me if he knew about the man's behavior."

He sounded as if he was discussing dealing with a runaway pig, and her temper began to stir. He was turning a source of pain and shame into an inconvenience. "You've been out of society for a long time, Lord Brandon," she said, liking the formality of his title. It kept him one more step away from her. "Selling one's body is not an act that is overlooked among 'good' people."

"People do what they have to do," he said, unmoved. "I presume you didn't enter the profession on a whim."

"No," she muttered. She wasn't going to make excuses for herself—be damned to them all. The only one who knew her history was Melisande, and it broke her best friend's heart. She certainly didn't want this man's pity. "Am I supposed to be grateful that you're noble enough to forgive my transgressions?" she said sharply.

His lids were half lowered on his ice-blue eyes. Not that she could see their color in the darkness, but she remembered that brilliant blue —for some damnable reason it still haunted her dreams. "You didn't transgress against *me*," he said mildly. "It's none of my business."

She'd worked herself up into such a state that his words deflated her. She was left with nothing to say, and she stared at him, at the beauty and ruin of his face, silent.

"But in fact I do appreciate your informing me," he went on in a purely practical tone. "I was going mad trying to think of where I'd seen you before, why your name was familiar, and now I know. I frequented a number of houses of ill repute—I must have seen you there." His forehead furrowed. "God, you must have been so young."

She froze. For a moment she recognized the nameless soldier she had cared so much about, and his casual sympathy twisted her heart. She wanted to cry, and she'd given up crying years ago. It accomplished nothing. He'd been to the house. Of course, he had—so had his older brother and any number of gentlemen. But he hadn't seen her there—once she took over the reins she never had to service anyone, and she ran the place behind closed doors, never venturing out among the customers. Some part of his brain was remembering her from the hospital, but her spontaneous announcement had successfully detoured him. Now that he thought he had the answers he wouldn't have to think of her again.

And then it got worse.

"Good God, I didn't sleep with you, did I?" he said in tones of absolute horror, and the man she'd cared about disappeared once more, leaving the cynic in his wake.

She glared at him. "You did not." And if he asked her how she could be certain she'd take the fire poker and bash him on the head. Or at least think about.

But he looked relieved, and she still wanted to hit him.

She managed a small shrug, ignoring her unruly reaction. "So, you can see why I'm persona non grata. Don't worry, you won't be required to be around me. I usually only visit when there are no other guests in residence. The family knows me and accepts me without question, and that's what matters." She started toward the door, desperate to get away from him. She couldn't bear that calm expression, she couldn't bear to be so close to him, to feel so panicked and angry and vulnerable.

Almost at the door, she realized she was being ridiculous. He'd made no attempt to stop her. Though he'd risen he simply stayed in the shadows, watching her, and she wasn't sure if she was relieved or. . . disappointed.

"You're forgetting one thing, Mrs. Cadbury. And I assume the Mrs. is a courtesy title, just as mine is."

She didn't bother to answer that question. "What?" she said testily.

And then he smiled at her, and her heart twisted. It was an honest smile, the way he had looked down at his infant goddaughter, with none of the cynical reserve that now seemed to be his norm. "I'm a member of this family."

She stared at him. What the hell did he mean by that? Was he going to convince the family to shun her, or was he saying he would agree with their acceptance? She wasn't going to ask.

"Good night, my lord," she said sharply, whisking herself out the library door and shutting it firmly behind her.

SHE'D ALMOST SLAMMED the heavy door. Brandon looked at it with real amusement—at least that explained her prickly attitude. If she thought a Rohan was going to disapprove of her, she'd picked the wrong family. Well, there was no telling with Charles—he was the most-staid member of their ramshackle tribe—but even he might just shrug. She was making a huge fuss over nothing, as far as he was concerned. Anyone who rejected her was someone not worth knowing. He remembered the house now; it had always been the height of elegance and good breeding, and the women there had been treated well, more like debutantes than hired companions. He was just going to have to do his best to convince Mrs. Emma Cadbury—he'd known perfectly well there had never been a Mr. Cadbury—that he had absolutely no problem with her past. For a moment he'd been horrified to think he might have bedded her and then forgotten, but who could forget a woman like her?

She was none of his business, he reminded himself. Granted, she was almost eerily beautiful, and he would have given anything to take her to bed and disrupt that cool, controlled expression. He could feel his body stir at the thought and he quickly controlled it.

In truth, he didn't want a dalliance and he certainly wasn't interested in anything more than that. If he were to stay in the south of England he could set her up as his mistress. No, that idea seemed very unpleasant, both staying in civilization and turning her back into. . . He might want to bed her, but it was a logical reaction to a beautiful woman, and he'd never found the need to act on those feelings if it seemed unwise. Not anymore.

Besides, she was a surgeon, of all things! He wondered if she cut off men's bollocks—she'd probably jump at the chance, and he wasn't sure he'd blame her. He'd seen what could happen to women who sold their bodies, and it was never pretty. He could remember nights with the Heavenly Host and the things they'd done. . .

He pushed that thought out of his mind, keeping it in the place he kept all his most appalling memories. He was far better off back in Scotland, away from reminders, from temptation, from the unexpectedly bewitching Emma Cadbury.

She must have run off to her bedroom, her bare feet flying across the floors. He'd liked those feet, her long toes, her delicate arch. Was the woman gorgeous everywhere?

He wasn't going to find out. He needed to make his way to bed as well if he had any hope of an early escape. That way he could avoid stuffy Charles and whatever nefarious matrimonial plans he might have.

He walked to the fire, damping down the coals, and he almost thought he could detect the faint scent of flowers and heat and woman. He closed his eyes for a moment, wondering what she might taste like.

"No," he said out loud, his eyes flying open in disgust at his maundering thoughts. "Just no."

CHAPTER 6

The sky was just beginning to lighten when Emma gave up trying to sleep. She washed and dressed quickly, then tossed the rest of her clothes in the one bag she'd brought. Melisande would be extremely cross with her, both for sneaking out when she'd promised to stay, and for dispensing with the help of a maid and doing everything herself. Then again, Melisande knew her better than anyone, and she knew that her best friend would accept her disappearance with no more than a slight grumble.

The servants were stirring—most of them rose well before dawn to begin their endless day and night of labor—and she gave a friendly smile to the chambermaid who scurried past her. It was Rosie, one of the girls from the Dovecote, but for some reason she didn't respond with her usual cheeky grin. Instead, with lowered eyes, she scuttled away, far too quickly, and Emma watched her go, frowning. What on earth could be wrong with her? Rosie had seemed happy with her new employment, which, despite the hard work, was better than the dangers of making a living on her back.

It had been difficult to persuade some of the girls. Some never changed, like Violet Highstreet, who now ran an elegant brothel in the heart of Mayfair, but at least she operated on more democratic principles, following Emma's example.

It seemed so long ago, she thought as she followed the long, empty hallways down to the ground floor. Mrs. Cadbury's house had been run along democratic lines—they all shared the profits equally, they catered to pleasant and clean gentlemen, and for a while she'd been lulled into a spirit of complacency. It had taken a random meeting with Melisande Carstairs to break her out of the trap, and the girls, who later became known as the Gaggle thanks to Benedick's sharp tongue, came too, complaining and arguing all the way.

She reached the ground floor, then headed down the last flight of stairs into the tunnels that led between the house and the stable. They had been installed fifty years ago by the previous owner, a dandy who hadn't wanted to get his coat wet before he went out riding in inclement weather, which had never made sense to Emma. The rider would be drenched the moment he left the confines of the stable—why would it make a difference?

The moment she stepped into the tunnel she breathed a sigh of relief. The only person she had to face was the head groom, and Lakeland had always treated her with deference and kindness. He had standing orders to take her wherever she wanted to go, and freedom was so close she could taste it.

The tunnel was unlit, and she'd forgotten to bring a lantern. She was a strong woman, impatient with her own weaknesses, but truth be told she'd never liked darkness much, and the pitch black of the corridor made her heart start pounding. She knew she was being ridiculous, and she sped up, determined to escape from the impenetrable shadows.

It was like running into a brick wall, something so hard it almost knocked the breath out of her, and she started to fall back when an arm reached out to catch her, pulling her back. Against him.

For a moment she couldn't move. She hadn't been pressed against a man's body in years, and never one so tall and strong and muscled. She knew who it was. There were any number of tall, strong men at Melisande's house party, as well as in the stables, but the way her luck had been running it could only be but one. Damn it.

And he wasn't letting go of her. She squirmed but he didn't release her and for one insane moment she wanted to close her eyes and lean into him, rest her head against his shoulder, put her arms around his waist.

Fortunately, she was of sound mind. "Would you please let me go, Lord Brandon?" she demanded in a frosty voice.

She heard an unexpected laugh and after an infinitesimal delay he released her. Stepping back, she suddenly felt the damp chill of the place when a moment ago she'd been so warm.

"What are you doing skulking around here, Miss Cadbury?"

"I am Mrs. Cadbury," she said stiffly, "not miss." She'd never been a miss.

"And I told you I didn't use my title, yet you persist in calling me Lord Brandon. Why don't we just dispense with honorifics entirely—you can be Emma and I'll be Brandon."

"I don't think so," she said tartly. "Our stations are so far removed that my mind can't even comprehend it."

"Oh, I think your mind can comprehend a great deal." His words seemed like a challenge, but she refused to consider it any further.

"Lord Brandon," she said with deliberate emphasis, "would you please allow me to pass?"

"Certainly, Miss Cadbury . . ."

"Mrs. Cadbury," she corrected in a repressive tone. Why was her heart hammering? Surely it wasn't as loud as it felt in this dank, tomb-like atmosphere?

"Miss Cadbury. I'll be happy to let you pass, I'll even escort you to your destination. As soon as you tell me why you're down here at the crack of dawn."

Blast the man! "I would think that would be obvious. I must return to the city."

"You must, must you? And what has caused this sudden emergency? Benedick informed me that you were staying for the week. What are you running away from?"

It was anger rushing through her body, she told herself, a sudden surge of emotion that was making her feel light-headed and shaky. "I do not run."

He gave a disbelieving snort. "You most certainly do. You ran out of the library early this morning as if the hounds of hell were after you. I promise you, I had no intention of following you."

It was a good thing they were having this totally inappropriate discussion in the dark—he wouldn't be able to see the way her face flushed. She took a deep breath, calming herself. "I'm sure you didn't. I was merely in a hurry to see if I could get some rest before I had to leave."

"Hurrying seldom leads to a good night's sleep, which I presume continued to elude you. That's something we have in common. I don't sleep when I'm around my family. The Highlands are a different matter —I sleep like a baby up there in the clean, cool air. You ought to try it."

Was he being deliberately cruel? "I don't foresee a trip to Scotland in my future, Lord Brandon."

"Why not, Miss Cadbury?" His voice caressed her name, and she wanted to smack him.

She didn't even have to force a polite smile—he couldn't see her. "I'm far too busy for frivolous jaunts. In fact, it's imperative that I return to London immediately, so if you would please get out of my way I'd be most grateful."

"I doubt that you have suddenly been called back to London. You seem to have taken me in dislike. I presume it's my ugly mug that's put you off."

"Don't be absurd!" she said, shocked.

"No? Well, you've probably heard dark tales of my degenerate behavior in years past. If you're as close a friend to Melisande as you appear to be then I imagine you know the full breadth of my wickedness." His voice was light, uncaring.

"Lord. . . Lord Brandon, I have not taken you in dislike," she stammered, appalled. "As far as I can tell you are a pleasant young man with an admirable record in the war that left you with battle scars of honor."

His laugh was both cynical and unsettling. "Really? I must assure you that I am most definitely not very pleasant, and I'm no longer young, and any claim I had to honor is long gone."

"Younger than me," she blurted out, then could have bit her tongue.

"Oh, really? You bothered to ask? I'm flattered. And what great age are you?"

"Thirty-two," she said repressively. "Old enough to view things with a little more distance. You have both arms and legs, you're not blind, and you seem fit. So many men are much worse off."

"You're right, of course, but I must admit that doesn't provide much comfort." His tone was sharp. "Don't worry, I no longer spend my time brooding and feeling sorry for myself. I've made peace with who I am."

"Have you?" It was for too intrusive a question. This was exactly why she had to get away from here—she kept crossing boundaries that were inviolate.

Whatever dark mood had hit him had vanished. "Of course." His tone was flippant. "Now why don't you turn around and head back upstairs? Melisande doesn't even have to know you tried to do a bunk."

"I told you I have to get back to London. Immediately. It's an emergency." She certainly sounded desperate enough—that much was real. "And what are you doing down here at this early hour?"

"I was planning on sneaking out as well. My family has been a little too. . . managing. . . for me, and I thought making myself scarce would be a wise idea. I'll tell you what—if you're equally set on getting away from here I'll take you with me. Who knows, you might like Scotland."

She was unprepared for how painful his light words were, as if she'd been stabbed in the heart, and she faced the dismal truth. A small part of her wanted him to scoop her up and carry her away, damn it. No matter how much common sense and cynicism filled her, there was some weak, longing strain in her that was still ridiculously in love with Brandon Rohan.

A man who didn't even recognize her.

"I should slap you," she said evenly.

"I wouldn't if I were you. I might slap you back. And don't give me any tripe about hitting a woman. I view you as an equal, not some frail flower of femininity. I'd give you the respect you deserve by treating you as I would any man."

She *would* hit him, damn it! Except that she didn't want her flesh touching his. Maybe if she had a gun. . .

That was enough to shock her. "Will you please move out of the way?" The intimacy of the darkness around them was only increasing her feelings of isolation.

"No need to, I'm afraid. There's a reason why I'm not already on the road. My dear brother has left word that none of the horses are to be made available to his guests without his express permission, even those that don't belong to him. I'm sure he knew I intended to bolt, and Melisande probably didn't trust you. I'm afraid you're stuck here for the moment."

She took a quick breath. "Doesn't that mean you're trapped as well?"

"Oh, I'm never trapped. I've already sent my man to the local inn to hire a pair of horses for us until I can buy new ones. He and I should be off fairly soon. I don't expect we'll meet again, which for some reason should please you. I don't know why—I'm perfectly amiable, but you don't seem to be particularly taken with me."

She ignored the odd pang that ran through her, just as she squashed down her instinctive protest. Let him believe she disliked him—things were much simpler that way. "And you'd simply leave your horse behind?"

"Of course not. Rohan will send Emma back to me when he realizes it's too late."

She dropped the bag she'd been clutching. "You named your horse Emma?"

"Indeed. Perhaps that's why I'm so taken with you. You're almost as pretty as she is."

She couldn't take any more. She picked up her bag, turning to leave, when he caught her arm again, not gently. "If you're so eager to escape I'll take you with me."

She yanked herself free, but she could still feel his strong fingers on her arm. "Go to the devil, Lord Brandon," she said fiercely, stomping back the way she came, shaking with anger and frustration and something that she wouldn't name.

"Only if you join me, Emma," he said with a soft laugh, and like a total coward she gave into temptation and ran.

CHAPTER 7

By the time Emma reached her room she'd slowed down to a decorous pace. The rain had settled in, the light was fitful even through the tall windows of Starlings Manor, and she felt like a ghost as she walked through the empty halls, drab and gray and lost.

Her bed was already made, the room dank and cold when she closed the door to turn and face it. It was a lovely room, always kept for her no matter how many guests were in residence. There was a large desk with excellent light where she could study, a comfortable chair where she could sit and read. She'd chosen the colors herself—a soft gray-blue that felt serene whenever she walked in.

Except for today. She felt rattled, unsettled, and she couldn't shake the last half hour from her mind, the feel of his body against her, his hands on her arms. Men knew better than to touch her—she'd cut an aspiring surgeon when he'd moved in on her while she was working. But Brandon was different. She'd felt his touch, long ago, and she knew it, deep in a place she hadn't realized still existed.

She needed to concentrate on what was important, what was good, when she was feeling so hopeless. Brandon Rohan was strong and healthy, no longer a wounded soldier clinging to life, nor the sickly skeleton of a man addicted to opium and whiskey. She didn't have to worry about him anymore—he would be fine. She could let go.

That he'd forgotten her was a blessing as well, she reminded herself, no matter how much it stung. The only connection between the two of them was known to her alone, and she could take care of it, dismiss it with no fear of it coming back to haunt her.

She was happy, she truly was. She had her work—she had saved lives at Temple Hospital, she would continue to save lives wherever she ended up living.

Admittedly, the situation at the hospital had become more and more difficult, and now, with Benedick's latest determination, it threatened to become impossible. As a major benefactor, the viscount had a great deal to say in the running of the institution, or Emma would never have found a place there.

But Benedick had decided that Emma would replace Mr. Fenrush, and no sensible argument would dissuade him. The surgeon was a venal, ham-handed butcher, but he'd been in control for decades, and his reputation, was impeccable, despite the fact that he killed more patients than he saved. He was a cruel, vicious little man, and she shuddered at the thought of what she was going to face when she returned. The sooner she did, the better. The fact that it took her far away from Brandon Rohan was merely an added benefit.

This place had been her haven, and it could be again, as long as she didn't have to spend time with him. He reminded her of too many things she could never have, but she hated being a coward.

Perhaps she could find a cottage of her own near Starlings. She could take care of the Gaggle, keep an eye on Melisande, glory in her godchildren, and never have to breathe the foul air of London again. Lord Brandon might occasionally come to visit, but it was just as likely he'd turn up at his parents' country house in Somerset for family gatherings. If he did return, she'd be living in her own house and she could easily avoid him. In truth, the future was looking quite satisfactory— nothing but pleasant times awaited her.

She had a headache, sharp and probing, and she pulled out her hairpins, letting her dark mane fall loose over her shoulders. She reached up to rub her scalp as she stared out the windows into the gloom. She'd planned to spend a week in the country, and it looked as if she was going to have no choice. The best she could do was keep busy, and the Gaggle were nearby.

Now that they'd finished the move, the country Dovecote was bursting at the seams, and Emma had gone down there almost every day. Most everyone had made the transition well, though Mollie Biscuits didn't think much of the kitchen. The others had settled in, and many of them, born and bred city girls, were now venturing out of doors simply for pleasure.

It was a good thing Starlings Manor came equipped with a large dower house. The estate was huge—the entire place covered more than a thousand acres. It had belonged to the Dukes of Bellingham, but the last one had died without an heir, and Viscount Rohan had been one of the few in England able to afford it. Melisande had immediately claimed the massive dower house and it served the purpose beautifully.

She needed some sort of distraction, she thought, leaning against the window. If Benedick Rohan was playing silly games with the carriages she could easily walk—after all, she'd been bred a country girl and her job required she spend hours on her feet instead of on her back, something she always considered with amusement whenever her feet were hurting her. She wouldn't melt in the heavy rain.

It was a perfect day to curl up by a warm fire and immerse herself in medical texts, but first she was going to clear her mind and her fancies by visiting the Dovecote, always a strong reminder not to feel sorry for herself. She'd be plied with ginger biscuits and hot, strong tea, surrounded by the only friends she had outside of Melisande. Why should a little rain stand in the way of that?

She was about to change her shoes when there was a soft scratching at the door, and a maid poked her head in.

"Beg pardon, Mrs. Cadbury," she said, "I hadn't thought you'd be coming back to your room. I'll lay a fire right now. . ."

"No need, Rosie. The rain appears to have stopped for the time being, and I find I'm in need of fresh air."

"Good day for a walk, missus," Rosie offered.

Emma glanced out the leaded-paned windows to the overcast sky.

"Whether it is or not, I should make another visit to the Dower House. I find the company more amenable there."

The girl said nothing for a moment, then took a deep, nervous breath. "If you're going to the Dower House you might want to take the shorter way past the orchards. Us girls all use it, and it's ever so much quicker."

"Excellent advice." Emma knew she sounded far heartier than she felt, but she'd learned years ago that brooding never helped a troubled situation. Action was always best.

"You simply turn left past the orchards and follow the path," Rosie said. "It will lead you to the Dower House."

Emma wrinkled her brow. "Won't that take me in the opposite direction?"

"It loops around. Just follow the path, over the footbridge and then left again and you'll be there."

The girl was unaccountably nervous, and Emma couldn't imagine why. Melisande had to be the most lenient of mistresses—Rosie would have nothing to be afraid of. "Are you all right, my dear? If you're not feeling well I'm certain you'd be allowed to go back to bed . . ."

Rosie's anxiety increased. "I'm fine, Mrs. Cadbury. No need to mention it to anybody. Lady Melisande makes certain that we don't work longer than twelve hours a day, and we get time off for meals and even a bit of a rest. She's the talk of London with her newfound ways. You wouldn't believe it."

In fact, Emma would believe exactly that. Melisande was the best woman she had ever known, the best person, and she had a scrupulous sense of the unfairness of life. They'd called her "Sweet Charity" Carstairs before she'd married Rohan—a society joke for her efforts to save various soiled doves, not to mention having a retired whore as a partner in the endeavor. Melisande had continued on, undaunted, and Emma had done her part. For some women the position as an upstairs maid was a dream come true, particularly for some of those who'd made their living on the streets. For others it might be a punishment.

Rosie looked as if she belonged in the punishment category, Emma thought, eyeing her. "Where did you come from, Rosie?" she asked suddenly, and the girl started, a look of panic flitting across her face before vanishing, so fast Emma would have thought she'd mistaken it. "I mean, originally."

"The north," Rosie said. "My family died and I came down here to live with my aunt, but then she died and I had nowhere else to go except the streets. You know the rest of it." It sounded reasonable enough, and Emma had no reason to disbelieve her, but there was something uneasy, almost furtive about the girl. Emma was used to those emotions, having seen them in the Gaggle, having felt most of them herself.

"Well, I'm glad you're here at Starlings. Go along now and get a cup of tea for yourself. If anyone bothers you tell them it's on my orders."

There was only the slight shadow of a forced smile as Rosie curtseyed. "Yes, miss. I'm very lucky to be here."

She watched the girl leave, her mind busy. Something was wrong with the girl, and she needed to discover what it is. She might be ill, or even in the family way, but no matter how great the problem, she would be treated well and fairly, hallmarks of Melisande's efforts toward them, toward all of the Gaggle.

Which reminded Emma that her own visit there was not without complications. The soiled doves were always trying to find a man for her, determined that she should have some kind of storybook ending. It touched her, though she never showed it, that women who had lived such a harsh, unforgiving life still had a naïve belief in love and marriage. She'd lost that belief years ago, and she hadn't suffered nearly as much as some of them.

She would be naïve herself to think that they didn't know all about the appearance of the viscount's youngest brother, and even the unexpected change in her own plans. Many were still illiterate despite Emma's best efforts, but they knew how to put two and two together. She decided not to take the shortcut, so she could spend the walk down there schooling her attitudes and expressions enough to fool most of them. Mollie Biscuits might be a challenge.

At least the shortcut would help later if the rain returned. Grabbing only her serviceable shawl, she left the room, in search of strong tea and warm hugs. Both would go a long way towards curing what ailed her.

THREE HOURS LATER, rain was soaking through Brandon's clothes, a fact which bothered him not in the least. He didn't mind the sharp wind, the constant downpour, even the sluggish horse that Noonan had been able to procure. They'd left Starlings Manor without a word to anyone and were already six miles away. They could probably make another ten before they stopped for the night, find a decent coaching inn, one with a bath and a fire, and be back in Scotland by the next week if they pushed.

No, he didn't mind the horse, the rain, the cold. All he could think of was the conundrum that was Emma Cadbury.

That should have been warning enough—for his mind to be so obsessed with a woman in such a short time was a clear sign of danger. He had no time for pleasant interludes in bed, and particularly not with someone like Emma Cadbury, who probably did an excellent job of feigning pleasure in an act that meant nothing but degradation to her. She was too much trouble on every level, and he had more important things to do.

Still, he didn't know why he was running. He had done terrible, hideous things in his life, things that his ramshackle but loving family had no inkling of, but he'd never been a coward. So what if Charles was ready to marry him off? He was no longer nine years old, being bullied by a stuffy elder. It had been child's play to avoid him, sneaking out of the house the moment Noonan returned, but maybe he'd been too rash. After all, there was no way Charles or Benedick could make him propose marriage—he was perfectly capable of simply refusing to do so. He said no on a daily basis to the indulgences that had almost killed him and others.

And he had no reason to run away from Emma Cadbury. He thought he understood her, or at least enough to satisfy his interest. Even if he were in the market for a decent shag she was the wrong choice. When he'd visited houses like the one where Emma had worked, he would take a particular pleasure in drawing his partners past their professional response to real pleasure, but that was when he'd been younger, foolishly carefree. Emma was no longer meant for dalliance—in truth, he couldn't imagine a time she ever was, despite her extraordinary beauty.

But it wasn't her beauty that was preying on his mind. He'd seen beautiful women a hundred times before—he could admire them and move on. There was something else about Emma that caught his attention, and that part was still a mystery. It was hardly her charm of manner—she seemed to dislike him the moment she met him. She always seemed to be struggling to be polite, and ultimately losing the battle.

Her slightly taciturn manner was both unexpected and fascinating. She said what he'd want to say if proper decorum hadn't been beaten into him as surely as his army training. Despite the rages that came and went, rages he kept under iron control, he did his best never to show emotion. He was a *tabula rasa*, a blank slate for people to accept or ignore. No one could get near him and that was the way he preferred it.

And yet with Emma Cadbury, his rigidly polite exterior seemed to crack. Any smart man would run.

He *was* a smart man, but he wasn't one who ran away, and he had to admit there was an irresistible challenge to her. He could show her how delightful sex could be if it was inspired by desire, not money—he had no doubt of it. His skills were beyond that of the average Englishman—his time in Afghanistan had taught him all sorts of interesting things, things he found himself imagining doing with Emma.

He wanted to prove that Emma Cadbury wasn't the cool, controlled woman she tried to present to the world. He could ruffle her feathers. He could shock the hell out of her by showing her what her body could do. And it was pure hell to be riding on a dull horse in the pouring rain with an erection.

He yanked on his reigns and glanced over at Noonan.

"You ready to go back to Starlings, me boy?" Noonan asked calmly.

Brandon shook his head in disgust at his own obviousness. "How did you know?"

"I know you better than I know meself. I was hoping you'd come to your senses hours ago rather than keep going in this soaking rain. I could use a dram of good Irish whiskey."

"Rohan's more likely to have Scotch," Brandon said imperturbably, turning his horse.

"That heathen stuff will have to do," Noonan said in an aggrieved voice.

"It's been good enough for the last three years," he pointed out. "Let's get going—it's going to take forever on this slug you brought me."

Noonan gave him a haughty look at odds with his craggy Irish face. "A good horseman knows how to get the best out of a horse no matter what the problem," he said loftily.

Brandon rolled his eyes. "I think this *is* the best she has to offer," he said glumly. "Let's go."

"In a bit of a hurry to get back to her?"

Brandon was done with denial. "Yes," he said, and gave the horse a swift kick.

CHAPTER 8

"You look like something the cat dragged in," Mollie Biscuits announced, setting down her rolling pin. "What made you walk all this way in the pouring rain? You be punishing yourself again? It sets an 'orrid example, it does, to the others. If you can't forgive yourself then why should they?"

Emma sank down in the chair beside the table Mollie used for kneading dough. The woman's meaty fists had the lightest touch when it came to baking, from thick, hearty slices of bread to delicate pastries that practically dissolved in your mouth. "His lordship decided that no one was to take any of the carriages out, and I couldn't stay in that house one moment longer."

Mollie pulled off the apron that covered her massive bosom, shook it until clouds of flour settled over the both of them, then took the other seat at the table. "What's up 'is arse?" she demanded. "And why did Charity let 'im get away wiv it?"

"Melisande," Emma said, putting particular emphasis on "Charity's" real name, "wants me to stay, and she doesn't mind if her husband is the one who makes it impossible to leave." She brushed the loose flour from her cheeks and nose, clapping her hands to rid herself of the rest.

"What's all this about leaving? You said you were here for a good long rest, something you sorely need, if I say so meself. You've been burning the candle at both ends and you know it, what with all that doctoring business while you were trying to watch over her ladyship's townhouse. I thought you were learning your lesson when you sent everyone down here. You know you can't keep up like that."

"Thank God I did send them," Emma said, wanting to change the subject. There were too many people who thought they needed to protect her from herself. "If they were still in residence they might have died in the fire."

Mollie made a clucking sound. "The more I thinks about it, the more suspicious I get. I lived there longer than anyone. That place was kept tidy. No loose rags or papers likely to make a fire spread. There were a lot of people who thought Charity had no business bringing a bunch for whores into her house, and we was always on the lookout for danger. You were the one what taught us that."

"I'm not very trusting," Emma admitted.

"No!" Mollie said in feigned shock, grinning. "Did they think it was an accident?"

"The police came and searched for bodies, but there weren't any, thank God. Someone from the Fire Brigade picked over the place, but no one mentioned anything suspicious."

Mollie shrugged her heavy shoulders. "Seems strange, is all." She peered at her through beetled brows. "The rest of 'em are itching to see you, but I thinks you need a strong cup of tea before you have to deal with them lot. Am I right?"

"You always are, Mollie."

Mollie accepted the praise as her due and rose to move over to the stove with her slow, rolling pace. She had once been considered the most beautiful woman in all of London and she'd lived very well indeed. By the time Emma met her she had already retired from the business, making herself useful in Mother Howard's kitchens and doing her best to keep everyone's spirits up with cakes and pies and simple good sense. In fact, it had sometimes been rumored that Mother Howard's brothel had retained its exceptional clientele with its pastries rather than its more traditional sensory delights.

She could also make the best tea—wickedly strong and powerfully sweet, a feat Emma could never duplicate no matter how hard she tried. She took the proffered cup with a sigh of gratitude, took a sip that burned her tongue and then slid back in her chair, at peace. "I just want to stay here," she murmured. "Can't you find me a pallet somewhere?"

Mollie snorted. "With all them new girls from London filling every nook and cranny? I think not. We've got two and three to a bed right now, and until the latest bunch get a placement it'll stay that way."

Emma sighed. It had been a desperate, unlikely attempt, and in truth she no longer needed to worry. Brandon and his ancient retainer would be gone by now, heading back to Scotland. Starlings Manor was once more a safe haven.

She took a deep swallow of the strong tea, and she could practically feel her backbone stiffen. He'd been a momentary distraction, a bit of longing for a time long past, and it was over. She would never ...

"Oh, Jesus Christ on a fucking fig tree," Mollie said bitterly, shoving herself to her feet. "They're here."

"Who's here?" Emma demanded, startled, and then realized the female voices she heard were not those of any former streetwalker, soiled dove, kept woman, or lady of the night; these were the purebred sounds of Mayfair. "Oh, Lord," she said weakly, having never developed the ability to curse in style of most of her friends. "Melisande's brought the ladies here for tea, hasn't she?"

"That's what it sounds like. I shouldn't be surprised—she drags people down here on any excuse."

"I should have remembered," Emma said wearily. "She wants to drum up support among her society friends, the ones who shunned her when she was simply an eccentric widow. Now that she's a countess they're more interested in listening, and she's always looking to take on new sponsors for the Gaggle Project."

"Gaggle Project?" Mollie echoed grimly, a dangerous look in her eye. "Is that referring to us?"

"I know—it's a wretched name, isn't it? I'll talk to her about it. In the meantime, I don't suppose I could sneak out the back door and. . ."

"Emma!" Melisande greeted her in a carrying voice from the door she'd just thrust open. "I thought you might be here. Come and join us

—you know even more about the program than I do. After all, you've been on the front lines while I've been here having babies." She smiled at Mollie. "You don't mind us dropping in, do you, Mrs. Biscuits?"

Melisande had been determined to address the sundry souls of the Dovecote formally, declaring that it gave them back some dignity, and all the arguments in the world couldn't convince her that "Mrs. Biscuits" was absurd.

Mollie had given up fighting it. "Not at all, your ladyship. I'll have tea ready in a few minutes."

"Come along, dearest," Melisande said to Emma. "You know you do a better job explaining the business aspect."

"I should help Mollie. . ." She tried to back up, but Melisande was as stubborn as she was.

"Don't need help," Mollie pronounced, the interfering wretch. "And if I did, don't I have three girls learning to cook as we speak? You go along now, Miss Emma. No need to worry about us."

She was trapped, and she threw Mollie a speaking glance as Melisande drew her into the front parlor. The room was crowded— usually Melisande's tea parties were small and female. The entire house party seemed to have descended on the Dovecote, including their male counterparts, as well as several people she'd never seen before.

She must have balked, because Melisande gave her a gentle push. "What's wrong with you?" she whispered in her ear.

"Nothing at all. I'm just tired. I should be fine once the sun shines and I get enough sleep."

"Those two things are never a certainty, given that we live in England," Melisande muttered. "And if you're to sleep peacefully then you need to drive out whatever devils are plaguing you."

He's already gone, she thought wistfully. "You're right," she said out loud, moving into the stately room that had once been the reception hall for whatever dowager was in residence. Now it served as a school room, meeting place, and even, occasionally, a boxing salon. Emma knew better than anyone the dangers a woman could face, and she did her best to see that each girl was equipped with the needed skills to protect herself no matter what circumstances she was thrust into.

"And tea helps everything," Melisande added.

Emma's smile was real this time. "I think a dram of brandy would be better," she said below her breath.

Melisande shrugged. "I can send back to the house if you truly want some. . ." She drew her over to the sofa under the window.

"You know I don't drink," Emma said quickly, sinking down beside her friend. "If I change my mind I can always make a midnight run if I need it, though I prefer tea and a boring book."

"Is that what you found last night?"

She didn't blush, but she could come close to it. "How did you know?"

"Benedick came down early, and Brandon was still awake. He mentioned that you'd been there."

She remained utterly still, not revealing any of the distress the sound of his name brought her. *He was gone*, she reminded herself firmly. *Get over it.*

Then she shrugged, seemingly at ease. "He was very pleasant."

"Brandon? Are we talking about the same man? Ever since he's come back he's been closed up tighter than a bag wig."

At least she was able to see some humor in the image, and she smiled. "He's hardly an ogre, Melisande. . ."

"Darling, look who I found wandering around." Emma jerked her head upward, panic slicing through her, at the sound of Viscount Rohan's voice.

A second later relief swamped her, and she felt almost dizzy with it. Standing beside Viscount Rohan was a man she'd never seen before, though she knew immediately who he must be. Only a Rohan would be that tall, that gorgeous, with the same bright blue eyes she'd last seen in Brandon's face. Unlike the others, though, he looked a little too smug, a little too sure of himself, as he walked over and took Melisande's hand in his, bringing it to his lips.

"My darling sister-in-law," he said smoothly. "I hope you don't mind that I and my guests are tagging along on your little charitable outing. Belated felicitations on the birth of your new offspring, my dear. I deeply regret I wasn't able to be here in time for the christening, but I'm hoping late is more acceptable than never."

"Hullo, Charles," Melisande said, and Emma knew her friend well enough to recognize the lack of enthusiasm in her voice. "I hope your wife and daughters are well?"

"As always. Elinor and the girls are in London, alas. Too many social commitments to allow them to escape."

"And you were afraid our sister and her wretched husband might be in attendance," Rohan interjected dryly. "You needn't have worried. Miranda is once again expecting—I think she and the Scorpion are planning to repopulate the entire Lake District—so your wife's delicate sensibilities wouldn't have been offended."

So the Viscount didn't care much for his sister-in-law, Emma thought, trying to sink back into the sofa, away from the new brother's flat, unfriendly blue eyes. It was slightly difficult, because Melisande's hand had grasped onto hers to keep her in place.

Lord Charles didn't blink. "Had I but known. . ." he murmured. He glanced at Emma and then looked away again, immediately, as if he'd come across a dead animal on the road. "And just where is our brother? I hear he is much improved."

Emma held her breath, but it seemed as if Brandon's absence had yet to be noted. "I imagine he's out somewhere," Benedick said lazily. "In the meantime, you will want to be introduced to Melisande's. . ."

But Charles had already turned away, very effectively halting Rohan's attempt to introduce them, and the slight was obvious to all of them. "Perhaps I should go find him. We have business to discuss."

"I know you do," Rohan said patiently, with only the trace of an edge in his voice. "But introductions. . ."

"Of course!" Lord Charles presented his profile rather than his back to Emma and spoke to Melisande "Allow me to present Miss Frances Bonham and her companion, Miss Marion Trimby. They are most grateful for your kind hospitality."

Emma could just see the two young ladies beyond Lord Charles's imposing figure. Miss Frances seemed sweet, shy, and pretty, her companion, whose arm was threaded through Miss Frances's, had a stiffer backbone and a protective aura. It was clear, however, that an introduction would not be forthcoming, so Emma sat back, content to be grateful that Brandon wasn't around to see his brother's attempts to humiliate her. It took a lot of achieve that, and Emma had no intention of succumbing to the attempts of a starched-up bully.

The polite protestations and welcomes went right over her head, and Melisande's tight grip on her hand loosened once she realized Emma wasn't going to bolt. Emma suspected what was coming, and she wished there was a chance in hell of diverting it, but there was no stopping Melisande when she was in defense of a loved one.

"Charles!" she said in a carrying voice, and in sheer surprise her brother-in-law whirled around, unfortunately bringing him face to face with the two of them. "You have yet to meet my dearest friend, Mrs. Cadbury. I know you will want to thank her for all she has done for Benedick and me, and I'm certain you'll look forward to a long and happy acquaintance. Mrs. Cadbury is family to me, just as you are, and we can expect to have many happy times together." Her tight voice suggested no such thing, but the room went silent, awaiting the outcome of this tense situation. Would Charles insult his sister-in-law and hostess by walking away? And how would Benedick react to such a breach of etiquette?

The moment that he hesitated seemed endless, and Emma was uncomfortably aware of all the eyes on her, including the innocent, curious eyes of Miss Frances and her companion, and then Lord Charles performed the most perfunctory nod in the entire history of perfunctory nods. "Mrs. Cadbury," he said in a voice so tight it could have cracked glass.

She knew the art of perfunctory nods herself, and she made hers both condescending and gracious, with the reward of watching Charles's lips compress. At least there was absolutely nothing to remind her of Brandon, apart from a superficial family resemblance. There'd be no reason. . .

And then the world was knocked from under her, as the man himself strolled into the room, as if he'd never left, and she froze.

She knew he had—his absence had been a palpable thing, and his hair was still wet from the soaking rain. His beautiful, damaged face was damp as well, but he must have changed his clothes before coming down.

She suddenly coughed, and her breath came rushing back—she hadn't even realized she'd been holding it.

"I hope you don't mind me barging in," he said lightly. "When I got back from my ride the house was deserted of everyone but the servants, and I was directed down here."

And then his eyes went straight to hers, past all the people in between them, and there was an odd expression in them, one she couldn't decipher. Was he angry with her? Why in God's name had he come back?

Charles moved between them, blocking him. Melisande had a frown on her face, though Emma had no idea what it signified, and she felt the tension in her body loosen just a trifle.

"Brandon, old man!" Charles was saying with what seemed like forced heartiness. "You're back and you look like a new man." He flung his arms around his younger brother, embracing him. He was a little shorter than Brandon, and Emma could still feel Brandon's eyes on her, opaque and watchful.

He detached himself with perfect politeness. "It's good to see you, Charles," he said in a neutral voice.

"And you too, m'boy," he said. "But enough about this—I know why you're here. Don't you want to say hullo to your affianced bride?"

The sudden silence in the room was crushing, and Brandon didn't move, but when she caught his eyes once more his expression was utterly blank.

And Miss Frances burst into frightened tears.

CHAPTER 9

There was momentary chaos in the Dovecote's salon. The Gaggle had been outside the room, waiting to be invited, but at the irresistible sound of tears they rushed in, a group of noisy, fluttering birds, and some of the guests drew back, as if a plague of unsavory vermin had descended upon the company. For a moment Emma concentrated on that—outraged that some of these weak, self-important people dared to think they might be contaminated by real life, but then Charles Rohan's words struck her. She'd risen when Miss Bonham had burst into tears, her instinct to help another female so ingrained that it was instinctive, but Charles and Melisande were already surrounding her, while her companion, Miss Trimby, was glaring at Brandon. It was time to bolt.

She wasn't quite sure how she managed to escape the room, crashing into Long Polly as she was carrying a tray full of the Dower House's best china tea service, and while Polly, ever resourceful, managed to keep the tray upright, Emma was past her in a flash, almost at the open door when Mollie Biscuits spoke out.

"Where are you running off to, Miss Emma?" she demanded in a disapproving voice. "What's all that uproar in the meeting room?"

Emma tried to say something, but her throat had closed up, and she pushed through the door into the kitchen courtyard of the place, without answering.

Mollie stood in the door, calling after her. "You've never been a one to run from a problem, Miss Emma," she chided.

Emma halted her mad dash for just a moment, calling back over her shoulder. "I am now," she said breathlessly, and then she was gone.

Brandon stood frozen, not about to rush into action as everyone whirled around him. There was too much going on already. Emma and Melisande had leaped up, and a young woman was sobbing quietly in the arms of her companion, while Charles blustered and did his best to take the attention away from the weeping girl, who was now lifting her tear-streaked face from her hands and peering at him She looked absolutely terrified. He realized that from her position she could only see the scarred side of his face, and he supposed that was what had horrified her. He could hardly blame her—he'd stopped looking at his reflection long ago, but he knew perfectly well that he was a monster. When Charles had cooked up this Machiavellian marriage plot he obviously hadn't informed his future bride about her proposed husband's deficiencies. A man who looked like him would be a nightmare to any young virgin. Most people he knew did their best to avoid looking at him directly—in fact, there were only two people who always looked at both sides of his face. Noonan, of course, without a squeamish bone in his body. And now Emma Cadbury.

Charles took charge, of course, grabbing his arm and steering him out the front door, leaving the chaos behind. Brandon had just enough time to notice that Emma had disappeared, and he could imagine the conversation in the room when he was safely out of the way. Everyone was gathered around the pathetic Miss Bonham, making soothing noises, and then the door closed behind him. He was not in the mood for this.

He turned to look at Charles, a saturnine expression on his face. "I assume the weeping creature is my bride-to-be? Clearly a match made in heaven."

Charles was furious. "Good God, don't use that tone of voice with me. You sound like Benedick. Or that damned Scorpion," he added, hoping to strike a mortal blow. Charles's hatred of his brother-in-law was legendary.

Brandon moved further away from the house—he had no doubt that people were spying out of the mullioned windows. It took everything he had not to show any sign of pain or discomfort—it had been a hard ride on that miserable horse. He and his mare, Emma, and he inwardly laughed at his use of the name, were perfectly attuned. The new one jarred and shook his bad leg, and his mood was not precisely amiable. He was still chilled, damn it, his leg ached, and he'd just terrified some poor child into tears simply by appearing.

Not to mention whatever was going on with the beautiful Emma Cadbury. She'd vanished before he'd had a good look at her. What had spooked her?

He glanced at his brother, determined to prove he was unmoved by all this fuss. "I happen to like my brother-in-law," he said, knowing it was family heresy. The notorious Scorpion, better known as Lucien Malheur, was persona non grata among the younger Rohans, though their parents seemed to tolerate him well enough. On the few occasions when Brandon had left the Highlands, he'd ventured as far as the Lake District and Miranda and Lucien's massive home there, and he'd felt welcome. The Scorpion was no beauty either, and the raft of children took Brandon's horrifying visage in their stride, unlike his pompous brother who was keeping his furious eyes a few inches past Brandon's scarred face.

"Don't play games with me. You deliberately frightened your betrothed."

"First of all, Charles, she is most definitely not my betrothed, nor do I expect she ever shall be. I have no idea why you took it upon yourself to arrange my marriage without bothering to consult me, but it was a waste of time. I have absolutely no interest in getting married."

"You owe it to your name!"

Brandon raised an eyebrow. "I doubt Mother and Father would agree with that. Benedick already has an heir—there's no need for me to sacrifice myself on the altar of Venus."

"One boy," Charles shot back.

"Then you go ahead and try again. Your two daughters are charming girls, no thanks to you, but I imagine you could. . . er. . . rise to the occasion."

It was a question whether Charles's red face was from embarrassment or anger. "That's not possible," he said stiffly.

"Really? Did you suffer some injury?" The moment the words were out a truly fiendish idea came into Brandon's head, and this time his smile was genuine, pleased with himself.

Charles growled. "Don't be absurd! My wife has a delicate constitution—having another child at her age would be difficult."

"If I recall she's probably not much older than Mrs. Cadbury. She married young."

Charles looked positively apoplectic. "Do not mention my beloved wife's name in the same breath as that whore."

Brandon's lazy smile vanished along with his sorely strained good humor. "And I would suggest you not use that word when you're discussing Mrs. Cadbury," he said softly.

Charles has never been one to notice subtleties in people's behavior. He sniffed. "And why not? Has she already become your mistress? Fast work, considering you only arrived here yesterday, but then, there's no need for seduction with a creature like her. It's just a matter of finding the right price. You needn't worry—I'm sure Miss Bonham won't object as long as you're reasonably discreet, though I could wish your choice was a little less notorious."

But Brandon was back under control now, even if he really, truly wanted to throw his smug brother out a window. "I'm not in the market for a mistress at the moment," he said coolly. "And I'm afraid your grand plans have come to naught. I have no intention of getting married, ever. I imagine that will bring a great deal of relief to that poor girl—who is she, by the way? She looked as if she were about to faint when she caught sight of my elegant visage. You might at least have warned her you were attempting to wed her off to a horror."

At least Charles didn't protest Brandon's description of himself—Brandon would have had to hit him if he did. "You mistake the situation," Charles said in an effort at civility. "Of course she'd be shocked by your appearance—it's almost impossible to prepare someone for it.

And she is Miss Frances Bonham." Charles looked at him, as if expecting him to react to the name.

Brandon didn't say anything. Emma Cadbury hadn't been shocked by his appearance. She'd looked at him, at both sides of his face, and she hadn't even blinked. "Agreed," he said.

"This marriage is a perfect arrangement for both of you. Your reputation is in the gutter, and you've dragged down all of the family's efforts to prove themselves respectable, ruined all the progress we made over decades!"

"All the family's efforts?" he echoed with a hoot of laughter. "I don't recall Benedick or Miranda doing much to walk the straight and narrow, and I think our parents would be greatly amused to hear they'd been trying to salvage the family honor. That was long gone generations ago, and even my sins, at least the ones you know of, are no worse than our grandfather's."

"Will you stop arguing with me?"

"No. Not as long as you're spouting nonsense."

Charles ignored him. "Miss Bonham is in a similarly difficult situation."

"You mean she's ruined herself? Soiled goods? She looks awfully timid for a scarlet woman."

"Of course not! Miss Bonham is all that is respectable. She's also an heiress."

"I'm very happy for her. She should have no trouble attracting an acceptable husband, and I expect you know, interfering sort that you are, that I have more than enough money on my own."

"No one ever has enough money," Charles said gloomily. "Her brother also left her a large estate that borders on the edge of Marchings, but there are strings attached."

Brandon's laugh was not pleasant. "Now we get to the crux of the matter. Her land adjoins yours, and you think bringing it into the family would be a good idea. Why don't you just buy the place from her if, as I understand, she's now an orphan?"

Charles gave him a sour look. He'd always been a pinchpenny, a changeling among the imprudent Rohans, and he never paid for something if he could avoid it. "It's more complicated than that. Although

Miss Bonham is twenty-two she should still be able to manage the rigors of childbirth, though as you can see she's a very timid soul. She'd never interfere with you in any way. You'll need to bring her companion along as well, but Miss Trimby gives Miss Bonham all the company she needs. You just need to marry the girl, get a couple of sons on her, and spend her money. That's hardly a great sacrifice, is it?"

"There's just one flaw in your clever plan, brother," Brandon said, enjoying himself.

"What's that? Whatever it is, I'm sure we can dispose of it."

"I'm impotent."

It was even better then he'd imagined. Charles looked aghast. The emotions that chased each other across his face were swift and revealing. First horror, then embarrassment, followed swiftly by distaste and frustration.

"You're joking."

"I'm afraid I'm not. My war injuries were quite severe. "

"But. . . but. . . you were part of the Heavenly Host! Licentiousness is. . ."

"I liked to watch." In fact, it was close enough to the truth. He'd found no pleasure disporting with the paid companions, and the opium had left him uninterested in doing more. It was an ugly memory, and he quickly banished it. "While I suspect that Miss Bonham would be more than happy to dispense with my stud services she might find that when she's older she develops an interest in bedsport."

"Brandon," Charles said, shocked. "She's a lady!"

"And ladies don't like bedsport?"

"Certainly not!"

Brandon's mood was much improved, and he laughed. "Poor, poor Charles," he said softly. "No wonder you only have two children."

"I request that you cease this discussion of such a private topic. It's in bad taste."

Brandon was unmoved. "Did you know your wife was going to be such a dud in bed? It certainly wasn't a love match. What a waste! And you're such a paragon that you probably don't have a mistress."

"Of course not! And leave my wife out of this!" Charles's color was high, and Brandon took pity on him.

"It's neither here nor there. You may as well accept it; your well-orchestrated plan has fallen to pieces. But you needn't worry about any lingering embarrassment—I plan to go back to Scotland the first chance I get and with luck no one will ever know a possible alliance was being considered."

"I sent a notice to the *Times*."

For a moment Brandon didn't move. The idea of fratricide had a certain appeal, but Benedick would probably stop him, and it would make his parents unhappy. "Then you're just going to have to send in a retraction."

Even Charles couldn't miss the menace in his voice, but his brother always believed that his version of "right" was incontrovertible. "I can't. Do you realize what it would look like? Everyone would think you jilted Miss Bonham, and she has trouble enough already."

But Brandon wasn't interested in Miss Bonham's trouble. "I doubt it. People have seen my face—it would be more unusual that someone would agree to marry a wreck like me."

"Women marry peers in their dotage quite happily. Miss Bonham needs your protection, not to be publicly humiliated."

"Not my problem. Find some nice, pretty boy for her if you're so inclined—with a fortune it should be simple. Trust me, she'll be much happier."

He should have known his brother wouldn't give up that easily. "Who's to say your. . . er. . . condition is permanent? In fact, a year or two without marital relations would probably be very good for Miss Bonham. She's extremely timid around men, and this would give her time to get used to the idea."

"Quite permanent," Brandon said wickedly. "They shot off my. . ."

"Enough!" Charles was looking a deliciously uncomfortable cross between bilious and embarrassed. "I get the point."

"Good," Brandon said.

Charles took a deep breath. "Hear me out. I told you, Miss Bonham is in a difficult situation. You know as well as I do that presentable heiresses are always in short supply, and she should have been besieged all year, ever since she came out of mourning. Now the only one who'd take her is a fortune hunter or a. . ."

"A monster," Brandon supplied, and Charles had the grace to look embarrassed.

"You know your situation is difficult. It's highly unlikely that anyone else would be willing to marry you, given your. . . I'll be blunt. . . given your appearance. You could go back to Scotland and Miss Bonham could stay here with her companion. She's a quiet little thing with no interest in society, and she'd be perfectly happy to live her life in the country. Since the prospect of children is not an issue there would be no reason to stay around."

"And you'd just as soon an inconvenient complication like your scarred brother disappear, wouldn't you?"

"Of course not." Charles's denial was perfunctory. "I appeal to your Christian charity, Brandon."

"I don't have any. Miss Bonham's difficult situation, whatever it is, has nothing to do with me."

"Actually, old man," Charles said, "It does."

He'd known this, Brandon thought. Charles was doing his best to tighten the noose around him, and deep inside Brandon had known that he was somehow to blame. He still wasn't done paying for his sins.

He sighed, weary beyond belief. He should have just kept going today, not turned around to come back. What was it about Emma Cadbury that had made him change his mind? Curiosity? Lust? That nagging bit of memory that kept eluding him? "So tell me about Miss Bonham," he said finally. "And I'll judge for myself just how culpable I am."

There was no missing the gleam of triumph in Charles's pale blue eyes, and it took all of Brandon's strength of will not to clock him. "Miss Bonham's half-brother was no other than Harry Merton, the late, unlamented mastermind of the Heavenly Host. You remember, the man who orchestrated rape and murder? The man you followed slavishly until you were so far gone in depravity that you tried to hang yourself rather than face the consequences of your own evil."

Brandon turned slowly to look at him, his face a cold mask. "And how does that concern me? I'm hardly responsible for that deranged scum of a human being," he said coldly. He could feel things slipping out of his control. He was drowning, and there was no lifeline to pull him to shore. Where was Emma?

The thought was errant and absurd. Why would he think Emma Cadbury could save him from his worst self? Why would he want her to?

"Your memory of that time is, of course, spotty," Charles continued, "and doubtless you've forgotten your drunken appearance at Tattersall's. You informed all and sundry that Harry Merton was the depraved head of the Heavenly Host. I believe your accusations were extremely colorful, and most of them were, unfortunately, true. However, degenerate though he was, he did not eat cats and dogs, he didn't commit treason, and he most assuredly not have sexual congress with his sister."

"Jesus Christ," Brandon said, shutting his eyes for a pained moment.

"Don't compound things with blasphemy," Charles snapped. "Of course people professed that they didn't believe a word, but then, when so many of the grotesque things you were ranting about were proven true, no one was ever certain about Miss Bonham. She was ruined."

Brandon opened his eyes. He managed a shrug. "For all I know it could have been true. I remember very little of that time, but enough remains that I know Harry Merton was capable of anything."

Charles had puffed out his chest a bit, clearly knowing victory within his grasp. "A woman accused of such an abomination would, of course, be considered unmarriageable, and that's your fault. Society wouldn't mind if it was the truth, wouldn't even mind gossip, but having it put out there so publicly makes her position untenable. She's been living in seclusion ever since."

"Why can't she stay in seclusion? She has as little enthusiasm for this marriage as I do." It was a last attempt at escape, and he knew it would fail.

"You know English laws of inheritance as well as I do. The estate was relatively simple—when Harry Merton died the title went back to the crown, and the estate will follow if Miss Bonham doesn't marry by age twenty-five. She'll be destitute, disgraced, with no hope of a decent marriage."

Brandon tried one last time, knowing Charles was about to open the trap door beneath him. "I'm surprised you consider me a "decent" marriage prospect, Charles. This is not my concern. If you want I can settle any sum of money on her—hell, she can have it all. I just won't marry her. That, or I have little doubt that Benedick could do something about her legal situation. You know how insidiously clever he can be."

"You think money her will solve the problem? You think everyone wouldn't find out, further blackening her reputation? You're to blame for this, Brandon. Be a man and face your responsibilities. Stop shaming our parents."

He heard the trap door squeak, and he knew he was lost. He could keep arguing, or he could accept the inevitable. He had destroyed so many things with his willful self-pity and nihilism, his weakness. Be a man, Charles said. This was one small way he could atone.

"And she wants this?" he said in a dead voice. "Even after she's seen my face?"

Charles had the sense not to show his triumph. "She wants this."

The trapdoor opened, and Brandon dropped through. "Then make the arrangements. I want to be back in Scotland by Easter."

CHAPTER 10

Emma made the mistake of running. After the brief respite the rain was coming down more heavily, and she'd neglected to borrow a cape from the Dower House, but she paid it no mind, racing across the fields as fast as she could until her clumsy boots caught her up, and she went sprawling in the mud.

For a moment she lay there, her eyes closed, listening to the breath rasping in her lungs, the heart pounding against her breast. She could feel the icy rain pelting her, soaking through her layers of clothing, chilling her to the bone, and she knew she had to get up, brush herself off, keep moving, but she lay face down, wondering if she were ever going to be able to cry again.

It didn't seem likely. Her eyes were hard and dry, her jaw set, and she rolled over onto her back, letting the rain pelt down on her body, rinsing some of the dirt from her face, filling her dry eyes with the water she couldn't produce herself. It was dark overhead, angry gray-black clouds swirling above, and there was no way the storm was going to pass anytime soon. She had no choice but to drag herself to her feet and make her way homeward.

She started slow, sitting up first, staring down at her muddy self in disgust. She'd brought two dresses, one for day, one for evening, knowing that despite all her protests Melisande would have new clothes waiting for her. It was a true luxury to have so many dresses, and she always felt guilty for accepting them, but the ability to put on fresh clothes everyday was something that was worth a little guilt. Fortunately, Melisande understood her austere tastes and the dresses were elegant, classic, and demure, devoid of ornamentation and immodest lines. Ever since Brandon had arrived she'd taken to wearing her work clothes, shapeless and drab, rather than the prettier clothes that hung in the wardrobe, but that wouldn't be possible tonight. This dress was a disaster, and the other one had a large rip under the arm. Dresses weren't made for ladies to move their arms, to reach for things, to exert pressure, and she was forever pulling seams. The dresses Melisande ordered for her corrected that problem, but she couldn't bring herself to wear them in the blood and sweat and even excrement that filled her days at Temple Hospital.

She slowly got to her feet, looking around her. She'd instinctively taken the short cut, but with the heavy rains she could barely see ten feet ahead, and the path was a trail of mud, slippery and dangerous.

She should go back—she knew it—and seek shelter at the Dovecote, in the arms of Mollie Biscuits and the others. They could make her laugh when everything was grim, they could remind her how lucky she was that she'd managed to climb out of the trap the others were still struggling with.

But the Dower House was out of sight, and she had no idea whether she was closer to the main house or the Dovecote. Starlings was a massive estate, and whoever had built the Dower House had clearly needed to keep his wife and his mother far apart, since they were situated at opposite ends of the demesnes. If she went back she might still have to face the others, people who had seen too much and doubtless surmised too much. With her appalling luck Brandon might still be there, waiting for the rain to let up.

Why hadn't he stayed away? He should have made his escape— what had brought him back? She'd been sure she could simply let go of him, now that she'd seen him. She'd known he'd gone up to Scotland after the Heavenly Host was brought down, and she'd subtly managed to ferret out the information that he was healing, both body and soul, and getting stronger every day. She would be content picturing him up there among the crags and bluffs, the crabby old Noonan watching out for him.

But he'd come back, come back to a fiancée! Why had no one told her he was engaged, why had that girl burst into tears, what in God's name was happening? Everything seemed unreal, as if the ground had shifted beneath her, and she needed time and quiet to sort things out.

If he was to be married then that should solve any problems she might have, not that she was admitting to any, mind you. She should be grateful for the arrival of Miss Bonham, but something felt faintly off about the whole thing, or maybe that was simply wishful thinking.

She was going to have to face all this when she got back to Starlings. Whether he had a fiancée or not couldn't be of any possible consequence to her, but it mattered, even if she wished it didn't. She would make Melisande clarify the situation, then head back to London, never to think of him again.

The sudden crack of thunder made her jump. God was calling her a liar, was He? She was made of sterner stuff than that, she thought, and plowed onward.

She was not, however, blessed with the ability to see through heavy sheets of rain. Water was running in rivulets across the ground, and there was no way she could simply sit down and wait, and enough of her country upbringing remained that she knew she couldn't seek shelter under a tree when there was lightning about. All she could do was slog onward and hope for the best, something she had little talent for.

With the capriciousness of English weather, the rain stopped as suddenly as it had started, and she stumbled in surprise. She was by the footbridge that Rosie had mentioned, and as the heavy, roiling clouds parted, a shaft of sunlight speared down at her, turning the water drops into sparkling crystals on her clothes, on the trees, on the narrow bridge. She paused, looking up into the sky, and sure enough there was a double rainbow, the colors bright and clear. It almost looked as if it ended in the general area of the Dower House, and she felt herself begin to calm. . .

A heavy hand clamped on her shoulder, yanking her around to face him, and she felt panic sweep through her, certain that Brandon had caught up with her. The reality was marginally better.

The man was huge, heavy-set and dark—an enveloping cloak covering his massive frame, a muffler wrapped around his face under the rain-soaked hat, and all she could see were tiny, evil eyes starting her with such malevolence that she froze.

And then she looked down at his hand, not the one that was still gripping her upper arm so painfully, but the other, ham handed, brutal, holding a knife.

She didn't hesitate a moment longer. Before he could swing that knife at her she spun again, trying to twist out of his grip, set to take off across the fields, as far and as fast as she could go.

She'd forgotten about the muddy ground. Her foot slid out from beneath her and she went down, pulling her attacker with her, so that they were sliding and rolling in the mud. She screamed, as loud as she could, not putting much hope in it, but experience had taught her to make as much noise as she could if someone was threatening her, and this man was more than a threat.

He definitely intended to kill her.

She, however, had no intention of being killed. She clawed at him, to little avail. She'd forgotten that her nails were filed down to the quick to make surgery more efficient, and she had no ability to rip flesh. She had a small knife tucked into her plain woolen petticoat— she never travelled anywhere without it—but whether she'd be able to get to it was a question. She tried to drive her knee into his bollocks. but he was too big, too heavy for her to manage. She thrashed, knowing one strike with his blade could end everything, but she refused to give up. She heard the knife clatter onto the rocks, her first piece of luck, until she felt his heavy hands planted on her throat, and death stared her in the face.

It had started to rain again. His hands tightened slowly, and she managed one more scream until he closed off all sound, his thumbs pressing against her throat.

She knew exactly how she would die. He would crush her trachea and her larynx, her voice box, so that no air could pass through, and blood would fill her throat, drowning her. She wanted to throw up, which, would, of course, only speed the process along. She struggled, knowing it was in vain but determined not to give up.

He was looming above her, and she didn't have to see his mouth to know he was grinning, his tiny dark eyes alight with pleasure. Those eyes were oddly familiar—none that she knew well, but she'd definitely seen them before. She went limp, deliberately so, and he leaned forward to increase the pressure, when she brought her leg up, hard, slamming into his crotch.

His scream was high pitched and comical, and he released her, unable to hold on as he rolled into the mud, giving her just enough time to scramble back, thanking God for her knowledge of anatomy. She struggled to her feet, prepared to run, when his hand clamped around her ankle, yanking her down again, and this time the fall was hard, face first in the mud. He was hauling her back to him, foul, vicious words coming from his voice, still breathless with pain, and that, too, was familiar. She tried to grab hold of something, anything that would keep her from moving, but he was inexorable. She slid through the mud, catching on to something at the last minute.

"I was going to make this quick and painless," he grumbled, "but you had to be difficult, so now I'm going to take my time with you. And it'll hurt. You'll be screaming so loud and no one will hear you, you'll be. . ."

And then he was the one who screamed, when she drove the knife she'd managed to grab up beneath his ribs, intent on skewering his liver.

It was a bad angle, and he was fast—it was far from a killing blow, and her arm went numb when he wrenched the knife away from her and slammed his heavy fist against the side of her head.

So this was it, she thought dazedly as his fists rained down on her body, feeling her legs give way. Wretched way to die, she thought dreamily, sprawling in the mud as he began to kick her. The rain was pouring down again, and she thought she heard someone call out, but she was losing consciousness, which was fine with her. If she were going to be beaten to death, she'd rather not be awake for the process, though she supposed she ought to, for the sake of science. She was no longer feeling pain, just a thumping sensation, a small comfort.

Another blow to the side of her head, and staying alert wasn't going to be a matter of choice. The next one would be the last she remembered, and she closed her eyes, unwilling to see her murderer's gleeful, strangely familiar eyes as she died. She should have fought harder, she should have gone for his throat, not his liver, she should have. . .

He kicked her in the side, hard enough to make her roll away from him, her skirts sodden in the mud, and he followed her. Those heavy, hob-nail boots would slam into her head, and she held her breath, ready to meet the angry God of her father.

The blow never came. She could hear it now, the pounding of hooves, feel the ground vibrate beneath her crumpled body, hear the shouting in the distance. Thoughts were drifting through her head, aimless, disconnected. So she was going to be saved after all, was she?

And she knew just who her avenging angel would be.

HIS MIND WENT BLANK. Brandon Rohan had been in battle too many times—it fell around him like a cloak, and he was nothing but action and instinct. The miserable horse beneath him managed to fly across the water-soaked fields toward the small stone bridge, and he focused on the mismatched battle taking place, the huge brute and the much smaller woman fighting back with the fierceness of an Afghan tribesman.

But then she was down, and the man was pummeling her, kicking her. Brandon let out a roar of pure fury, digging his heels in as he drove the horse forward, one last spurt of energy from the sorry creature before he flung himself off, onto the huge, dangerous brute, knocking him away from Emma's prone body.

The red haze in front of his eyes was familiar, direct, as he acted purely on instinct, driving the man into the ground, pummeling him with mindless rage. He might have killed him had not his stupid horse decided to intervene, looking for one of the sugar cubes Brandon had used earlier to goad him into a reasonable pace.

He fell back, unwilling to shove even the sorriest of horses, and the motionless pile on the ground suddenly came back to life, scrambling to his feet and taking off before Brandon could get to him.

He stood, panting, staring after the fleeing man for the briefest of moments, cataloguing his shape, his gait, everything he could, before turning and sinking to his knees beside Emma's crumpled body.

There was blood everywhere, on her face, soaking into the neckline of her dress, reaching to her hands. It looked as if most of it was coming from a gash on her temple, and he knew from his military experience that head wounds bled copiously. Shoving a hand into his jacket, he pulled out a handkerchief and began dabbing at the cut on her face, trying to ascertain her injuries.

To his cautious relief her eyes blinked open, and she stared up at him without focus, clearly disoriented. And then her gaze sharpened as she recognized him, and he sensed her instinctive recoil.

He felt his instinctive surge of fury, remnants of his killing rage, and let it fade back, dissolving as civilization took hold. "Yes, it's me," he said, sounding more pragmatic than he felt. "I just saved your life, so you don't need to look at me like I'm a dyspeptic python." It was a lame attempt at a joke, but she managed the ghost of a smile, some of the hardness fading from her eyes.

"I could have stopped him." Her voice was wispy, slightly raw, and it seemed to surprise her far more than it surprised him.

"Don't try to talk," he said. "Clearly you don't have a great deal of experience fighting for your life."

"That's what you think," she muttered, and a little more of his tension eased. She was still fighting back—she couldn't be at death's door.

"You couldn't have taken him," he said calmly. "He was twice your size and he was playing with you. He could have broken your neck at any moment, no matter how many blows you got in—he was simply taking his time, enjoying himself, like a cat with a juicy little mouse."

There was no missing her nauseated expression, and that was the last thing he needed to complicate matters. He didn't bother asking her permission, he scooped her up in his arms with as much gentleness as he could muster, and she lolled back against him, fading out again, sending a dread chill through his chest.

The damned horse was standing nearby, a disgruntled expression on its face. The grass was matted into the mud surrounding them, and if Brandon had learned one thing about the wretched nag it was that it loved to eat. He hesitated only a moment—the horse wouldn't carry both of them, and even if he put Emma's limp body up in the saddle he'd have to hold her in place as well as lead the damned slug.

Looking past the bridge, he could see the towers of his brother's house. He started off at a quick pace, moving as swiftly as he could without jarring her unnecessarily. Her breathing was shallow, and he wondered whether her lungs had been punctured by a broken rib. He moved faster, the horse trailing behind them.

The rain had started again, and his efforts to shield her were wasted. It was cold and miserable, chilling him to the bone, but he was inured to it. She was a Londoner, pampered, protected from the harshness of life—this weather could mean the difference between life and death.

He was barely aware of the fact that he'd almost made it back to the house when people began crowding around him, his brothers, the guests, innumerable servants surrounding him in the rain. Hands reached out to take Emma from him, but he snarled something vicious, and most people fell back, staring at him like he was some sort of wild beast. And then Benedick was there, a strong hand on his shoulder, forcing his attention.

"Let me take her, Brandon. You need looking after as well," he said gently.

Brandon shook his head fiercely. "I'm fine. Send for a doctor."

"Already done. And you're bleeding."

The man must have nicked him—it didn't matter. He'd gone through far worse without noticing. "Show me where to take her," he growled.

Charles made the mistake of interfering. "Don't be ridiculous, Brandon! Let one of the servants carry her. . . I have no doubt she'll be perfectly fine. . ."

Brandon looked at him, and Charles stumbled, shaken. "She stays with me," Brandon said, his voice flat and expressionless.

"Then get her the hell in out of the rain!" Melisande said, pushing ahead of Benedick. "And stop wasting time terrifying your brothers."

His humorless laugh surprised him—his sister-in-law was making more sense. Following her into the house, he simply ignored the people that followed them out of the biting rain.

CHAPTER 11

Someone was trying to lead them up toward the bedrooms, but Brandon kept moving on through the ground floor of the house. Emma had begun shivering, and he needed to get her near a fire, fast. He felt her stir in his arms, and then she opened her eyes, the gray shadowed with pain and confusion.

"You're awake," he said. *Idiot.* "What hurts?"

She managed to focus on him. "Everything."

"Good," he replied. "If everything hurts then with luck you'll just end up with a few bruises."

"Heartless bastard," she said with a soft groan.

"That's me," he said firmly, holding her a little closer.

She dropped her head against his shoulder, and he felt the last of his blind rage draining away. He'd known animals, babies like that, creatures who'd sink against you in absolute trust, knowing you'd take care of them. For some reason Emma Cadbury, despite her caustic tongue, trusted him.

"What in the world made you decide to go that way?" Melisande was hurrying to keep up with him, and she tried to peer at Emma. "It's much longer, and likely to flood if this rain keeps up. If Brandon hadn't found you, you might have been drowned."

"Rosie," Emma said faintly, "the maid. She said it was a short cut."

"It isn't. It takes your way out of your way. What's wrong with that girl? Randolph, have someone go find her, would you?"

"And why the hell were you out on your own?" Brandon felt his temper began to rise again, an odd emotion.

"Brandon, dearest, don't swear at the girl," Melisande said plaintively. "Can't you see she's hurt?"

Emma stirred before he said something he'd regret. "Don't. . . squawk," she said sleepily, increasing his worry. He'd seen how trivial a bloody head wound could be, but he'd also seen men take a blow to the head, walk around and joke for hours afterwards, and then suddenly keel over dead. He wasn't going to let it happen to his Emma.

His Emma? What the bloody hell was wrong with him? He could feel Benedick behind him as he moved quickly down the hall, careful not to jolt her more than necessary, and he knew he ought to hand her over, walk away, but he couldn't bring himself to do it. He'd worry about his foolishness later—right now getting her safe was all that mattered.

"Bring her in here, Brandon," Melisande said, pushing open a door, and he headed into Melisande's salon. He still didn't want to release Emma, which was patently absurd, so he set her down on the chaise, reluctantly giving way as Melisande moved ahead of him, but he drew the line at the tall woman who pushed past him as well. "Who are you?" he demanded rudely, prepared to stand his ground.

"Miss Bonham's companion." Her voice was acerbic, her eyes sharp behind her glasses. "I have experience in treating injuries."

"So have I," he said tightly.

The woman looked at him, and her withering expression might have daunted another man. Not even a hoard of furious Afghanis would make *him* blink.

"You're a man," the woman said, as if that explained everything.

"And. . .?"

The woman just rolled her eyes, and he remembered that she was part and parcel of his marriage deal. He'd told Charles "yes." God, what had he done?

"You're bleeding," Melisande said in a practical voice. "Someone needs to look to you as well."

"I'm fine. It's a scratch, nothing more," he said, still on the edge of fury and a panic that was completely foreign to him. Never in his life had he been afraid, but he was now.

"Sit," Melisande snapped, fully as bossy as the tall woman whose name he couldn't remember. He sat, reluctantly, unable to tear his eyes away from Emma's pale, blood-streaked face when he realized there was someone else in the room. Oh, Christ, it was his so-called fiancée, looking everywhere but at him.

"You look awful, Emma," Melisande said briskly.

"I expect she looks worse than she feels," Brandon offered, hoping to goad Emma into a reaction.

Sure enough, it worked. "Nice of you to speak for me," she said weakly. "How do you know how much I'm hurting?"

"You told me." He turned his gaze to his sister-in-law, wanting to reassure her, wanting to reassure himself. "Head wounds always look terrible—they bleed like. . . bleed like the very devil," he amended his speech for his fiancée's delicate ears. "Once we clean her up she'll look a lot better."

Melisande fixed him with a fierce stare, not unlike some of the ones his mother had offered him in his adventurous youth. "There's no 'we' in all this. Leave the room and Randolph will see to you."

"I'm not leaving her until I'm certain she hasn't been seriously injured."

"I thought you said she wasn't!" Melisande snapped.

"I'm not a doctor." He rose from the chair, moving to Emma's side. She did look like hell. Picking up her filthy hand in his, he searched for her pulse. It was a little fast, but steady. Knowing battlefield medicine was necessary for any soldier who wanted to survive, and Brandon had never wanted to die. Not until he returned to England.

"I need to wash her, put her in something clean and comfortable, and you can't be here," Melisande said stubbornly. "Besides, you need your own wound looked at."

"My damned wound can wait—it's a scratch. I won't leave." He could be stubborn too. If he hadn't decided to go after Emma, if the disapproving cook hadn't told him which way, she might not have been found. The logical assumption would have been that she found a way to get back to the city, and no one might have found her body for weeks.

"I'll have Benedick remove you," Melisande threatened, her eyes narrowing.

"Benedick is ten years older than me and he's never been a soldier. I doubt that he and Charles together could make me leave if I'm determined to stay. And I am, you know. Very determined."

There was a long, pregnant silence between them, broken only by the soft crackle of the fire. Melisande was someone who didn't like to admit defeat, he thought, and if it had been up to him he would have avoided such a confrontation. Emma's attempted murder changed everything.

He could practically see the possibilities flitting through Melisande's face. After a moment she nodded briskly. "All right," she said. "But you are to go to the corner and keep your back turned while we change her clothes."

He glanced at the two other women, expecting severe disapproval, but they ignored him. It didn't matter, as long as he got his way. "As you wish," he said curtly. He was still holding Emma's wrist and hadn't even realized it, and he started to release her and step back when her hand turned and caught his, holding on to him like a lifeline.

"Don't go," she whispered. Her eyes, usually sharp and hostile, were frightened. She'd be kicking herself later when she remembered she'd held on to him, and that was incentive enough.

"I won't," he said in a low voice, looking down at her. A mistake, he realized too late. For the first time she looked as vulnerable as he had suspected she was beneath her spiky exterior, and he wanted . . . God, he wanted all sorts of things he could never have.

Pulling his eyes away from hers was almost painful, but the moment he did hers closed again. He looked at his sister-in-law. "I'm staying," he said again, his hand clasping Emma's. She had strong, capable hands, but they still disappeared in his rough, scarred one.

Melisande let out a long-suffering sigh. "You will avert your gaze," she said crossly. "And don't try to tell me she has nothing you haven't seen before—that's neither here nor there. If she realizes you've seen her in dishabille, she'll be horrified and embarrassed once she's feeling better."

"You may blindfold me," he said flatly, sliding one foot under a nearby chair and dragging it closer, all without letting go of Emma's hand. He sat, glaring at everyone and not exactly sure why, as the nameless companion decided to get down to business, washing the blood and dust off Emma's face while Melisande was beginning to undo her severe jacket.

His unwanted fiancée was watching all this with no expression on her face, keeping out of everyone's way, and he wanted to laugh. He couldn't have chosen a more useless bride. Then again, she'd hardly been a choice. She was a duty that he had no way of avoiding.

He had more important things on his mind than the woman who was now his burden. He turned back to Emma, watching as the other woman. . . Miss Trimby, he suddenly remembered. . . cleaned her bloody face.

It was almost as pale as the white sheet someone had placed beneath her. He cursed beneath his breath, accepting the tightness in his belly. "Be careful," he told the woman. "She's got some kind of head injury."

"I know how to deal with injuries." Miss Trimby didn't bother to glance at him, but Melisande was giving him a look that could have sliced his bollocks off.

"Kindly keep your mouth shut if you stay here, Brandon," she snapped, trying to pull the wet, blood-soaked jacket down her arms. "But I take leave to tell you that you are an arrogant bully, forcing your way on helpless females."

"My dear sister—" his voice was a deliberate drawl, "—I have never known anyone less helpless than you in my entire life, and that includes war-hardened soldiers. Except," he added, "for Mrs. Cadbury, who I imagine could rule the world if given half a chance."

Melisande's grim expression softened infinitesimally. "You're not as big an idiot as I thought you," she said, forcing Brandon to release Emma's hand so she could free her from the jacket. "There we go. Miss

Bonham, would you please hand me a clean rag? I want to get the blood and mud off her arms."

Miss Trimby stepped forward, a fresh rag in her hand. "Frances is unused to this sort of thing," she said. "I think it best she sit by the fire while we take care of this woman." She looked down at Emma's limp body, and Brandon waited for some snippy, disparaging comment—after all there was no chance she wasn't fully aware of Emma's history. If she dared pass judgment on Emma, he would remove her and her charge from the room by force.

"She's a strong woman," Miss Trimby continued. "I admire strong women."

"But Marnie. . ." came his fiancée's soft voice. "You know what she was!"

Miss Trimby cast her a quelling glance. "I do not feel we are in a place to judge," she said. "Let she who is without sin cast the first stone."

Oh, Christ, was he going to be leg-shackled to a religious fanatic? Now was not the time to worry about it, not when Emma was making an occasional soft, distressed sound, her hand jerking in his. He rose, looking over into the wound, ignoring Melisande's hiss of disapproval. "It could be worse," he said. "She's got a deep little cut across her eyebrow—those always look worse than they are. She'll need stitches, however. Are you up to it, or would you rather I did it?"

"I am perfectly capable of setting stitches, Brandon. I've done it more times than I can count. And now that you know what's wrong with her you could always. . ."

He sat down again before she could continue her helpful suggestion. "We'll need some laudanum for her to help with the pain. You must have some on hand."

"No." The word was soft, a little hoarse, but very, very clear. Emma opened her eyes. "I don't need it."

"It's going to hurt like the. . . like the dickens," he amended. "You'll need something to take the edge off it."

"No!" It was only a whisper, but it was firm and clear. Her eyes were still closed, and there was dried blood stuck to her eyelashes.

"I could make you."

"You will do no such thing!" Melisande forced herself between them. "Don't worry, Emma, my dear, I won't let him."

His irrational panic had now turned to annoyance and frustration. He knew exactly what she needed, and he could take care of her with a great deal more dispatch than Melisande was offering. "You're being a fool," he said, more to Melisande than to Emma, since his sister-in-law would be the one to enforce it. "There's no need for her to suffer needlessly. . ."

"We are in agreement that Emma is a strong woman, are we not? She has little fear of physical pain. You may distract her while I take care of the wound."

"Oh, may I?" he countered, sarcasm heavy in his voice. "What would Benedick say if he knew you were going to torture your friend unnecessarily?"

"I agree, my lady," Miss Trimby said. "Surely she should have something. . ."

"Enough!" Melisande raised her voice, and he felt Emma's jerk of pain. Oh, yes, she was going to have one monster of a headache. The thought of a needle slicing through her skin made him wince, he who had, on one occasion, had to assist in the amputation of a soldier's leg and done so with sang-froid, and he opened his mouth for one more protest, when Melisande silenced him for once and for all.

"If you were in her position, would you want me to dose you with opium?"

He stiffened. "The situations are entirely different."

"No," said his sister-in-law, "they're not."

He closed his mouth with a snap. "At least get her some brandy."

"No," Melisande responded sharply.

Emma's whispered voice drifted into their argument, though her eyes were still closed. "Stop fighting and get on with it. I feel like a bone between two dogs."

"A very pretty bone, my dear," Melisande said tenderly. "Even if you're a little worse for wear. Brandon, go find one of the servants and have them bring fresh clothes. . ."

"Trying to get rid of me! I'm staying right here. Send a maid, or Miss Bonham."

"Oh, for God's sake!" Emma's weak outrage stopped them. "Just get on with it. I want to curl up in bed and sleep for days."

"That's the last thing you'll be doing, my girl," Brandon said with no attempt at compassion. Emma would prefer plain speaking, he was sure of it. "Head injuries need to be watched constantly, and you won't be allowed to sleep for long periods in case there's some hidden injury."

It was a fortunate thing that Emma's response to that was quiet enough that it didn't reach Miss Bonham's ears, though he suspected that Miss Trimby heard. He fought back his grin. Sinking back in the chair, his eyes never left Emma's angry face. "Don't worry, *darling*," he said deliberately. As long as he could annoy her, it would keep her alert. "I won't leave your side."

He was expecting another shocking, whispered outburst, but she simply closed her mouth in a thin line. He glanced over his shoulder at Melisande, who was busy threading a needle. And then he saw Miss Bonham's expression.

She hadn't missed his term of endearment, and she had no way of knowing it was mocking. As if he would ever call a woman *darling*, ever again. Not when he was incapable of offering anything but shame and sorrow to someone he loved.

Loved?

Where the hell had that come from? He tore his gaze away from his troubled fiancée to look down at Emma Cadbury. Her eyes were open, and she was looking up at him.

"Don't," she said in a whisper, and he didn't pretend to misunderstand. *Don't stay by me, don't care about me, don't get in my way, don't love me.* But her grip on his hand was strong.

And he wasn't going anywhere.

CHAPTER 12

"Hell and damnation," Emma said in a rough, raspy voice. It was twelve hours later, the middle of the night, and once again she couldn't sleep. Despite the uproar of the day, which should have left her a little pool of exhaustion, she was awake, staring at her ceiling once more.

She'd been bathed, stitched, and put to bed, and she'd immediately fallen into an exhausted sleep as her body started to mend her injuries. She should have known, though, that sleep would again elude her, and now it was probably two or three in the morning.

Perhaps it wasn't that surprising. She wasn't in pain, per se, but the aches of her wild struggle were reminding her every time she tried to turn over. The stitches at the edge of her scalp were a more insistent throbbing, but she'd learned to soldier on no matter what insult her body or soul had been subjected to, and nothing had changed.

She could ignore stitches, twisted ankles, body blows that left ugly bruises. She had a harder time with her stomach.

She was starving. She'd grabbed a biscuit from Mollie's kitchen, but she'd skipped breakfast in her hurry to escape, and she'd fallen fast asleep once Melisande and the surprisingly efficient Miss Trimby finished with her. She'd had the hazy idea that she should talk to Frances Bonham's companion to see whether she might be interested in furthering her education in the healing arts. She was tired of being the only unicorn in a herd of jackals, and she knew Benedick would be more than happy to sponsor the woman, particularly if Miss Trimby's mistress was going to be part of the family.

She refused to think about that, though it doubtless would have destroyed her appetite. Instead the thought of strong tea with lashings of sugar and cream, fresh warm buns, and even some cold chicken and cheese were filling her head with sensual dreams, and the longer she lay still in the darkness, the more her stomach protested.

She gave up the battle, trying to pull herself up in bed, but dizziness and pain hit her with brute force, and she almost sank back on the soft mattress. She knew if she did she wouldn't be able to try again, so she braced herself with her left hand, staying utterly still until the dizziness abated. So far, so good.

Swinging her legs over the side of the bed was a little more challenging. Everything seemed to hurt, even her teeth, and she wanted to moan. Strong women, survivors, didn't moan, and she clamped her mouth closed, ignoring the tenderness. Lifting her hand, she touched her skin, checking for swelling, tenderness. She must look a fair sight, which was probably a good thing—her so-called beauty had been nothing but a curse to her and those around her.

She pushed herself to her feet, then quickly steadied herself. She was already feeling a little more human—a short hike down to the kitchens and a decent bit of food would do wonders.

The hallway that encompassed the family rooms was shadowed. It wasn't pitch black—the sky had cleared after the torrential downpour, and a sliver of moonlight came in through the tall windows at the end of the hallway. The family staircase lay at the center of the hall, and she started forward, moving slowly, waiting for her customary brisk energy to return, but she was breathless, dizzy, exhausted. She had just reached the top of the staircase when her strength deserted her entirely. Feeling her legs give out beneath her, she put out her arms in a blind attempt to stop her fall, only to have them caught in someone's strong hands as she was pulled back against a strong, male body.

She knew who it was. Fate wouldn't be kind enough to have Charles or Benedick Rohan wandering the family corridor—oh, no.

Besides, Charles would have let her fall. For a moment she let Brandon hold her, closing her eyes and breathing in the scent of him, the heat of him, before she turned, trying to push free.

"What the hell are you doing wandering around in the middle of the night in your condition?" Brandon demanded in a rough, low voice. "You could have fallen and broken your silly neck."

Move away from him, she ordered herself, but that other Emma wasn't listening, too weary to fight her own base nature. As long as he held her, she didn't have to meet his gaze, and for all his voice was harsh his hold on her was infinitely tender.

"I was hungry," she said to the clean white linen of his chest. He was not wearing a coat, and she wondered whether he was in his night rail. The thought was disturbing, but instead of pulling away she pressed just a little closer. No, the feel of his breeches through the thin material of her own nightgown was. . . confusing. Reassuring, disappointing, disturbing. . . God, she must have been concussed after all.

He sighed. His chest rose and fell with it, and she could feel her tangled hair stir. "Why didn't you just ring for the maid?"

"I don't ring for maids," she said, trying to sound brisk but failing miserably. Maybe he'd carry her back to bed. Maybe he'd climb in bed and hold her, and she could keep breathing him in, feel the strength of his arms around her, holding her, keeping her safe where nothing could harm her.

She pushed back, wobbled slightly, and then gave up as his hand clamped around her arm, pulling her away. "Let's have this conversation away from the stairs, Emma," he murmured. "I don't want you breaking your bloo— your silly neck."

"You can say 'bloody.' I do." Her verbal efforts to keep him at a distance were failing miserably, and she shook her head, trying to sharpen her mind, but it only succeeded in making her feel dizzier.

"Emma." In the dark his voice was even more mesmerizing, rich and deep. It was the kind of voice that could soothe her to sleep, warm her, enchant her. . .

"Don't call me Emma," she muttered, squirming a bit to break free of him. He didn't let go. "What are you doing up here?" Was he going to say, *looking for you, Mrs. Cadbury?* And she would ask *why*, and he would say. . .

"My rooms are here. In fact, I know for certain your rooms are in the opposite direction. Allow me to escort you back and I'll have some food brought up to you."

Noooo, she wanted to shriek, but she kept her inexplicable panic under control. "I assure you there's no need," she said, pleased to sound more alert. "I'm not really hungry after all."

"There's every need. You must have met my mother on one of your many visits—she would box my ears if she heard I was capable of such shabby behavior." There was a moment's silence between them. "I know what you're thinking. I've done far worse than a slight lapse in courtesy, worse than you could even imagine. Nevertheless, I am doing my best to atone for at least some of my misdeeds, and you are being escorted back to your room whether you like it or not."

The darkness was disorienting. She could make out his outline, and he seemed to loom over her, for all that she was a tall woman. "I don't need imagination to know of the hideous things men are capable of. I doubt it would hock me." She was trying for a practical note. "Anyway, I've visited here far more often than you have, and I'm sure I know it better," she said. "You'd probably get lost getting back."

"I never get lost. Not even in the Afghan mountain passes." His voice was expressionless. "What are you afraid of, Emma? Do you think I intend to force my way into your room and ravish you?"

"Most people wouldn't believe it possible to rape a whore." She should never have said such a thing, she thought belatedly. Standing there, cocooned in the dark with him, the last thing they should be discussing was sex.

She sensed more than saw him shrug. "That's a matter requiring vigorous intellectual debate and I'm not in the mood. If you don't want to prolong our time together you should stop arguing."

"I'd adore to have you escort me to my room, Lord Brandon," she said promptly in a breathy little voice, a perfect imitation of a society miss.

His short laugh was more disturbing than almost anything else—it was warm and good-humored, sounding more like the wounded soldier and less like the embittered man who'd returned to her life. "I should have threatened you earlier." He released his grip on her. "Your arm, Mrs. Cadbury?"

It was too dark to see him clearly, and the last thing she wanted to do was touch him more than socially necessary. Maybe Mr. Perfect who never got lost had excellent night vision in those quite remarkable eyes. She raised her arm blindly, only to accidentally hit him in the chest. She tried to leap back but he caught her, pulled her back against him, his strong arm going around her waist.

"You are the most skittish female I've ever known," he said dryly. "I can't believe you're capable of slicing into human bodies without a qualm when you can hardly stand to be in the presence of a male. Unless, for some reason, it's just me who seems to unnerve you."

"Given my previous profession, I have a very reasonable fear of your sex, Lord Brandon," she said, inwardly groaning at her inadvertent use of the word "sex."

There was a moment of silence. "I assure you, Emma, that you have absolutely no reason to fear me," he finally said, and in the darkness her heightened senses thought she could hear guilt and regret in his voice.

No reason at all, she thought, letting him guide her through the darkness. She needed to get away from him so desperately that she was willing to do anything. He could even slam her up against a wall and take her if that would hurry things along—at least it could clarify her unsettled feelings. Then she could simply hate him.

He wanted her, and she knew it. He wanted her body, she clarified in her mind as they moved through the darkness, and he was a soldier, a gentleman, someone used to taking what he wanted, and she was a whore. If he decided to take her there was little she could do to fight him. She'd survive, as she'd survived far worse.

But if her sweet, broken boy forced himself on her that might truly break what tiny portion of her heart had remained whole. He wasn't the gravely wounded, charming man in the hospital bed who spent the long dark nights of pain holding her hand and telling her stories. Once they'd taken him away from her he'd sunk to the very depths, and then managed to patch himself up, an inexpert job, to be sure, but serviceable. The lost boy was gone forever, and the man with his strong arm around her waist was a dark, troubled stranger.

They traversed slowly, in silence, so close that she could feel her skirts brush against his long legs, so close that she could feel the almost infinitesimal hitch in his left leg. She'd seen the ruined disaster, she'd changed the dressings on the torn muscles, the shattered bones. The fact that he could walk at all was astonishing—that he could disguise the lingering effects of such a wound so well was a testament to his strength and will.

Suddenly he halted, and his arm dropped free, so that she was alone in chilly darkness. "Tell me one thing, Emma, and if you lie to me I'll know it."

"I don't lie," she said stiffly, a perfect lie. *Oh, God, what now?* The truth was a dangerous commodity, one she used sparingly. She was so versed in dissimulation that he would never guess.

"Did we meet during that dark time in my life? Did I cause you some injury? Those months are clouded in my memory, but I know full well I did terrible things. Did I do them with you?"

She didn't have to feign her shock. "Of course not, Lord Brandon. Don't be ridiculous."

"Call me Brandon."

"No!" She moved a step back, and he let her, still close enough to catch her if she wavered again. She was still in danger. It had been so long since she'd been near a rutting male, but she recognized the breed. It didn't matter if he was a far cry from the soft old men she'd pleasured. Her body could feel his tension, his desire. "How would I have ever frequented your circle of acquaintance?"

"Emma, I was a member of the Heavenly Host. We had orgies, we hired women, we debased them and ourselves in unspeakable ways. Were you one of them?"

A measure of relief swept through her. She didn't even need to lie. "I was never in the company of those depraved 'gentlemen.'" Her voice dripped with contempt. "And I had ceased practicing my profession years before you returned to England."

He was silent for a moment, and she congratulated herself. Too soon, she thought, when he spoke again. "And we never met before this week?"

"Never." Her voice was strong, sure, incontrovertible. "Now that's settled will you guide me the rest of the way to my room or allow me to find it myself?"

"We're at your door." He moved toward her, brushing against her, and opened the door, letting the faint glow of the fire out into the hall. She could see him then, his dark and light beauty, his troubled eyes.

Don't, she thought desperately. *Please don't.* "Thank you for your assistance this evening, Lord Brandon."

"Brandon," he corrected her.

The moment stretched. "Are you expecting me to invite you into my room, Lord Brandon?" Her voice was steady, and she congratulated herself on sounding so unmoved. "I don't think you have the price."

"You're right," he said slowly. "The only man who's going to get in your bed is going to have to love you, and I'm afraid that's a part of me that never healed."

It felt like a blow. Why should the word "love" even be mentioned between them? "You're stronger than I am," she said calmly enough. "You could take what you wanted. I'm a professional, remember? I know when a man wants me."

His smile was wry. "Oh, I want you very much. I doubt there's a man who sees you who doesn't want you, with the possible exception of my brother Benedick. Even a stuffy old prude like Charles wouldn't be immune. But you've been hurt, you're weak and trembling, and I don't make a habit of taking advantage of frightened little girls."

"I'm not. . ." she started to protest, when he bent down and brushed the softest, sweetest kiss against her mouth, gone almost before it had begun, so quickly that she could do nothing more than stare at him in astonishment.

"You are," he said softly. "Good night, Emma."

She stood outside her door, bemused, as he faded into the shadows. She put a hand to her lips, expecting some monumental change. They were no different—soft, slightly open. He'd kissed her, and life would never be the same.

CHAPTER 13

She climbed into bed with his taste on her mouth. The feel of his body against hers as he caught her before she tumbled down the stairs. The warmth of him. . .

Stop it, Emma Margaret, she reminded herself sharply. *There's no room in your life for such lollygagging. Concentrate on your work, not schoolgirl fantasies.*

But she looked at the heavy medical tome on the desk and simply sank deeper into the bed. She felt peculiar, almost dreamy, and she wanted to hug that feeling to herself for just a little while. Oh, she had a thousand plausible excuses not to get up and get her mind back where it should be, but she knew the essential truth. She wanted to curl up in bed and think about Brandon Rohan.

IT HAD BEEN A COLD, rainy evening when she'd arrived at St. Martin's Military Hospital. She'd rolled up her sleeves and put on one of the unfortunate leather aprons they were required to wear, not unlike those worn by butchers to repel blood. There were few women who worked as volunteers at night—most of them were required to earn their living in the dark hours, either on the streets or in a house and they couldn't afford the time. Yet the nights were hardest for these poor lost boys, and that was when she was needed.

"You'll need to go stay with Number Thirty-seven," the nursing sister told her. "He won't make it through the night and he's restless. See what you can do to soothe him. The rest are all doing as well as can be expected."

She'd nodded. Number Thirty-seven had come in with a new shipment of the wounded from the Afghan Wars. The worst ones died on the trip and were buried at sea. Few in his condition survived this long, though there were a handful who held on until they reached their home shores—only to die once they'd accomplished that. Death was a strange thing, she'd observed. The body made its own decisions, regardless of medical wisdom, and when a patient decided to die all the brilliant treatment in the world couldn't save him.

Number Thirty-seven was one of those. He had no name or memory, in fact the thirty-seventh in that condition to die like that. She wove her way through the parallel rows of beds to the alcove near the fire—the place the patients ghoulishly referred to as "the Styx" in reference to the Greek river leading to hell. It was believed that moving a mortally wounded patient there eased the others, but in truth it only made the entire process more mysterious. Death was a fact of life, Emma knew, and it was only through these checks and balances that things began to make sense.

The boy was still and silent when she sank down on the stool beside him. He was very bad indeed—the entire left side of his body had suffered terrible damage, including his face, but he had managed to survive the long trip home despite it. He'd spoken very little since he'd arrived, and she had known he wouldn't be with them long.

She reached out and put her hand on his thin, almost claw-like, one —not bothering to wonder at her compassion for these poor, lost boys. As a rule, she despised men, but these were the wounded who needed nurturing, not unlike the women she lived with in Melisande Carstairs's vast house. Their need put everyone on an even footing, and she looked at him with tenderness.

He'd opened his eyes then, looking up at her. They were clouded with pain and acceptance, and he pulled his hand from hers. "Don't waste your time on me, sister," he said. "The living could use your sweetness more than I."

If she'd taken his dismissal, things would have gone very differently in her life, but her contrary nature had kicked in, She caught his hand in hers, holding it tightly. "I'm not a sister," she'd said. "I have no medical training—I come in here to help."

"Then help me by leaving me alone." His voice was far from strong. He *would* die that night—she recognized all the signs. Except that she wasn't going to let him.

And he wasn't a boy, though they all seemed like boys to her, help-less and dying. He was probably near her own age, and he didn't have the hard look of a life of toil. He didn't belong in this hospital—some-where he had family looking for him, and they would never know he died.

He wasn't strong enough to pull away from her, and she could see his frustration. "Go away," he choked out.

"Stay," she said to him.

Her single word seemed to startle him, and he looked at her in shock, no longer struggling. "Why?" he whispered.

It seemed as if the two of them were alone in the vast building, the moans and snores simply background like the crackling of the fire. "Because I did," she said simply. "I stayed. Dying is easy. It's making a good life, despite all the terrible things you've done, that's hard."

"You don't know the terrible things I've done. The things you do in a war. You can't even imagine it."

She'd been thinking of herself, of her choice to sell her body, because at one point it had been a choice. His words hinted at things that were far, far worse.

"You can't change what you've done," she said. "You can only accept responsibility and move forward." Her hand tightened on his. "You do not strike me as a coward, Thirty-seven."

She almost thought she saw his grim mouth curve at the name. "I am everything despicable," he said flatly, his voice weak. "If you knew what I'd done you would agree."

"Tell me, then. And I will tell you honestly if death is what you deserve. There are a great many men here who are fighting to survive. My time could be better spent with them."

"Go then. I told you to."

"Tell me," she repeated. And he did.

In fact, that had been the last time she could remember even coming close to tears. He made his confession in a rough whisper, holding her hand in the darkness, and while he talked he held off death. He talked for hours, alone in the darkness with her, and when he was done the sun was coming up, a faint glow coming in the windows set high in the walls, and he had made it through the night.

Death had left him—he seemed as if a huge weight had left him as well, and his eyes were clearer when he looked up at her. "You're a harpy, you know," he said, his voice stronger. "What's a man to do to get a little peace in this world?"

"Not die," she replied flatly, hiding her emotions.

He had surveyed her, considering. "I will make a bargain with you. I won't die today. Come back tonight and convince me to last another day."

"Perhaps," she said, planning on doing just that. She stood up. The day was beginning, and she needed to return to Melisande's household to see what needed to be done. Whether he lived or died, she would still be back.

"And one more thing. Give me something to live for?"

She eyed him warily. "What is that?"

"Kiss me, sister."

She'd frozen. "I told you, I'm not a sister. And I'm not someone who kisses strange men." She wasn't someone who kissed any man. The men who had bought her favors hadn't been interested in kisses—to them paying money had precluded the need for kisses, or kindness, or tenderness. The dismal, unlikely truth was that she had never kissed anyone.

"I'm not a strange man. You know me better than anyone in this world."

She could sense rather than see the wariness in him. He was testing her—his injuries, the terrible things he'd told her should have made most women recoil in horror.

If she hesitated, she wouldn't do it, and she knew he would be dead when she arrived that night. Leaning over, she cupped his bandaged face gently in her hands and pressed her mouth to his.

His lips were cracked and dry from fever, and when she drew back he'd closed his eyes, tension leaving his body. There was even the faintest trace of a smile on his mouth. "Tonight, Harpy," he'd said.

She'd wondered then whether she'd misjudged things. Whether he'd wanted the kiss as a last blessing on earth, and she half-expected that there'd be a new soul in the Styx when she arrived the next night. She was right.

The man lying in the alcove was a stranger, one whose amputation had turned septic, who'd been secured to the bed with straps to keep him from tossing himself onto the floor. She stood at the entrance, her eyes barely seeing the poor man, as grief filled her heart.

"Don't waste your time with him, Emma," Sister had said as she pushed past her into the little room. "Thirty-seven's been asking for you."

She'd managed to compose herself by the time she found him at the far end of the row of beds, a rough curtain shielding him from the others. "You decided to delay your departure, I see," she said caustically from the foot of his narrow bed.

His smile was faint but clear. "My own harpy! I'm counting on your torment to keep me alive."

"I'm more than happy to oblige." She sank down on the chair beside him. And so had begun almost two weeks, where he had slowly improved, where each night he had demanded a kiss, insisting he wouldn't be alive when she returned if she didn't give him one.

She knew it was hogwash, just as she knew he didn't belong in the rough wards of St. Martin's Military Hospital. He had the voice of a gentleman, and she had yet to meet anyone who could falsify those tones. She had kissed him anyway, the soft brush of her mouth against his—harmless, innocent. Until the last night, when the kiss became something quite different.

He'd grown stronger, he'd been sitting up in bed, and she'd moved her chair closer, night by night. For some reason she continued to hold his hand—the human touch kept him tethered to this earth, she thought, never realizing it kept her tethered to him. Until the last night, or early morning, when she rose to leave him, and leaned over to give him her chaste, affectionate kiss.

Instead he'd caught her arm, tugging her off balance, and deftly managed to slip his hand behind her head to hold her in place while he deepened the kiss, pushing her mouth open with his, using his tongue.

She'd been too shocked to react, had simply let his kiss her, long and slow and hard, so thoroughly she felt. . . she felt. . .

His grip loosened, and she stumbled back from him, her hand to her mouth. "Harpy. . ." he'd said, laughter and concern in his voice, but she whirled and ran, through the crowded ward without a backward glance.

For six days she didn't return. Six long days while she relived that kiss, the feelings that had flooded her body, the disgust, the fear, the longing, and then she knew she couldn't stay away any longer. She'd returned to the hospital in the middle of the night, and for a panicked moment she hadn't been able to find him.

He was in a small room off the hall, a room with a bed and a table and nothing else, and in the lamplight she could see he slept deeply. There was laudanum on the small table, in reach if he needed it, and she knew from experience that he'd been using it too freely.

She climbed onto the bed, careful not to jar him, but he slept on, the siren drug keeping him captive. She lay against his undamaged side, watching him. His hand lay on the bed, and she took it in hers, held it while he slept, and it was hours before she drifted off, content just to watch him breathe.

When she had awoken he was gone, the bed empty, and the kindly sister was looking at her in pity.

"His family came, Emma," she had said. "He remembered who he was. His family was in Somerset, but we sent a message, and they arrived this morning, full of relief and tears and rejoicing."

Emma had felt nothing, nothing at all. "Did he say anything?"

Sister had shaken her head. "He was still sleeping when they took him – I don't think he knew you were here. He'd been missing you— kept asking for you, but I told him we never knew who'd be helping. I thought it would be better not to say anything to the family."

"Very wise," she'd mumbled, climbing off the bed.

He had forgotten her, had her lovely boy. The moment his memory had returned her existence had been relegated to a trifle, not even worth a word of thanks or farewell, and she could thank God he'd been too deeply drugged to realize she'd been there last night.

She hadn't been surprised. Apparently, he was the son of a marquess, a lord himself. No wonder he'd wanted to distance himself from the dingy hospital and the soiled doves who worked there.

She'd been grateful, so grateful that his leaving had prevented her from making a very great mistake. He had gone, and she had accepted it, determined to move on with her life.

Until she found him again, in the house of Melisande's lover, and known, to her joy and despair, that her life wasn't through with him yet.

CHAPTER 14

"Bloody hell," Melisande, Viscountess Rohan, said succinctly, and at another time Emma would have laughed. For some strange reason her sense of humor had vanished. She'd fallen asleep thinking about Brandon, remembering things she'd done her best to forget, and she awoke late in the morning feeling unaccountably bereft, only to have Melisande swan in an hour later and plop herself in the nearby chair.

"Benedick's been teaching you terrible words," Emma said instead, leaning back in her bed. She was actually feeling better. She had the gift of healing quickly, though right now she wanted to hide in her bed rather than join Melisande's guests. "Don't let your children hear you."

"In fact I learn more from the Gaggle," Melisande countered cheerfully. "I particularly like the word 'fuck.' You look better, at least. Not quite so much like death warmed over. Everyone will be glad to hear it. How are you feeling?"

Emma closed her eyes. All things considered, she was feeling more than adequate. Her ribs were bruised, not broken, and the cut above her eye was minimal, despite the fact that it had provided the most gore. Her hands hurt from fighting off the man, but they were strong and used to abuse. Her entire body ached, but she'd do. Clearly her attacker had expected someone with ladylike demeanor, not the sort to kick him in the bollocks. If she'd been that kind of lady she'd be dead.

"Better," she said. "I believe I might even be able to travel by this afternoon. I must get back to London."

Melisande gave her a long look. "Maybe that knock on the head did more damage than we thought. You're not going anywhere. Someone tried to kill you, you ninny! You can't seriously expect me to believe you just happened to meet up with a brute who spends his time murdering women? On a path that no one takes? I don't think so."

"Why in the world would someone want to kill me?" Emma countered patiently. "I have no money, no power, no secrets. . ."

"Oh, you must have secrets," Melisande protested. "Some particularly juicy ones, I don't doubt, though you've never given in to my entreaties to share them. I have to rely on Mollie Biscuits and Long Polly to hear all the naughty details about the most proper gentlemen of my acquaintance."

"I'd rather not think about it," Emma said in a quiet voice.

"My dear," Melisande said gently, covering her hand with hers.

Emma smiled, quite without bitterness. "It's in the past, love. I've moved beyond it and prefer to keep it that way. But as you can see no one would have any reason to hurt me. If I were the keeper of secrets I would have used them by now. Besides, men tend to discount women —they don't realize how dangerous they can be."

Melisande laughed. "True enough. So you're convinced this was simply random? You were in the wrong place at the wrong time?"

"Of course."

"Then tell me why Rosie has disappeared," Melisande said.

Emma shrugged, ignoring the pain in her head. "She's probably terrified that her bad advice almost got me killed, and she ran off rather than face you or Benedick."

"Good thing she has," Melisande muttered. "I'd box her ears."

"You would not, and you know it. You're a ridiculously understanding mistress."

Melisande didn't deny it. "Not when they put my dearest friend in danger. But you're insisting this was entirely random?"

"What else could it be?" Emma said faintly.

"Then perhaps you could tell me what in the world is going on between you and my brother-in-law."

The question shouldn't have been unexpected, but it felt like a blow. Fortunately, she was quick to recover. "I've never met Lord Charles before in my life," she said, pleased with her own cleverness. "Don't imagine intrigue where there is none—he's not some shadow from my working years returned to embarrass me."

"Of course he's not—Charles is too stiff, and not in the right way, to ever take himself to a brothel."

"We're really having a lowering effect on your language," Emma said, shaking her head.

"To hell with my language. You know perfectly well I'm not talking about stuffy old Charles. I'm talking about Brandon. And you. What in the world is going on? He was more than politely concerned about you —why, he spent the rest of the evening pacing, refused to come to dinner, avoiding everybody. When I went to look for him he was down in the servants' hall, questioning the servants."

She did her best to ignore the treacherously warm feeling that filled her. "Don't go imagining things, Melly. There's nothing between us. I imagine he was simply concerned that someone had been hurt. Truly, I've never seen Lord Brandon before he arrived."

"Liar," Melisande announced succinctly. "I may have been in distress at the time, but I know perfectly well you saved his life that awful night three years ago. You stopped him from hanging himself. Did you think Benedick wouldn't have told me? Brandon thought it was some angel who'd come, and I didn't bother to disabuse him of the notion."

Emma didn't blush—she had grown skilled at schooling any errant emotions. *So he'd remembered that much, had he? What else had come back to him? Clearly not enough.* "I prefer not to talk about it."

"Aha! That proves there's something more to it! If you simply met him then, there's no reason you would want to avoid the subject. What is it between you and Brandon?"

Emma sighed with false ennui. "Nothing! How could there be? As it is, I only saw him that one time and he was barely conscious. He has no memory of me, and I have only the faintest recollection of him." The moment she spoke she cursed herself. If she'd had her wits about her she could have said "Oh, is that the man I helped?" in an artless tone. Not that it would have done any good—her friend knew her too well.

"I doubt you're disgruntled about that," Melisande said judiciously. "And now that I think of it, you've always seemed a bit more interested when we've discussed Brandon than anything we've said about Charles or Miranda or their parents."

"Well, isn't that only logical? I hadn't met the others."

Melisande was like a terrier with a rat, and she wasn't about to let go easily. "You met his parents at my wedding, you met Miranda and the Scorpion when everything exploded with the Heavenly Host. Charles is the only other one you'd never seen before—he wasn't sure he approved of me enough to make the journey to our wedding, so that won't wash. You've been on edge ever since the christening, when Brandon arrived, and you ran off when Charles mentioned Brandon's fiancée."

"I hadn't realized he was betrothed. It surprised me."

"He's not betrothed!" Melisande corrected her automatically. "And simple surprise isn't enough to make you go haring off in a storm like that. Not only is he not engaged to that pathetic little girl, I doubt he ever intends to do such a thing, ever. This is just some scheme that Charles has cooked up. I told Benedick he needed to put a stop to it, but you know Benedick. He's the opposite of Charles—he doesn't want to interfere."

"It scarcely matters. Your brothers' matrimonial plans have nothing to do with me," Emma said.

"I wonder." Melisande was eying her speculatively. "In the end it's just as well, I suppose. Brandon will simply say no, and Charles will sulk. There's no way Charles can compel him to do anything. I'm sure Miss Bonham will be much relieved—she looked quite terrified when she saw Brandon, and he deserves better than that. It will be up to us to make the poor girl feel comfortable. Charles hinted there was some sort of scandal attached to her name—well, there'd have to be, wouldn't there? For her to come out here to meet an unknown fiancé?

She and her companion are very close, but we must do our best to help the situation."

"I need to get back to London, today. I'm sure you'll provide excellent support, and the smaller this house party is, the better."

"You're not going anywhere," Melisande said firmly. "Not until you can provide me with a good enough reason."

Emma couldn't still a desperate laugh. "You can't keep me hostage here, Melly."

"Of course I can. I have the Rohans at my back. So tell me why you ran. Why you're still so desperate to run. It's not like you—you're the bravest woman I know."

"Hardly," Emma said, but she knew that look on her friend's face, that stubborn, determined expression. Melisande's determination had served her well in the face of public disapproval—she had established the Dovecote, both here and in London, she had embraced a former whore and madam without question, giving Emma her first experience with unqualified love and acceptance. Emma owed her the truth, or at least a good portion of it.

"Perhaps I. . . might have met Lord Brandon before that night he tried to hang himself," she said carefully.

Melisande's eyes lit up. "Oh, my goodness! Never tell me he was one of your customers? I gather he was quite the wild one before he went into the army, giving his dissolute ancestors a run for their money. I've even had a hint or two that he was a favorite of the ladies. Apparently, he was particularly adept with his. . ."

"No!" Emma said in a strangled voice. "He was never one of my. . . um. . ."

Melisande sat back, staring at her. "Why are *you* being so missish?"

"I didn't fuck him, if you prefer me to use more colorful language. It's a word I know particularly well; I just don't happen to like it very much."

"So?" Melisande was unabashed. "If it wasn't in your professional capacity, how did you meet him and when? And why is he acting like you're a complete stranger?"

Emma's head pounded, her heart ached, and she just wanted Melisande to go away. There were times when she wished she could cry—if she could just burst into tears Melisande would go into maternal mode, comfort her and stop with these incessant, painful questions. But Emma was not about to beg for mercy. She made it through life by facing difficulties head on and that wasn't going to change.

"To him I *am* a complete stranger." She took a deep breath. She'd learned that when something would be painful it was best done quickly, and she went on. "I used to volunteer at the soldiers' hospital, remember? That was how I discovered my affinity for the medical arts. Your brother-in-law was one of the men I looked after when he first came back from the Afghan War. He was very ill, and he had no memory of who or what he was."

"And?"

"Isn't that enough?"

"No. Taking care of an unconscious man is not the sort of thing to make you react like this. It's most uncustomary."

"I didn't say he was unconscious," Emma muttered. "He was in a great deal of pain, but he was able to talk. And we did. Talk that is. It helped him get through the long nights."

For a long time Melisande looked at her, saying nothing. "I see," she said eventually. "And what happened?"

"Absolutely nothing. I came back to the hospital and he was gone. His family had discovered him, and he was whisked off to be properly cared for like the aristocrat he is, and his memory came back and he forgot all about me."

"So you had this connection with him all this time, while Benedick and I were going about trying to stop the Heavenly Host, and you never said a word to me?" Melisande's voice was prosaic, but Emma knew her too well not to miss the well-hidden strain of hurt.

"What was the point? He'd forgotten me, he was doing his best to kill himself with opium and anything else destructive he could find. There was nothing I could do, and you had enough going on. You didn't need an unimportant fact like that distracting you."

"An unimportant fact like you'd fallen in love with a lost soul who was bound up with licentious, murderous degenerates?"

"Don't be ridiculous! Who falls in love with someone they barely know?" Emma's mouth twisted in a grim smile. "Whores know better than to fall in love."

Melisande slapped her. The blow was swift and unexpected, though more shocking than painful. "That's my dearest friend you're talking about," she said sternly. "Don't you dare call her names."

Emma managed a shaky laugh. "You're far too good to me, Melly."

"Don't be ridiculous." There were bright tears in Melisande's eyes, and the ache in Emma's heart deepened. Melisande was uncharacteristically silent for a few moments, and then sighed. "You know, it would probably be better if you weren't in love with him. And don't waste your breath saying that you're not—I've known you for many years—I can tell when you lie. If he ever did marry, his wife would have a lifetime of emptiness."

Emma shot a glance at her. "She would not!" she said, knowing it was unwise of her.

"No intimacies, no children. . . his wife would have little useful role in the household."

"No intimacies, no children," Emma echoed, perplexed. "What in heaven's name are you talking about?"

"Why, his injuries. I hadn't realized they were quite that extensive until Charles told me. He cannot perform a husband's duties, he cannot father children. He's a eunuch. But if you tended him you must already know that."

Emma stared at Melisande in shock. "What?"

Even outspoken Melisande blushed slightly. "His wounds. He lost his. . . that is to say. . . well, Benedick was most upset."

"I imagine he was," Emma said grimly.

"I expect Charles managed to communicate the distressing situation with great delicacy to Miss Bonham," Melisande said doubtfully. "Though a small, evil part of me would have loved to have heard him try."

"Hmph," Emma said.

"You don't find the situation at least somewhat tragic?"

"Not particularly. I helped bathe him. He's not missing a thing, and all would have been in working order. He's been having somebody on."

Melisande looked nonplussed for a moment. "Really? How odd. He must have been desperate to avoid Charles's matchmaking skills. I shall have to reassure Benedick. . ."

"You will say nothing!" Emma shot back. "Brandon has forgotten who I am, presumably he's forgotten his entire time in hospital. There's no earthly reason why I or anyone else here would know whether he was intact or not."

"But Benedick is so distressed!"

"The perhaps Brandon will tell him the truth. In the meantime, you are not to say a word! Promise me?"

"I promise," Melisande muttered in a grudging voice, and Emma was content. Whether her friend liked it or not, she would never break a promise. "So you aren't going to say anything either?"

"I'm going to be gone, I told you. The entire situation is much too complicated. I think that it's better if I leave and let the family work this all out. . ."

"You *are* family, Emma. You're my sister, just as important as Benedick's assorted siblings. And you love Brandon."

"Would you stop saying that? Of course I don't. I just. . . I just. . ." Words failed her.

"Exactly. And you're in no fit state to travel. You're going to stay right here for the next few days while you recover and we find where Rosie ran off to. The girl has some questions to answer."

"I'm not the frail flower you imagine me to be. I've survived a lot worse than this and been back on my feet in less than a day."

Melisande shook her head. "When did you. . . I don't want to know, do I?"

"You do not. I'm better off not remembering. Just leave it. I promise you I'll be fine."

"And I promise you that you aren't going anywhere." There was a stubborn set to Melisande's jaw. "Don't worry—you won't have to see anyone. I can have a tray brought to you."

"You are not to say or do anything," Emma said fiercely, and there was no missing the edge in her voice. "Do you understand me, you are not to interfere in any way. I would never forgive you. That is not hyperbole, that is the simple truth. I would still love you, but I would never forgive you."

Melisande nodded, the light fading. "I know. I still wish. . ."

"Don't," Emma said flatly. "Wishing is a waste of time."

BENEDICK WAS STANDING IMPATIENTLY at the head of the breakfast table when Brandon came down in search of coffee, and three other men were in attendance, including Charles, dressed for riding. "What a slugabed you are, Brandon," Benedick greeted him. "It's good to know that some things never change. Mother used to make me try to get you up in the morning and you resisted every effort."

For a moment Brandon remembered those long-ago days of youth with the three of them tumbling around their country estates. He'd been the youngest, of course, and he'd made it his mission in life to annoy his older brothers. "I believe I even slept when you poured a bucket of water over my head. Mother wasn't best pleased with that."

"You weren't asleep," Benedick said. "You were feigning it."

Brandon's mouth curled in a seraphic smile. "You'll never know. What are we all doing here?"

"We're going to continue our search for Mrs. Cadbury's attacker. Also, Rosie, one of our maids, has disappeared. She's the one who told Mrs. Cadbury to take that roundabout way, where it appears that the man was waiting for her. I want to know who paid her and why." His face was grim.

"Give me a moment and I'll join you," Brandon said, tossing his coffee back ruthlessly.

"I need you to stay here." Benedick was as autocratic as only an older brother could be. "With the rest of us gone, I'd like at least one Rohan on site to make sure the women feel comfortable."

Brandon nodded, accepting the decree without pleasure. "And you believe I'm less able bodied than the others."

Benedick's laugh was unrestrained. "Hardly. I may not have been a soldier, but I know how to apportion my troops, and one leaves one's most powerful weapon in charge of one's most precious assets. If that man shows up here I want you to be the one he has to face, not Charles here."

"I say," one of the other men objected, clearly not wanting to be relegated to the rank of less dangerous.

"Put a sock in it, Duckworthy," Charles grumbled. "It's bad enough we have to go out."

That explained why Charles was going—Benedick hadn't given him any choice. Brandon accepted his fate with more grace.

"Just promise me one thing," he said, pouring himself another cup of the strong coffee and seating himself.

"What's that?" Benedick demanded.

"Let me kill him."

IF MELISANDE THOUGHT Emma would remain meekly in bed then she didn't know her nearly as well as she thought she did, Emma decided, pulling on her clothes with minor difficulty and only a few curses. She'd dispensed with all but the lightest of corsets years ago—they constricted her movements— so she had no difficult laces to deal with, just a general stiffness. She glanced around her comfortable bedroom. Someone else had come in and laid her fire, another had dealt with her ruined clothes. Where in the world was Rosie?

She had no difficulty understanding yesterday's mistake—Rosie was fresh the city, coming out only a few weeks ago and taking up her first position at Starlings Manor. She would hardly be the one to know shortcuts, and she must have gotten the directions wrong. Although, considering that the one place she'd go would be to the Dovecote to visit her old friends, it seemed odd that she'd be so mistaken about it.

It also made sense that, realizing her mistake, she'd run off. Rosie had been one of the youngest they'd found on the streets. By her age she was well-experienced—at sixteen she'd been selling her body for five years—but she'd retained a curious sort of innocence that would have been unusual in a ten-year-old, and God help them, they'd recovered ten-year-olds on the streets.

The younger girls were sent to schools and decent families, and only half of them returned to the street. Melisande bewailed that so many did, but Emma viewed the matter more pragmatically. When they'd first begun they'd only saved a handful.

Her shoes were nowhere to be found, and she vaguely remembered the squelching mess as she'd picked her way through the muddy field. She slid on stockings and tied them, then looked down. She could go into Melisande's dressing room and filch a pair of slippers, but Melisande's feet were smaller, and she'd end up hobbling. She didn't bother with the small bustles that were just going out of style, nor was she tempted by the new, wide crinoline cages, so her lone remaining gown—a simple one of an unfortunate rose color that flattered her much too well—hung close to her body and down to the floor. With luck no one would ever notice she was without shoes.

"Ha," she said out loud, the sound startling in the stillness of the early afternoon. Brandon would know. The man was the very devil.

It would be too late to leave today, and she had no choice but to accept it. Her arrival downstairs would, however, signal her recovery. She would leave the next morning if she had to walk all the way back to London. The longer she remained here the more likely it was that Brandon would remember, and she doubted he'd be happy about it. She should have told him, she should have brushed it off as a stray coincidence. Instead she'd held the truth to her breast and yet treated him with far too much intimacy. She'd been an idiot, but then, it hadn't been entirely her fault. The moment she'd seen him she'd tried to leave. He had never been at any family gathering, not in the last three years since Benedick and Melisande had fallen in love, and apparently not much before that. He'd been a soldier, never at home. His sudden appearance in the church had shocked and numbed her. If only she could still maintain that deadness of spirit, instead of the roiling, twisting ache deep inside.

Shoes or no, she was going downstairs. She paused in the door, glancing back at her room. It was safe, warm, a place of study and reflection and better sleep than she knew anywhere else.

It was also now a place of writhing torment and sleepless nights, and she wondered if she'd ever feel safe here again.

The rare, sunny day was encouraging, though dark clouds lingered ominously in the distance, and there was no sign of Melisande or her guests when Emma reached the main floor, clinging to the railing as long as no one could see her. Melisande's favorite green salon was empty, as well as the larger drawing room, and looking out the floor-length windows that fronted the house, she could see a rousing and obstreperous game of croquet being held in the still-muddy lawn, the women's skirts splashed liberally with mud that would take a maid hours of labor to remove. The men weren't in sight.

"You're becoming a humbug, Emma Cadbury," she informed herself out loud. "You're in trouble when you start finding fault with simple pleasures."

Emma Cadbury didn't reply. It wasn't her real name, of course. She'd taken it in honor of what had once been her sole pleasure in life —cups of steaming hot chocolate. The Quaker, John Cadbury, sold the very best chocolate in town, as well as tea and her other delight, coffee, and when she'd been prodded for a last name it had been the first to come to mind, though her family name, Brown, had been anonymous enough to use safely.

"You should be in bed."

The deep voice startled her, the words setting up the all-too-familiar churning inside her, and she turned to look at Brandon Rohan. He was dressed casually—no carefully-tied neckcloth, his unfashionably long hair awry—and she imagined that was what he'd look like when he was home in the wilds of Scotland.

"You should be out there playing croquet," she countered, sinking just slightly to make sure her stockinged feet were covered. He'd kissed her. The memory, which she had managed to put from her mind, came sweeping back, along with so many other memories, and her cheeks felt warm. Impossible, she reminded herself. Whores don't blush.

His eyes narrowed, as if he recognized her move. "It's too muddy," he said. "My leg's not strong enough to support me if I slid."

His casual acknowledgement of his wounds surprised her. No one ever talked about anything as personal as scars, of course, but given his rapid descent into self-destruction after he left the hospital she had assumed his leg would be a matter of sensitivity as well. He certainly made a concerted effort to disguise any hindrance or discomfort, but she was too well-versed in the surgery not to recognize just how difficult it might be.

Not sure what best to say, she simply nodded. "I was feeling trapped in my room," she offered. "I'm stronger than most of the women you know, and I heal quickly. I'm suffering from no more than slight discomfort and hiding in my bedroom was growing tedious."

He cocked his head, looking at her. "Then why don't you go out and join the rollicking festivities?"

"I'm not a fool, Mr. Rohan. My ribs are bruised and I feel rather like a large cur has taken me by the scruff of the neck and shaken me thoroughly. I believe spending the afternoon curled up with a cup of tea would suit me very well, particularly since I intend to spend tomorrow in a coach on my way back to London."

His eyes narrowed. "Is that wise?"

"Of course it is. I'm perfectly fit to travel," she snapped, then wanted to kick herself. She was angry again, when she really shouldn't be. As far as he knew she had no reason to be hostile, which was simply the truth. With luck he might have forgotten all about that midnight kiss. . .

What kind of idiot had she become? Of course he hadn't forgotten, and her only defense was to distract him from that ridiculously potent memory. "Indeed, I'm feeling quite well," she said, belying her recent assurances. "Though perhaps I should go out and join them."

"You can't without shoes," he said, and she wanted to do something childish like stamp her stockinged feet. She'd known he would notice.

"My shoes have disappeared," she said stiffly.

"I imagine they have. They were caked with mud and blood. And there's no way you can be feeling as sprightly as you maintain—I've seen grown men laid flat by what you went through."

"Men are notoriously bad patients."

There was something ridiculously melting about his rare smiles. Only one side of his mouth turned up, the other frozen in place with scar tissue, the devil and angel in his face incredibly alluring. "I won't deny it. I imagine I was a baby like all the rest."

She was about to assure him that he was a far better patient than he supposed, but at the last second remembered there'd be no way she could know. She smiled politely and lied. "I would have no idea."

It came out oddly. His comment had been random, seeking no reassurance, and her denial had been unnecessary. She really had to get away from him.

"I believe I might return to my room after all," she added. "I can't imagine anyone would be pleased if they returned to the house and found us together, particularly your fiancée." *Another unwise choice of words*, she thought.

"I don't care."

Before she could respond the door was pushed open, and Richmond appeared in all his august glory, a maid following behind him with a heavy-laden tray. "Your refreshments, Mrs. Cadbury."

"But I didn't request any. . ." she had begun when Brandon spoke.

"I did."

She was not going to stay and pour tea for the both of them, she was absolutely not. "I'm not in the mood for tea," she said, torn between not offending Richmond and a desire to stop Brandon.

"Neither am I. Would you prefer coffee or hot chocolate?"

It had taken her that long to recognize the two seductive scents, and her stalwart soul let out a helpless wail. Tea she could have easily turned her back on. Her twin weaknesses were another matter.

She sighed in surrender. "Just one cup," she said, moving quickly to the sofa by the window. At least the possibility of an audience would keep him from kissing her again, assuming he had any intention of doing so.

The two small silver pots sat nestled in snowy linen, and she cast an inquiring glance at him. "Coffee," he said in response, taking a seat that was just far enough away, and then moving it closer. "Black like the devil."

It was an unnerving comment, when she'd just been thinking of him in terms of his Satanic Majesty, but her gestures were smooth and practiced as she poured him a cup and handed it to him before turning for her own. She almost never had the supreme indulgence that lay before her, and there was no way she could resist the rare temptation, filling the delicate Limoges cup with half a cup of thick, creamy chocolate, then filling the rest with coffee and stirring it with one of the tiny spoons. She took the first sip and closed her eyes in quiet ecstasy. And opened them again at the sound of a soft, strangled moan.

BRANDON HAD NEVER BEEN SO DAMNED uncomfortable in his life, and his inadvertent sound betrayed it. Her soft, orgasmic expression had turn his awakening cock into a full erection, and his breeches, although loose enough for working in the field, were still too tight for such doings. He leaned forward, folding his hands over his lap as casually as he could manage. "What the hell are you drinking?" he demanded, hoping his voice didn't sound as raw as he felt.

"I believe it's called mocha," she said, still looking at him oddly. "It's quite sinful."

"You don't look like you know much about sin, Emma," he said. He meant it, but he hasn't thought it through.

Her mouth hardened, and he wanted to kiss it back to softness. He wanted to taste that wicked concoction on her skin. "I'm a professional at it, Lord Brandon."

There she went with the damned "Lord" bit again, showing her displeasure. "In actuality, you've changed professions. You're a surgeon, Emma, which makes you more likely a professional at pain."

Her mouth curved in an unhappy smile. "Who's to say that wasn't part of my previous profession?"

And that set off all sorts of thought. Sweet Emma with a whip and shackles, taking her anger out on the flesh of willing supplicants. It was only marginally potent—he'd played with every sexual variant that could be thought of during his time with the Heavenly Host, and after the first time he hadn't found the whole punishment game that interesting. But every thought of Emma and sex made his current situation more difficult.

He shrugged, managing to look unimpressed. "Well, at least you received some recompense for the assaults you suffered."

He'd surprised her. But then, that was a central part of their relationship—a battle between them to prove whom could shock the other.

Her smile then was real. "True enough," she allowed, taking a healthy drink of her concoction. Ladies sipped their drinks, they poked at their food, they had no bodily functions. Thank God Emma wasn't a lady, though he thought far more highly of her than the very peak of society.

"Why did you kiss me?"

He jumped. That was the very last thing he expected—he'd assumed she'd ignore the incident, skittish as she was, and he wasn't prepared for her flat question.

He knew he hadn't shown it though—he was an even better master of his reactions than she was. "That's an inordinately silly question. I wanted to. There's something about your mouth, I think. Why? You didn't seem to mind."

Her face had whitened, which he found extremely odd "You didn't give me a chance to mind," she mumbled, taking another hasty drink. He was going to have to tell Noonan about it. In the north they usually got by on gallons of hot, strong tea, but given that he allowed himself no other liquids, Emma's drink might be a worthy addition to Noonan's limited cooking repertoire.

"I'm sorry," he said softly. "Should I have kissed you longer? Harder? Deeper?"

She squirmed. He'd been about to call himself an ass for his sugges- tive talk, but her squirm made his self-respect die a quick death. For all her seeming disinterest in the male sex, she reacted to him. In the far too quick brush of his mouth against hers he'd felt it, the spark of response that she was too startled to hide.

"Hardly." She was trying for asperity, but her choice of word was unfortunate. She looked flustered, and she didn't strike him as the kind of woman who flustered easily. She rose suddenly, setting down her empty cup, and there was just the faintest bit of chocolate on the corner of her lip. "I really need to go back upstairs," she said hurriedly. "I feel unwell. That is, if I'm to leave tomorrow I should probably rest. . ."

She'd been backing away from him, with good sense, since he'd risen as well and was moving toward her. He caught up with her just before she reached the door and casually pulled her away from it, backing her into the corner of the room away from the windows. Near a divan.

"I'll let you go," he said softly. "In a minute." And he set his mouth against hers, his tongue licking out to taste that tiny bit of chocolate.

She shuddered, but it wasn't in disgust. Her hands had come up to his shoulders, but they'd moved beneath his jacket, clutching the soft cloth that covered his shoulders, and the sound she made was one of soft, unexpected pleasure.

It was simple enough to slide his tongue into her mouth, kissing her with such thoroughness it could have melted the bones in his body. He lifted his mouth for a second, and her gray eyes were staring up into his with glazed wonder, making his need even more powerful. He could lock the door to the hallway and take her there on the divan, but the silly women noisily playing croquet outside would be certain to come back at the most inconvenient time. He kissed her again before she could protest, pressing into her, wanting to absorb her into his very bones.

He tried to coax her tongue into play, but she was either very reluctant or simply ignorant of the intricacies of kissing, but that could hardly be possible. She'd been paid for this, a fact which bothered him not in the least. This wasn't a commercial encounter—she was reacting to him on the most basic, carnal level, pushing her soft breasts against him, and he wanted to cup them with his hands, but he didn't dare release her arms. She had relaxed into his hold but it wouldn't take much to make her skittish.

Using his teeth, he tugged at her lower lip, trying to draw her closer still into the late day shadows, and she moved, eager, seeking him, until she froze, and some sound intruded on his carnal haze.

There were voices, noise coming from the adjoining front hall, men's loud, excited voices, and he wanted to groan in frustration. He lifted his head, looking down at her, hoping she'd show some of that same emotion, but she'd already drawn her defenses back around her, and she pushed at him. For a moment he didn't move.

Her smile was cool and acid and for some reason it made him want to kiss it off her set mouth. "I can't wait to get back to London to report on your miracle, Lord Brandon."

He blinked, confused. "Miracle?"

"I've been informed that your war wounds were more extensive than outward appearance. Apparently that essential part of your anatomy that was blown off in the war seems to have regrown and is now pressing into my stomach."

He stared at her for a long, incredulous moment, and then he threw his head back and laughed, releasing her, his amusement almost stripping away his desire. Almost. God save him from a woman like her —she was the kind of woman he could love.

Even that hideous prospect couldn't deflect his laughter, not her stony expression, not the women herding in through the French doors as the day turned stormy, not the men crowding in from the hallway, looking grim and curious. He wanted to collapse on the sofa, but that was impossible with ladies and older men present, so he simply stood there, trying to contain his mirth.

And then Benedick spoke, his face dark with disapproval. "What do you find so entertaining, Brandon? I could use a laugh at this point in time."

Brandon had known his brother all his life, and he knew the difference between simple bad temper and real trouble. This was real trouble, and the last of his delight left him.

"Nothing of any import. What's happened?"

"Don't miss a thing, do you?" Benedick muttered. "We found the missing maid."

"Rosie?" Emma spoke up, ignoring protocol. "What did she say?"

"Nothing," his brother Charles interrupted, practically sneering with disapproval, and Brandon had the errant desire to punch him in the face. "She was dead."

There was a piteous shriek, and he turned to see his sapskull of a fiancée swoon into her companion's tender arms, as all the women surged around her.

All except Emma, who stood still as a statue, her face white, her mouth, that mouth he'd just kissed so thoroughly, grim. "How?"

Charles grimaced. "She'd been. . ."

"Charles!" Benedick snapped. "There are ladies present!"

Charles didn't have the grace to look abashed. "Well, then, perhaps we should wait until the ladies depart and then I can relate the gruesome details to Brandon's doxy."

Melisande's soft cry of barely registered in Brandon's blood-maddened haze as did just what he'd been longing to for so many years and punched Charles. Someone pulled him away as Charles crumpled to the floor, shrieking that his nose had been broken, and there were various cries of distress from the women, sounding more like a flock of silly birds than anything else.

"Enough!" Benedick thundered. "Melisande, my dear, perhaps you might escort the ladies to the salon for tea, while Miss Trimby sees to Miss Bonham. Brandon, your behavior is inexcusable; Charles, you deserved it. How dare you insult a guest in my house? First, I must apologize to you, Mrs. Cadbury, for both my brothers' boorish behavior. They shame themselves and they shame me. Let me apologize to all my guests for my deplorable family, but we are, after all, Rohans."

It was just the right thing to say, and as Brandon's fury lessened to a cold anger he had to marvel. The other men were chuckling knowingly, his family's excesses over the decades well-known, and even the fluttering women were tittering. His hand hurt, which seemed absurd, and he couldn't bring himself to look at Emma.

When he did, she was already gone.

EMMA WAS RUNNING. Running away from the scene in the salon, the women who looked at her with their sideways, pitying glances, from the man who lay crumpled and shrieking on the floor, blood gushing from his nose, from Melisande's concern, from Benedick's grim knowledge. Most of all she was running away from Brandon.

Brandon, who'd kissed her so thoroughly, his hard body pressing her against the wall, and she'd wanted to kiss him back, so badly. She didn't know how. Men didn't kiss whores—she knew nothing about it. She was aware that tongues were used, and it all seemed part of the general messiness of the business, but she kept tasting him, wanting more of him, wanting his mouth on hers once more, his long, lean body against hers.

What in God's name was happening to her?

And he'd hit his own brother. No one had ever done that, defended her with a violence that was both shocking and arousing. Not that any other guest had dared be that rude in front of Benedick and Melisande, but with any other confrontation she was on her own. It was dangerously seductive to be championed, almost as seductive as those kisses had been.

She could sleep with him. She could give him her body and the pleasure men seemed to take from it. There was no possibility that she could enjoy it, but with Brandon she could endure, as long as he kissed her like that. It was a frightening, enticing thought.

She reached her bedroom, slammed the door and went straight to the window seat overlooking the courtyard. It was raining again—the brief sunshine had been only a small respite—and she leaned back against the wall, closing her eyes, catching her breath, letting her racing heart return to normal. She could still feel his hands on her, and she crossed her arms to touch where he'd touched. She wanted to cry, but her eyes were stubbornly dry. If Melisande and Benedick didn't let her leave tomorrow she would run, and keep running, until no one could find her.

Common sense returned like a slap in the face. Of course she couldn't run and hide. She was a woman who had always dealt with life head on—she didn't run.

She let her head rest against the cold window, closing her eyes in weariness. Why was she fussing about Brandon Rohan? In the scheme of thing he was no more than a peripheral distraction. Dismissing him would be easier when she was back in the stimulating atmosphere of Temple Hospital, her mind absorbed in work. No, her problem was far greater than Brandon Rohan.

Someone was trying to kill her.

She couldn't believe how dense she'd been. The fire at Melisande's house in London had started when she was alone in the building. It had seemed like a random coincidence—there'd been threats for years about the place. No one had any charity for the soiled doves who took shelter there, and men with power never liked living with the fact that women knew their secrets. Once they no longer served their purpose, those women were disposable, and there'd been threats aplenty. That had been one of the reasons all the women had been relocated to the country, thank God, so no one else would have died but she.

Except it was starting to look like she'd been the target in the first place. That hadn't been an accidental push into the Thames, as she'd conveniently believed. She had no idea who had pulled her out, but Dr. Fenrush's man had been in the crowd, and if he'd known about Benedick's plan to have her supplant his master he probably would have thrown her back in again.

And now the attack in the secluded field, one she'd wanted to convince herself was random. Random, except that Rosie had told her particularly to take that path, a longer, more out of the way path, and now Rosie was dead.

Emma might prefer to ignore inconvenient distractions, but she wasn't stupid. When you put all those incidents together it meant only one thing, and if she continued to dismiss it, other people might get hurt as well.

She sighed. There was always the possibility that the London attempts had no connection with the danger she'd faced six hours to the northeast, that those incidents were, as she'd first believed, mere accidents, and she'd somehow run afoul of a deranged killer when she'd come here.

She hadn't endured and survived without a willingness to face ugly truths. It had become even more urgent that she return to London— the answer must be there, somewhere. She could talk to Fenrush's man, Collins, his name was, and see if he'd noticed anything odd that day by the river.

And she could be secure in the knowledge that her escape from Starlings House would have absolutely nothing to do with the man who had just kissed her so thoroughly that she felt. . . claimed. There was no claiming going on, not by anyone, she reminded herself, and the sooner she got home and concentrated on this mess the better.

CHAPTER 15

Brandon would have had a great deal to say about it if he'd been informed. As it was, his mind was caught up with the events of the day as he changed for supper with the dubious help of Noonan.

"When the hell are we getting back to Scotland?" the old man demanded. "The longer I stay down here in this place the more nervous I get. Throwing rocks at the British Army can be considered treason, you know."

"It was twenty years ago if it was a day, and no one even remembers," Brandon replied. "I've still got things to do down here. Besides, I'm supposed to get married."

Noonan dismissed that particular notion with a colorful phrase. "You're no more going to marry that dishrag of a girl than you're going to win a beauty contest," he said with his usual devastating frankness. "Just leave off and let's go home."

"Trust me, there's nothing I'd like better." But was there? Was there any other woman whose lithe, strong body felt made for his, whose mouth tasted of paradise? He'd been an idiot and a rare bastard for kissing her this afternoon, but he hadn't been able to help himself. He'd been wanting to for so damned long, and the chaste kiss of the night before had only whet his appetite.

But he couldn't have her. Even if he managed to find his way out of this absurd marriage idea, he still couldn't have Emma Cadbury. She didn't even like him, for all that she'd put her arms around him and almost kissed him back, and she would have no interest in. . .

"What do I do with this thing?" Noonan interrupted his conflicted thoughts, clenching a spotless neckcloth in one hand. Brandon grabbed it away.

"You don't crush it," he said, tying it haphazardly around his neck. "Damned things."

"You're right about that, me boy. Those things could strangle you, and there's no way you could fight in one."

Not even with a blink of an eye did he show his reaction. Noonan brought up the war at regular intervals, and each time a part of him wanted to recoil. He'd accepted it: the things he had done, the trust he'd betrayed, the monstrous things. . .

Deliberately, he looked in the mirror. In Scotland they had no mirrors, at least, none in the gamekeeper's house where he and Noonan had lived for the last three years. The main house was shuttered, the furniture covered, and they could have walls and ceilings made of mirrors for all he cared. Noonan didn't give a damn, and Brandon hadn't wanted to look at his ugly mug, the constant reminder of all he wished he could forget.

In truth, though, he wasn't ready to let go of it, of the harsh, damnable past. He looked at the monster in the mirror with steady regard. It was no wonder his pathetic little fiancée had screamed and almost fainted at the sight of him. The thought of being forced to look at him across the breakfast table must have horrified her.

"No beauty contests, eh?" he said out loud, surveying himself.

The left side of his face had looked like raw, bloody minced meat in the beginning, but now it was merely a spider web of scars, his nose had been broken several times before the last battle, and he couldn't say much for the rest of him. The scars tugged his mouth into a perpetual glower, his left eye was tilted, though praise be he still had vision in it. He could stand there and catalogue the deficiencies, the damaged ear, the deep vertical scars, but he didn't bother. He was repulsed enough by his reflection, knowing that he deserved it. It was the outward sign of all his inner torment, a punishment for the horrors he'd committed. He'd never shirked responsibility—he took his punishment like a man.

"I pity that poor girl having to look at the sight of this every morning," he said.

"She'll get a crick in her neck if she keeps trying to avoid the sight of you," Noonan said with a certain malice. "I've always told you that if someone won't look you in the face then they aren't worth knowing."

Brandon grinned, turning from the mirror. "You think I'm pining for my lost beauty, Noonan? I mind my bad leg more. And I'm more than used to people staring at my shoulder instead of meeting my gaze. It no longer bothers me."

"I know, laddie," Noonan said, and there was an unexpected note of sympathy in his scratchy Irish accent. "You know one thing that's odd? That woman—the pretty one, what used to be a doxy. What's her name?"

"Emma Cadbury," Brandon said in an expressionless voice. For some reason he'd bristled at the word "doxy" but it was nothing more than the truth, and a man like Noonan would pass no judgments.

"Aye, that's the one. That one looks you straight in the eye and—she doesn't flinch. To my mind she's worth ten of anyone else here, saving your family." He took a step back and ran his eyes over Brandon. "You look as pretty as you're going to, though I don't know why you bother. I'm going down to the kitchen to get meself a drop of good whiskey and maybe an armful of that plump scullery maid while you have to sit all stiff and proper. When you come to your senses and are ready to head north all you have to do is say the word and I'll have our horses saddled."

It was tempting, so tempting, just to run away from this mess his once simple life had become. Running away from Emma Cadbury made even more sense—she upset his hard-won equilibrium.

"Soon," he promised. Turning away, he moved toward the window as the door closed behind Noonan. It was still raining—did he need to build an ark to get out of here? He was used to rain in Scotland—liquid sunshine, they called it, and then ignored it, going about their business anyway. Here it seemed to call a halt to everything, and he was ready to explode.

Damn, damn, damn. Why had he kissed her? She was broken, perhaps as broken as he was, and despite her prickles she needed to be treated gently, and instead he'd been on her like a teenage boy, ignoring her injuries, perhaps even ignoring her dislike of the whole situation. He'd been so aroused, had been fighting it for so long that once his infernal lust had slipped its bonds he might have been too far gone to notice her dislike.

But no, she'd put her hands on him, closer than he'd expected, and her body had melted against his, and he'd felt, absolutely felt her own longing. He wasn't a man who deluded himself, and he knew that, despite her antipathy, despite her very rough history, she was as deeply attracted to him as he was to her. Strange—he'd never had such an instantaneous feeling that someone was important to him, someone seemingly so strong, yet he suspected was far more vulnerable than she let on.

He'd once had a baby hedgehog when he'd been a boy—he'd always been collecting animals back then. His mother had told him his room was like a zoological garden, but she never forbade him to bring in the wounded birds, the motherless rabbits, the companionable ferret with the missing leg.

Emma was like a broken bird, he thought, staring out into the rain. A raven in a wren's costume, that mesmerizing beauty banked down and hidden.

She was neither a raven nor a wren. She was a robin—bright and smart and strong, but she was hiding, and he wasn't the man to lure her out into the sunlight, not when he lived in darkness himself.

She'd tasted so good, so right. It had felt like coming home, that kiss, all those kisses behind the door of the salon, and his head kept filling with fantasies so depraved he should be ashamed of himself. He wasn't. He'd always had strong sexual appetites, ones he'd done his best to bank down since the horror of his time with the Heavenly Host, but Emma Cadbury woke something in him he'd forgotten.

A visit with the discreet Widow MacKinnon would take care of it, he told himself. All cats were gray in the dark, and Fiona MacKinnon was a talented and enthusiastic lover. If anyone could put Emma out of his mind it would be Fiona. If anyone could.

In the meantime he had to go downstairs and be attentive to his meek little fiancée, unless someone had been kind to her and set her at a distance from him, and he'd try to remember his duty, when all the time he was wishing he was in the kitchen drinking whiskey with Noonan. No, he didn't miss the whiskey, he thought, prodding that old desire like one prodded a sore tooth to see whether it still hurt. He just missed his simpler life.

Would Emma even come down to dinner? Could he sit, expressionless, pretending? He had no choice in the matter, and Benedick would skin him alive if he knew he'd kissed his wife's best friend.

He straightened his shoulders. He was a Rohan, more than anything. He did what he had to do, by conventional or unconventional means, and he tried not to let anyone bear the results of his wayward desires and morals but himself. His grandfather Francis would approve, the old satyr.

THERE WAS a definite pall over the group gathered for dinner that night. Charles was gone, and Brandon neither knew nor cared where. To the devil, he hoped. His absence was about the only good thing about the evening. He entered the grand dining room, Miss Frances Bonham's tiny, gloved hand on his arm, looking around for Emma. He couldn't decide whether her absence was a blessing or a curse.

He'd done his duty with the perfect air of courtesy and amiability, meeting with his intended to give her a chance to get used to him. After the debacle in the reception room he'd been sure she'd cry off, but his hopes were in vain. She didn't like this any more than he did, but she had fixed her gaze on his shoulder, determined not to see the ruination of his face, and she made the proper responses as if she'd memorized them, while the dragon beside her kept a strong, comforting hand on the heiress's shoulder. She seemed to like their proposed marriage even less than the bride and groom did, and he wondered if there was something she could do that would put an end to this. Miss Marion Trimby was in her mid-thirties, and she looked like someone who was used to being in charge. If he really was forced to marry Miss Bonham, there'd be a battle over who controlled her. It was quite clear that young Frances had no interest or ability to assert her independence.

The other guests had already been seated when he escorted her into the dining room, and they all immediately rose, applauding politely as he led Frances to her seat between Benedick and one of the chowderheads who'd gone in search of the maid and apparently became violently ill over her remains. He settled the girl carefully, the perfect husband-to-be. The word was out, then, not that it made any difference. Once a Rohan agreed to something he didn't renege—he had promised to give this terrified young creature the protection of his name, what little protection it was. As a married woman she would exist on a completely different level of society, and while there was no way to erase his hideous accusation, the fact that he married her would speak for something. This was her only way to return to the kind of life she'd been born to.

"Is something wrong?" his nervous fiancée whispered when his arm jerked.

He smiled down at her with determined benevolence. "Nothing at all, my dear." He couldn't call her Frances, and Miss Bonham seemed ridiculously formal. He looked up, and there were two empty seats at the table. Correct social behavior was automatic, and he headed toward the proper seat, wondering who could be even later than he had been, when there was a shadow at the door, and whom he had been looking for, whom he had been dreading, had arrived. Emma Cadbury stood in the door, murmuring abject apologies, never sparing him a single glance.

She had her thick black hair scraped back away from her face, and the bruising near her temple did not show as prominently, although he thought she had helped that along with rice powder. There were still shadows under her eyes, her mouth was tight and thin with determination, and the gray dress she wore was even frumpier than her previous ones, something he wouldn't have thought possible. She was breathtaking.

He moved behind her chair, ready to pull it out for her, and for a moment the memory of their afternoon kisses flared in her eyes before it was quickly extinguished.

Everyone had, of course, risen again, including his sister-in-law, and for some indiscernible reason Melisande had a truly miserable expression on her face. "Emma!" she cried, and there was an odd tone in her voice. "I didn't think you'd be able to join us for dinner."

Emma looked suddenly alert. "A short rest improved everything," she said, and Brandon could attest to it. He wanted to cross the room, take her hand and pull her out into the hallway, back to the salon with the divan and the door to hide behind, or back to his vast room and his empty bed. He didn't blink, his face impassive.

Melisande had already started around the table in Emma's direction. "You cannot be too careful, my love. You've been through an awful experience—I can't imagine even being out of bed, much less coming downstairs twice in one day. Why don't you retire and I'll have a plate brought to you?"

The extreme oddness of the conversation didn't escape the other couples at the tables, but then, Melisande was known to be eccentric and egalitarian in her views and behavior. For some reason she seemed intent of sending her friend away from the dinner table. All eyes swerved back to Emma, awaiting her response. As he was, he realized, not even glancing at Frances.

Emma narrowed her magnificent eyes for a moment, as if trying to understand what Melisande was hinting, and then she did something very interesting indeed. She cast another glance at him as he stood there waiting, as if *he* had something to do with Melisande's very odd behavior.

Benedick caught Melisande's arm before she could reach Emma, and he shook his head, frowning at her. *What in Christ's name was going on with them*, Brandon thought. He had enough frustration on his own without some new disaster involving his brother.

Emma wanted to run, he knew that as well as he knew his own name, even if her expression remained politely blank. He didn't blame her—if he could get his horse out of Benedick's clutches he would take off like a bat out of hell. He could even offer Emma a ride to escape whatever she was trying to avoid, and the two of them would head to Scotland, with Noonan barely able to catch up.

But he wouldn't do any such thing. He had too much to atone for, so many things that he couldn't do anything about. He could do something about Frances, and he would do his duty.

Emma straightened her shoulders and smiled politely. He wasn't sure if he'd ever seen a real smile from her, one that reached her eyes and her heart. He had the odd sense that she had smiled at least once, but that was impossible. He would have remembered.

"I'm feeling well, my lady," she said formally. "I wouldn't have come down if I weren't up to it."

"Perhaps we might change the seating, and you could sit by me. . ."

"My dear," Benedick murmured, and Melisande seemed to come to her senses.

"I'm fine," Emma said meaningfully.

"Of course you are," Benedick said, releasing Melisande and moving to take Emma's arm. "Don't mind my wife—she has her moments of extreme silliness." He brought her over to Brandon's side. "You'll take care of Mrs. Cadbury, won't you, Brandon? She's not the frail flower my wife seems to think she is, but if she seems ill you might see her out and find a maid to assist her."

Emma was stoic once more. "What a huge fuss over nothing. Good evening, Mr. Rohan."

Brandon looked at her. He almost missed her calling him Lord Brandon, simply because she did it to annoy him. "Good evening, Mrs. Cadbury," he replied, helping her to the chair before taking the seat beside her.

Everyone at the table had been watching this little drama with avid eyes, including, he noticed, his fiancée. Conversation immediately began again, but rules were rules and Frances was following her hostess's lead and making desultory conversation with the elderly knight on her right. Halfway through the meal the very polite guests would then turn and talk to the person on the other side, rather like a stately court dance his parents might have been involved in.

Then Frances had left his mind completely. He was damned if he was going to wait until the fish or roast course to talk to Emma.

"What's going on?" he demanded in a whisper. The lady on his other side, Mrs. Beauchamp, had a consuming passion for rolls, and the wise server had put three on her plate. She was busy ripping small pieces off them and slathering them with butter—she wouldn't want to be interrupted with polite conversation.

Emma's face was expressionless. "The weather is positively dreadful, is it not? It is a great deal too bad that you missed getting out while the sun shone."

Considering that those who'd been out had found the mangled body of the murdered maid, that was less than felicitous, and there was a troubled murmur around the table. She flushed for a moment, realizing her mistake.

"The company in the house was more appealing," he said in the same polite voice.

"I'm so glad," she murmured, and there was just a trace of malice in her rich, sweet voice. He liked it. She was angry with him over those kisses. That made two of them—it had been incredibly foolish of him. He'd do it again in a heartbeat.

He watched her clever gray eyes sweep the table, linger for a moment on Benedick's taut expression, then at Melisande's clear misery, and then light on Miss Bonham, who looked only half as terrified as she had earlier. Emma turned back to look up at him, her beautiful gray eyes serene. "I gather we are to wish you happy," she said softly. "Will you be taking your bride to Scotland?"

EMMA HAD KNOWN the minute she'd walked into the room. It had started as a sinking dread, and Melisande's less than subtle behavior made it more and more clear. Despite Melisande's certainty, Brandon Rohan, Lord Brandon, was indeed going to marry Miss Frances Bonham, half-sister of the late Harry Merton. Which was lovely, absolutely right, he'd do well with a sweet, unquestioning young virgin to adore him, once she got over that look of cornered prey in her unremarkable eyes.

Which begged the question—why did Emma suddenly want to throw up?

Brandon was frowning at her simple words, not looking the slightest bit gratified. In fact, he had barely glanced at his new fiancée once since Emma had entered the room.

Emma was concentrating on her water, the voices surrounding her, when she realized he hadn't said a word. She was used to being rebuffed, but not even this new Brandon would behave so badly. She lifted her gaze to glance at him.

"I doubt it," he said, and he gave his future bride the briefest of glances before turning back to Emma. "She seems much too civilized a creature for the wilds of the Scottish Highlands."

At that moment Emma wanted to use Benedick's vile curse herself. "Then London will have the pleasure of your company? Or will you reside in the countryside?"

Another moment of silence, and she realized she'd been far too inquisitive. There was a fine line between polite conversation and rampant curiosity, and she was stomping all over it. She should have said nothing—what business was it of hers where Brandon Rohan chose to live—but she had a desperate need to know, in order to fortify herself if she was doomed to run into him.

Doomed. Such a dramatic word, she chided herself, glancing up at him. When had she become so infantile?

Brandon was as good as she was at hiding his thoughts. "I will arrange for Miss Bonham to live wherever she chooses, be it London society or a quiet country estate. I intend to return to Scotland posthaste, which I expect will make my wife extremely happy. Would you care to come with me?"

The question was added so casually that for a moment Emma didn't understand him. "I beg your pardon?"

"I asked if you wanted to come with me. To Scotland. To stay," he clarified. "It's cold and rainy and miserable a great deal of the time, and I live in the moldering ruins of a gatekeeper's cottage, but we manage to keep warm and Noonan does all the housework. He's not a half-bad cook."

She had slowly turned to stone at his abrupt words. Stone, with a ripped-up, bleeding heart inside. "I thought I explained to you, Lord Brandon, that I was no longer for sale."

She saw him blink, but instead of offense she saw a flash of humor. "Oh, I had no intention of paying you, Mrs. Cadbury." He returned tit for tat. "I rather thought you might like it."

Her expression could be withering indeed, and she gave him the full benefit of it. "Clearly you rate your attractions a bit too highly, my lord. If performing such services are not worth the money that's usually offered then I would hardly be tempted to perform them for free."

She could have remained cold and offended and walled off, except that he smiled at her, and for the first time she saw a glimpse of the old Brandon, the wounded soul who had made light of his grievous injuries, the young man who teased and enchanted her. "Now that's definitely going too far, sweet Emma," he said. "'Lord Brandon' is bad enough, 'my lord' is impossibly stuffy. And I could most definitely change your mind," he added softly, and his low voice beneath the hum of conversation made her flesh heat. "Have you forgotten this afternoon so quickly?"

It was instinctive, a bad move, but she didn't stop to think, she simply kicked him, hard, under the table, and then let out a little yelp of pain. He was wearing riding boots, the bastard, and her soft slippers only did damage to her own foot.

He made a soft, disapproving noise, his eyes still alight with mischief. "Temper, Emma," he chided. "You don't want to give anyone the wrong idea."

"What wrong idea?" she whispered fiercely. "That I kicked you? I don't care who knows it—my mere existence is already considered highly inappropriate. I could hardly make things worse with my behavior."

There was a faint softening in his expression, and it was even more painful than his mockery. "Emma. . ." he began gently, but she interrupted him.

"Say one more word to me, Lord Brandon, and I will spill my water in your lap."

His humor was back. "A cooling off might prove beneficial." He glanced down at his lap, and before she could stop herself she did the same. Oh, he was a gorgeous man, with those narrow hips, long legs, his. . .

She jerked her eyes away, then reached out and picked up her water, contemplating it meaningfully. "Your supposed injury isn't going to pass muster if you keep finding yourself in that condition," she said dryly.

She heard his soft laugh. "Don't worry—it only happens when I'm around you," and in the next minute he was deep in conversation with the matron on his left, dismissing her.

The rest of the meal passed in a painful blur. He never addressed another word to her, nor glanced her way as far as she could tell, though it seemed to her fanciful mind that she could feel his eyes on her. Every now and then she stole a glance at Frances Bonham, trying to imagine her with Brandon. Trying to imagine her in bed with him, beneath his large, strong body, taking him inside her, reveling in the act.

No, that was unlikely. Miss Bonham was small and slight and easily frightened—she would not be eager for bedsport. Brandon would force himself on her on their wedding night, but at least then he'd probably leave her alone.

It didn't matter that she couldn't really see Brandon forcing anyone. In fact, she couldn't even imagine that he'd ever had the need to. With his deep, rich voice, his gorgeous eyes, his strength and power he probably had women throwing themselves at him. His ruined beauty would be an aphrodisiac to a discerning woman—she imagined he'd been simply too pretty before he'd gone to war. She knew men—it had once been her business—and she knew he'd be a good lover, a generous one, the kind of man who found little pleasure if his partner didn't. During the years she'd spent on her back she'd never run into that sort of customer, but the other girls had, or so they swore, and indeed, a number of them had tried to stop charging their favorites.

Emma rubbed her head. It was throbbing, though whether from the blow or something else she wasn't quite sure, and she wanted to go back to bed and bury herself in the covers. She'd had such hopes for this week—a quiet time with Melisande's family, playing with the children, walking in the woods for exercise, taking Benedick's favorite, smelly old spaniel with her for company. Instead she'd found rain and Brandon Rohan, and Brandon was definitely the worse of those two trials. She'd be better off in the city.

Melisande wouldn't fight her any longer. At least this would put paid to any fantasies her best friend might harbor. A man would never cry off from an engagement, particularly not a good man, and she was convinced that beneath everything Brandon was a very good man.

There was no doubt in Emma's mind that Miss Bonham would accept him. She had always been an expert of eliciting gossip—it was an important part of her former trade. She knew all about the young woman's reputation, about her brother, she even knew about the legalities that tied up her inheritance. Men talked to their whores, and women talked among themselves. No, Frances Bonham had come here, accepted him, despite being completely spineless and terrified.

Emma immediately felt wicked. Despite Miss Bonham's very rational fear of Brandon, she had accepted his haphazard suit. She was braver than she seemed. She wouldn't cast him off lightly, and she didn't to be judged.

Emma barely touched her food, pushing it around on her plate with desultory disinterest. Usually she was blessed with a healthy appetite, particularly in London when she was working. Missing a meal or two would do her no harm.

She looked up suddenly, and her eyes met Melisande's speaking ones across the table. The men on either side of her had broken protocol in the face of her abstraction—Brandon listening with polite interest as the matron described her eligible daughters, and the elderly knight next to her attentive to the woman who'd accompanied Frances Bonham, who presumably was accompanying her into her marriage as well. It left Emma in a quiet sort of bubble, free to observe, free to feel sorry for herself, she thought with a fair amount of mockery. Melisande's bright blue eyes were troubled, and there was a tightness to her usually full mouth that signaled her distress as they looked at each other across the table.

Abruptly Melisande rose, causing a flurry of scraping chairs and clanking silverware. By rights she should have waited until the last course was removed, and normally the husband would then dismiss his wife and her female friends so they could smoke cigars and drink port and crack nuts.

Emma was fond of walnuts and white port, and she found the scent of cigar smoke oddly comforting, but no lady was allowed in the sacrosanct dining room once they'd been dismissed. It was different when it came to whores, and she'd worked two such gatherings in the past. Her own memories were far from pleasant, but there'd been something enticing about the ritual, at least, until she and her friends were put into play.

She shuddered. "We'll have dessert in the salon," Melisande was saying, her lush mouth tight with anger. "You gentlemen may enjoy your various indulgences. . ." and to Emma's horror she cast a fulminating gaze at Brandon. To Emma's relief the man beside her either didn't notice or didn't care.

Trying to extricate herself from between the two gentlemen, she momentarily found herself trapped. The knight was stolid and unmoving, his back to her as he conversed with Miss Bonham's friend, but Brandon Rohan was standing, looking down at her, making no effort to pull out her chair or guide her from the table as the other gentlemen did.

She knew the rules of society—her family had been seemingly proper, and the rituals of the upper class had been simple to assimilate. Brandon was flaunting the rules, his big body trapping her.

She knew how to behave, but she also knew that at least half of polite society didn't feel similarly obligated when it came to her. Melisande's house had usually been a safe place, and if, for a scant moment, she considered whether Brandon was treating her as the vicar and his ilk did, she dismissed it. Brandon didn't a damn who she was or what she had been, which was both a relief and . . . something else she refused to name.

She looked at him, wondered if kicking him at this vantage point would have any more effect. Probably not. "If you please, Lord Brandon," she said in a cool voice.

He still didn't move, looking at her, his expression totally unreadable, and he gave that cynical half smile, and shrugged. "Of course, Mrs. Cadbury," he said, pulling the heavy chair out of her way so she could join the other ladies. She moved quickly, her skirts brushing against his long legs, and to her shock she felt his fingers close around her wrist, just for a moment, slowing her pace, and she felt his thumb stroke the inside of her wrist, where her blood was hammering wildly. "That's better," he murmured, and releasing her, he turned away.

Once the door to the dining room was closed behind her she stopped, taking several deep, calming breaths. She had no idea why she had allowed him to rattle her—it was probably lack of sleep and general exhaustion that had made her so vulnerable. She was behind the other women, and she could see Miss Bonham and her companion with their arms linked, their heads close together. It looked like nothing more than an intimate chat, until she saw the panic in Miss Bonham's eyes, the despair in the other's, and Emma felt sympathy rush through her. It was like that, was it? There would be no happy ending for Miss Bonham and her friend—society wouldn't even admit such feelings existed, much less condone it. Miss Bonham was being traded to the highest bidder, Brandon, and the best Marion and Frances could hope for would be if he kept his resolve, married her, and then removed to Scotland.

It wasn't a particularly happy group of women in the salon. Mrs. Beauchamp had found the cookies and was devoting her attention to them, and Melisande's neighbor, Elizabeth, Lady Carlyle, was leaning back in a chair with complete disregard for those around them, her pregnant belly burgeoning in front of her. She had about five weeks left, Emma decided, and her color was good—she was, as most expectant mothers were, simply tired.

The others weren't much livelier. Melisande looked murderous, Frances Bonham tragic, her friend Miss Trimby defensive, and Emma herself wasn't certain whether she wanted to laugh or burst into tears.

She took her seat beside Melisande and a moment later polite conversation became the norm, aided by the social lubricant of tea. "I don't know what happened," Melisande muttered under her breath between declarations about the weather. "I never thought he'd go through with it. I'm going to kill Charles."

"He's simply looking out for his baby brother," Emma said calmly. "And I have no idea why you consider it a problem."

Melisande let out a quiet breath of exasperation. "Don't lie to me— I've known you too long. You're. . ."

"Felicitations on your engagement," Emma said to Frances, speaking over Melisande's whispered speech. "You must be looking forward to the happy day." It was the first thing she could think of to say, more of the social piffle so beloved of society, but Frances's martyred look reminded her it wasn't the best topic.

"They have yet to set a date," Miss Trimby announced repressively.

Frances managed to summon a wan smile. "It's all so new. I imagine Lord Brandon is in no particular hurry."

Oh, my. She was calling him by his title—that didn't auger well for the future. "I'm certain you'll be very happy," she said with complete insincerity. Brandon would be kind to such a meek creature, but completely bored, and Frances didn't appear as if she'd get over her terrors easily.

Miss Trimby surveyed her with a piercing look. "Have you hurt your wrist, Mrs. Cadbury? You keep rubbing it."

Dropping her hands to her lap, Emma felt embarrassed heat rise to her cheeks. She'd been holding her wrist where Brandon had grasped it, rubbing the skin, caressing where he'd touched her. She was going mad.

"How kind of you to notice," she said stiffly, and then managed a smile. She recognized Miss Trimby as well as if she knew her life's story —living on the edge of society as Emma now did, prickly and defensive and devoted to her best friend.

But Emma had lived among women who were open and honest with their affections, and she had no doubt that Miss Trimby's feelings for Frances were more passionate than sisterly, and those feelings were returned. That was all well and good in the world Emma inhabited, but there was no way for Miss Trimby and Frances to find happiness together, more's the pity, though if Brandon gave her the protection of his name and then abandoned her that would go a long way toward it.

And why was she so busy trying to come up with happy endings for everyone else when her own were to be forever denied? Not that she actually knew what she wished for. The chance to work, to practice medicine without having to hide behind some incompetent man, would be enough. The chance to help her friends and the women who'd survived by selling their bodies, either out of choice or necessity, would add to her satisfaction with a hard life.

She'd learned ways to compensate for the things she could never have. She had never had to resort to the kindly old lady down by the docks who assisted professional women whose less than reliable protection had failed them. In the beginning there'd been no protection at all, until the other women had taken her in hand and told her what little she could do to keep herself from the unwanted consequences of their profession, but she knew she hadn't needed it. She would never be able to bear children, but she could revel in Melisande's growing brood. She had no interest in the attentions of men, but she could enjoy their good points with the company of Benedick and . . . and . . . surely there must be other good men, though at the moment she couldn't think of any. Except, strangely, Brandon.

In fact, she should be delighted that she would never have to worry about men and their invading bodies again. The one man who had stirred unwanted, unrecognizable feelings inside her was now safely out of reach, engaged. She should be feeling happy and relieved.

Instead she was anxious, uneasy, restless, wanting something and not knowing what it was.

She did know what it wasn't. It wasn't sitting in an overheated drawing room with a group of torpid women in the throes of various emotional upset. Melisande was still simmering with rage, even comfortable Lady Beauchamp's love affair with the biscuits seemed to wane, and Lady Carlyle was doing her best to hide her worry about her first confinement, taking refuge in a not quite believable somnolence. Emma knew she would explode if she didn't escape.

She rose abruptly, and Melisande stared up at her in alarm. "Is something wrong?"

"I'm exhausted," she announced, even if she felt as tightly coiled as some hideous foreign snake. "I pushed myself a bit today, and if I'm to leave tomorrow I'll need a good night's rest. If you don't mind I think I should make for my bed."

No one in the room protested her early departure from the house party, she noticed with slightly grim amusement, though it might, perhaps, have nothing to do with her inconsequential self and more with the unhappy preoccupations of the women. It didn't matter—soon she'd be back in her own world, facing Mr. Fenrush and his coterie of bullies, and she wouldn't have to waste a moment thinking about the people here.

Melisande rose beside her, a smile on her face, rebellion in her eyes, and Emma knew that escape was still going to require an effort. "Of course, my dear. Would you like me to call for a maid to assist you?"

It was an infelicitous choice of words, reminding all what had happened to the young woman who had previously taken care of her, and the tense atmosphere in the room heightened.

"I'll be fine," Emma said firmly. "I'll bid you all good evening, and if I'm gone by the time you arrive downstairs, then a goodbye as well."

Miss Trimby was watching her with that peculiar fellow feeling of the classless, and even young Miss Frances looked a little distressed at her defection, which was ridiculous. She might be terrified of her new fiancée, but she could hardly think Emma might be the one to distract him.

She was ready to collapse when she finally made it to her bedroom. All her clothes were loose, designed to be easily removed without the aid of anyone, and she almost left them on the floor where they dropped. The dress she'd worn when she'd been attacked was hanging up, and it appeared that most of the blood had been successfully removed, though there were still some faintly darker patches. From now on it would be her primary work dress—even with enveloping jackets, surgeons tended to get splashed with blood. With a sigh she scooped her clothes from the floor, flung them across a nearby chair and crawled into bed, the heavy linen sheets cradling her.

She stared up at the ceiling in the darkness, only the faint flickers from the damped fire making any movement. It was warm enough there, though it would doubtless chill during the night, but in the meantime she was safe, tucked away, and if luck was with her she might never see Brandon Rohan again.

Turning her cheek, she buried her face in the pillows, letting the night close around her, and for a rare, precious time, she slept.

CHAPTER 16

Emma opened her eyes, blinking in the murky darkness. Her dreams had been so vivid—the man with the knife, slashing at her, his familiar eyes vivid, but this time they were someone else's eyes, someone's uncovered face, and she sat up in sudden panic.

It took her a moment to catch her breath, and then she forced a shaky laugh. In her nightmare the marauding attacker had been no other but Mr. Amasa Fenrush, chief surgeon at Temple Hospital, his eyes mad with murderous fury.

Which was, of course, a total absurdity. Her attacker had been huge, Fenrush was a small, bird-like man. He had almost colorless blue eyes, her attacker's eyes had been small and black, like currants. On top of that, the thought of such a fastidious man as Fenrush lowering himself to a brawl in a rain-soaked field was simply absurd.

It was no surprise that her sleeping mind had chosen Fenrush. If she had to name one person who truly hated her it would be her erstwhile superior, and a part of her was dreading what was awaiting her when she returned to London. He wouldn't take his demotion with any good grace, particularly by a woman, and she rather dreaded facing him.

And then there was Brandon. His appearance in her dreams had been no surprise—he'd been haunting them since he'd strode back into her life. If she were truthful she'd admit he'd haunted her for almost four years, but she steadfastly refused to consider it.

She tried to summon up the healthy irritation that kept him at arm's length, but she couldn't remember why she was angry with him. He hadn't done anything to hurt her. In fact, it seemed as if he'd actually been kind to her, in his own way. In her sleep-drugged state she couldn't remember much, she just had a general sense of unease, but the memory of Brandon was different. He somehow felt . . . right.

She opened her eyes again, growing slowly more alert as her memory filtered back. Brandon Rohan was the farthest thing from "right." He was engaged to marry a very sweet, very unhappy girl. And yet he'd kissed her—several times, very thoroughly, and she hadn't fought him.

Hadn't fought him? She'd gone willingly, damn her idiocy! Hadn't she learned after all this time?

The house seemed almost unnaturally still, even for the dark of night, and then she realized what was different. The lashing rain had finally stopped.

It was well after midnight—she'd always had an instinctive sense of time, whether it was close to dawn or dusk, and it didn't fail her now. It was the depth of the night, the time she usually woke when her sleep was troubled. A sound finally came to her—the muffled wail of a miserable baby, and she recognized her unhappy goddaughter.

The floor was cold beneath her feet when she rose, reaching for her heavy shawl. The crying was getting louder now, and she pushed open her door, making her way slowly down the hall, wishing she'd at least had stockings to warm her bare toes. When she finally returned to her self-contained rooms in London she'd appreciate the tight confines that enabled her to stay warm. One always assumed the wealthy had the best in life, but those who lived in these grand old houses were probably freezing to death. She'd take her rooms in the slums any day.

She slipped into the nursery, closing the door behind her silently, only to stop short, wishing she were anywhere but there. Nanny was nowhere in sight, neither were any of the nursery maids. Instead a man leaned over the cradle, speaking in a soft, soothing voice to his infant niece and goddaughter, and Emma wondered whether she could slip out of the room before he noticed.

Brandon didn't lift his head, but his warm voice carried across the room. "Are you going to just hide there in the shadows, Emma, or are you going to help me with this squalling brat?"

While the words were harsh, the tone was at direct opposites, and there was no mistaking the tenderness in the man as he reached down toward the crying baby. She didn't need to see this. She was already having a difficult time sorting out her feelings for this unpredictable man—there was nothing more guaranteed to melt her heart than the sight of a big, strong man caring for a baby.

He looked beautiful in the candlelight as he reached down and picked up the infant. His too-long hair was loose, he was wearing only breeches and a shirt, and he was everything she had ever dreamed of, cradling the infant against his chest before he turned to look at her, and the undamaged side of his face came into view.

It was only then that she realized she'd been mooning over his scarred face, seeing the man, not the damaged flesh, and it was one more reminder that she was in deep trouble.

"Where are the servants?" At least she could sound cool and controlled.

"Benedick sent them away. We'd managed to calm the wee scrap, and my brother wanted to check on Melisande. Apparently she's been having difficulty sleeping and he didn't want to disturb her."

Wee scrap. The Highlands must be having a subtle effect on him. It was no wonder—he'd been up there for more than three years. The last thing she wanted to do was move closer to him, but the cries were growing louder, and she crossed the room in efficient strides before she could give in to the temptation to run away. He was hardly going to start kissing her again when a baby was crying, and a small part of her regretted that fact. "Why didn't you send for someone?"

He glanced down at her. "She's eaten and had her nappies changed —there's nothing anyone can do that I haven't. You don't have to have tits to care for a baby."

"They do help," she said dryly. "Give her to me." She reached out her arms, and Brandon raised an eyebrow.

"You think you can do better with her?" he said, rocking the baby gently as she nestled against his broad chest.

"Of course." In truth, she wasn't sure. There seemed no better place in the world than resting against his shoulder—but Alexandra didn't seem to be enjoying it properly, the foolish wench.

"You'd best sit down first, and I'll give her to you. You're still looking a bit pale," he said, surveying her critically.

"It's too dark for you to see that," she said crossly, moving to the large chair Nanny used when the children needed rocking.

He leaned down and put the infant in her arms, and he was suddenly too close, too warm, his mouth. . . "I've been paying attention," he said. Then, thank God, he moved away.

Alexandra squirmed against her, mewling in unhappiness, rooting against her breasts with blind need. "She's still hungry," Emma announced. *Trust two men to think they knew a thing about babies!* "You'll need to get the wet nurse back, quickly, before she works herself up into a full-blown tantrum."

He glanced around him. "Where's the bell-pull?"

She let out a long-suffering sigh. "That would take too long. A footman would answer, he'd have to go to Richmond, and then Richmond would need to find someone to rouse the wet nurse. Go yourself."

Another man would have been affronted but Brandon simply grinned. "Yes, ma'am," he said, and a moment later he was gone, leaving her alone with the snuffling babe. She leaned back, rocking, murmuring softly to the little one, and together their bodies warmed to each other, relaxing in the shadowy room. He'd come back. The baby would sleep. And they would be alone together, with the memory of those heated moments in the salon fresh in their minds. What if he touched her again? What if he didn't?

BRANDON HAD NEEDED an excuse to leave her. Watching the infant root at her breast through the thin cotton shift had been far too arousing, and she was an inconveniently observant female. He had little doubt she'd notice his condition, and whether her reaction would be fear or disgust, he didn't want to go there. And if she responded with interest. . .

He'd been unable to sleep. When the gentlemen had eventually joined the ladies in the salon he'd been informed that Mrs. Cadbury had retired for the night due to her early departure the next day.

The hell with that, he'd thought. She wasn't going anywhere until they'd had an honest talk. He'd made a royal mess of it all, when he'd only been wanting to do the right thing and then get the hell out of there. Now, for the first time in his memory, he found he was thinking of someone other than himself, someone who felt like she belonged to him, someone he wanted, not just her body, but her heart and soul and brain.

He wanted to pound something, perhaps his own thick skull. Charles would have been even more worthy of a pummeling, but he'd already been banished. Brandon couldn't even acquit his closer brother of wanting the best for him—Charles's only interest was in securing the land next to his for his family. He knew perfectly well that Brandon had no interest in the English country estates he already owned, much less those of Harry Merton, the man who had almost killed him and so many others. He wanted nothing to do with it, and Charles would somehow manage to secure it, sly bastard that he was.

Brandon didn't want to be thinking about Harry Merton or his sister. He wanted to think about Emma Cadbury, wearing the thin nightdress, a shawl trailing from her shoulders, her bare feet peeping deliciously from beneath the hem.

In fact, he'd been lying in bed, in the midst of a truly immoral fantasy about her, one hand wrapped around his cock, when he'd heard the baby crying and gone in aid of the situation. It had been organized chaos, with Benedick trying to hush everyone, Nanny and the nursemaids clearly in the midst of some power struggle, and the poor little infant wailing her head off. At any moment he'd expected his sister-in-law to charge in, but not even her baby could rouse her from her long-denied rest.

Things had settled down relatively swiftly, and everyone returned to their beds until an hour later the cries came again, cries he'd been doing his best to deal with when Emma had entered the room, looking only slightly the worse for wear, her thick, black hair tumbling down her back, her feet bare, her shift too thin for the chilly air and his peace of mind.

Christ, he had to get out of there, get back to Scotland, before he did something he regretted! He was half-tempted to simply scoop her up and take her with him, which wouldn't go over too well with his fiancée, he thought sourly, moving through the halls as swiftly as his bad leg would let him as he followed orders and went for the wet nurse.

It wouldn't take much to finish things up—Benedick was probably more than ready to see the last of him. Tomorrow he would ignore the temptations pulling at him and head back to Scotland until the time came for his marriage ceremony, assuming he couldn't avoid it. Neither he nor Miss Bonham spent time in society—no one would expect them to make the rounds that an average engaged couple normally would. In fact, he might insist on holding the wedding in Scotland. He wanted the business handled with the least amount of disruption— anyone could marry them in Scotland, and then she could go back home a safely married matron and he wouldn't have to think about her again. He had no intention of ever living with her. No intention of bedding her either, though he supposed he might have to, sooner or later. She was too meek, too pale, too. . .

Too not Emma. Jesus, he had to get out of there!

It was relatively quick work to arrange for the wet nurse, and he started back slowly, favoring his leg, but even so, he reached the hallway outside the nursery before anyone else did. To his astonishment there were no howls of fury, no baby screams of despair. Just a soft voice, almost inaudible, singing.

He pushed open the door, and he froze, unable to move. He'd faced down charging lancers, deranged Moghuls, murderous Afghan tribesmen, and the fathers of innocent girls. Nothing compared to this.

Emma was sitting in a chair, the baby in her arms, rocking gently. She was smiling down at the dozing infant, and she looked like a Madonna as she sang an old Welsh lullaby, one he knew as well as he knew his own name, even as everything else in his life seemed suddenly upended.

Sleep, my child, and peace attend thee, all through the night,
Guardian angels God will lend thee, all through the night.
Soft the drowsy hours are creeping
Hill and dale and slumber sleeping
I, my loving vigil keeping
All through the night.

Her voice was beautiful, clear and sweet and low, and it danced through his brain, through his body like a wicked taunt. He knew that voice, that sound, that lullaby, and the knowledge went through his body like a bolt of lightning.

He'd heard it before, from a woman who had sat by his bed, night after night, holding his hand while he fought against a death that had seemed so enticing. A woman who had talked to him, made him laugh, kissed him, made him want to live again. A woman who had disappeared when he'd needed her most. His Harpy.

She sat there, all innocence, as if she hadn't been lying to him for days now, as if she hadn't been acting a part, pretending there was no past, nothing between them. She hadn't forgotten—he knew that full well. So why had she lied?

No wonder he'd been like a moonling over her. His mind may not have remembered that dark, confused time, but something more elemental had. She had come to mean so much to him back then it had almost frightened him. She was his nebulous dream for the future, his reason for enduring the vicious pain and shattered bones. She was his hope, and then she'd taken it away, gone between one moment and the next. He'd ended up ensconced with his family, the last few weeks of his life vanishing, concentrating instead on the opium pipe and draining his brother's cellars, concentrating on decadence and indolence and the darkest of desires.

He tried to die, then, by any means necessary, but it was already too late. She'd been with him long enough to nurse him past the danger point, then abandoned him with nothing to live for, and he'd survived in broken fury.

He'd even gone to look for her one day, when he'd made himself sick on the foul stuff he was taking, when he'd seen things at the gathering of the Heavenly Host that he could never scour from his memory. His orders from their anonymous ruler had been disturbing enough that even he had balked, and he'd gone out, lame, staggering, in the early morning rain in search of her at St. Martin's Military Hospital.

How could he have forgotten all this? The insidious power of the opium had even more wide-ranging consequences than he'd realized—she had vanished, along with his time in that miserable hospital, in a puff of sweet-scented smoke.

He never should have been sent there in the first place, of course. If he'd been properly identified when they shipped him back to England he would have been taken up by his family and given the kind of care the brother and son of peers should receive. By the time he awoke in that crowded, stinking ward, awash with the screams of pain and the misery all around him he'd said nothing, pretending to have no memory, simply awaiting death.

Until his Harpy had come along and ripped it away from him.

But when he returned to the hospital it had been almost a year since his family had found him and carted him out of there, and no one remembered the woman. The kind of women who worked in hospitals tended to be anonymous, from the dregs of society and quickly forgotten. Even the celestially beautiful woman who spent nights by his bed, holding his thin hand, teasing him, chiding him, exhorting him to live.

Celestially beautiful? He'd thought her some kind of angel. Now he could see her for what she was, his eyes no longer blinkered by sickness and vulnerability. She was a woman, nothing more, one who derived pleasure from taking a helpless man and making him rely on her, then abandoning him. In truth, a part of him couldn't blame her. It was the only revenge against the abuse she'd suffered at the hands of men, and if he hadn't known her he might even have applauded it.

But he did know her, finally, even with her deceitful games throwing him off-track. Never once had she tried to find him, never once had she reached out, even though his own brother married her closest friend. She'd kept herself aloof, indifferent, as he'd been drowning in a morass of decadence and addiction. After she'd saved him she'd been willing to stand back and let him die by his own hand.

No wonder she'd been as desperate to leave this place as he was. She'd probably been terrified he might remember her.

The wet nurse arrived through the door off the servants' stairs, and Brandon drew back into the shadows abruptly. He should be well satisfied, he thought as he returned to his room, not even bothering to hide his limp. The nagging question about her had been answered—it explained his fascination with her, his obsession. It answered the question that had haunted him until he'd smoked enough and drank enough to drown it out—what had happened to the beautiful woman who sat in the shadows and had somehow become everything to him.

Whores' tricks had served her well. She was well versed in the art of bringing a man to his knees, and she'd played him very well. He could salute her—she was a worthy adversary, and she'd managed to win their first encounter.

She'd won the second as well, playing her games again, the only pleasure she allowed herself to accept from the opposite sex. He mentally bowed down to her—he'd been in the presence of a master of manipulation and deceit.

But in the end he'd won, because he'd remembered, and he could now see her in all her duplicitous glory. He would leave first thing in the morning and never have to see that lovely, lying face again.

She would believe he'd forgotten her completely. It was a paltry revenge, but it was the least he could do. He'd return to the Highlands and do everything he could to make it the truth. He had no idea why he felt so angered by her lies, but he welcomed it. Anger was something he was used to—it fit him well enough.

Regret was far too troubling.

CHAPTER 17

He didn't come back. Emma had been sure he'd return, to banter with her at the very least, perhaps even to flirt, to kiss her again, to perhaps. . .

And she might let him. She could allow herself so little, but that one night would tide her over for years. She could survive giving herself to him—there was no question that he wanted her. And she wanted him to hold her.

She might as well accept the fact: she was like a green girl in raptures over a pair of broad shoulders. And his shoulders were very broad after the years in Scotland, his strength returned to him in abundance.

But this hadn't started with broad shoulders. This had all started with a deeply damaged man barely clinging to life, to long hours in the darkness as she did everything she could to bring him back from the precipice. With soft, harmless midnight kisses until they became something more. The man whose charm and wit had surfaced and enchanted her, until it was too late to defend herself.

She'd spent many long hours of the last three years, trying to understand her unlikely infatuation, she who despised most men, and she'd come across a simple answer. When she first met him, he was so frail he was no danger to her, not on any level, and she'd let down her guard. He wasn't the enemy, as most men were, he was simply a damaged boy in need of comfort, and she'd tried to convince herself her feelings were only maternal. After all, she loved children—she found both boys and girls delightful.

But as Brandon returned to life, growing stronger day by day, it was already too late. When he'd first managed the pale ghost of a grin she was smitten, and nothing had been able to scour that unlikely attraction from her soul.

And his kisses. They were innocence and charm, and she'd never been kissed like that in her life. Growing up, she'd been kept close to home. The lurid dangers of the male species had been explained to her in such harsh and explicit terms that she'd viewed every man with distrust, relying on her stern father's guidance, until he'd turn those same, lustful eyes on her and she'd known her presence on this earth was a curse.

Why had she let herself forget? For years she'd believed that her inconvenient beauty had tempted her saintly father to attempt something so heinous she refused to think about it. It wasn't until many years later that she recognized the fault wasn't in her, it was in the male of the species, and she'd been absolutely fine since then, armored in her dislike and distrust.

That is, until Brandon had slipped into her heart.

She'd always been a great reader, and she adored travel books, the vicarious adventures almost enough for a woman who would doubtless never leave England, and she read of a strange phenomenon in the desert, something called a mirage. It happened when the sun grew so abominably hot it seemed as if cool, refreshing water was floating on the sand. The idea had always fascinated her, and the knowledge that when the thirsty traveler arrived at the fantasy oasis they only found barren ground.

That was her relationship, for want of a better word, with Brandon. A mirage, a brief, tantalizing glimpse of cool, refreshing water, only to find it turn to sand in her mouth. She was a fool to ever let herself be so vulnerable.

She waited in the nursery for over an hour, but he didn't return, and she told herself it was a relief. Tomorrow she could leave—she was feeling well enough, and Brandon would marry Miss Bonham, and she and her companion would be miserable. . .

It wasn't her problem, she reminded herself. She was already dealing with enough—the girls at the Dovecote, her patients, her nemesis, the cow-handed Dr. Fenrush. There was no place in this world for unconventional attractions, be they between two women or a gentleman and a whore.

As luck would have it, she slept late into the morning, only waking when the sun moved overhead, the sun she hadn't seen in so many days. She struggled out of bed, landing on the floor in a tangle of covers, bruising her backside, before she could fight her way out of the linen and throw off her nightclothes. Dressing normally was a matter of a few short minutes—she didn't bother with voluminous petticoats, tight corset or a myriad of buttons, and her hair was usually screwed into a tight knot at the back of her head. She'd been primping the last few days, and she knew why, knew she should make her way downstairs looking like a drudge. And knew she wouldn't.

She stared at herself, frustrated. She looked her age—two years older than Brandon Rohan, and a century beyond that. Perhaps she should just stay in her room to pack and have the maid bring her something to eat.

And then Melisande would come traipsing in, asking her all sorts of uncomfortable questions, and she surely didn't want Brandon to think she was avoiding him. She was happier if he didn't think of her at all, something he seemed to have mastered last night, even if his afternoon kisses had shattered her.

She yanked her hairpins out, twisted the long length of her hair into a knot and secured it with a few hairpins, secure in the knowledge that now she looked like herself, a sensible woman with no interest in attracting the attention of anyone. She could convince Brandon, and she could probably convince Melisande as well. She just needed to convince herself.

"Darling, you shouldn't be up!" Melisande greeted her when Emma wandered into the small green salon. Young Adrian was playing at her feet, entranced with a set of wooden blocks, and Alexandra Emma lay curled in her mother's arms. "Surely you aren't still intending to leave? Only two days ago you were attacked and almost killed."

"But I wasn't killed," she said, squatting down besides Adrian and handing him a block, accepting his toothy smile as reward. "I had a restful day yesterday, a good night's sleep, and I'm more than ready to get on the road. I have work to do.

"What about Brandon?"

"What about him?" Emma said innocently.

Melisande wasn't so easily distracted. "I don't suppose he's remembered you yet, has he?"

It had taken years of practice, but Emma knew how to keep her expression serene and unruffled. "I hadn't thought about it," she said airily. "It doesn't matter, Melly. You're making a romance where there is none, and he's engaged to be married. Really, I can't put off leaving any longer—I must return to the city. I can't leave the women in town to the tender mercies of Butcher Fenrush."

Melisande laughed, distracted. "Do you think he's going to be a problem? Being replaced by anyone is always difficult, by a woman is worse, though I agree with Benedick's decision completely. Sooner or later he was going to kill a patient."

"He kills patients every week," Emma said. "It's the only reason I agreed to Benedick's high-handed decision, and I have no intention of staying in charge any longer than it takes to find a more suitable surgeon. The sooner I get back the sooner things will settle down."

"All right," Melisande said, giving in more easily than Emma would have expected. "In fact, that should work out quite well. Brandon plans to leave for London today as well. You can travel together."

"Oh, God, no!" she cried before she could stop herself. She cleared her throat, trying to sound more reasonable. "I wouldn't want to be a burden. I'm certain Lord Brandon would prefer not to have a female on his hands."

"Lord Brandon, as you so formally call him, would be more than happy to assist you. He has a great deal of penance yet to perform, and looking after you. . .

"I don't need looking after!" Emma's voice was fierce.

"Of course you don't," Melisande agreed. "But men like to think they're useful, and it would help Brandon put the past behind him."

"I think he's already managed that quite well. His upcoming marriage is proof of that. Where is he, by the way?"

She didn't like Melisande's sly grin. "Miss him already, do you?" The grin faded when she saw Emma's stony expression. "Did something happen between you two?"

"Of course not. Nothing ever would. We are far removed on the social scale—he's a peer, I'm a. . ." she remembered Melisande's slap and amended her words ". . .a working woman. There is no common ground, and our history is just that. Over for me, already forgotten for him."

"So why are you running away?" Melisande asked calmly.

In fact, she didn't have to leave. If Brandon truly was heading to London, then she was better off here in the country. Danger seemed to come from all sorts of unexpected directions—at least here she wouldn't risk running into Brandon.

She was being absurd, she reminded herself. London was a vast, sprawling city, and they would travel in much different circles. This wasn't her life—she needed to get back to her shabby rooms, her work, her place in the world, to deal with Butcher Fenrush and move on. Those things were what she needed to ground her, remind her who she was, to sweep away any errant fantasies and dreams.

"I'm not," she said. "If I was trying to get away from Lord Brandon . . . Mr. Rohan," she amended, too aware of Melisande's scrutiny, "then staying here would be the wiser choice. But I have to get back."

"I see," Melisande said, and Emma was afraid that she did. "Well, it is his loss."

"Life is full of losses."

Melisande rolled her eyes. "Leave off, Mrs. Siddons! Life is a healthy mix of joy and sorrow, and if you didn't spend your time running away you'd realize it."

This was far worse than the much-needed slap. "I don't run away!" she insisted in a raw voice. "I'm no coward."

"No? What are you doing right now? You've been trying to get away from here the moment you set eyes on Brandon, because he makes you *feel*. You've been able to divert all your love and caring to the women who've suffered as you did, as long as you keep everyone else at arm's length."

"I haven't kept you at arm's length," Emma said stiffly. "Perhaps I should have."

Melisande didn't relent. "I'm safe to love. The Gaggle is safe, my children are safe, even Benedick is safe for you to let down your guard. And that guard is formidable. Brandon somehow managed to get past it at some point, and you're terrified. Don't run, Emma! Stay and face him, face your own feelings! What's the worst that can happen? Do you have a heart left to break?"

The pain from Melisande's words was so sharp it took her breath away. She stood frozen, staring at her best friend, when the door to the salon opened and Benedick strode in. Behind him, Brandon stood in the doorway.

"Up so early?" Benedick greeted Emma, coming over and giving her a kiss on the cheek. "Shouldn't you be resting?"

"Emma must get back to the city, my love," Melisande announced before Emma could say anything. "She's needed at the hospital. She has to deal with Mr. Fenrush."

"That's probably wise," Benedick said, giving his wife a more lingering kiss and dropping down beside her. "We're sad to see you leave, Emma, but perhaps it's for the best."

"I thought Brandon could accompany her, since he's leaving for London as well," Melisande added artlessly.

Brandon had not entered the room, and the expression on his face was shuttered. "I don't think that's a wise idea," he said before Emma could protest.

His flat words startled her. She would have expected amenability, even light flirtation at the suggestion, not that cool dismissal.

"Why ever not?" Benedick's brow furrowed.

"I'm going on horseback, for one thing. . ."

"You asked to borrow my carriage."

"That was when I thought my fiancée would accompany me. Since she and her companion plan to travel on to Cambridge to visit her old nanny, I changed my mind. Noonan and I would prefer to be unencumbered." He didn't look at Emma—in fact, his gaze hadn't settled on her once this morning. It was so unexpected that some of her initial distress began to fade, replaced by annoyance. *Unencumbered?* How dare he?

Melisande and Benedick were looking equally surprised. "Take a damper," Benedick said impatiently. "Mrs. Cadbury is my guest and you will show her every courtesy. You will provide her escort back to London and be gracious about it! What the devil is wrong with you?"

That was Emma's cue to leave. Benedick had no qualms about airing private matters in front of her, and the last thing she wanted was to be witness to a family quarrel with her as the bone between two squabbling dogs. "I don't wish to be a bother," she said, following Brandon's lead and avoiding looking at him. "In fact, I'm sure your brother would make much better time on horseback, and there's absolutely no need to hover over me. I hate to sound ungracious. . ." *Take that, you surly bastard!* ". . .but I'd prefer to travel alone, and the public coach would be preferable. I have work to do during the trip, and I don't wish to be forced to make idle conversation." *Another slap at him*, she thought with irritated pleasure. *Idle conversation indeed.*

She did truly love Benedick like a brother, perhaps the only male she'd allowed herself to care for, but she'd forgotten how dictatorial even the most enlightened man might be, particularly if he were a peer and an older brother. "You will ride in my carriage, Emma—what kind of host do you think I am? And my very rude baby brother will accompany you to your destination. He will be absolutely silent if that is what you prefer, or he can entertain you with his version of polite discourse. Do you understand me, Brandon?" He directed his impressive glower on his younger brother, and reluctantly Emma followed his gaze.

She expected mutiny, but Brandon still had that cool, detached expression on his face. Even his startlingly blue eyes seemed to have turned a shade icier. "As you wish, Benedick. At your service, Mrs. Cadbury."

She bared her teeth in the approximation of a smile. It would be a waste of time to argue further, and only mire her deeper into the morass of confused emotions that seemed to tighten in her chest. "Your escort would be most *gracious*. . ." she dug the knife in ". . .but you may, of course, feel free to simply ride beside the carriage with your friend. I have no need for entertainment, and indeed, would prefer my own company." *Take that, you swine!*

He looked neither relieved nor annoyed at her subtle barbs. "As you wish, Mrs. Cadbury."

She glanced at Melisande, part of her heartsick that they had fought, a stronger part still affronted by the accusations. Her friend looked equally unhappy, and not best pleased with her brother-in-law. He was not going to find a warm welcome when he returned to Starlings Manor.

The tension in the room was unbearable, and Emma had no intention of continuing to enjoy it. "I must finish my packing," she said abruptly, knowing that this efficient household would have overheard her plans and already taken care of that little matter. It was a small annoyance compared to everything else.

Melisande didn't contradict her. Benedick was glaring at his impassive brother, who was blocking the doorway to the center hall. She could always leave by the side door, but that would put her much farther away from the family staircase, making it clear to everyone how unsettled she was. She wasn't going to give her erstwhile weakness the satisfaction.

Turning, she advanced on the door, expecting him to move out of the way. He didn't. In fact, she came right up to him, too close, so that her skirts brushed against his riding boots, and she would feel the warmth of his body, absorb the faint, leathery scent that clung to him, mixed with fresh air. It was enticing. Or, it had been, before she'd abruptly come to her senses.

She looked up, her face as stony as his. "Are you going to let me pass?"

For a moment he stayed, blocking her. She was wondering if she was going to have to put her hands on him to push him out of her way when he stepped back.

"I beg your pardon," he said in a bored voice that she'd never heard from him. "I was wool-gathering. Thinking of my fiancée."

If he was thinking of his fiancée then she was a goat's breakfast. "Instant love is such a glorious thing," she said icily.

This time the barb ricocheted, hitting her in the heart. She could see the look of satisfaction on his ruined face—he knew that he'd upset her, and he was pleased to have done so. She had no idea why. Yesterday he'd kissed her as if she was the only thing in the world that mattered. Now, for no discernible reason, he seemed contemptuous.

It wouldn't matter. In six long hours, possibly longer given the state of the roads, she would be quit of him, her irrational weakness scrubbed clean, the last vestige of an old life, an old dream vanished. She would return to her work with a clear mind, free of any entanglement, even if it had been of her own making. She'd been a fool, allowing herself furtive daydreams, but she was over that now. She was probably just as deluded about any sinister connotations to her recent accidents. She would be wary, of course, but in the cool light of day the very notion of someone trying to hurt her was simply absurd. Especially since Brandon Rohan's casual words could do a much more effective job.

Dropping a perfunctory curtsey to Melisande and Benedick, she left, traversing the broad hallway and the private staircase with a speed that made her head pound. As she disappeared into the darkness his eyes followed her, she knew it, and this time not from appreciation. Unlikely as it seemed, she had suddenly been declared the enemy. She would accept that role with relish.

CHAPTER 18

The trip started well enough. Emma had parted company with Melisande, both of them crying, their argument put to rest, at least temporarily. Brandon Rohan had mounted his horse, his ruined face like granite. Now he rode ahead of the carriage beside the craggy old man who was apparently his servant. Even the rear end of Brandon's horse expressed his disdain, Emma thought sourly. In fact, *he* was the horse's ass, something she'd never realized before, and she could count her blessings that his true, obnoxious self had finally been revealed, freeing her from her inconvenient emotions. She could hardly call it an obsession, since she'd gone for days without thinking about him during the last three years, and she rejected the thought that she'd had any tender feelings at all for the miserable creature.

In truth, it had been mere curiosity, a bland interest that had stirred within her and nothing more, and now that she realized there was nothing beneath the usual masculine bravado she was content to dismiss him. Craning her neck, she peered at his strong back for the dozenth time, reminding herself that she didn't care, and then sank back on the cushioned seat, trying to ignore the tight feeling between her breasts.

The early sun had vanished and the day was now cloudy and overcast. There were signs of the storm everywhere—fallen trees, sodden fields, the road rutted to an uncomfortable degree. It was a good thing it was well before planting, or this year's crops could have been ruined, she thought. She hadn't thought about crops or farming since she'd run away from home—it was odd to suddenly remember the devastation that bad weather could wreak.

There was no way she could sleep in the carriage, not with the deplorable condition of the roads, so she simply held on and rocked back and forth, her healing body beginning to ache. Cook had packed a lavish hamper, clearly meant to be shared with her unwilling escort, but the constant motion had turned her own stomach, and she wasn't about to offer Brandon Rohan a thing. If he grew hungry then he could ask, and it was clear that he would starve before he'd speak pleasantly to her.

But why? It was a mystery, and much as she ought to she could never leave a mystery alone. He could scarcely have discovered anything new about her—she'd told him she'd been a whore and he hadn't even blinked. If his sudden antipathy made any sense then she could easily let go, but instead her mind kept going back to him, even more often than her gaze, as she tried to puzzle out what had happened, and no matter how often she told herself it didn't matter, it was none of her concern, she couldn't leave it alone.

They were making miserable time, and darkness was coming early. Eventually exhaustion took over—she need to be back home in the safety of her rooms so badly that she wanted to weep with the need— and she fell asleep even as her body was tossed and shaken. When she woke with a start some time later, it was pitch black and the carriage had come to a stop.

She had no vain hope that they'd reached the city—even at this dark time of year there were street lamps to illuminate London's gloom, and the noise was almost constant. A light rain had begun to fall, splashing against the roof and sides of the carriage and she sat up straight, determined to hide her dismay. With any luck they were simply stopping to exchange horses before continuing on with the final lap of their journey. But luck hadn't been with her recently, and she had the gloomy feeling that wasn't about to change.

She had just grasped the door handle when it was suddenly flung open, pulling her with it, catapulting her straight into Brandon Rohan's strong arms, and there was no way she could stop her forward motion, particularly when the steps hadn't been let down yet. She needn't have worried—he disengaged from her as if her very touch were poison, setting her on the muddy ground and taking a step back.

"The road's washed out," he said, ignoring the cold rain that was pelting down and freezing Emma to the bone. "We have to stop for the night."

Not the best news she could have heard, but under the circumstances she wasn't surprised. He was blocking her way again, keeping her from seeking shelter as the rain began to soak through her wool gown and the mud oozed around her feet. He still had his hat on, protecting his face, but she'd left hers, along with her enveloping shawl, in the carriage.

If he expected her to complain he would have a long wait. She was a country girl at heart—a little rain never harmed anything more than a silk gown. "Where are we?" she demanded, her voice almost as cold as her feet.

"Just north of Chelmsford. Noonan found an inn that will take us, so we won't be forced to spend the night in the carriage."

Her eyes flew open at that horrible thought. "They have rooms for us?" she inquired delicately. If he told her they would be forced to share a bedroom then she was going to climb back into the coach and not leave it until they reached London.

He was looking at her with such anger and contempt from beneath the rain-soaked brim of his hat. *Why*, Emma thought, bewildered. *It made no sense.*

"The inn has no other customers—it appears that most people were wise enough not to attempt travelling while the roads were in such a mess."

His tone of voice suggested she was the one who'd forced the journey, when he'd already been planning to leave that day. She controlled her instinctive retort. "Indeed?" she said, her catchall phrase to put anyone in his place.

But of course Brandon didn't react. "In fact there are three bedrooms, so even Noonan gets a decent bed rather than sleeping in the stables with the driver, and the landlord has promised a good meal compliments of his wife."

It took all her strength to keep from shivering. She needed a fire, a strong cup of tea, and now that they were no longer moving she discovered that she was famished. She was about to murmur something vague and move around him when he spoke.

"And in your case we needn't worry about your reputation being compromised, need we?"

It felt like a slap in the face, and not the light one Melisande had given her. No, it was like a hard fist across the jaw, and the shock of it took her breath away. She jerked her head up to look him straight in the eyes, but she only had a glimpse before the heavy rain blinded her, just long enough to see momentary remorse, as a reproachful voice behind him said, "Laddie!"

It didn't matter how shocked Brandon might be at his own cruelty. He could roast in hell for all she cared, her entire body suffused in a warming rage. "No, we needn't," she said, her voice brittle. "I'm delighted that my years of selling my body makes the situation more comfortable for you." She didn't hesitate, shoving him out of her way with the strength her anger had given her, and he fell back easily enough. "I find I'm not particularly hungry," she tossed back over her shoulder. "I'll see you in the morning."

"Emma. . ." If he sounded regretful she didn't give a rat's ass. She ran the last few steps to the door of the tavern, her feet squelching in her muddy shoes, and burst forth into warmth and light and safety. She allowed herself a hopeful glance behind her, just in case there was some way to bolt the door and keep him out in the harsh weather, but there was nothing.

"Welcome to the Hawk and Cock, miss," said a voice, and she turned back, pushing the rain and her bedraggled hair away from her face. "Bosomworth's the name."

He looked every inch a solid country innkeeper: round-bellied, rosy-cheeked, immensely cheerful. She knew how that look could change if Mr. Bosomworth suspected his prospective guest was far from respectable, but Brandon Rohan had already made arrangements, and no one would dare to question someone with his address. Just another thing different between them, she thought. Brandon had that easy self-assurance that Benedick and Melisande had, the kind that came with being born into that class, while she was a ruined woman from the country.

"Thank you, Mr. Bosomworth," she said, striving to sound brisk. "I'm very tired—would it be possible for you to show me my room? I think I'll simply retire for the night." The moment the words were out of her mouth she knew she'd done it wrong—guests make demands, not pleas.

The innkeeper didn't react. "Certainly, miss. But my wife's a fine cook—she can make up anything you want, and she's got a roast chicken just out of the oven. Can I tempt you. . . ?"

She heard Brandon fiddling with the door behind her, and she quickly stepped away. "I'm not hungry," she said with a twinge of regret. She could smell the chicken now, and it made her mouth water. "Just my room, if you please."

"Certainly, miss," he said leading her across the room toward the staircase. "I'll be right back, Mr. Rohan," he called over his shoulder.

"I'm in no hurry," Brandon said, and the sound of his voice was so dearly familiar, so deep and enticing, that she wanted to cry. But there was nothing to say or do, and she followed Mr. Bosomworth's sturdy backside up the stairs, escaping.

He'd brought a branch of candles with him, lighting the way, and he led her up another flight to the third floor. "Mr. Rohan said I was to put you as far away from him as possible," he said apologetically as he fought to catch his breath on the top landing. "For respectability's sake, of course. I had the girl get the fire going, and it should be comfortable enough." He pushed open the first door, and blessed heat wafted out, enveloping her in its embrace.

She walked in ahead of him, looking around, and her throat tightened. It was a small room, beneath sloping eaves, and the narrow metal bed, the threadbare rug on the scrubbed floors, the bright fire blazing in the small fireplace were so familiar. Her own room had been like this one—clean, comfortable despite its Spartan furnishings, before she'd traded it for the deceptively fancy surroundings of a London cathouse.

There was even a cozy-looking chair by the fire. "This is perfect," she said, meaning it. She moved to the fire, holding her chilled, gloveless hands out to the flames. "How far are we from London?"

"London? Why, miss, in the best of weather it's no more than four hours, but as you can tell the weather is far from good."

She stared at him in shock. "How is that possible? We left Rippington in the late morning and we were only five hours from the city. Surely it didn't take a goodly portion of the day to achieve an hour's worth of progress?"

"Main roads are out, miss. They're all right for horses, but a big fancy coach like yours would never make it. Your coachman would have had to take back roads to get to London, and those send you either north or south. I'm thinking he took the northern way trying to avoid the worst of it, and that can add a full day onto the journey."

Shit, she thought, reveling in the word Long Polly had taught her, a word she never used. "Oh, dear," she said faintly.

Mr. Bosomworth looked sympathetic. "As long as the rain stops you should be past the worst of it. With any luck you'll be in London before dark tomorrow. But what shall I tell Mr. Rohan if he asks after you?"

He wouldn't, the rat bastard, she thought. "Oh, he knows I prefer to be by myself. For respectability's sake," she added, trying to keep the savagery from her tone. And then she smiled like a demure young female. "And I should warn you, he's not *Mr.* Rohan. He's Lord Brandon Rohan, the son of a marquess and the brother of viscount. He's very starchy about his title—he'll insist he doesn't wish to be called by it but he's still very affronted if you don't."

Bosomworth looked worried, and Emma almost felt a pang of guilt, but the very slight revenge was little enough to ask. "Thank you so much, Miss," he said. "I'm glad you told me—I wouldn't want to cause offense."

"I thought you wouldn't," she said. "I will see you in the morning, Mr. Bosomworth." Her tone was final, and the innkeeper had no choice but to accept it, bowing himself out of the room with repeated promises to provide anything she might desire.

She closed the door behind him. "Like Brandon Rohan's head on a platter?" she muttered beneath her breath.

There was no lock on the door, but that was of no importance. No one would be trying to get into her room. She was cold, she was wet, and her entire body ached from the rough day's travel. She would kill for a warm bath, but nothing would make her do or say anything that might bring her near Brandon again. He'd just have to make do with his precious Noonan's company. The old man had looked at her like she'd crawled from under a rock as well, though she suspected that was simply an old bachelor's distrust of females, and at least he'd been surprised by Brandon's casual cruelty. Let the two of them enjoy each other. She just had to survive another day of travel and then she'd never see Brandon or his man again. Melisande and Benedick would simply have to come to her in London.

Sinking down by the warm fire, she pulled up her sodden skirts and attacked her wet, muddy half-boots. They were sturdy enough, made for moving through London's filthy streets, and they'd survive this rough treatment, but she needed them cleaned and dried for tomorrow's long day. She pulled them off and set them on the hearth, then slid her wet stockings off her legs and dumped them in a sodden pile next to the shoes.

She leaned back against the chair, shivering. She needed to get out of her wet dress and pull a blanket around her to ward off the chill, but for the moment she couldn't bring herself to leave the fire. It was too hot against her face, while her back felt cold and pinched, and she leaned her head against the wing of the chair, sighing. Presumably someone would bring up her bag, but if they didn't she would survive that as well. She'd certainly survived far worse.

She wasn't sure how much time had passed when she heard a soft knock on her door, and she struggled to her feet. It wouldn't be Brandon—he'd have a more peremptory knock. And why should he be at her door anyway? For some reason he'd discovered he despised her, which made her blissfully happy. She could despise him in return.

As soon as she figured out how to achieve that happy emotion.

She was almost at the door when she remembered that a woman in her situation would be unlikely to answer the summons herself, and she stopped where she was. "Who is it?"

"Bosomworth, miss. We've got a bath for you, orders from his lordship," came the innkeeper's booming voice.

She hesitated for a full five seconds. Pride demanded that she send him away, but she'd abandoned pride long ago, and she would frankly kill for a warm bath at that point. "Come in," she said, quickly returning to her seat by the fire.

The copper tub wasn't huge, but it would easily encompass her, and she watched as two servants dumped heavy buckets of steaming water into it, bringing it halfway full. "Tim will be back with another bucket and your bag, miss, and afterwards Sally will be bringing you a tray of chicken, cheese and biscuits, orders from his lordship. Would you like wine or ale?"

Now that she'd already compromised her principles for a bath it would be foolish to turn down a meal. "You're very good, Mr. Bosomworth," she said, unable to bring herself to drop the honorific. "I would prefer something without alcohol. Perhaps some new cider?"

His forehead creased. "Are you and his lordship members of some new religion? Never heard of two people refusing good ale before."

His words almost made her smile. "It's not on moral principles, Mr. Bosomworth. Beer and wine disagree with my digestion."

He looked doubtful. "If you say so, miss. Funny that Lord Brandon would suffer from the same affliction."

It was slight, harmless, and he'd never know she'd trashed his reputation. "Oh, in his lordship's case it's simply that he has no head for it. One glass and he's crying like a baby."

By that time the two servants had returned, laden with even more water and her bag. "We don't have bells in this place, miss, but I'll have them come bring you dinner. Will that be acceptable?"

Might as well be hung for a sheep as a lamb, she thought. "That would be lovely."

"I'll let Lord Brandon know. He was worried about you."

She almost told him she changed her mind. Worried about her, was he? She sincerely doubted it. It was most likely a last remnant of his mother's teachings—Lady Charlotte, as she was known in Melisande's household, was a stickler for kind behavior, and no matter what sudden bugaboo Brandon had developed towards her, his instincts would be at war over his sudden contempt.

Besides, accepting a bath and a meal was hardly compromising her any further. As he had pointed out, that ship had already sailed.

She slipped into the steaming water with a moan of utter bliss—if she were ever moved enough to cry this would be the sort of thing that would motivate her. The heat was so delicious it made her chilled bones ache with it, and she was astonished the water didn't turn muddy after she dunked her entire head. For a brief moment she was tempted to stay that way, but the small bath required her to contort into an uncomfortable position so reluctantly she sat up again.

The soap was heavenly, scented with thyme and roses, and she washed every part of her with an unexpected vigor, determined to start her life from then on with a clean slate, physical as well as mental. She could wash Brandon Rohan off her quite easily, just as she'd managed to scour him from her mind.

The Hawk and Cock was a well-run hostelry—no sooner had the water begun to cool than the maid reappeared with a tray of food, just as Emma had pulled her wrapper around her. "Oooh, you have lovely hair," the girl breathed. "Would your ladyship allow me to brush it?"

She was young and country-bred—she probably thought all women were ladies. "Just miss," Emma said, hesitating. "Of course."

One more favor she was going to accept, but at least this time Brandon had nothing to do with it. Mollie Biscuits use to brush her hair when she'd first joined Old Mother Howard's establishment, and the simple comfort of it did wonders to stop her endless tears that first year. Mollie had continued the task when they were all living in the Dovecote, and it reminded her of peace and affection, two things that were sorely lacking in her life right now.

The food was wonderful, and she ate every scrap on her plate, sipping at the tang of fresh apples in the cider that accompanied it. While she ate they removed the tub, and when she was done Sally, who it turned out was even younger than Emma had thought and was Bosomworth's oldest daughter, insisted on taking her muddy dress and shoes along with the dinner tray, determined to clean them for her before she left the next morning.

Emma could no longer resist. She was warm, well fed, and drowsy, and she hadn't even thought of the bastard below more than once or twice. She would sleep well tonight, and tomorrow she would be done with him.

CHAPTER 19

Hours later Emma lay staring up at the slanted ceiling of the unfamiliar bedroom, stubbornly awake. She should have expected it—sleep was always elusive in the best of times, and not only had she slept most of the day away in that blasted carriage but her spirits were completely disordered. Whenever she began to relax, the memory of the man below would return, and it would require all her effort to dismiss him again, reminding herself that he meant absolutely nothing to her.

There was no way she could tell the time, but she'd always relied on a kind of inner clock, and she knew it had to be midway between midnight and dawn. She'd heard Brandon retire to his bedroom several hours ago—his footsteps heavy and uneven on the stairs and the old wooden floor of the place.

Uneven. Of course they were. When one looked at Brandon's strong, lean body one assumed he was whole. No, that was wrong, she reminded herself. Most people had only to see the ruined half of his face to know he'd suffered grievously. Odd, but she never saw it. It was simply part of who Brandon was. She'd never pitied him. Even when he hovered close to death, she'd known he was a fighter, and she'd goaded him into doing just that.

She didn't want to think about it.

He hadn't favored his leg at all while he'd been at Starlings, and she knew he had to have been hurting. For some reason the thought of him still enduring that kind of pain, never letting on, caused her heart to clench, and she wanted to go to him, soothe him, talk to him and distract him from the pain as she had so long ago in the hospital during the empty hours of night.

She wasn't going anywhere but to sleep, she thought with steely determination, and she'd lain in bed, summoning oblivion.

Oblivion never listened, and eventually she was forced to give up. She had no slippers, and Sally had taken her stockings. It would have to be barefoot, something she was used to, and she climbed down from the high bed, determined not to put it off any longer. There was bound to be milk in the kitchen of the old inn, fresh from the evening milking, and the stove would doubtless retain enough heat that she could warm herself a mug of the stuff. She might even find a bit of cinnamon to spice it, though dabbling in a cook's precious spices might be too presumptuous. She had no idea whether the hot milk would be efficacious or not, she only knew that once she made the effort she could finally sleep instead of tossing and turning and dwelling too much on the past.

The house was silent, and she knew her footsteps didn't carry as she crept down the narrow attic stairs, past Brandon's closed door and on to the main stairs. There were only two rooms on that floor, and one of them remained open. Noonan must have chosen to sleep in the stables with the coachman after all, and the Bosomworths would be sleeping in another wing of the building. It was far from troubling— she could be alone with Brandon on a desert island and have no fear for her. . . her inviolability. She paused on the stairs, looking back, and then stuck her tongue out at his door. The childish gesture entertained her until she reached the bottom of the stairs to come face to face with her nemesis lounging by the banked fire, watching her.

"Why were you sticking your tongue out?" he said lazily. "Did poor Noonan offend you in some way?"

She froze where she stood. At least she'd grabbed her shawl before she'd left her room, and now she wrapped its enveloping folds tighter around her body, awash in conflict. She wanted nothing more than to run back upstairs, which was out of the question. Her hair, always the bane of her existence, had dried into a mass of uncontrollable curls, her feet were cold, and she wore nothing but the very thin shift beneath the shawl, leaving her self-conscious and vulnerable. She could turn and stalk away in dignified silence, expressing her displeasure, but already her heart was pounding, twisting inside her. She wouldn't give him that satisfaction. He was nothing to her, she reminded herself. She was hardly going to change her plans because of him.

So she was silent, heading toward the kitchen door, averting her gaze and pulling her skirts away from him, though they were scarcely close. A detached, clinical part of her catalogued his appearance—she could appreciate beauty wherever she found it, she hoped. Brandon Rohan was most definitely beautiful. He was lounging back in the chair, his long legs propped on a chair in front of him, no stockings or shoes, just long, narrow feet. One wouldn't have thought feet could be beautiful, but his certainly were. The loose, open-necked shirt revealed far too much of his tanned, muscular chest, an arresting sight when she was accustomed to seeing him so thin and pale, and his breeches seemed too tight for comfort, but she wasn't going to think about that. His hair was long and loose, and the unblemished side of his face was presented to the fire, not to the world at large. If she tried very hard perhaps she could think of him as some monster, some gargoyle. . .

Even in her dreams that felt horribly petty and disloyal, if not to him then to the countless other visibly wounded patients she'd dealt with. His scars had nothing to do with his perfidious soul—in fact she was perverse enough to imbue them with their own kind of beauty. No, she would simply have to accept the cruel vagaries of fate. Not only was there only one man on the face of this earth who had the power to move her past her anger and fear, but he was so far above her in station, above even the proper young girl she'd once been, and if he hadn't suddenly seemed to despise her, that nothing. . .

"You're not speaking to me," he observed before she made it through the door. "I can't say that I don't blame you. What I said was inexcusable, no matter what the circumstances."

She stopped where she was, then pivoted to face him. "If that constitutes an apology, you should endeavor to refrain from throwing in a new insult. Your new wife will not appreciate it." She said it to goad him—most men would be appalled that she dared to even mention his wife.

That didn't seem to bother Brandon, to her regret. He was watching her warily. "What are you doing up?"

"If you remember, Lord Brandon," she said spitefully, "I have trouble sleeping."

"I do. We first met when you were wandering my brother's house in the middle of the night."

"That's not when we first met," she said, and he looked suddenly arrested.

"It isn't?" he said, his eyes sharp and searching.

"Of course not. We met at the church. You drove me back to Starlings."

For some reason he looked disappointed. "So I did. I'd forgotten. How very odd of me—I usually have a stellar memory."

She wanted to hoot with laughter at the thought. He'd managed to forget her quite handily. "Do you? I rejoice to hear it." She started for the kitchen once more.

"What about your memory, Mrs. Cadbury? Do you find yourself forgetting important things?"

She narrowed her eyes. "My memory is equally stellar. In fact, I might be bold enough to suggest that my own recollections far exceed yours."

"Do they indeed?" There was a silky undercurrent to his voice, and she stared at him. She was no fool. Was it possible he'd finally remembered her, and was now somehow furious with her for nursing him back from death?

But surely if he remembered her at all it should probably be with the same affection she had felt. They had been friends. They had hovered beyond friendship. If he disliked the fact that he'd once seemed to harbor tender feelings for her, he could hardly blame her for it, could he?

In her experience men could do all sorts of heinous, irrational things, but looking into Brandon Rohan's cool eyes gave her no hint.

There was no reason for him to dissemble—if he remembered he would say so.

She straightened her back, keeping the shawl wrapped tightly around her. "I'm going to avail myself of a mug of warm milk and then I plan to return to bed. Doubtless you'll have retired by then, so I wish you a good night."

Where had that sardonic expression come from? It was nothing she remembered from those weeks so long ago. "Are you offering me a mug of warm milk, Mrs. Cadbury?"

"I am not. You seek out your own means of procuring sleep and I will attend to mine."

"I can only think of one way to ensure a good night's sleep, and I doubt you are about to offer it to me."

To her absolute shock, her face warmed. When in her life had she been so missish as to blush at the suggestion of sex? She fought back the only way she knew how. "I'm not about to fuck you so you can rest comfortably. Your hand will have to suffice."

He looked neither shocked nor angry—in fact she thought she spied a trace of reluctant amusement before she whirled around and stormed away. She didn't want to think about it. She slammed the kitchen door behind her, not caring if she woke the household, and leaned against it, her heart hammering. She needed to get away from the man, more desperately than she'd ever had to escape anything, even her coerced presence at Mother Howard's establishment. Nothing had been able to tap her deeply sealed vulnerability like Brandon Rohan.

The room was shadowed, dim light coming from the cast iron stove, and her eyes adjusted quickly. It would suffice—she was feeling admittedly low in spirits and sitting alone in the dark suited her very well indeed. She would simply wait until he left.

She found the milk in the larder, scooped herself a tin cup of it, and set it on the warm stove. It wouldn't take long to heat, and she found a seat nearby, her toes curling in the delicious warmth. She had no choice —she was alone in the dark with nothing but her thoughts and the object of them just beyond the door. She hated him. She truly hated that man, more than she hated her holier-than-thou father, the vicious vicar in Melisande's parish, or the group of men who'd paid Mother Howard to take their turn with her during her first drugged night in the brothel. None of them had ever been able to touch her soul.

Brandon had. The heart that she had managed to wall off had somehow developed cracks that first night at his bedside, when she thought he was dying, and perhaps therein lay the explanation. The young man who lay in the darkness would be gone before her sudden affection could grow troublesome.

But he hadn't. He'd pulled back from the abyss, and she'd found herself kissing him, the first kiss she'd ever given or taken despite her years in men's beds, and it was too late.

She closed her eyes in the darkness, accepting the miserable fact that she'd denied so long. She'd fallen in love with him that first night, when she'd been so certain that she had no heart. She'd loved him, and it had been her own, personal disaster.

At least she was quit of it at long last. Each time she thought she was free something had reminded her that she wasn't, not quite. Something kept pulling her back to him, like a homing pigeon or a faithful dog.

That was at an end now. Tomorrow he would leave her and disappear, and whether she liked it or not, and she liked it very well indeed, she would never see him again. He would avoid her even more assiduously than she would return the favor. It was going to be just fine.

So why wasn't she feeling happier? Oh, there was the small problem of three attempts on her life in the last four weeks, something she'd been paying far too little attention to. Now that she could dismiss Brandon from her thoughts it shouldn't take long to discern whether it was merely a series of unlikely coincidences or someone truly trying to harm her. Now that she would no longer be distracted, it shouldn't take long to find out what, if anything, lay behind it all.

She drained the milk, shuddering slightly, and then rose. He'd had to have gone up to bed by now—he had no more desire to be around her than she did, and while she hadn't heard him leave she could be relatively certain she was safe. There was no way he could still be waiting for another confrontation with a woman he despised.

HE WAS TIRED OF THIS. Brandon paced his small bedroom at the inn, trying to stretch his cramped and aching leg. If he were home in the Highlands, and God knows he would have given anything to be there and never to have left—he'd go swimming in the coldest water he could find, never a difficult feat in that climate, and then lie by the fire with his spaniel Tammas stretched out beside him, and by the next day he'd be capable of anything.

But down here he had to improvise, and he'd discovered the best he could manage was to try to walk it off, ignoring the pain that sliced through his knee and thigh as he'd been ignoring it for years. And so he paced.

He'd wanted to follow Emma into the kitchen, grab her and make her tell him why she'd lied. It was the one thing he couldn't abide, and by doing so she'd betrayed his returning memory of the Harpy who'd saved his life.

Then again, she'd already betrayed him when she'd disappeared. He'd waited, day after day, for her to return to his side, so that he could tease her, flirt with her, continue with that deep, soul-shaking kiss. But instead she'd run away, and the sister in charge of the ward told him that she had no idea where his Harpy had gone, or even if she would return—that was the way of things, and so finally, reluctantly, he'd told them his name.

Of course he'd remembered it early on, remembered his adoring, ramshackle family including his tempestuous sister Miranda, stuffy Charles, and irascible, impossibly caring Benedick, not to mention his beloved parents. They didn't need a hideous shell of a man who'd broken every law of decency, even by Rohan standards, and the more time he spent with his Harpy the less tempted he was to confess his background.

He'd had no illusions. He knew the kind of ruined women who came and worked in the hospitals. They were soiled doves, abandoned wives, even criminals. It had been easy enough to know what she was— no man would ever be fool enough to abandon her, and with her looks she'd never have to resort to crime. She was a whore, plain and simple, though there had been nothing plain or simple about her, and he didn't care. She had become his reason for living, and he didn't even know her name.

When she'd abandoned him without a word she'd taken that reason with her. He'd had foolish fantasies about carrying her off, finding a place in the countryside where no one knew them and marrying her. Everything had been hazy and completely impractical, but he'd had nothing else to do while he lay in bed but build castles in the air. Those castles tumbled into dust when she disappeared.

Her crimes were manifest—not only had she vanished when he'd needed her, after her implicit promise of . . . what? She'd never promised him anything, and yet he couldn't let go of his fury. She'd spent days in his company that week and never uttered a word, as if they'd never seen each other in their lives. If he hadn't actually. . . cared for her then the betrayal wouldn't feel as deep. Snapping at her was accomplishing nothing. He needed to confront her, have it out, and then he could abandon her once they reached London.

Couldn't he?

He'd been so lost in thought he hadn't heard the furious muttering or the stomped footsteps on the creaky old floor, but there was no missing the way his door slammed open, and Noonan stood there, his wispy gray hair straight on end, creating an unlikely halo around his face, his eyes ferocious. "What the bloody hell has got into you, if I may ask? I spend the whole bloody day in the bloody rain because you're so bloody determined to get away from that place and then when I try to get even an hour's sleep you bloody well stomp around your room, muttering to yourself! What's gotten into you, you bloody pissant?"

It was enough to startle Brandon out of his brooding, and he even cracked a smile. "That's more 'bloodies' than I've ever heard in one speech. I'm impressed, old man."

"I'll impress me bloody boot into your bloody backside," Noonan snarled. "It's that woman, isn't it? She's leading you around by the cock hairs and you're like a randy boy with his first taste of quim. Get over it! Take her or don't—I don't give a royal fuck. Just get it out of your system so life can get back to normal. No piece of scrumhole is worth this much fuss."

"Don't talk about her like that!" Brandon snapped before he could stop himself.

Noonan looked at him with a combination of affronted dignity and pure pity. "By the cock hairs," he repeated. "I'm sleeping in the stable." The door slammed behind him.

Brandon stood in the center of the room, frozen. He'd actually considered hitting Noonan at his coarse term for Emma. The old man was right—he had lost his bloody mind.

He stalked back across the room, looking out into the courtyard. The moon had set, and everything was dark and deserted. He was alone in the main part of the inn with the woman he'd wanted so badly it had kept him alive.

He still wanted her.

He tried to remember the aphorisms his nanny had drilled into him. Beauty is only skin deep, pretty is as pretty does, looks fade but character persists. Nanny had had to deal with the way-too-beautiful Rohans, whose looks and wildness touched every generation. Emma's loveliness hadn't faded in the years since he'd last seen her—if anything she looked even more luminous, and she would be beautiful, to him at least, when she was seventy years old.

He heard her soft footsteps on the stairs. She'd been barefoot again, he'd noticed, despising the fact that he found her long, perfect toes erotic. She was as quiet as a mouse creeping around, but she was far from mouse like. She would be hoping he would be in bed by now, and that was exactly where he should be. He should let her float silently by his door, up the narrow stairs to her bedroom. It would be best for both of them.

It wasn't going to happen. He moved to the door.

CHAPTER 20

Emma didn't realize she'd been holding her breath as she tiptoed past Brandon's bedroom. She'd almost made it when the door was shoved open, into her. She let out a panicked squawk, jumping backward, and if he hadn't caught her arm she would have gone tumbling backward down the stairs.

He yanked her up, then released her with unflattering speed, and she put an instinctive hand to her breast, trying to catch her breath. He was watching her with that same, cynical expression, the one she had learned to hate so much in just one short day.

"You scared me," she said crossly. "Now I've probably gone and woken the household."

"I doubt it. Noonan went to join Tillerson in the stable, and the Bosomworths live in a wing off the back of the kitchen. No one would hear you if you scream."

Her eyes shot up to his cool face. "That sounds like a threat, my lord. Is it, by any chance?"

"No. I was thinking about making you scream in pleasure."

She glared at him. "You don't know me very well, then, do you?"

She didn't like that small, sardonic smile that twisted his face, the ruined half as well as the beautiful one, the face that once held such a different smile. "Oh, rather better than you might expect," he said.

"What's that supposed to mean?" She wanted to edge away from him—he hadn't moved any closer since he'd released her, but he was too big in the small, shadowy hallway. If she moved backward she'd hit the stairs, and this time he might not stop her from falling. The door to his room was between her and the small stairway that led to the upper floor, and she wasn't going to count on latent manners to get him out of the way. Most gentlemen didn't consider manners necessary for women with her past, no matter how punctilious they were with their friends and wives and daughters.

"Take it however you want it. I'm very good at reading women. I've had a great deal of experience." Oddly enough it didn't sound boastful —more a simple statement of fact.

"I'm not an ordinary woman," she shot back.

"On that we're agreed."

Thank God he couldn't see the flush that had risen to her face. Another veiled insult—why wouldn't he leave her alone? She drew herself up to her full height, usually imposing enough, but little defense against Brandon Rohan's. "Did you open your door for a reason, my lord?" She used the title deliberately. "Or did you simply not want to miss a chance to insult me?"

She could see the look of frustration twist his face, and for an odd moment she wanted to reach up and touch the scarred side, to stroke him gently, and it must have shown in her eyes.

Of course he misread it. "Feeling sorry for me, Mrs. Cadbury? If I'm with a woman I do my best to keep the good side of my face in the forefront. I know people have delicate constitutions and they're not interested in the souvenirs of war."

His words distracted her from her need to escape. She wrinkled her brow, remembering. "You do keep your face turned, don't you?" she said. "I don't think I noticed." Indeed, he was a man of two sides, and she saw both of them equally, accepting both.

"Again, we're agreed that you're no ordinary woman. My fiancée can't bear to be in the same room with me, much less be forced to look at my scars. I don't imagine she'll find my body any more reassuring once she's in my bed."

A host of emotions swept through her, anger at Frances Bonham, sorrow at the burden he bore, and sheer, unadulterated pain at the thought of him, stripping off his clothes and taking that cold little girl to bed with his big, strong body.

She was far from an idiot—she had a very good idea where her own pain was coming from. Later, alone, she'd take it out and examine it like a laboratory specimen, looking for signs that she could cut out. For now she could do nothing but ache.

"Then she's a fool," she said flatly, before her customary good sense could interfere. "You're a strong, beautiful young man whose scars are a badge of honor. If she can't see that then perhaps you shouldn't marry her."

There was an arrested look in his eyes. "I'm far from young."

"Younger than I am."

"Not by much," he said. "I hardly think that makes a difference."

"I've seen more of pain and. . ." The words failed her as she remembered his confessions in the chill light of dawn as he was fighting off death. He had been through much worse than she had, she realized suddenly.

"And if I'm so strong and beautiful why don't you come into my room and demonstrate your appreciation?"

The words were a shock, another blow, as clear an insult as he could have offered, and the pain was searing. "You're joking!"

"I never joke about fucking. I need release and you're the only one who's available."

This had taken on the air of unreality. During that first, endless night when together they had kept death at bay, he had confessed to all sorts of things, including the torture he and his fellow soldiers had inflicted, tying the victims by the ankles and hauling them up, in order to lash them with canes and whips and batons. And swords. Emma felt like one of them—helpless, hit by blows from every angle.

She let out a soft, silvery laugh, the sound bizarre in the shadows. "Now I understand you, my lord," she said lightly, finding just the right tone. After all, she'd had years of experience playing a part—this would be her finest performance. "You're one of those people who derive sexual pleasure from pain. Do you like to receive it as well as deliver it? Or do you simply need to debase and insult and *torture* your partner in order for you to get it up?" She used the word "torture" deliberately. Mrs. Cadbury wouldn't have known what he'd done, but of course he would, and reel from the memory, unless he was too far gone in his own darkness to care.

It hadn't been a good idea to give in to the temptation to taunt him. His eyes were black, inimical as he looked at her. "I have absolutely no interest in those particular variations, though I imagine you're well versed. And I have no problem in getting it up." Before she realized what he was doing, he caught her hand and pressed it against the front of his breeches.

She froze. She wasn't sure what she should do. The smart, hard woman she wanted to be would give him a laugh and a stroke, turning the tables on him, and then there was the odd need to let her fingers touch him, explore that rigidity. He was very hard, and very big, and she just stood there, her hands pressed against his erection, doing nothing to pull away.

It seemed like ages, though it was probably no more than a few moments, until she was able to say, "Release my wrist or I'll scream loud enough to wake London."

He did just that. In fact, he'd barely been holding her in place, his fingers loose, and she could have pulled free at any time.

She did, and without thinking she slapped him.

He blinked. "I take it that's a no?"

Her hand was tingling, her heart was pounding, and in the cool night air she felt blisteringly hot. She couldn't feel the cold outline of his face against her hand—instead she could still feel the shape of his cock—hard, insistent. "No?" she echoed. "What are you talking about?" She was getting angry now, really angry. "You seriously want to bed me?"

He just watched her, though the imprint of her hand was clear on his face. The only time she ever slapped anyone was during her first year at Mother Howard's establishment, the time when her veil of oblivion had fallen and she'd realized what was being done to her.

Mother Howard had been a relatively kind abbess, but there was no room for disobedient whores, and the men . . . she didn't want to think about that.

"I don't want to bed you," he said, but her momentary relief didn't last long. "I want to fuck you. Hard and long and deep."

She crossed her arms, her face set in stone. "Of course you do," she purred. "How silly of me not to recognize your problem. But you're forgetting one thing. I'm a professional, and my services come at a high cost."

"How much?" he said abruptly.

This was getting out of control. What had been pain and confusion at his sudden coldness had sharpened into simple rage. She curved her mouth in a mocking smile—it felt strange, unfamiliar—and looked up at him.

"Five . . . thousand . . . pounds."

It was an absurd amount. Obscene. A decent dowry for an aristocratic bride, the price of a small country home with tenant farms. No man in his right mind would even contemplate such a sum.

But Brandon merely smiled. "I believe the highest sum ever spent for a night of pleasure was registered at a thousand pounds. Are you that good?"

"Make it seven." Her voice was like steel.

"Done."

That small, shocking word took her breath away, and when he caught her up in his arms she was too startled to resist as he carried her into the bedroom and kicked the door shut behind them. A moment later she was tossed onto the bed, and stunned, she simply lay there,

The fire was the only light in the warm, cavernous room, and he looked huge, menacing in the shadows. Finally her wits returned. "No," she said.

"You named a price, I agreed, the bargain is done. Surely you wouldn't renege on a business deal?" he said silkily.

She stared up at him, and the sudden knowledge hit her with the force of a boulder. He had broken her heart once more. Just when she thought it inviolate, if not extinct, he had managed to get beneath her cool defenses and break her, just like that. She'd been so sure she'd never feel that searing pain again, was incapable of it, and now she lay in his bed feeling shattered. She had no idea whether he was simply ruled by lust or had some inexplicable need to punish her, but she didn't care.

She could bring an end to all this in a matter of moments. He could climb on top of her, rut and sweat and grunt like all the others, and it would be over. She lifted her eyes to his face. She couldn't see him well in the darkened room, but she knew there would be no mercy, no tenderness, no emotion whatsoever, and she was ready for the coup de grace. Her face was set like stone. "I await your pleasure, my lord." She braced herself.

She'd expected he'd rush her. He didn't move, still lost in the shadows. "Take off your clothes." His voice was muffled.

She didn't hesitate. She was paying the price to destroy any last bit of feeling she had for the man, and she sat up in the wide bed, tossing her shawl on the floor. Her nightdress was a thing of beauty, with tucks and lace and tiny pearl buttons, made by the aspiring seamstresses at the Dovecote, and she didn't want his hands on it. She might never be able to wear it again, but she treasured it, so she slowly lifted her hand and began to unfasten the neckline.

She had learned her lessons well, so long ago. Delay, tease, linger, and by the time she was ready her customer would be so overwrought that it would take but a minute or so of frantic effort and he would spill. She moved her fingers down, taking her time, exposing more and more of her flesh, prepared for him to rush her at any moment.

He didn't. He didn't move from his spot in the darkness, though she thought she might have heard a hitch in his breathing. The buttons stopped at her waist, and she paused, hoping she wouldn't have to go further.

He stayed where he was.

There were buttons on the long sleeves, and she took her time unfastening them, then she paused, waited. Pulling the gown down to her waist, exposing her shoulders and breasts was marginally less humiliating, but she wanted and expected the worst from this encounter. She reached down and caught the hem of her nightdress, yanked it up, lifted her bum to free it and pulled it over her head so that she sat there, completely nude.

And then she remembered that wasn't how it was done. Gentlemen, for want of a better word, preferred their whores to wear little naughty bits of clothing—useless underwear that did nothing to impede access, bits of fluffy scarves. In fact, she'd usually worn a great deal more than that for the men who wanted the fantasy of debasing their wives, and she couldn't remember if she'd ever been completely naked.

She could feel the heat suffuse her body. Surely now he would launch himself at her, finish this mockery.

"You're blushing," he said softly, and she cursed his night vision, his sudden gentleness. He broke it a moment later, thank God. "I didn't know whores blushed."

She could feel the color drain away, until she was cold and hard. "As you can see, you don't know much." She sank back on the bed, staring up at the ceiling. "Have at it."

He laughed, he actually *laughed*, making no effort to approach her, and she was filled with sudden horror. Had he been playing a game? Was this simply one more way to humiliate her?

She waited, her heart hammering, the silent prayer repeating, over and over again, in her mind. *Please go away, please go away, please go away. Tell me you didn't mean to do this, tell me you aren't this man.*

She didn't expect her prayers to be answered, and they weren't. She felt him approach the bed. "All right," he said, his voice taut and emotionless, and the mattress dipped as he stretched out beside her, his clothed body pressing up against her side. She closed her eyes, wanting to weep. For a moment there was silence, only broken by the sound of their breathing, his heavy, tense, hers shallow. "Do you have any specialties? Are you particularly good with your mouth? Perhaps you like to take it up the. . ."

"Shut up," she said fiercely, rolling to her side to face him. She needed this done, and quickly. "Unfasten your pants and finish this."

She was trembling, practically vibrating, but she doubted he'd notice. She reached for his clothes, realizing too late that he'd stripped off his shirt and there was only warm flesh beneath her fingers, the feel of the scars that she had once tended a rough reminder of what was lost forever.

He caught her hands in his larger one, holding her still. "I'm thinking this might be a mistake," he said evenly.

She wanted to wail, to beat at him. She couldn't bear it if he suddenly became decent once more. "Surely you wouldn't renege on a business deal?" she quoted back to him. "Or do you perhaps have performance issues? I suppose there are things that I could do. . ."

A moment later he had rolled her onto her back, and he lay on top of her, between her thighs, the fabric of his breeches rough against her soft skin, his erection pressing against her. He was too damned big. She'd bathed him in the hospital, unperturbed by sick men's bodies, and he'd seemed no more endowed than the men she'd serviced. That assumption had clearly been wrong.

He cupped her face with his strong hands, and his warm breath touched her face. "You're shaking," he said quietly.

"I'm cold."

"The room is warm, and your nipples are soft. You aren't cold and you aren't aroused."

"Oh, for God's sake," she cried in desperation. "Just get this over with."

He did the very last thing she expected. He kissed her.

CHAPTER 21

The woman lying beneath him was terrified. He had no idea how that was possible—there was no doubt at all that she'd spent a number of years running a brothel after spending time working in one. He'd heard the stories of the youngest Madame in England, never guessing they were talking about his beloved Harpy.

And she had been his beloved. Even when'd she abandoned him and disappeared, he'd still loved her, longed for her, until the opium and the brandy had scoured her from his memory. He hadn't allowed himself to think of her when he'd been in Scotland, determined not to waste a moment's thought on anything that might deter him from his goal, and he hadn't even recognized her when he first met her, apart from that odd sense of familiarity.

He tried to summon his fury, his sense of betrayal that had fired him for the last day, but it had vanished. All that existed was this naked, trembling woman lying beneath him, and he knew what he had to do. Remove himself, cover her, and go back downstairs, leave her to put on her nightgown and retreat to her bedchamber. They could pretend this had never happened, and tomorrow would be the very last time he would see her.

But he was only human. He'd wanted her when his body had barely been clinging to life, he'd wanted her as they'd danced and played around his brother's moldering old country house. He wanted her now, and there was no way he could do what he ought to do and walk away.

Her mouth was cold beneath his, her lips quivering as she tried to hide her fear. She obviously hadn't expected to be kissed—most men didn't bother with it unless they had to, and in a brothel the patron ruled. He wasn't most men, and he suddenly wanted to taste her, to feel her lips soften beneath his. He wanted what he had before, the hot, roiling heat of desire pulsing between them. He wanted to explore her, seduce her with his kisses, he wanted her shivering to stop and her body to melt against him, and damn, he wanted her pale nipples hard against his bare chest. He brushed his lips softly against hers, feathering them, then touched the tip of his tongue to them, dampening them. She was holding her breath, he realized with belated amusement, and if he didn't get her to breathe she would pass out and he'd have no choice but to be a decent human being. He was going to hell for this night, and he intended to see it through.

He moved his thumbs against her jaw, pressing lightly, and her mouth opened like the blossom of a snapdragon, and he heard her raw, sudden intake of air. He gave her a moment before he set his mouth against hers again, and he deepened the kiss, using his tongue to gently stroke hers.

She quivered, a different reaction from her panicked shaking. Her head tilted back on the mattress to give him more access.

She tasted like spring flowers and innocence, she tasted like darkness and sin, and he moved against her, needing her, kissing her with slow, deliberate intent. He could tell that she was forgetting her doubts, forgetting her fears and her anger, forgetting that she probably hated this. He moved his mouth away for a moment, nuzzling her neck, giving her time to catch her breath before kissing her again.

He was still holding her hands against the mattress, but he released them, needing to touch her. He slid his fingers down the silky skin between them to cup her breast. When he felt the tip harden in his hand, his cock twitched in reaction. He pressed against her, getting her used to the feel of him, even though he was so hard, so damned packed into his breeches he wondered if he could do himself an injury. He longed to strip down as well, but he knew what would happen. The moment his pants were off he'd be inside her, and she needed to be handled carefully. He'd told her he would make her scream in pleasure, and he was going to do just that if it killed him.

He kissed her again, deeper, and she kissed him back with an absurd lack of expertise. She really didn't know what she was doing. Kissing had definitely not been part of the services offered, as he expected, but for some reason her tentative clumsiness was more arousing than all the practice in the world. He wanted to keep kissing her, but even more he wanted to taste her skin, and reluctantly he released her, sliding his mouth down, kissing, licking his way down until he came to the small, soft, perfect mound of her breast. He ran his tongue over the pebbled nipple, and her entire body jerked. He licked it again, swirling his tongue around the tip like it was some delicious bit of candy, and then he sank his whole mouth over it, sucking it in, pulling on it, so aroused he thought he might come in his binding breeches.

But damn, he could stay here forever, just sucking at her perfect tit. Her hands had come up to his shoulders, her grip slowly tightening as he sucked at her. Much as he hated to leave the first one her second breast needed attention, and he moved over, putting his hand on the first one to pull and tease at it while he took the other one in.

Oh, his girl liked that, she did. Her fingers were digging in now, and she was making soft, anxious sounds of pleasure that he wanted to drink from her mouth, if only her breasts didn't taste so wonderful. He wanted to put his mouth between her legs, lick her there, see what reaction he could get when he sucked her clit into his mouth, but he'd never make it through that in one piece. He'd do that the next time, he thought dimly, ignoring the fact that there'd be no next time.

She had strong hands, a surgeon's hands, ones that could cut through flesh and bone, and he found he liked those strong hands on his body, wanted them on his cock. She slid them down his side, brushing across the scarring that marred him, almost seeming to stroke that rough flesh with especial tenderness before reaching the edge of his breeches, and she was pushing at them, trying to slide them off his hips, clearly in a hurry to get this done.

He was always agreeable to a lady's wants, and he pulled up, unfastening the buttons, letting his cock spring out with a groan and a sigh. He was finally free, and he wanted nothing more than to bury it again, inside her tight cunt, and pump into her for hours, goddamned hours, until she exploded around him.

That wasn't going to happen. He was going to go off like a schoolboy unless he concentrated on something else. He tried to think of farming practices and the Scottish parliament, but then she touched his cock, and he was lost, ready to come in her hand.

He couldn't wait any longer. He reached between her legs, and she jerked in surprise. He should have gotten her used to his touch again, like dealing with a nervous filly, but he was past the point of rational decision. She was wet, slippery, thank God, for all her fears, and he had to feel inside her. He slid one finger into her, and she squirmed, startled, and then he withdrew and thrust two in, rubbing against her clit as he went, and her sound of need was the most erotic thing he'd ever heard. No latent decency could stop him now—hell, the building could collapse and he'd take her anyway. His need was that bad.

He caught her thighs in his hands and spread them, just enough. He hadn't said a word to her, and he wasn't going to—anything would be a lie or a reproach, and he'd been cruel enough already. He needed bliss, he needed forgetfulness, he needed her, and always had.

He caught his randy cock in his hand and brought it to her, rubbing the sensitive head against her dampness, against the folds and creases of her, and she made that soft, strangled noise again that he wanted to echo. This was too much, too good, too important. He looked down at her, and she still seemed faintly terrified, her eyes wide and beseeching, wanting something and not knowing what it was. But he knew. He levered forward and pushed, feeling the tight, clinging warmth surround his cock, closing his eyes at the exquisite pleasure that was better than anything he had ever felt.

He sank into her, slowly, so slowly that it was going to drive him mad, filling her inch by inch. He was bigger than usual and he knew it, she was much tighter than he would have imagined. He didn't want to hurt her, but he couldn't stop, not until he was deep inside her, his bollocks resting against her, his body covering hers. He kissed her again, afraid to move and set off an imminent reaction. He needed her to relax against this invasion, and he put all of his attention to her mouth and his need to lure her into this game, this dance. He wanted participation, not endurance, and the shiver that ran across her body had nothing to do with fear but more with undeniable desire.

He'd wanted to throw himself at her, pump furiously until he was spent, but this was enough to slow him down. He rested his weight on his elbows, cupped her face with his hands and kept kissing her, nipping at her, his mouth dancing across her skin as he began to thrust into her, slowly, with exquisite care, and his own body started to shake with the power of his need.

And she was responding, raising her hips to meet him, growing wetter still, a thin sheen of sweat on her beautiful skin, unexpected desire warring with her resistance. She hadn't meant to respond like this, probably hadn't thought she could, but there was no denying that her arms were around him, clinging tightly, and the soft, reluctant moans were urging him onward.

Words began spilling from his mouth then, when he'd been so determined to be silent. "Yes," and "fuck" and "more" and "yes" as he moved faster, his own body beginning to shake with the power of his overwhelming lust. He couldn't, wouldn't say the word "love" but he could push into her, with dirty words whispered in her ear that made her tighten around him. He was fighting a losing battle with self-control, and he wanted to lose it, but she wasn't quite ready, though he knew from her breathing, from a thousand other physical signs that she was near. "Don't," he said, his mind blank, "give it," he muttered, and the battle was lost. "Now," he groaned, feeling his seed boil up from his balls and spurt into her, and the last word he spoke, as he pulled free and collapsed beside her, was even worse.

"Harpy," he said, and fell into an exhausted sleep.

EMMA LAY STILL, unmoving beside him in the bed. Her body felt raw, invaded, oddly incomplete, her mind and emotions were a merciful blank. She wouldn't think about it. She refused to. She would just lie there for another few minutes and let the numbness settle around her.

She had no idea how long she lay like that. It was only when he stirred, muttering something, and reached for her that she made herself move. She scuttled out of his way so fast she ended on the floor, but she fell lightly, and he slept on, oblivious.

She had to haul herself to her feet—her legs felt weak, her heart was pounding, and when she leaned down to pick up her discarded nightgown she almost blacked out. She wasn't going to think about it. She was going to go up to her room and bathe, that's what she would do. There was no reason to think.

She held on to the walls on either side of the narrow stairs, and when she finally reached the top she wanted nothing more than to collapse on her narrow bed.

She couldn't. She felt unclean, violated, wrong, so very, very wrong, and she couldn't rest until she scrubbed her body clean.

Because she'd liked it. The most deplorable, shameful thing of all was that she'd actually begun to feel alive as she'd wrapped her body around his, taken him inside her, and she'd wanted more. She knew that some rare women could reach their peak as men did, and she could feel it just outside of her reach. She'd struggled, almost there, his filthy, arousing words in her ear, when he said the one thing that would destroy her.

Harpy.

He knew who she was.

She shook her head, hard, trying to banish the thought, and her sudden dizziness increased. She couldn't bear it. She'd borne everything else, but this was too much—she had to wipe it from her brain. She began to sing beneath her breath, the effort of remembering the words occupying her mind enough to keep her sanity in place. It was an old song—"Come Haste to the Wedding"—and she sang it without thought, all the verses, quickly changing over to a sturdy hymn, "Come Thou Almighty King" as she poured the cold water into the bowl, on to a silly children's song as she scrubbed between her legs, drowning out conscious thought, memory, the stretching and the unexpected glory of something she'd always hated. She wasn't going to think about anything. She started on "Bonny Light Horseman" but when she got to the line, "in the war he was slain" she stopped, her voice breaking. Life would be so much better for her if he'd died of his injuries, if she'd never met him at all, but there was no way she could wish it. She had survived things no woman should ever have to face. She could survive this as well.

When she finally stepped away from the washbowl she was shivering. The fire had gone out, she was wet, bedraggled, and she could still feel him inside her. Scrubbing wouldn't help. Nothing would, nothing but time.

She pulled the rough linen sheet from the bed and wrapped it around her, then sank down in the chair and closed her eyes. *It will be all right*, she told herself, the words she had used to soothe herself. She'd come across an old prayer one time, written by an ancient English nun. *All shall be well, and all manner of things shall be well.*

She said those words over and over again, pushing everything out of her mind, as a hard-won calm descended. All would be well.

It just might take time.

CHAPTER 22

It was cold as a witch's tit, Brandon thought numbly the next morning, staring out across the countryside. The Hawk and Cock was deserted, a waystation on a heavily travelled road, but most people had had enough sense to stay home. He should go back into the taproom and grab his greatcoat against the bitter chill, but at that moment he would rather freeze his bollocks off than face Emma Cadbury, and chances were she'd be down any minute.

What a monumental idiot he'd been! What a complete arsehole, treating her like garbage and then offering to buy her sexual services. Even worse, he'd taken her, losing his self-control so completely that he'd ignored his semi-noble determination to bring her pleasure and just gone at her like a lust-maddened dog. He'd even come inside her, an act of stupidity that rivaled few others.

For the first time in his life he'd lost that little bit of control he'd always held onto, but she'd felt so good, so warm, so tight that he could no more break away from her than he could fly.

He'd called her by name. By his name for her—he remembered that much, and he cursed beneath his breath. It was out in the open now, and a good thing. He'd acted like a school boy, throwing a tantrum, treating her like one of the punching bags his father had set up in the abandoned cheesery.

And what terrible thing had she done? Saved his life in that little hospital, held his hand when he'd been frightened of death, forced him back from its beckoning shores. So she'd left him without a word, abandoning him in that miserable place until he could stand it no longer and sent word to his family. There were worse things. She'd kissed him, and he'd done all sorts of wicked things to her in his mind while he lay there, slowly getting stronger, wicked things he had every intention of doing the moment he had the chance.

But she hadn't come back. And then, to compound her guilt, she'd looked him straight in the eyes less than a week ago and pretended not to know him, making every word, every gesture a lie.

Who was he to sit in judgment? It mattered not that he felt betrayed and abandoned—in truth she owed him nothing, and yet he'd stormed and railed like a petulant child, compounding his wretched behavior by offering to pay her for sexual favors. He'd just meant to anger her, but she'd already been angry, and it hadn't been his fault entirely, though he bore the brunt of the blame. She'd taunted him, deliberately—she'd fought back, and he'd made it worse still, until they'd goaded themselves into bed. He still had no excuse.

Tillerson was leading the carriage out into the courtyard, Noonan was stomping around, looking like the wrath of God, the horses were fresh and restless in the cool morning air. If his mare was equally . . . Jesus fucking Christ, why hadn't he made that connection before? He'd named his horse Emma. The only creature he loved and trusted without reserve, and he'd named her Emma.

"You all right, m'lord?" Tillerson had come up to him, and Brandon realized he'd shaken his head rather violently at the unbidden thoughts that were flying at him like poisoned darts.

"Fine," he said shortly. "You and Noonan already had something to eat, I assume?"

"We have indeed, my lord. Very kind of you to ask." Tillerson said mildly. "They're all set and ready to go. Is the whore ready?"

Brandon hit him. Without thinking he slammed his face into

Tillerson's face, and the man went flat on his arse, looking slightly stunned.

"Do not ever let me hear you refer to Mrs. Cadbury in such terms again," he snapped.

Tillerson scrambled to his feet. "Begging your pardon, my lord," he said hastily. "I misunderstood the situation."

Brandon cursed again, under his breath. Of course Tillerson had—he'd heard all the stories and he'd watched and listened as Brandon had treated her as less than dirt beneath his boots. Tillerson wasn't the one who needed hitting—he was.

By that time Noonan had joined them. "Here, now," he said sternly. "What's all this about?"

"Nothing," Tillerson mumbled, looking sheepish. "I'll go finish checking the traces."

Noonan looked up at Brandon, his eyes beady with anger. "You're the one who needs to be horsewhipped, you young idiot. What did you go hitting Tillerson for? The man's a fool, but he's older and smaller than you. Despite your behavior this week, I thought better of you."

He'd thought better of himself. He had two choices—tell Noonan it was none of his damned business or appear an even greater fool by telling him the truth. "He insulted Mrs. Cadbury."

He expected Noonan to say something equally bad, but the old man just looked at him, and then he sighed. "You hurt the lass?"

Guilt swept over him. "Of course not! What kind of man do you think I am? Don't answer that—you've already told me. No, I did not hurt Mrs. Cadbury."

"So she just went to your bed on her own accord? That don't seem likely, me boy."

He didn't bother to wonder how Noonan knew what had happened last night. He'd never been able to hide anything from the man. "If you're thinking I'd force her. . ." he began.

"You'd also be flat on your backside in the mud if I even suspected such a thing. I'm not too old to give you a beating when you deserve it, and I'm thinking now might be the time."

The very thought should have been amusing, but Brandon didn't feel like smiling. He knew he deserved a horsewhipping, and he knew just the man who'd do it. All he had to do was tell Benedick what he'd done and his brother would take him out to the stable for a lesson that was long over-due. The last time Benedick had done that, Brandon had been sixteen and he and a group of his friends had trampled a farmer's field in an excess of ale-infused high spirits. The next time he'd tried Brandon had fought back.

This time he wouldn't. He'd take his punishment like a man who deserved it, because he did. If Benedick proved reluctant he could always ask his brother-in-law Lucien, better known at The Scorpion. Lucien had never needed encouragement to rain down fire and brimstone.

He glanced at Noonan's pugnacious scowl. "Someone will see to it soon enough. I expect my brother will be the first in line. Are the horses ready? Mine seemed to be favoring her right hock." He couldn't refer to her by name. For one thing, Noonan probably knew very well that Mrs. Cadbury was Emma, and for another, he didn't want to remind himself.

"You've got that right," Noonan said. "She's got something going on. I'm thinking it might be better if you didn't ride her today till I have a chance to poultice it."

He almost shut his eyes in desperation. As if things weren't bad enough, he would now need to be in close quarters with Emma, the real Emma, for hours as they completed their journey. He glanced at the carriage. It was one of Benedick's infernal inventions—a little heavier than the popular landaus of the day, with a collapsible roof that nevertheless allowed for long-distance travel and room for only one on the box. That roof might collapse beneath his weight if he tried to sit up there as on a stagecoach, and the perch in back, made for a stable lad, was ridiculous. He had no choice.

"I'll use yours then," he said somewhat desperately.

Noonan laughed in his face. "Meggie's not up to your weight, and even if she was I'm not letting you get your hands on her. You'll ride in the carriage and try and undo some of the damage you've done. You'll be nice to the girl. It don't matter where she came from or what she's done—she's a sweet young lady and she doesn't deserve the likes of you acting like a spoiled brat."

Brandon kept his face stoic. Noonan had clearly seen far too much over the last few days. "What if the best thing for her is my absence?"

"She'll have that as soon as we get to the city. In the meantime you have some making up to do."

He supposed he could always order Noonan to give him his horse, but Noonan would probably laugh in his face. Besides, he'd been a total ass already—he didn't have to compound it.

"Are we almost ready then?" he said, hoping he'd have a little while longer in the cold air, but Noonan simply nodded. It would take but a moment to bring his mare out and tie her to the carriage, and it was too cold to leave the horses standing around for long. Looking toward the door to the cozy inn, Brandon straightened his back and moved forward.

He almost hoped she wasn't down yet, and he could send Bosomworth up with a message, but when he stepped inside the warmth of the taproom she was sitting at one table, drinking a cup of tea. She looked like a little girl, her feet neatly together, her dark hair two smooth wings on either side of her perfect face. She was utterly still, looking up at him when he came into the room.

"You're ready?" he said roughly, unable to think of anything else to say. He was going to have to find some way to apologize, but everything that came to mind would only make things worse.

"I am," she said, her voice as expressionless as her face. "Did you require breakfast, my lord? I'm certain Mrs. Bosomworth would be happy to make you some of her delicious gammon and eggs."

"Have you eaten?" he said warily.

"Yes," she said, and he knew it was a lie. She was too pale, too fragile looking to have eaten a substantial meal, and he wanted to curse. He didn't. From now on he had to treat her like a perfect lady in a belated attempt to . . . he wasn't sure. Redeeming himself seemed an unlikely goal. At least he could refrain from behaving like a wounded child again. Though once he'd put his hands on her there had been nothing childlike about their encounter.

He growled, low in his throat, as he felt his cock began to stir. Last night was over, he reminded himself, pulling his greatcoat in front of him. The best thing he could do to atone was to keep his distance and having wood in his pants was going to make things difficult.

She rose, graceful, and started toward the door, and without thinking he was there ahead of her, holding it for her. The look she gave him should have shriveled his erection, but his member was perverse enough to grow harder. "After you, my lord," she said coldly, and he remembered that he'd barged ahead of her when they'd arrived.

"Don't be ridiculous," he muttered. "I'll be right behind you." Of course, that probably wasn't much comfort.

But Emma was having none of it. "It's a matter of precedence, my lord. You are my better in every sense of the word—you're titled, wealthy, a war hero, and a man. A woman like me is of little consequence. I'll follow you."

He wasn't sure if he'd ever felt such shame in his entire life. He looked at her, and knew she wasn't going to move until he did, so he shrugged and went through the door.

She was carrying her bag, and he reached for it automatically when she jerked it away from him. "Do not trouble yourself."

He had to stop himself from yanking it back. He didn't move, knowing that if he let down the stairs for the coach or opened the door she'd refuse to precede him, and that would annoy him no end, so he waited until a repentant Tillerson got her settled before approaching the coach.

"I'm afraid you have company for the last bit of our journey, Mrs. Cadbury. My horse seems to have gone lame." He was almost amused as he saw her lurch forward, as if to escape, but he was standing in the door and there would be no way past him, so she sank bank in defeat.

"My condolences," she said in cool voice, taking the leather satchel she'd left in the coach into her lap. A moment later she'd pulled out a heavy tome with the disconcerting title of *The London Guide to Severing Limbs* and ignored him as he heaved himself up into the carriage, dropping onto the seat opposite her.

It was going to be like that, was it? He slouched down, tilting his hat over his head, his greatcoat still clutched around his waist. *Fine with me.*

He was exhausted. Yesterday's endless ride should have been enough to have sent him into a sound sleep and last night's debacle could have been avoided. But no, since he'd recognized Emma, sleep had been almost impossible.

He'd ended up sleeping for a few hours in the bed that smelled of sex and flowers, and he hated himself for that. He could have started to mend things as she lay beside him, perhaps even finished taking care of her the way he'd wanted to, had her gasping and writhing in his arms. Instead he'd fallen asleep, and she'd run. Damn his soul to hell.

He should talk to her. Somehow make peace with her. He just couldn't summon up the requisite repentance. Oh, he was sorry he'd made such a mess of things, sorry he'd hurt her. But he couldn't regret those moments in the bed with her.

It was going to be a long, miserable drive, with his mind awash in guilt and his body still awash in lust.

He was asleep in five minutes.

HE WOKE WITH A START, filled with panic that immediately subsided when he saw her asleep across from him. Her papers were scattered beside her on the seat, the morbid book still open in her lap, and the illustrations would have made anyone but a former soldier blanch. She looked as exhausted as he felt, and for a while he sat as still as the coach would let him, watching her beautiful, troubled face.

He'd put that look on her, damn his hide. It would be up to him to remove it, though he had no idea how. The first step would be to give her a little time, keep away from her for a few days, despite how the very thought made his gut twist.

It was cold in the coach—he'd insisted on leaving so quickly they hadn't even stacked lap rugs and throws to keep the passengers warm. She was wearing fingerless gloves, and he expected that her fingertips were cold, even as she slept on.

He scooped up the papers first, as silently as he could, tucking them back in her worn leather satchel. Then he lifted the heavy book from her lap, but she didn't move, and when he'd placed it with the papers he looked back to see that she'd curled up in the corner, her breathing steady and shallow. She had her shawl wrapped tightly around her, but it wasn't enough to keep her warm, and in the harsh light of day he could see the bruising on the side of her head.

God, he'd forgotten all about the attack. He'd been so mad with lust he hadn't done anything to protect her injuries, he'd just rutted. He was going to purchase his own horsewhip and hand it to Noonan.

Stripping off his heavy coat, he draped it around her sleeping form. He shivered slightly and then scolded himself. He lived in Scotland— he was used to the cold. He swam in weather like this. He settled back on the opposite seat, watching her. It might very well be the last chance he got, and he felt the knife twist inside him again. How had he managed to screw up his life so badly? He had a weeping, unwanted fiancée and a range of sins impressive enough to earn him reentry into the Heavenly Host, he thought with almost abstracted horror. He needed to get the hell away from everyone, back to Scotland with Noonan, and his spaniel and the Widow MacKinnon. Who, he realized, looked a fair bit like Emma herself, tall and pretty, though no match for his Emma.

But Emma wasn't his. Never would be. And that was the curse of it.

CHAPTER 23

Emma always woke quickly, ready to face whatever the day threw at her, and today was no different. The carriage was dark—he hadn't lit the small lamps on either side of the seats—and she could feel the roughness of the cobbled streets beneath them. They had reached London.

She lifted her gaze to her companion. She'd been instantly aware of him, everything flooding back before she even opened her eyes, but he was in the shadows, and she could only hope he was still asleep. She felt uncommonly . . . safe. There was no other word for it. Warm and protected and cared for. Despite her instant alertness, that false sense remained, but she forced herself to sit up, even though she wanted to stay exactly where she was and hold on to that ephemeral feeling.

Something was over her, keeping her warm. Pushing it aside, she realized it was his huge greatcoat, and her heart twisted in sudden pain. She threw it across the small space, straight at him, but the dark figure caught it deftly, clearly wide awake.

"Where are my papers?" she snapped, with no intention of thanking him.

"They're in your satchel along with that distressing book you were reading." His voice was light, conversational. "The thought of you sawing through bones is quite terrifying."

"It wouldn't be your *bones* I'd be cutting off," she shot back, and he had the temerity to laugh. "We're in London?"

"Indeed. We're almost at your lodgings."

Light was coming from the street outside, light and noise, and he leaned forward, looking out the window, momentarily silhouetted before he sank back into the shadows once more. It would be her last glimpse of him, she thought. The moment they pulled up outside of the house she would be ready to scramble out before he could pretend to be polite, and she could sweep inside with the knowledge that Noonan or Tillerson would bring her bags. This part of her life was over, completely, irrevocably over, and she should feel nothing but joy.

She wanted to weep. It was a good thing she couldn't—every tear in her body had dried up long ago. If he'd seen her with tears in her eyes he might make the foolish mistake of thinking that she cared for him, which she didn't, not any longer, not even a little.

The carriage finally rumbled to a stop, and she could hear the voices from the streets, sounds that she knew so well she never paid any attention. She did now. The smell was overpowering as well—garbage, human waste, unwashed bodies, and horse droppings. Her taller boots came in handy as she made her way to and from work, but those boots were still recovering from her dunk in the Thames, and she had only her sturdy shoes, which would probably be ruined by the detritus on the street. So be it. She began to gather her things, ignoring the simple fact that her hands were shaking, ignoring Brandon.

The door had been opened, but no one had let down the steps, and Noonan stood there blocking her escape, deep in conversation with Brandon, who was now fully visible. She wished he'd stayed in the shadows. The left side of his face was to her, the scarred, damaged side, and deep, unwanted emotions rushed through her. It would have been so much better if the unmarked side of his face was in evidence—the pretty, perfect bit of him that was like everyone else. That wasn't the man she had . . . that wasn't Brandon to her. This was, and it hurt.

"Could you please set down the steps, Mr. Noonan?" she said, interrupting their hushed conversation. "I'd would very much like to get inside and settled."

Brandon nodded at Noonan, leaned back, and to Emma's complete horror the door was slammed closed. "You're not going there," he said flatly, and the carriage jerked, slowly moving forward through the shifting groups of people, proving his point.

She leaped for the doorway, determined to simply fling herself out, but he caught her, *caught her*, damn it, pulling her against him and keeping her flailing arms imprisoned with his own. She swore at him like a veritable fishwife, and her command of profanity was extensive, but it made no difference. He had hauled her onto his lap, and she kicked her heels back at him, hoping to do some damage, but he seemed impervious, and even her attempts to move down and sink her teeth into his arm got her nowhere. She struggled until she was worn out, until the warmth and strength of his body around hers grew too distracting, and then she sank back against him, unable, or unwilling to fight.

"That's better," he said with a pragmatic tone that made her frankly murderous. "Fighting me won't do you any good, my girl. I'm not letting you stay at that pesthole with criminals all around, any one of them capable of cutting your throat before you realized what was happening. Why in God's name do you live in the slums?"

"Those are my people! That's where I belong, not set up as a rich man's doxy. I'll take the honest slums over anything you have to offer."

He sighed, and she could feel it, held as she was against his chest. "First of all, you cannot really insist that those are honest slums. People who live in poverty can't afford to pay attention to such niceties when they're trying to survive."

"And how would you know, *my lord?*" she said, emphasizing his title.

"Because I have lived far from a blameless life since I returned from the wars. Melisande must have told you I was once a member of the Heavenly Host. Trust me, I have spent more than my fair share of time in the slums, doing unspeakable things."

She was shocked into stillness. Exactly what did he remember? She had assumed, by his deliberate utterance of the word "harpy," that he remembered everything, including the night when he'd tried to kill himself in his London bedroom. Apparently that bit of information was still missing.

And she was not about to offer it up. "It doesn't surprise me," she said darkly. "Nevertheless, where I choose to live is none of your business or your concern."

"That's where you're wrong. My brother entrusted you into my care with clear orders that I was to see you safe. Why aren't you living in their house on Bury Street? The place is huge, and I have little doubt they would have wanted you staying there."

She squirmed, but instead of releasing her his arms simply tightened again. "They've done enough for me," she said, trying to ignore the way her body was warming, softening in his arms. "I prefer to rely on myself."

"Why didn't you stay at Melisande's house, then? You used to live there—Melisande told me."

And just what else has Melisande told you, she wondered. His arms were like loose iron bands around her body, not hurting her, crushing her, but an inescapable shackle.

"We ran out of room, and the women needed a sanctuary far more than I did. Please let me go." The last was added, almost against her will. She was surrounded by him, encased in him, and she wanted nothing more than to sink back and absorb him into her very bones, one last time. She stayed rigid.

"Not yet." His voice was implacable. "All the women are out in Sussex. What's your excuse now? Or do you simply prefer to be a martyr?"

His words hit her with the force of a blow as the truth sank into her, unavoidable. Unbearable as the thought was, she had seen herself as a woman doing penance, deserving of nothing. She couldn't bear to think of it right now. "The Dovecote burned," she said, her flat voice giving no hint to her emotions.

He went very still, and then, to her mixed relief and sorrow he released her, so quickly she almost slumped to the floor before landing on the opposite bench. The London streets were uneven, the carriage lurched, and she stumbled, but he was no longer holding her, touching her.

"When did that happen?" His voice was flat and cold.

"A few weeks ago." She hunted for something to say, to belittle the disaster, but nothing came to her.

"Somebody set it on fire?"

It would be useless to deny it. "Yes."

"Was anyone hurt?"

"No."

He was relentless. "No one was there at the time?"

She was an excellent liar—it would have been such a simple thing to do to distract him. "I was," she admitted.

"I rejoice that you decided to stop lying to me. Were you hurt?"

"I told you the truth—no one was hurt. I breathed in a bit of smoke, but I managed to escape quite easily."

"How?"

"Do we have to continue with this?"

"How?"

"I jumped," she said defiantly. "The stairway was blocked, and my only choice was to throw a chair through the window and then jump out. People were already coming to help, and I had no more than a few small cuts from the glass."

There was silence in the carriage as it made its way through the streets at a snail's pace, the milling nighttime crowds getting in the way. Finally he spoke. "So that's a second attempt on your life."

"Well, technically the first." She was trying to sound breezy and failing utterly.

"Were there any others?"

"Other what?" she said, stalling.

"Other attempts on your life?"

"I'm not agreeing they were personal attacks."

"Any other?"

She took a deep breath. "I did fall into the Thames," she admitted.

"Christ! Fell? Or was pushed?"

"The crowd jostled me."

"You were pushed," he said grimly. "And with all this happening you wanted to return to your miserable rooms in the slums with no protection? Just how great an idiot are you?"

"I'm perfectly able to take care of myself! I've done so for more than half my life."

"It doesn't appear that you've been doing a very good job of it," he muttered, and the usual guilt swept over her.

She shrugged, knowing her face would give no clue to what she was feeling. "I didn't feel I should kill myself after I ended up in a whorehouse, which was morally weak of me, I agree, but I was more interested in fighting back."

She couldn't see him that well in the fitful light from the nighttime city, but a flash of teeth made her think he might have grinned at that. "You *are* a fighter," he said, and it almost sounded like admiration in his voice.

"I want you to take me back to my rooms," she said.

She couldn't see much more than his silhouette in the darkness, but he looked perfectly at ease. "No," he said flatly. "Have Benedick and Melisande even seen that place?"

She was silent. "I thought not," he said. "I'm already due a horse-whipping from my older brother—if I let you stay there he'd probably kill me. I'm taking you to their house."

It could be worse, she thought, her brain scrambling for an escape. "And where will you be?" She tried to make her distaste clear in her voice, but she could only hear her own wistfulness.

"My house is closed up, with only my caretaker and his wife on the premises. It would take too long to open it up. I really should get rid of it—I have no intention of ever living in the city again."

"What about your wife?"

"Wife?" There was no missing the confusion in his voice. "Oh, you mean Miss Bonham."

"Do you have any other affianced wives?"

Just a moment's hesitation, before he answered. "I'll make suitable arrangements for Miss Bonham."

She really wanted to hate him. "I'm sure you will."

The carriage was finally slowing. When it pulled to a stop the footmen were already waiting, opening the door and letting down the steps.

She considered refusing to leave the questionable safety of the coach. Brandon couldn't just haul her out, kicking and screaming, in the middle of Mayfair.

"After you, Mrs. Cadbury," he said in a silken voice. Yes, he probably could. The sooner she appeared to be following his high-handed orders the sooner she'd be able to escape.

Sighing dramatically, she pulled her shawl around her shoulders and clasped her heavy satchel to her bosom, only to have it snatched away. "I'll bring it," he said.

The under butler was already waiting for her. "Welcome back, Mrs. Cadbury," he said warmly. "Will you be. . ." His words vanished as he suddenly saw the man who accompanied her, and then his pleasant face turned into a dazzling smile.

"Lord Brandon!" he cried, momentarily ignoring her. "We had no idea you were coming! How wonderful you look."

Brandon came up beside her and caught her elbow. "Good to see you, Michaels. Richmond sends his regards. We'll be staying here for the time being—will you let the housekeeper know?"

"Mrs. Patrick is already waiting, sir." Michaels seemed slightly affronted that he'd need to be reminded. "She'll be overjoyed to see you."

"I'm sure she will," he said wryly. "It's a good thing my sainted mother is so strong, or Mrs. Patrick would have insisted on raising me."

"She's very fond of you," Michaels agreed in his precise voice.

Just how fond was amply demonstrated when Brandon guided her into the front hallway. Mrs. Patrick, a seemingly placid woman of impressive girth and indeterminable age took one look at Brandon and launched herself at him like a young girl, bypassing Emma completely.

"My boy!" she cried, bursting into tears. "You're back! I was that worried about you. You would never have gotten into all that trouble if I'd been here, I know you wouldn't, and I could have cursed my sister for getting sick at just that time, or I could have saved you."

He smiled down at the old woman with real affection. "I was heading for hell any way you looked at it, and even your tender mercies couldn't have stopped me. And how is your dear sister?"

"Dead," said Mrs. Patrick with no particular regret. "Just like her, too, stirring things up and then popping off. I'd never been so annoyed."

Emma felt her eyebrows rise at this, but Brandon seemed well versed in Mrs. Patrick's attitude toward life. He detached her gently. "I've brought Mrs. Cadbury. We'll be staying for a few days."

Mrs. Patrick finally recalled her duties. "Mrs. Cadbury, a pleasure to see you as always."

"Put her in her usual room, would you?" Brandon said.

Emma tensed.

Mrs. Patrick cast him a quizzical glance. "Well, I'm afraid I can't," she said. "Mrs. Cadbury always prefers to use your room."

He glanced down at her, hopefully unable to read her blank expression. "Does she really? Well, then, continue to indulge her, and put me anywhere you please.

"Don't be ridiculous!" Emma broke in. "Of course you must take your own room. It merely seemed convenient during the times I stayed here. I didn't even realize it was yours," she added hastily, praying Mrs. Patrick would keep her mouth shut.

That hope was in vain. "Oh, no, Mrs. Cadbury! You've forgotten, but I told you all about Mr. Brandon since you two had never met."

A little of Emma's anxiety left her. At least Mrs. Patrick had been nowhere around during that long, terrible night when she'd found Brandon hanging from a rope in that room and managed to save him.

She'd spent most of that night holding him in her arms, dry eyed, mourning, hurting so much inside she thought the pain would devour her. "Really?" she said vaguely. "It must not have made much impression." She refused to meet his gaze. He would know very well that she would have paid close attention to any information about him, even if he'd been only one of her random patients, but she refused to think about it. He hadn't brought up the subject of their earlier acquaintance, though he'd made it clear he knew about it, and she had no intention of doing so either. "If you don't mind, Mrs. Patrick, could I perhaps have something on the third floor? I like my privacy."

"She takes my room," Brandon said, and Emma knew it would be a waste of breath arguing. "I'll use the blue room."

She jerked her head to look at him as an obedient Mrs. Patrick scurried off. "That's next door. No."

She couldn't read his faint smile—was it derision, contempt, or actual amusement? "I'm not about to creep into your bed in the middle of the night, Emma, so you may rest easy. I just happen to know you'll take the first chance you get to run off back to that viper's nest you've been living in, and I don't fancy retrieving you time and again. If you try to run away I *will* tie you to the bed. Yours or mine is still up for discussion."

She froze. "I thought you weren't interested in those sorts of variations."

He moved in on her unexpectedly, crowding her, but she stood her ground. He put a hand under her stubborn chin, tilting it up toward him, and said, "You, of all people should know there's a difference between the enjoyment of pain and the more delicious possibilities of measured restraint. Then again, your practical knowledge of fuckery is surprisingly scant. You didn't even know how to kiss."

There was no reason she should feel shame at the criticism. "Men do not kiss whores, my lord."

"I do."

The words left her still, breathless for a long, silent moment, and then she came to her senses.

"Taken from a business point of view, I must tell you that whores do not like or expect kisses. They want to get things done quickly and efficiently before they move on to the next one."

"Do they really?" He sounded amused, and she had to give him that. If any of the women she knew had been servicing Brandon Rohan they probably wouldn't be in any kind of hurry. Even she wouldn't.

"Well," he continued, "taken from my point of view I must tell you that you're dead wrong. Women like to be kissed, no matter what the financial arrangements are, and I kiss very well."

She had to give him that as well. That man could seduce a nun with his mouth. He came absurdly close to seducing her.

"I find this conversation distasteful," she said, turning her back on him and starting up the stairs. She should have known he'd immediately be by her side. In fact, distasteful was not the word for talking about kissing with Brandon Rohan. Disturbing might be more accurate.

He followed her up the staircase, down the long hall without a word, and her skin prickled at his nearness. His room was at the end of the hall, and she stopped outside the door.

"Do you want me to carry you across the threshold?" he inquired politely.

She wanted to hit him. She wanted to distract him, send him away, she wanted to be in the dubious safety of her rooms down by the docks. She pushed open the door.

The huge room was warm, spotless, inviting, a fresh fire burning merrily in the grate, the big bed turned down, and the telltale scrap of brown cloth lay on one of the pillows. Emma's heart sank. This room had been prepared for her. The information delivery system of Melisande and Benedick's excellent servants was impeccable—a footman would have seen the Rohan carriage pull up outside, and they would assume it had to be her, returned from the countryside. Someone would have rushed to inform Mrs. Patrick before Emma set one foot out of the carriage, and a small army of maids would be at work by the time they reached the door.

At least Brandon would have no idea how houses worked. Men tended to be oblivious, particularly in someone else's house. He'd assume the room was set for whoever had arrived.

He was standing behind her just inside the room, and she could feel his presence like a warm robe wrapped around her. A stifling one, she reminded herself swiftly. She glanced up at him and froze when she saw the expression on his face.

CHAPTER 24

Brandon stared at his old bedroom with a sense of unreality. It was so familiar—he'd spent his childhood, when he wasn't roaming the estate in Hampshire, in these confines, thinking up mischief, playing with his tin soldiers, holding onto. . .

"Oh, my god," he said, his voice reverential. "Morley."

The woman in front of him had moved away, turning to stare up at him. "Morley?" she echoed.

He crossed the wide room in quick strides to pick up the disreputable bundle that for some unknown reason was lying on one of the pillows on his bed, and an unreasonable shaft of longing went through him, for a simpler time, a simpler life, when everything made sense. "Morley," he confirmed, staring down at the moth-eaten stuffed bunny in his hands. He'd lost one eye, his fur was rubbed off in numerous places, and his stuffing had either leaked or compacted, because he was a far cry from his plump, sassy old self. If Emma hadn't been there he would have hugged him.

He cleared his throat. "A childhood toy," he said casually. "I used to sleep with him every night. He looks rather the worse for wear. I should probably burn him."

"Don't you dare!" Her protest was so fierce he half-expected her to try to snatch the toy away.

He looked at her curiously. "If you developed an attachment to this bundle of rags then you may certainly have him."

"Don't be absurd." She moved past him to the window, looking out into the rainy night. "He's not *my* childhood companion."

"Then shall I toss him on the fire?"

She said nothing, but he could see then tension vibrating through her, and he decided he'd done too much already. "No, I won't," he said. "I'll keep him with me. He's a fond memory."

He looked around the room, and he felt it, an eerie sense of what the French called *déjà vu*. Highly ridiculous, he told himself. He'd spent half of his life in this room—there were too many memories. But there was something else there, just at the back of his brain.

Normally he'd ignore it, dismiss it. But he'd known there was something about Emma Cadbury, even though he'd been idiot enough to forget her, and he hadn't paid proper attention. If he had they might not have gotten into such a mess. He'd known he should keep his distance, and for a soldier who relied on instincts to keep him alive he'd done a piss-poor job.

He looked at her stiff back as she stared out the window, obviously waiting for him to leave, and then he glanced at the bed. He could see her on that bed, her arms around him while he wept.

But that was absurd. For one thing he couldn't imagine weeping—he'd done with that after his first battle, when he'd killed. And killed and killed.

If they'd been on that bed it wouldn't have been he who was weeping. Emma and beds had an obvious connotation—in fact, the idea of any bed made him think of Emma. Any flat surface. Up against a wall. In a chair—he hadn't done it in a chair for years. . .

He slammed a door on his thoughts. "Did I ever bed you in this house?"

She turned, and he couldn't read her expression. "I assure you, until last night I had been blissfully celibate for eight years."

He froze. "That's not possible!"

She turned, calm and controlled, raising an eyebrow. "How so?"

"You . . . that is . . . you . . ." he hadn't been at a loss for words since he'd be a callow youth, and he simply stared at her in disbelief.

"I retired from the day to day tasks of a bordello and concentrated on the business side. Once a whore, always a whore, but in fact my hard-learned skills have not been put to the test for a very long time. I hope I proved satisfactory, my lord. I would hate to receive money for inferior performance."

The goddamned money! He'd forgotten all about it—it had vanished in the haze of lust that had surrounded him. He would have agreed to anything last night. Good lord, he'd agree to anything right now.

He smiled faintly. "I'll need to write a draft on one of my accounts."

"No hurry. I gather you have disposable income, and I don't come cheap."

He had never seen such a cool, practiced smile in his life, a perfect curl of the lips that he wanted to kiss so badly, and nothing in her eyes at all. Suddenly he was angry again—at himself, at her for valuing herself so little, at the whole messy, confusing fiasco that he couldn't figure how to get out of.

"No, you don't," he agreed. "You are, however, worth every penny." The moment the words were out of his mouth he knew they were the wrong ones. He'd only enforced the notion of a commercial transaction when he'd been trying to tell her how much he wanted her.

In for a penny, he thought. "Would you be interested in doubling that amount?"

Her face drained of color. "Get out."

He knew how ridiculous he must look, looming over her in his old bedroom, his much-loved childhood bunny in his hand. For some goddamn reason he couldn't keep his mouth shut when he really needed to.

He shrugged. "You'll need to give me the direction of your bank so I can have the money transferred."

"I don't want your goddamned money," she said between her teeth. "I just want you to go away."

Instead of walking away he moved closer, but she held her ground. "You were the one who brought money into our relationship."

"We don't have a relationship."

He moved closer. "Of course we do," he said. She was right there, so close, tension radiating through her body. He dropped the bunny, took her arms and pulled her close. "Harpy," he added softly, and kissed her.

He was prepared for a battle. He was prepared for rage and then, please God, an eventual melting. He never expected she would slide her arms around his waist, holding him tightly, as she let him kiss her, as she started to kiss him back with such endearing awkwardness that his blood caught fire. He wanted her, needed her, so badly. He needed to lose himself in her, drown in her, die in her, he loved. . .

She yanked herself out of his arms, a second before the door opened and Mrs. Patrick appeared, a young maid behind her. "There you are, Master Brandon!" she said jovially, missing any tension between the two of them, Emma's reddened mouth, the brightness of her eyes, his own upheaval. "Your room's all ready for you. Would you two be wanting dinner down in the dining room, or would you prefer a tray up here?"

"If you don't mind I'd prefer a tray," Emma said before he could say a word. "I'm very tired. I'm certain Lord Brandon would like to go out this evening. He must have old friends he wished to visit."

And with those simple words she broke him.

EMMA WATCHED Brandon walk out of her room without another word, and she felt sick inside. Why had she said that? She had, in effect, told him to go out and try to kill himself again. She knew his old friends had been deviants and satyrs, she had seen the results of their work when she'd found him in this very room, trying to put an end to his existence. What if she'd been too late? What if she'd opened the door and he'd been hanging there, dead, gone forever, lost to the dark world he'd entered.

And now she'd just told him to go back there. He hadn't missed it, either. His face had gone still, blank, and he'd simply walked away from her.

She could feel him on her mouth, the taste of him, the demand of him. She could feel him on her breasts, pressed against his hard chest as she'd held on to him. She could feel him in her belly, the growing hardness pressing against her, something she no longer thought of with revulsion. He'd been warm and strong and hard and she wanted him back.

She turned away, hugging herself, cursing herself and then she stopped thinking, moving on instinct alone, through the door and out onto the landing that looked down over the broad staircase. He was going quickly down the steps, his head bowed, and she couldn't stand it. He was going out to die, all because of her wicked tongue, and she couldn't let that happen. If it did, she would die too.

"Brandon!" She leaned over the railing, not even considering what she was doing.

He stopped his headlong pace, turning to look up at her from that endless distance. She was the slightest bit nearsighted, and she couldn't read his expression, but she could imagine it.

"Mrs. Cadbury?" His voice was frosty, and she should have been abashed that she'd used his given name for the very first time.

"Lord Brandon," she amended hastily. He didn't move, and she cleared her throat. She felt like such an idiot, such a thoughtless, evil fool. "Lord Brandon," she said again. "I . . . I didn't . . . forgive me . . ." She couldn't put her regret into words.

She squinted, trying to draw him into focus, but it was hopeless. "There is nothing to forgive, Mrs. Cadbury," he said with stiff politeness. "I will wish you a good evening."

"Where are you going?" She heard the intake of breath behind her and knew that Mrs. Patrick had overheard her grossly inappropriate question.

There was a long moment of silence. "I haven't yet decided," he finally said. "To church or to the devil or someplace in between. Pleasant dreams." Before she could say another word he was gone.

CHAPTER 25

Emma was alone. There was no one to keep her from walking out the door and heading straight back to her rooms by the docks. She could hire a hackney, or she could even walk, straight out of his life and this time he wouldn't come after her.

It was beyond stupid to even consider it. She'd been so fixated on getting away from him that she hadn't examined the situation with her usual calm deliberation. She'd spent her life surviving by sheer grit and her ability to use her wits. Now was hardly the time to stop using her brain, even if it did have the unfortunate tendency to turn to pudding any time she got near Brandon Rohan. She needed to be practical, not let herself get distracted by what she could never have. Something she shouldn't even want.

Whether she wanted to admit it or not, it appeared as if someone was most definitely trying to kill her. There was a chance that all three incidents—the fire, the near drowning, the attack at Starlings—were coincidental. There was a likelier chance that dogs could talk and pigs could fly. She'd been going around with blinders on, fixated on the one man who had ever been able to make her feel, make her long for some-thing more, and she'd been foolishly reckless.

Resolutely she pushed him out of her brain. *Discipline, my girl,* she told herself firmly. *Your first task is to stay alive. Mooning over Brandon Rohan is a complete waste of time if you end up dead.*

Of course, mooning over Brandon Rohan was a complete waste of time, no matter what, but she refused to think about him right now, about the way his hands had touched her, about the way his body had moved over her, inside her, so very different from all those other times, all those other men.

Enough! Going over to her worn leather satchel, she pulled out her heavy book, the sheaves of paper covered with her neat script, until she found a blank one, along with her pen and tiny bottle of ink. She sat down in a chair by the fire, and then jumped up again at the feel of something beneath her.

The stuffed toy. Morley, he'd called it. She'd spent many nights in Brandon's bed in the last three years while he'd been banished to Scotland, and she'd slept holding the worn bunny rabbit, a pathetic talisman of someone who would never be a part of her life. Tucking it under her arm where it rested comfortably enough beneath her breast, she set the paper in front of her, using the book as a makeshift desk, and began to write.

She started with three columns, neatly arranged. First, anyone who had reason to hate her. Next to that, the ability to carry out the three attacks, followed by what her enemy had to gain by her death. When she was done she looked down at her pages of handiwork in frustration, no closer to a solution.

"Hello, dearie." Mrs. Patrick pushed the door open, followed by a thin, very young maid carrying a heavy tray laden with covered dishes. Unfortunately the tempting aromas were lost on Emma, though she knew she needed to eat, if for no other reason than fuel. "You must not have heard me knock. We've brought you a bite to eat, and Jenny here will see to your bath. You'll have a good night's sleep, and tomorrow everything will look ever so much better."

She didn't bother to question Mrs. Patrick's accurate assessment of her current state of mind—in the years she'd known her Emma had discovered the housekeeper had an almost preternatural gift for homing in on feelings and emotions she'd rather keep hidden. "I'm not terribly hungry," Emma said, setting her papers aside, "but I'll try. And a bath would be lovely if it's not too much trouble."

"No trouble at all, miss. We're here to take care of you—it's our life's work to make things a little more pleasant for you. Heaven knows Lady Melisande has wanted to coddle you for years now, but you always refuse. She'll be very happy you decided to spend some time here, I'm sure. And I'm so glad you haven't changed your mind and decided not to stay. Lord Brandon left strict orders that you were not to leave the house, but the footmen are in distress, worried about what they might have to do to keep you here."

Emma had never learned the gift of accepting a servant's work as her just due, and the thought of the nervous footmen, afraid to put their hands on her but terrified to disobey Brandon, made her feel guilty. At least now she knew she couldn't have left even if she wanted to. He hadn't looked in any mood to stop and issue warnings when he'd stormed out of the house, but maybe her stupid words hadn't sunk in.

She sighed, reminding herself one more time that she wasn't a stupid woman. "I won't be going out until tomorrow, Mrs. Patrick. I have work at the hospital."

Including the new, unpleasant task of dealing with Mr. Fenrush about the seismic shift in responsibilities. The man was going to be enraged, but Fenrush was a ham-handed butcher, a spiteful fanatic who took lives with his carelessness and taught his sycophantic staff to do the same. Splitting the control between the two of them should lessen some of the unnecessary deaths, but she foresaw a battle royale that wasn't going to end anytime soon. The sooner she began to deal with it, the better.

"That'll be up to Lord Brandon," Mrs. Patrick said, her brow creased, and Emma felt a fresh, cleansing rage sweep through her.

"No," she said firmly, "it won't. I will be going to the hospital first thing tomorrow morning, and you may tell the servants that Lord Brandon would not want anyone to touch me." That much she instinctively knew was true. He might want to control and imprison her, but he wouldn't want anyone laying hands on her. Anyone else.

Mrs. Patrick shook her head. "Well, now, that's between the two of you, or I miss my guess. I always find that it's the gentlemen that know best."

The ire simmered nicely beneath her breastbone, keeping Morley company. "And I always find the gentlemen couldn't find their arse with both hands."

Mrs. Patrick let out a huff of shocked laughter, and the very young maid grinned before quickly wiping the expression off her face. "Well, that's as may be," the older lady said vaguely. "Speak with Lord Brandon. He's a dear boy."

He's a rat catcher, she thought, giving Mrs. Patrick a dulcet smile. "Of course," she murmured, and the gullible woman believed her.

The bath went a long way towards improving her mood, and the cold chicken, fresh rolls and cheese managed to woo even her fading appetite. It wasn't until she climbed into bed, Morley still tucked under her arm, that the thoughts began to flood her mind once more, worry and guilt and longing. What if he'd gone straight to an opium den? There were both pubs and private clubs where he could drink, and bordellos.

With a whimper she rolled over in the bed, burying her face in the soft pillow as she hugged the toy. A mistake—the night before came rushing back, his long fingers on her skin, his teasing, questing mouth, his tongue, his. . .

She rolled onto her back with a moan. He was probably dead, she told herself bitterly, and she didn't care. Anyone who let a woman's harsh, careless words decimate him wasn't long for this world anyway. Of if he'd gone to the devil once more, he could still return as he had managed to three years previously.

She stared into the room, lit only by the banked fire. It was much quieter in Melisande's neighborhood—the docks were never silent but Bury Street might almost have been in the country. Except for the birds.

She heard the unmistakable call of the ravens, back and forth, and she was suddenly very cold in the big bed. They were nowhere near the Tower of London with its permanent flock of the birds, and yet the sound was clear and loud. They were a harbinger of death—she'd known that since she'd been a young child. It was nothing but a country superstition, and she was a woman of science, but the calls came again, and she curled up around herself, unable to quell her panic. He was going to die, and she had never told him she loved him.

Yes, she did love him, no matter how much she didn't want to, no matter how much she pretended it wasn't true. She loved him and he was going to die.

She heard the church bells toll midnight, echoing in the night, one more song of the city. He was drunk in a pub.

They tolled one—he was lying in a gutter, beaten and robbed.

They tolled two—his body was floating in the Thames.

They tolled three—his body was being picked apart by the ravens that had warned of his death.

They tolled four—he was . . . he was back! In the silent household she could hear him—the front door closing quietly, the steady steps on the stairs, barely a trace of a limp, moving on the landing, coming closer, past his door now, at hers.

She held her breath, frozen, waiting for the knob to turn, waiting for him to come to her, but the silence held, he moved, and she heard the quiet opening and closing of the door next to hers.

She closed her eyes, but they flew open immediately. She spent exactly one moment considering the ramifications of her act, then dismissed it entirely.

The hall was deserted, and there was no footman dozing downstairs. No witnesses, no gossips, no one to know.

She hadn't brought a candle, and she didn't knock. She simply pushed the door open and stepped inside.

He wasn't there. Pain and fear swept over her—she'd been so sure he was back, but no, he was dead somewhere and. . .

"Why are you here?" His voice came out of the shadows, flat and expressionless.

He was over by the window, the pale moonlight silvering his body. He'd been undressing, and he wore only his breeches, his chest bare, the scarring clearly visible. She loved his scars.

"I was afraid something had happened to you."

His derisive laugh broke the night. "What, did you think I'd gone off to find the remnants of the Heavenly Host? I went to a pub with

Noonan and sat watching him, drinking tea, for God's sake, while he got rip-roaring drunk on Irish whiskey. He's a fondness for it and you'd have a hard time finding it anywhere in Scotland."

She, who never prayed, offered up a silent prayer of thanks to the God who had never listened. She took a tentative step toward him. "I brought Morley back to you." She held out the floppy little bundle.

There was a long moment of silence, as if he were considering whether he was going to tell her to throw the bunny on the banked fire or get the hell out of his room. He did neither.

"Come here," he said.

She did.

EMMA CADBURY WAS QUITE the most beautiful thing he'd ever seen in his life as she moved toward him on quiet, bare feet. God, he loved her feet! Her rich, dark hair was hanging down her back, the flowing night-dress was ridiculously fancy. It must have been a gift from his sister-in-law. She should wear something more classic, simpler, silk against her glorious body. Or nothing at all.

She came up to him, and the moon shone down on her upturned face. She had the hint of faint creases around her eyes, and he could imagine what she'd look like when she was old. She'd still be beautiful, sitting at a table, drinking tea, looking at the man opposite her. That man was going to be no one but him.

She held out Morley, and he wanted to laugh. He didn't want a bundle of stuffed rags in his bed, he wanted Emma there. Needed her. Forever. He just had to convince her that she needed it too.

He took his boyhood companion from her and tossed it lightly onto the chair, and there was nothing between them but inches. He shortened the distance, and she didn't retreat, and he was almost touching her, so close he could smell the soap on her, so close he could feel her warmth, so close.

"You're so beautiful," he said. "You're perfect." There was almost wonder in his voice that he couldn't hide.

She didn't flinch. "I hate it. I hate being pretty, I hate that that's all people ever see, I hate that something like my face causes men to do terrible things. I wish I were a troll."

He wasn't sure if he wanted to laugh or cry. This was a confession so intimate he wondered if even Melisande had heard it. But she was telling him.

"Well," he said judiciously, drawing out the word. "I didn't say you were *that* pretty."

She laughed, her voice light and silvery, and it hit him directly in his heart. They were so close. And then she said the most astonishing thing. "I think you're *that* pretty."

It was absurd. One didn't call a man pretty, and God knows he was a monster who scared small children. He kept his tone light. "Perhaps the part of me that hasn't been ravaged might not be too bad, but. . ." Before he knew what she was doing she'd risen to her tiptoes and pressed her lips across the scarred side of his face. The feeling in his skin was strange—both numb and exquisitely sensitive, and her soft lips were miraculous.

She leaned back. "Pretty," she said, and this time he believed her. "I love your scars."

"Why?"

"Because I never would have met you if you didn't have them. Because you get to show your darkness on the outside, where mine is stuck in my heart. Because the other side of your body is too handsome and you needed something to give you character. A thousand reasons." She placed another kiss on his jaw and he wanted her hands on him.

It was simple enough to reach down for them, to pull them up and set them on his shoulders. "I don't want you to lose your balance." His voice had lowered to an intimate growl. Her hands held on.

"I don't like this," she whispered, making no effort to move away.

"What don't you like?" He lowered his head and kissed the side of her neck, so gently, then her cheekbone, then her forehead, slow, soft kisses that demanded nothing, and he heard the hitch in her breathing. "This?" He moved over and kissed her perfect earlobe, sucking it into his mouth for only a moment. "Or this?" and his mouth brushed her eyelids.

Her sigh was soft on the night air. "I don't want to be here."

Their bodies were almost touching. "Then why did you come?" he whispered back.

Her eyes opened wide, meeting his gaze in the silvery moonlight, and he could read so many emotions there. Fear, anger, longing, sorrow. And love. He could see love. His Harpy was here with him, now, and she loved him.

"I don't want to." Her voice was only a breath of sound.

"Don't want to what?" He didn't worry. This time she wasn't going to run—he knew it. This time she was here.

"Anything. Everything."

"But you're here."

"I'm here," she said.

"Why?" he said again. "Penance?"

He could tell by the way her eyes darkened that that was one of the whips she'd used to drive herself. But it was a goad, an excuse, nothing more.

She didn't deny it. "I should never have said such an awful thing."

"You're my harpy. You always say awful things. Do you want to leave?" He would let her, of course. He would let her out of his life if he had to, if she had to. He would die, but he would do it. For her.

"I want to stay," she whispered.

The buttons on the night dress unfastened easily—the fussy thing wasn't without merit. He could feel the tremor in her body and he knew she had to be handled carefully, not with the brute passion of the night before.

"I won't hurt you," he said.

She was holding very still as his hands moved lower and lower, the tiny pearl buttons releasing with just a flick of his shaking fingers. The gown parted to show her moon-silvered flesh, and he caught his breath. "I could wish you weren't so perfect."

"The ugliness is all on the inside," she said.

"There's no ugliness in you anywhere. There's only pain."

Her eyes flew up to meet his, and he knew he'd shocked her. She'd tried so hard to hide it. He reached up and pushed the gown off her shoulders, and it pooled on the floor around her bare feet. A moment later he scooped her up, because he wanted to cradle her against him, and she was so light in his arms when she was so heavy in his heart. He carried her across the room, pushing open the hidden door to the adjoining bedroom, his room, his bed, kicking the door shut behind him. He held her for another moment, then set her on the mattress. "I want you in my bed," he said. "I've always wanted you there."

The shadows were deep, and he wanted to see her. Stepping back, he pushed the curtain aside, letting the moonlight flood in. He turned to look at her, the glorious picture she made, stretched out on his sheets.

She was naturally, inherently graceful as she lay there, looking up at him, and while he wanted to savor the sight of her, he needed to touch her more.

He knelt on the bed, grimacing as his breeches pressed against his rampant cock.

"I've seen one before, you know," she said with what was close to laughter in her voice, but to her this was still a very serious matter. "I know what to do. I'm out of practice, but I was a professional."

He didn't bother correcting her—she used her constant reminders to keep him at a distance, and it had never worked. He simply didn't care, except that it had hurt her.

"I imagine you're very proficient at fucking if you put your mind to it," he said. "But I don't think you've ever made love before."

He shouldn't have been surprised by the sudden fear in her eyes, as if the very thought was a threat. "I don't. . ." she started to say.

"Yes, you do." He looked at her with such tenderness.

"I'm . . . I'm frightened."

He knew how much it cost her to admit it. "I know." He kissed her then, soft, sweet, so that her lips clung to his, her body rose into the kiss, and her mouth opened when he tugged at her plump lower lip. Her nun like kisses were getting more adventurous, and she was a quick study. There was a certain desperation about them, but he understood, and he sank down on the mattress with her, pulling her into his protective arms.

He had all of her laid out before him, warm, naked, acquiescent if not eager, and the wealth of her was overwhelming. While part of him, a particularly insistent part one, wanted to push her back and throw himself on top of her, the rest of him wanted to take his time, discovering her, pleasuring her, warming her frozen soul.

But then her hands were on his chest, pushing back, and he wanted to howl in despair that she was going to run, and he would have to let her go.

She wasn't. "I want to see you," she said in a small voice. "I want to touch you."

There was no way he could argue with that. He began to unfasten his breeches, but she pushed his hands away, moving to the buttons and releasing them.

For a moment he'd been afraid of whores' tricks—she would know them all, but that was another woman, not this shy creature in his bed. She pushed his breeches down clumsily, until he sprang free like a goddamned cork on the water, waving in her face.

She didn't move, she simply surveyed him, and he realized with sudden amusement that this must by what she looked like when she was examining some strange medical growth she was going to remove. Even that unsettling thought didn't inhibit him, though he'd be careful not to have scalpels around when she was angry. He lay perfectly still, letting her look her fill.

She rose up on her knees, pushing her thick, dark hair behind her ears, and moved closer, examining all of him with a distracted eye, and damned if it didn't make him even harder, something he hadn't considered possible.

She frowned, still that surgeon's look in her eyes. "That is a great deal larger than the ones I've seen," she observed. "Do you have some medical condition?"

This time he did laugh. "Yes," he said. "Exposure to you."

It took her a moment to realize what he was saying, and she smiled faintly. "Obviously everyone I've ever seen has been in my presence," she pointed out.

"I'm more enthusiastic."

She even managed to laugh at that, though he could see she was still trembling, just slightly, for all she was trying to appear scientific and matter of fact. "I won't touch you until you give me leave to," he rashly promised, wondering if he was signing his death warrant. He would keep that promise, even if it killed him, which it damned well might if she changed her mind.

"I'm not afraid," she said, contradicting her earlier words.

"Of course you are, my poor darling. But I promise you won't be."

She looked at his face, not his raging erection, thoughtfully. "All right," she said, sinking back. "I think I can stand it now. Go ahead."

She really was going to kill him, he thought. "No."

For a moment it seemed as if she hadn't heard him. She was resting against the pillow like some virgin sacrifice, and she was probably trying to send her mind to that secret place she'd gone all those other times, with all those other men, just to survive. And then her eyes flew open. "No?"

"You came here. You got this far—it's time for you to go all the way. If you want this, if you want me, then you'll have to show me."

God, was he the world's greatest idiot? She was ready and willing—why was he demanding more?

Because she deserved more. It was that simple. If she couldn't move past her fears, just a little, if she couldn't even bear the thought of. . .

She moved so swiftly he was taken off guard, as she put her hot, sweet mouth against the scarred side of his face. She moved her lips slowly, carefully, down his neck with soft, little bites, and he moaned.

She pulled back quickly. "Did I hurt you? Old wounds can contain a kind of phantom pain, as if the wound were new. . ."

"Do it again," he said in a choked voice. "Please." No one had ever touched his scars. He didn't blame them—they were repulsive, and he'd come to think of that part of his body as dead. It wasn't. The torn, damaged skin was exquisitely sensitive, and her soft mouth felt like water in a desert.

She wanted to refuse—he could sense her reluctance, and he bit back his longing. "You don't have to do anything you don't want to do," he said again, and she was watching him, her expression unguarded and . . . needy.

"I want you," she said simply.

He reached out and cupped her face gently, his fingers twining her beautiful hair. "Then what do you need me to do?"

"Show me. Show me what lovers do."

A vast tenderness came over him, so different than his burning need for her. He'd never thought so much about sex in his entire life—he'd always been single-mindedly intent on rutting, though a woman's response did heighten his. Now he was determined to give Emma pleasure if he died trying.

He tugged her down, deepening the kiss. Her breasts were soft against his chest, the sweet nipples just beginning to bud, and he slid his hand down to cup one soft, lovely mound. She pushed against him, clearly needing more, and his fingers closed around the nipple, tugging slightly. Her quiet moan was his reward and her nipple hardened. He gently pushed her down on the bed, leaning over her body to gorge himself on her richness.

Her eyes were solemn as she watched him, and he dropped his head down and licked across the tip of her breast. She jerked, surprised, and he allowed himself to wonder if no one but he had ever done this for her, to her. His licked again, teasing her, feeling the nub harden against his tongue, and then he gave in to temptation and put his mouth on her, sucking at her sweet breast as he covered the other one with questing fingers.

She practically rose from the bed as the pleasure spiked through her, and if his mouth hadn't been so deliciously busy he would have smiled. He let his teeth lightly scrape against the edge of her nipple, and he heard her muffled shriek. She had sensitive breasts, he thought, but she liked an edge, and he bit down carefully.

"Oh, God," she gasped, and he realized her fists were clutching the bed sheet beneath them. He wanted those strong hands clutching him as he drove into her, he wanted it so badly he would have wept.

But if he rushed things he'd ruin it. He had to go slowly, to ready her, to show her what pleasure could be had.

He lifted his head, releasing her nipple with a soft popping noise and kissing her mouth, swiftly, sweetly, before taking the other breast into his mouth, the nipple already tight. He was in a desperate hurry, he had all the time in the world, and he stopped thinking, trusting his instincts, his emotions, his. . . love for this beautiful, wounded creature who was somehow stronger than anyone he had ever known.

THEY WERE SKIN TO SKIN, his mouth tugging at her breast, and she felt swamped with the strange, restless feelings of the night before. She wanted to close her eyes, to disappear and let him simply have her, but he was demanding more than that. She couldn't refuse him and her fingers tightened on his shoulders. A shudder ran through him, and she knew without doubt it was a reaction of pure, carnal pleasure. But how could something be pure and carnal at the same time? This was sin and wickedness, all she was good for, and if she took any more pleasure in it she deserved the eternal damnation that would be her lot.

He lifted his head to look down at her, and she could see him so clearly in the moonlight, the beautiful, half-ruined face. "Don't think," he whispered. "Just feel." And before she realized what he was doing he'd moved down her body, kissing her belly and her hips and her thighs, and then, to her horror, he put his mouth between her legs.

She let out a muffled shriek of protest, trying to pull away, but his hands were holding her still, pushing her thighs apart as she felt his tongue against her most private flesh. He lifted his head for the briefest of moments, but she didn't have the presence of mind to try to close her legs against him. "Don't think," he said again, and put his mouth, his tongue back.

Thinking was her only chance of salvation. As head of the brothel, and with a natural bent toward medicine, she had taken care of the others, and she was better educated in the details of what lay between a women's legs than most people. She tried to isolate her mind, concentrate on what he was doing. His tongue was wicked, tasting her, for heaven's sake, and she knew he would attempt to arouse the small bit that gave a woman pleasure. It would be useless—her own efforts in that regard had ended in an embarrassed sort of failure, even though she'd been alone in her shame. He was wasting his time and hers.

She could feel his hot breath against her, and then the slightest brush of his teeth, his strong, white teeth, and she frowned. What was he doing? Why did he. . .?

She heard her own scream with shock, and she quickly slammed her hands over her mouth, as a fierce, hard response rocketed through her, strange and untenable. "Don't—" she gasped, but he was past listening, and then she was past protesting as she felt a sharp energy begin to build, to suffuse her body with something that surely was wrong. She was past fighting it, past worrying about it, and when she felt him slide two long fingers into her as he licked and sucked and bit, then she was gone, unable to stifle her response as it took over her body, leaving no room for herself there.

It was like being thrown over a cliff, sailing through dark, powerful winds and ending in a storm-tossed sea, and she could do nothing but hold onto him like the life raft he seemed to be, the only thing solid and safe in her mad, swirling world. Every muscle in her body had seemed to lock, as those waves crashed over her again and again. She couldn't stop it, she couldn't control it, and then she no longer wanted to, giving herself over to the wash of feelings. She hadn't even realized he'd moved up, over her, until she managed to open groggy eyes to stare at him, at the triumph, the satisfaction on his face, things she could rail at, except for that shocking streak of tenderness in his eyes.

"I hate you," she said in a soft, broken voice.

"Of course you do," he agreed amiably enough. "You're about to hate me even more. Unless you tell me no."

He was very still, resting just above her, but she thought she saw anxiety in his eyes. The moonlight had leeched them of color, but the blaze of feelings was a shock. He truly would stop if she told him.

She let her hands slide up his strong arms, her fingers clenching and grasping as she moved them, wanting to catch him in her strong hands, to keep him and hold him. It was madness.

But for now she was willing to run mad. In truth, she had no other choice. "Yes," she said. "Now."

This time she meant it, not because she wanted it over and done with, but because she couldn't wait. She wanted that feeling back, the one that was just leaving her shaken and helpless when she'd sworn she'd never be helpless again. She could feel him against her, waiting, a shock in itself. Men thrust blindly, hurtfully.

But he was waiting, looking down at her expectantly. "Then touch me."

She didn't hesitate, afraid that if she did she might not go through with it, and her long fingers reach up to touch him. He was so different —warm, satiny skin over iron hard flesh that pulsed in her hand, and for once she didn't want to pull back in disgust. He let her fingertips touch him, test him, the strength and resilience of him, and it was a marvel it seemed to fit in such a narrow space. Encircling it, her fingers barely able to close around him, she tugged slightly, as Mollie Biscuits had once explained to her.

"Jesus Christ!" he moaned, pushing against her hand. "You are going to kill me, love."

Love. He called her love. For right now she would pretend that it was true. "Come to me," she said, tugging at him, bracing herself, knowing that there'd be pleasure.

He didn't slam into her. He was at her entrance, and slowly, so slowly he began to push inside her, his eyes locked with hers as each invading inch took possession of her, for now, forever. Pinpricks of reaction were running over her skin, and her body was responding on its own, tightening around him, clasping him, her very flesh seeming to pull him in deeper, deeper, until he finally rested against her, all of him sheathed deeply inside, filling every bit of her with thick, male power that should have disgusted her as it always had before. Instead she wanted more, wanted to own that power, own him as he owned her. He lay with his weight resting on his elbows, his brow resting against hers, damp with sweat, his eyes closed, and she could feel the tremors that ran across his body, small, involuntary jerks of that hard invasion within her softness. They stayed that way for a long moment, and then she felt him begin to withdraw, and she wanted to shriek in protest, to clutch at him with desperate hands. What did he want now, what test did she have to pass?

But when he pushed back in it was even more wonderful, and her hips rose to meet his, the walls of her sex tightening around him as her hands clutched his biceps. This was possession, but a different kind, a glorious one that she could hold in her heart. He took her, claimed her, but she took him as well, into her body, into her heart, into her soul, where he would always stay, no matter what happened. She finally let go, giving herself to him, to the rampant, building pleasure, to the joy of love that had cracked her guarded heart, as he thrust, each push a promise he couldn't keep, but it no longer mattered. Deep and harder and harder and she wanted more, craved more.

"Yes," she whispered fiercely. "Again. Again. More."

The darkness that was closing around her split with lightning, and suddenly everything ceased to exist, only man and woman, elemental, eternal, as she seemed to burst apart in a shower of pure sensation. She could feel him with her, her love, her soul, joining her, flooding her, and she took everything in savage satisfaction and a guttural sob of triumph.

BRANDON RETURNED TO HIMSELF, slowly, not certain he wanted to. Every part of him was weak, shaking, damp with sweat and perhaps even tears. She lay beneath him, her legs still locked around his hips, and he couldn't even remember how they'd gotten there. He must be crushing her, and he pushed himself up quickly. He had never lost himself so utterly, so completely, and he felt odd, almost disoriented.

She lay beneath him, her beautiful hair framing her face, her eyes closed. When she opened them she looked as shell shocked as he felt.

"Are you all right?" he questioned urgently, his voice hoarse.

She closed her eyes again, shaking her head. "No," she whispered.

He was still hard within her, or maybe he was hard again, but he knew she'd reached her limit. He might have as well. He withdrew, slowly, reluctantly, and he saw the momentary distress that crossed her face as he left her.

Pulling her into his arms, he rolled on his side, taking her with him, tucking her against him with exquisite care. "I love you, Harpy," he whispered in her ear, stroking her hair back from her face, stroking the worried expression her face.

She put her arms around him, trusting, but when she opened her eyes he could see the doubt and sorrow in the deep gray depths, the mournful acceptance, and he waited for the words he knew were the truth, the words that never came.

Instead she kissed him, and it was no longer an untutored, nun like kiss. It was a woman's kiss, deep and full and sure, a woman in love, and then she sank back against him, closing her eyes, and they lay that way until the early hours of the morning, neither of them sleeping for a long, long time.

CHAPTER 26

Emma slipped from the bed, determined not to wake him. He'd held her the rest of the night, and she'd pressed her face against his shoulder, burying herself in his skin, his scent, his body, letting the temporary peace fill her.

It wouldn't last. Nothing lasted, neither the good nor the bad, and she would survive this, the loss of him, as she survived everything else. It didn't matter that this loss would be the hardest.

He didn't want to let her go. In sleep, his body relaxed, but he still held her, and she moved by small increments until she finally slipped from his protective grasp. She stood in the early morning light, not reaching for anything to cover herself, and looked down at him. The unscarred side of his face was against the pillow, and she looked down at the war's devastation and wanted nothing more than to climb back into the bed, to stay there, to stop fighting, stop trying.

She couldn't do that. Not to him. Not to herself. He would marry quiet Miss Bonham and learn to love her, he would live a good life without the shame Emma would bring him, even as his whore. And she would have been his whore, gladly, sold herself on the streets for him, die for him.

But she would only bring him disaster. She loved him, had loved him, probably from the first night she'd seen him, and she would love him until the day she died. Loving wasn't about selfishness and pleasure, it was about wanting the best for someone. It was about letting them go.

They had ended up in his old bedroom, though she couldn't remember how. Her clothes were hanging in the clothes press—she moved swiftly, gathering them in an armful and then slipping back through the adjoining door. No one had brought fresh water or tea—they probably had strict orders not to disturb either of them. Mrs. Patrick was a wise woman who saw more than most people, and no one would bother them until they were called. At least there was an ewer of cool water in the basin, and she washed herself quickly, doing her best to ignore the tenderness in her breasts, her hips, between her legs, sensitivity that squeezed her heart and brought back a shocking arousal. It would pass, she told herself, pulling on her clothes with shaking hands. It had to.

She almost escaped the house without notice. She'd stayed there often enough to know that the servants would be down in the basement having tea at that hour, and she was almost at the door when a familiar voice startled her.

"Where do you think you're going, young lady?"

She turned to face Noonan's disapproving glower, keeping her own expression blank. "I doubt it's any business of yours, Mr. Noonan,"

"Anything that affects the boy is my business," he growled.

"He's hardly a child," she said briskly. "He doesn't need your protection."

"He's got the heart of a boy, true and good, even though he hides it. I won't have you troubling him."

"Trust me, I won't have the slightest effect on his heart."

"Trust me," he mocked her, "you already have. We do just fine up in Scotland without a bunch of women running around. You're no' good for him."

"I know that."

Noonan looked startled. Despite the hard night of drinking Brandon had mentioned, he looked no more ill-tempered and craggy than usual. "So what are you planning to do, then, miss?"

"I'm planning to let him be."

She expected satisfaction in his faded blue eyes. Instead his frown deepened. "And if he doesn't want that?"

"It's not his choice. Goodbye, Mr. Noonan." She hesitated. "Look after him."

"I'm thinking he won't want you leaving without a word."

"Then tell him I said goodbye."

The old man was already racing up the front stairs by the time she closed the massive front door, and she knew she had to hurry. Within a matter of moments she'd blended with the crowds, gone before Noonan could wake his precious "boy."

Her precious boy. Her angry man, her broken soldier, her salvation and destruction. *Let him go*, she thought fiercely. *Let him go.*

She had never taken a hackney cab in her life, and this wasn't the day to start. She could walk for miles, in both city and country, and she knew the way to Temple Hospital well enough to cut through neighborhoods and alleyways and shortcuts, reaching there in half the time a vehicle might take, well before Brandon might arrive, if he even wanted to. She paused in the shadows of the old hospital, built by one of the Stuarts hundreds of years ago, and stared up at its imposing stone walls. She'd been happy there, fulfilled, infuriated, heartbroken. If it hadn't been for Mr. Fenrush and his underlings, her life would have been perfect.

But that time was gone as well. Taking over from Fenrush would mean a battle she was no longer willing to wage—and if she didn't care, then she would never win, even with Benedick's power and money behind her.

It was time to find a new place, a new way to bring her gifts, such as they were, to people. Melisande would be hurt and furious if she disappeared, but perhaps, after a few years, Emma would be able to contact her, beg her forgiveness. By then Brandon would be settled in his new life, her existence forgotten once more.

She pushed herself forward. She needed her book on anatomy, the most important one, and some of her instruments, but most of all she needed the change of clothes and the cache of money she kept hidden in her private changing room. Leaving anything of value in her rooms by the dock had never been an option—here, everyone had kept their distance as if she'd carried a plague. They would avoid her today as well as she retrieved her necessary possessions.

But in this, at least, she was mistaken. Emma had no sooner set foot inside the door that had been allotted for her use when she ran into Mr. Grimley, the young surgeon she'd stabbed with a scalpel when he'd tried to interfere with her. Not the best luck in the world, she thought, but she had given up any hope of luck long ago.

He was a plump young man with a red face, soft hands, and watery blue eyes that always seemed filled with petulance or lust or occasionally both, and he'd been wanting revenge for a long time.

"What are *you* doing here?" He also had a nasal, high-pitched voice and a tendency to lisp his r's, and she honored him with the haughty expression that had always infuriated him.

"I believe I work here. I assume the hospital still has the misfortune to employ you?"

He was rubbing his hand, the spot where she'd pricked him that time, and she felt a moment's regret. Her own pain didn't give her the right to hurt other people, even someone like Grimley, and she was about to apologize when his eyes narrowed in triumph.

"You'd best not let Mr. Fenrush see you," he said. "The trustees told him you were going to be in charge of the students, and he was . . . displeased."

Emma could imagine it. "I have no interest in meeting with him. I'm simply here on an errand. I don't believe I'm scheduled to work for. . ."

"You won't be working here again," Grimley said triumphantly.

Emma had concluded the same thing, but irritation managed to sneak through her misery. "Is that so?" she said coolly. "According to whom?"

"You'll see." He turned away from her, addressing an approaching figure. "Here's Mrs. Cadbury, Collins. She just showed up without warning."

"I hardly think I have to give notice. . ." she began as Mr. Fenrush's huge manservant loomed in front of her, and she took an involuntary step back before she could stop herself.

He put one heavy hand on her arm, and she looked down at the bruised knuckles, the scratched skin, before searching his face. That was bruised as well, as if he'd suffered at the fists of someone in a fury, and a strange sense of familiarity washed over her. Of course he looked familiar—she'd seen him skulking around the hospital building for the last two years she'd been training there. But it was something else, the dark eyes like currants in a pasty face, the. . .

"No," she said, frozen in shock. Those eyes had been staring into hers as those hands tried to choke the life from her. But it was impossible, it made no sense. . .

"She's going to faint, Collins," Grimley said.

The hell I am, Emma thought, but she felt her knees dip slightly as if she were about to collapse, and immediately those huge, vicious hands yanked at her.

Clearly, not a man who learned his lesson. Even hampered by her skirts her kick hit her target, and Collins doubled over with the same girlish scream she'd heard a few short days ago. Grimley stumbled back in gratifying panic, and she thought she might have a chance to escape when Collins rose up in a roar, launching himself at her and then she was falling, falling and everything went dark.

IT WAS THE SMELL. Horse dung, urine, unwashed bodies and something else that she couldn't quite recognize, pushing into her mouth, her nostrils, her lungs. It was the motion—she was cramped, restrained, unable to catch herself as she rolled back and forth in what had to be some kind of conveyance. It was the darkness—everything was an unbreathable blackness. Her arms were clamped to her body with heavy rope, her wrists tied even tighter.

Someone had thrust a gag in her mouth, and if she thought about where that rag might have come from she *would* vomit, and then she could very easily choke and die. She'd seen it happen in patients who hadn't been carefully tended. Her stomach was roiling with an onslaught of revulsion, but she willed herself to think of cold, cool things as she was tossed back and forth in the blackness and filth.

Her first sense that she wasn't alone in whatever instrument of torture they'd placed her was when someone kicked her, hard, in her already bruised ribs. "Can't you keep her away from me?" came Amasa Fenrush's fretful voice.

"Could have finished her back in London," the slow voice of his manservant answered. "Then when I dumped her in the river this time there'd be no one around to fish her back out again."

"And when is the riverside ever deserted?" Fenrush's tone was waspish. "She's the one who created this debacle, and you've failed time and time again. We can't risk another mistake."

"Your mistake in the first place, telling a whore about your side business," Collins said. "Anyone knows you can't tell a whore anything, but no, you had to go and talk about our side business while you were having at her. What did you think, she was some holy nun and you were making your last confession?"

"She was a whore," Fenrush said stiffly. "She shouldn't have known what I was talking about, and besides, most trollops are dead by the time they reach twenty-five. I never thought I'd see her again."

Collins made a disgusted noise. "Life doesn't work out so nice, gov'nor. It's a good thing that toff sent her to your hospital to learn her trade—else who knows who she might have told. You're boneheaded, is all I can say."

"May I remind you that you are my servant?" Fenrush said frostily.

"And may I remind yer bleedin' worship that I've killed for you, time and again, and if those Rohans find out you have something to do with this bitch's problems then you may as well kiss your comfortable life goodbye."

"I'm dying of syphilis. My comfortable life is over anyway."

Collins expressed no sympathy or regret. "At least you're taking Mrs. Cadbury with you. Should have kept to cleaner whores, but you like a bit of the mud, don't you?"

"It was her fault. After that young girl died she wouldn't allow me into her tawdry establishment, and I had to make do with the filthiest of streetwalkers. If her life wasn't about to end I'd rape her myself to make sure she died of the same disease."

"I thought all whores had it." Collins sounded no more than mildly curious.

"Not the delicate flowers of Mrs. Howard's establishment. That's why they could demand the highest prices. They were very particular about their clientele, as if the sluts had any right to be." He cleared his throat and spat. "And she was a worthless lay."

All right, now she truly was going to throw up, Emma thought, thinking of frozen lakes and snow-covered hills. She had never looked at the men who'd been led into her room, never noticed who she'd been servicing in her drugged stupor. The very thought that Butcher Fenrush had once touched her was enough to make her gag.

"I might take a poke at her before I finish her off," Collins said in a thoughtful voice. "Dunno whether I have the French disease or not, but if she dies being afraid of it then so much better. She owes me for the beating I got."

"You should have finished her off before Rohan's brother rescued her."

"I likes to take me time."

She felt the boot again. "Think she's still knocked out?" Fenrush said.

"Hard to say. Might be dead already—she hit the marble floor hard."

"She's not dead," Fenrush said grimly. "You said yourself, life's doesn't work out so conveniently. Haul her up and take a look."

Oh, Christ, Emma thought, letting her body go completely limp. If she had to look at the man she might really throw up.

It took what little fortitude remained her to keep from reacting as Collins wrapped his big, cruel hands around her arms and hauled her up, but she managed to remain limp, eyes closed, as she was dumped onto a seat and the covering was ripped from her head.

She wanted to suck in the fresh air, to blink as murky light penetrated her eyelids, but she did nothing, simply lolled on the seat like a rag doll.

Someone kicked her leg but she didn't react. At least it was an improvement over her ribs. If those splintered she'd have a hard time running, and she was going to need to be able to, sooner or later.

She felt a hand on her breast, tweaking it cruelly, but she still remained passive, and she heard Fenrush's snort of disgust. "How hard did you hit her? She's still out cold."

"I didn't hit her—I told you, she smashed her head on the marble floor. T'aint my fault if it scrambled her brain. She's going to be dead in a short time—what does it matter to you?"

To her disgust she felt the seat shift as Fenrush moved closer. He stank of body odor and formaldehyde, and she couldn't react, mustn't react, when he put his doubtless filthy fingers on her face and pried up an eyelid.

That was one thing she couldn't fake. "I thought so," he said with a little crow of triumph. "She's faking. She's been awake all this time."

But Mr. Fenrush's knowledge of human anatomy had always been imperfect, and he wouldn't know a sign of life if it bit him on the arse. She let her eyelids drop to half-mast, staring at him blearily and making a mumbling sound from behind the revolting gag, then sank back and closed them again, seemingly succumbing to unconsciousness once more.

"I dunno," Collins said. "Looks kinda half dead to me."

She heard Fenrush's snarl. "You are hardly a respected medical professional."

Neither are you, Emma thought, allowing her body to sway a bit. Since total insensibility was denied to her, she could instead appear dazed, *non compos mentis,* and an idiot like Fenrush wouldn't know the difference. Collins said nothing, and Emma didn't dare let her eyes do more than flutter open. He was picking his teeth. She closed them again.

They were in a carriage, or what passed for one, though it couldn't be the fancy conveyance Fenrush travelled to work in each day. This one had no springs, the seats were torn and stained, and the smell was appalling. It must have . . . *oh, god.*

She knew that smell. Fenrush had risen to the top of his profession on the strength of his ability to procure one of the most needed of medical commodities. He'd been able to deliver hundreds of cadavers to the surgeons' academy, some dead not more than a couple of hours, and no one had asked where they came from. They'd come from this carriage—the unmistakable smell of putrefying flesh was everywhere.

She gagged, unable to help herself, and no matter how hard she tried, visions of mountain streams and snow couldn't stop her. If she vomited she would die, and Fenrush and Collins would watch her, unmoved. She gagged again, trying to swallow her bile, trying to think.

The mountain stream came again, and the snows, but the vision was clearer, and she knew where she was, even if she'd never set foot there in her life. She was in the Highlands of Scotland, by a deep, icy mountain burn, and Brandon was in the water, naked, long hair flowing behind him, swimming, impervious to the cold, impervious to everything as his eyes met hers across the distance, blue and calming, and she felt tendrils of comfort seep into her bones, cool, clean, washing away the horror.

The slap across her face jarred her back, but the crisis had passed, and she was tired of not fighting back. Her eyes flashed open, her hatred piercing through Fenrush's smug face.

"I told you she was awake," he crowed.

He was an unexpected-looking man, bluff, seemingly cheerful, full of bonhomie for his staff and the world at large. No one would look at him and think he was a monster.

"Of course you were lying," he went on. "Women always lie and whores are women."

She could have come up with an argument for that if she hadn't been gagged, but instead she simply put all her fury into her eyes.

"I knew you remembered me," he went on, his voice hurried, anxious, so at odds with his cheerful face. "I was just waiting for you to make your move, to try to take me down. You knew I wasn't going to let you, didn't you? I could see you watching me, see you planning your attack, but you should have known you could never hurt me. Good always triumphs."

He was mad, Emma realized without a trace of sympathy. This wasn't rational—she still didn't recognize him or remember anything of a past encounter, and the man actually thought he was on the side of the angels. If Collins recognized his employer's delusions he didn't pay any attention, still picking at his blackened teeth.

Fenrush's eyes were bulging slightly. "Why aren't you saying something? Haven't you got more lies, more excuses, aren't you going to say you love me, that you never wanted. . ."

"She can't talk," Collins weighed in. "You told me to gag her. If you want her to speak then you have to take off the gag. In fact, this'd be a good time to get rid of her."

Fenrush's look of disgust was laughably patrician. "I am not going to 'get rid of her' as you put it. I couldn't expect a man of your limitations to understand, but I have a *plan*. Dumping her on the side of the road is not part of it. Fire, Collins. Only fire washes away all sins."

Fire and washing were pretty much opposites, Emma thought, letting her contempt distract her from her current disastrous position. She had to content herself with giving him a look of withering disdain, then leaning back and closing her eyes as if he bored her.

It worked. He yanked her forward and tore the gag away, spittle flying from his mouth as he screamed at her. "You will not ignore me! You are worthless, a travesty, a mockery of all that is sacred and noble in the medical profession! You filthy, disease-ridden trollop!"

"I gather you're the one who's disease-ridden," she said calmly, surprised her voice sounded so normal. "I myself am quite healthy, and signs of the illness would have been noticeable by now if I had it. You kill more patients than you save, I save more than die, and as for all that is sacred and noble, you provided a never-ending supply of freshly-killed bodies for research, enriching your pockets and leading to your appalling appointment as head of the surgeons' hospital, when there should have been little doubt you were murdering people for their corpses." It was a wild shot across the bow, but it hit its mark, and there was no way she could hide her horror.

"Fact is, he didn't kill 'em," Collins pointed out. "I did, me and me mates. Though occasionally he'd have to finish 'em off if we got sloppy and delivered some still twitching, but I thinks he enjoyed that."

"Shut up!" Fenrush screamed. "They were worthless, the dregs of society. They gave their lives for science, they. . ."

"They gave their lives for your pockets," Collins said. "Admit it. And they weren't all low-lives—you sent me after some of the gentry when someone paid you enough. There was that young man—son of a duke, he was, and those two old ladies. What'd ya want them for?"

Fenrush no longer looked like a cheerful shopkeeper—he was pasty, pale, and sweaty. "I admit there is no use for female cadavers in science," he said loftily. "But I have benefactors, and small favors must be dispensed to keep them happy."

Emma opened her eyes. "Small favors like killing their wives?".

"Shut up, bitch," Fenrush snarled.

"More like their mothers—both of them were too old to fuck before I did 'em," Collins said. "You're a different matter."

She didn't even blink, looking at him like he was a slug. "I'd be surprised if your bollocks are still up to the task."

He lunged off the opposite seat, but suddenly there was a blade between them—and not a small one. Fenrush held the saw used for cutting through bone, and it would slice through Collins quite easily. "Sit down," Fenrush said icily. "I told you I had plans for her. She'll go with the others. That is, if this time you did your job right."

Collins sat back, disgruntled. "It's taken care of. One spark and it'll go up, with all them dollymops inside. But not this one. I deserve my go at her."

"Especially this one," Fenrush said. "She must burn the brightest."

Emma promptly vomited.

CHAPTER 27

He couldn't find where she'd gone. He'd been dead asleep when Noonan had come barging into the room, and his immediate, groggy thought had been to protect Emma, hide her from intrusive eyes, but the bed was empty, cold without her, and Noonan ripped the covers off his naked body.

"You've done it this time, me boy," he said. "She's run off, and if you have any sense you'll let her go." He paused, running his eyes down Brandon's length. "Though it seems you enjoyed yourself well enough."

He got out of bed slowly, not bothering to glance down at his body. There would be small bites, scratches, love marks. He'd managed to drive her into a frenzy, and each mark on his body was a badge of honor, far more than his battle wounds. "What are you talking about?"

"Your girl's gone. Run off just a minute ago—told me to tell you goodbye. What'd you do—bungle the job? That's not like you."

Brandon didn't waste time with niceties—he washed himself with the bowl of cool water, splashing it liberally on the floor before looking around for his clothes. They were scattered over the floor, and Noonan was already handing him his drawers. "Where was she going?"

"She didn't tell me, you young fool. I don't guess she wants you to know."

He yanked his breeches on over the drawers. "What did she say? Was she angry?" He was having trouble thinking straight—why had she left? He was going to . . . he wasn't sure what he was going to do, but one thing he'd been certain of. He wasn't going to let her go.

But she had gone anyway.

"Let her go," Noonan said again. "What have you got to offer her, eh? She's nothing but trouble, when you've got that nice girl to marry so you can settle down and become a good, solid gentleman around town."

He cast Noonan a dangerous look. "That sounds like pure hell."

"Then what *do* you want?"

"I want her!" The words burst from him, and the simple truth shocked him. "I want to take her to Scotland and never come back. I hate the city, hate the south. I want her and the glens and the lochs and the cold rain, and by God that's what I'm going to have."

"And what if she doesn't want the same thing? Maybe she's a soft southern girl."

"She wants the same thing," he said, knowing he was right. "She's just afraid to fight for it."

"A woman who won't fight isn't worth having."

He considered hitting Noonan, but the man was twice his age and half his size. "I don't know why she ran, but she's fought all her life, and if something is right she'd do it, no matter what the cost. She just needs to realize this is right."

There was a pause, and then Noonan laughed. "Glad you figured that out, boy. For a smart one you can be thickheaded as a goat." He tossed him his jacket. "She went on foot, heading toward the docks. I expect she's either gone back to that doss house she was living or on to the hospital. You want a horse or a carriage?"

"Neither. If she's walking then we'll be faster going the same way. Go fetch me a cup of tea while I find the rest of my clothes. I'll meet you at the front door."

"Aye, aye, cap'n," Noonan said, disappearing from the room, leaving Brandon to berate himself for falling asleep.

Emma was nowhere near her rooms, and no one had seen her for days. The people in the shabby neighborhood were neither villains nor whores in the light of day, but solid working class, and they spoke of Emma with pride and affection. She'd made a difference there as well as in the lives of what his brother had called "the Gaggle," and his rage at himself grew exponentially.

"Must be the hospital then," Noonan observed. "Or we could wait for her here—she'll have to come back sooner or later. We could get breakfast in that tavern and watch for her." There was a plaintive note in his voice that Brandon ignored.

"The hospital, it is. It seems to be the only thing she cares about besides the women she's helping."

"And you think she'll turn her back on all that and come to Scotland with us?" Noonan's voice was caustic.

"Yes." It was that simple, he was that sure. He should have told her, should have asked her, but the night had been overwhelming, and he hadn't been able to do anything but hold her, lost in her. It wasn't too late to fix that. It couldn't be.

The streets were growing more crowded as the day progressed, and they threaded their way through the crowds as quickly as they could, slowed down by a group of toughs who took exception to being jostled and weren't interested in an apology.

It had delayed them almost ten minutes but in the end he was exhilarated, his fists bruised, a cut on his mouth, and the sense that he was finally doing something simple, something right. Noonan was an able fellow warrior, and the five toughs were laid out in various states of disrepair as the two of them moved on, faster now.

Temple Hospital was a gray stone building, dark and depressing, so grim Brandon wondered how Emma could stand going there every day, but Benedick had assured him that she loved it, and his brother never lied.

He'd have to build her a surgery in Scotland, something a bit more cheerful, with lots of windows to let in whatever light the contrary Scottish weather felt like providing. If she didn't mind this dismal place then the frequent overcast skies up north shouldn't bother her.

But there was no trace of her, and no one seemed to know anything, even when he mentioned Benedick's name. Emma was gone, and he had absolutely no idea where she was heading.

Back to Melisande was a possibility, but he didn't think so. If she wanted to avoid him that would be the last place she would choose. Rage and hopelessness filled him, and he wanted to hit something, someone in his fear and frustration. Didn't she realize she was in danger? Didn't she know. . .?

"Begging your pardon, sir," a small voice said, and he turned to look at a tiny scrap of a female, bucket and mop in hand, standing a few feet away in the deserted hallway of the surgery. It was little more than a whisper, and when he didn't move she gestured him closer with one small hand. He went.

"Are you looking for Mrs. Cadbury, sir?" she said in a low voice, casting a furtive glance around as if to make certain no one overheard her.

He barely managed to keep his voice calm. "Yes, I am. Apparently she hasn't been here today—at least, that's what everyone tells me."

"Not true," she said. "She was here, all right, talking to one of them doctors, when Mr. Fenrush's man came up and pushed her. She fell and hit her head, and then Mr. Collins picked her up and took off—it looked like it was to Mr. Fenrush's office. They wouldn't let me follow, but I kept me eyes out, and not long after Mr. Fenrush and his man took off in the old carriage, the one they use for bringing the bodies in." The woman shuddered. "Not nice, that carriage. They had me clean it one time and you couldn't get the smell out of it."

"Was Mrs. Cadbury with them?"

"Couldn't see—just Mr. Fenrush and Collins were sitting on the seats, but that didn't mean they didn't take her. I mean, where is she, if not with them, I ask you."

Cold resolve filled him. "Did you see which direction they were headed?"

"Dunno. Up north, maybe."

North. The carriage was heading north, toward Suffolk where Starlings and the Dower House stood. Brandon had no proof they were headed there, he had only his instincts to rely on, but he had learned to trust them.

He reached for his pocket, digging for money to give the girl. "Thank you very much, miss. . ."

"Just Ermie, my lord. And I don't wants no money—Mrs. Cadbury —she saved my life, and got me this job too, with a good wage. She's a good woman, far better than that sorry lot." She cast a contemptuous eye at the huddle of men who were watching them. "You find her and keep her safe."

"I'll do that, Ermie," he said, clasping her hand in thanks, and she looked aghast. The gentry didn't touch the lower orders. Too bad. He didn't live by the rules. He'd made a stab at it while he'd been down here, but he'd had enough. "You need anything, you apply to Viscount Rohan and he'll see to it. Will you do that?"

She nodded, pulling her hand away and looking at it gingerly, as if had turned into a foreign object. "I do just fine, my lord. But if something happens, I'll tell the viscount."

"Good girl," he said, deciding it was better that he didn't touch her again, though in truth he wanted to hug her in gratitude. He turned his head to his companion. "Noonan," he said. "We need a fast carriage."

Noonan nodded. "That we do, lad. That we do."

THE SMELL HADN'T IMPROVED, Emma thought with bitter satisfaction. Fenrush was sitting opposite her, crammed onto the bench seat with the bulky Collins, clad in vest and shirt sleeves, his ruined coat tossed out a window. She'd manage to direct the entirety of her stomach disruption on the man, and if he hadn't been so disgusted he might have killed her on the spot.

"You're awfully squeamish about a little indigestion for a man comfortable with hauling corpses," she observed in a tranquil voice. Her wrists were tied too tightly in front of her, so there was no way she could work at the knot, and the bonds around her body kept her movement limited, but her spirits had improved. She wasn't defeated yet, for all that things looked dire.

"Cadavers," Fenrush corrected her sullenly. "They were entirely for medical purposes."

"Except for the women, because treating women is of no importance."

He glared at her. "Any medical advancements we discover with men are applicable to women's bodies. They're essentially the same."

She managed to produce an actual laugh at that. "No, they're not. I would have thought with your predilection for whores you might have realized that."

"You were one of them."

She didn't even blink. Now wasn't the time to get distracted. "So I was. Actually I'd forgotten you. But then, I never paid the slightest attention to my clientele. There were simply a pack of rutting dogs, and I had better things to occupy my mind."

He flushed, and she felt another trace of satisfaction. Whether she could escape or not, she could use her sharp tongue to weaken him as best she could.

She knew about syphilis and the terrible affects it had on the mind and body. Many of the women under her care had died from it, and the mental instability was one of the hallmarks of its latter stages. There had always been pressure to send the dying women to Bedlam, to end their lives in squalor and misery, but she had done her best to keep them at Temple Hospital, where they could be looked after until their death.

She had no idea how close Fenrush was. His normally high complexion was pasty, with a sallow undertone, and some of his bulk had lessened, leaving the waistcoat loose around his once-massive paunch. His hands trembled, his feet twitched, and he grimaced in pain. His initial infection could have been as recently as five years ago, as long ago as twenty, and she knew a moment's panic. They had always done their best to keep the women safe when she ran the house, but after the first outbreak of the vicious infection came a period when all symptoms vanished, and there'd never been a guarantee.

And then her bitter amusement took charge. Chances were she was going to be dead in twenty-four hours, so anything else hardly mattered. In truth, had she been infected, symptoms of the early stages would have cropped up. Several of the women they'd rescued had contracted it, but none of them had earned her living under Emma's care, and her oldest friends were safe.

"There's no treatment for it, you know," she said lazily, leaning back as best she could.

He didn't pretend to misunderstand. "Do you think me a complete fool?"

She decided not to answer that.

"Don't listen to her," Collins advised. "She's just trying to get yer goat."

"I know that," Fenrush snapped. He glared at her. "You know, I could be merciful. I could have Collins snap your neck before he sets the fire, but now I don't think so. I want you to feel the flames licking at your skin, your eyeballs melting." He was drooling.

"Eyeballs don't melt in a fire." Her voice was flat, prosaic. "Everything singes, then chars. Have you never examined a cadaver . . . oh, wait. You're more than familiar with them. Perhaps you contracted your disease from one of them. I gather there are a specialized few who prefer relations with the recently deceased. . ."

This time it was Fenrush who lunged at her, and Collins who held him back with seemingly little effort, which could mean that Fenrush had been weakened by his disease. It was a useful thing to consider—any bit of knowledge might help.

"Now, now, Mr. Fenrush," Collins chided in a soothing voice. "You don't wants to go losing your temper, do you? She ain't worth it, she ain't, and you know it. You don't want to be doing anything that might throw things off, do you now? These things can be very difficult, very difficult indeed, I can tell you. How many times has she managed to escape your careful plans? First, she breaks out of that rats' nest of whores that Charity Carstairs set up. Then she makes such a fuss when I push her into the river that someone fishes her out again. Then, when I've got her dead to rights in a deserted field what happens but that ugly soldier with the torn-up face comes, and I've got no choice but to run."

"You're forgetting I kicked you in the bollocks," Emma said helpfully. "You must admit that slowed you down a bit."

The look in Collins's tiny dark eyes promised a particularly evil retribution, but otherwise he ignored her. "And now everything's set in motion. No one has any idea we're behind this—the girl lives a dangerous life, after all, and it's no wonder she's had a few accidents. And these old buildings are bound to be firetraps, and what do whores know about anything? One untended candle and the place goes up in flames, taking everyone with it."

"You said it was foolproof before." Fenrush sounded like a sullen child, deprived of a sweet.

"Well, we learned from that, didn't we? Everything's been taken care of, all nice and tidy like, and the men we sent from London said everything was ready. The fire should burn so hot there won't be anything left of the whores to bury. We've got some of them new Rockite kettles to bring the coals, and it won't be but the work of a moment to move the debris to the doors, trapping them inside. It'll burn, all right, and her and all the others with it."

"What if one of the women wakes up and tries to stop you?"

Collins let out an exasperated sigh. "I'll club her senseless and get on with me work. But I knows how to be quiet. You don't live to be my age without a lot of experience—that's why you hired me so long ago, and I haven't failed you yet."

"She's still alive," Fenrush pointed out fretfully.

"She won't be for long."

The carriage was slowing, and Emma's empty stomach began to tighten. The drive to Suffolk, usually endless, now seemed to have been over in a blink. She had no idea how long she'd been unconscious, she only knew that they were already nearing their destination. There was still some light left outside—it had been early when she'd stumbled into the hospital, and while shadows were looming it was not yet dark enough to enact the events that Collins had obligingly outlined. They would have to wait, and waiting gave her time to think, to plan.

She didn't want to die. Brandon wouldn't like it, and Melisande would be distraught. If she simply disappeared, as she'd first intended, they would be angry rather than grieving, and they would both recover.

Even more important, she didn't want the Gaggle to die in the flames set by a madman. Each and every one of them had been through enough horrors, and they'd dragged themselves up and out of an almost inescapable world. She knew far too well that they'd already paid dearly for a life that hadn't been of their own choosing, and she was damned if she was going to let them suffer any more.

Not the least, of course, was her iron-hard determination not to let monsters like Fenrush and Collins win in the end. Too often the poor unfortunates, usually women, suffered while the men enjoyed the results of their cruelty. She wasn't going to let that happen again.

The carriage pulled to a stop, and Fenrush slid down the window, letting in a blast of chilly, wonderful fresh air, enough to make a small dent in the miasma of the cramped space. She had her first look at the coachman, and she knew he wouldn't be of any help. If anything he looked more evil than Collins, and he merely glanced at her, as if a bound woman was normal in his daily duties.

"I've parked us in an outcropping," he said, standing in the open door of the carriage. "No one will see us in the shadows, and it should be full dark in an hour. The lads will be meeting us with the kettles just before midnight—you want me to go check on them?"

"Yes," said Fenrush.

"No need," said Collins at the same time. "They know what will happen to them if they fail me—that little chippie from the big house paid the price already. No one wants to end with their parts scattered from here to the coast like she did."

The coachman looked unfazed. "I expect not. No worries. This is all going to go smooth as silk. You've got the best working with you."

Fenrush sniffed, and Collins chuckled. "I know I do, me lad. And you know what might happen if something goes amiss. I made the mistake of working with amateurs before. Wouldn't do it again."

The man jerked his head in her direction. He had a small, rat-like face, a long, thin nose and broken teeth. "She up for some entertainment before we set to work? She's a prime piece."

Emma held herself very still, refusing to look at him. She'd survive if he raped her. She'd survived worse.

But Collins shook his head. "Himself says we're to keep our hands off her. Don't rightly know why, but there it is."

Fenrush had lapsed into a mumbling silence, ignoring everything, and Emma's stomach tightened further. Too bad she didn't have limitless food to spew over everyone, but she hadn't eaten much in the last few days. She'd been too busy thinking about Brandon.

He might never know what happened to her. If the flames were as hot as Collins had said, there might be no way to identify the bodies, and she would be buried as one of the nameless women who had tried to better themselves. In a way it would be fitting.

But that wasn't going to happen. She glanced at Collins from beneath half-closed eyelids, then at Fenrush. He still had the surgical saw tucked into his pants, more visible with the loss of his fancy coat, and she suspected he might have more of his surgical tools tucked on him.

Fenrush lifted his head and caught her watching him. She quickly lowered her gaze, but he was alert now, sounding marginally more rational. "How long do we have to wait?" he said plaintively.

"No more than a few hours," Collins said. "Why don't you sleep a bit while we wait? Beedle, you go make sure the fires at the back doors are ready to go. It's late enough that no one would be using them, and I don't wants any more mistakes."

"There'd better not be any," Fenrush growled, his eyes narrowing, and Emma accepted his mood swing with resignation. She'd have an easier time of it if she only had to deal with Collins, but no matter what the circumstances she had every intention of surviving, and saving the Gaggle as well.

"What say we take her out into the woods and have a little fun with her?" Collins suggested, seemingly ever hopeful. "We've got hours of waiting."

Fenrush shook his head, and Collins made an exasperated sound. "Why not? She'll be dead by midnight—why not enjoy her in the meantime while we wait? You can't have any reason to spare her."

The man outside the coach was looking avid, his mouth open, and Emma could barely control her shiver of disgust.

"No!" Fenrush snapped again.

"Why not? We can all take turns, mebbe have 'er at the same time. . ."

"I can't!" The words came out in a cry, followed by a shocked silence. Then Fenrush managed to calm himself. "I find I am unable to perform adequately, due to my illness," he said in precise little voice, "and I have no intention of sitting and watching."

"You've liked it well enough before," Collins pointed out, unmoved.

"Do not dare to question me!" Fenrush cried. "You will follow my orders or I'll find someone who will."

The possibility of that was far-fetched, but no one remarked on it. "Yes, sir," Collins muttered, then lumbered down from the coach to join his accomplice. "Just keep her company, Mr. Fenrush, and we'll be back."

The voices, the coarse laughter faded quickly, and she was alone with the man who wanted her dead. She raised her lids and looked at him calmly, racking her brain for distraction, but words failed her when she saw his face.

Tears were pouring down his fat cheeks, splashing onto his soiled shirt and stained waistcoat. His lower lip was trembling, like a child's, but he made no sound whatsoever, he simply sat there and wept.

She blinked, momentarily at a loss. Was he regretting the horrible things he'd done, the things he'd planned? Should she feel compassion for him as well, for a life gone so terribly wrong?

Fuck that, she thought succinctly, using the word she'd always tried to avoid, as she eyed the surgical saw. Could she throw herself on him, somehow manage to grasp the knife with her bound wrists and free herself before he could stop her? Was that her best chance, when the two more able-bodied men weren't around? How likely would it be that she'd succeed?

And then Fenrush raised his weeping face, his eyes meeting hers, and she froze. Those eyes, overflowing with tears, held no sorrow. Instead, they held a mad glee, and Emma knew she was going to die.

CHAPTER 28

"You'll kill yourself!" Noonan shouted at him.

The light carriage was in a ditch, one wheel thrown a dozen feet away, and if they hadn't jumped in the last minute they both would have been dead. That wouldn't have helped Emma, Brandon thought, scrambling down into the ditch to help Noonan release the panicked horses.

"We survived, didn't we?" he shot back, running a soothing hand along the back of one of a matched set of bays Benedick kept for the light, fast curricle. It took all he had to keep from communicating his panic to the gelding, but he knew he had to take the time or he'd end up sabotaging himself again.

"If you hadn't been driving like a madman and taken that corner too fast we wouldn't have lost that wheel. Now we've got to find a new carriage somewhere, and we're miles from the nearest village."

"No, we don't," Brandon said grimly, leading one of the high-strung horses up the embankment. "If you tell me you can't ride without a saddle I won't believe you."

Noonan looked horrified in the early evening shadows. "It's a carriage horse, lad! Not one for holding your weight or mine!"

"They're strong enough to pull the curricle with two passengers.

You can stay behind—I won't. We're still a good two hours from Rippington, and I need to stop that bastard before it's too late."

He surveyed the horse for a moment. It was nervous, eyeing him warily. He'd ridden bareback often enough as a child—he and his brothers had tumbled around their country estates like wild savages, his mother used to say, and his sister had joined in as well. They would ride, swim in the ocean, play bandits in the forests and wizards and fairies in the caves. He'd been Oxtaine the Foolhardy, Benedick's name for him, and he'd need every ounce of that foolhardiness to get to Emma in time.

Noonan was watching him, skepticism writ on his face. "He's not used to being ridden—he'll try to buck you off."

"He can try." He surveyed the horse, which stood at least fifteen hands. Somehow taking a flying leap at a pony in a field had always seemed simple enough when he and his siblings had been ready for a lark. It no longer looked quite so easy.

"And how are you planning to get up on that big monster? His back is as high as your shoulders."

He swung his head to look at Noonan. "You're giving me a leg up."

"And if I refuse?"

"Then I pummel you and climb on your fallen body," he snapped.

"You and what army? You may be bigger and younger but you've forgotten one thing."

"And what's that?" said Brandon.

"I fight dirty." Noonan then let out an exaggerated sigh. "You don't even know the girl is there—it's just a guess."

"I know," he said, completely certain. He didn't dare consider any alternative.

Noonan scowled. "There's no making you see sense, is there?"

"Is it sensible to let the woman I love be murdered?"

"Love her, do you? You should have thought of that earlier," the man grumbled. "I wish to bloody Christ we'd never left the Highlands. Our peaceful life is at an end. You'll be saddled not only with a wife but a mistress as well, one you lo-o-o-ve," he mocked the word, "and we'll never have any peace again."

"There'll only be one woman in Scotland, or wherever she chooses to live, one wife, and that will be Emma."

"You'll marry a whore?" Noonan took a step backward. "Don't give me that look, my boy. I'm only saying what everyone else will."

"To hell with you and everyone else," Brandon said succinctly. "Are you helping me or getting in the way?"

He half expected more argument, and time was flying by. At least Aristide, the gelding, was growing calmer by the minute. He wouldn't like being mounted, but he'd survive it well enough. He was a strong horse with good heart, enough to carry him the last two hours of hell-bent riding. He had to be.

But Noonan moved forward and cupped his hands, and Brandon didn't hesitate, vaulting onto the horse's back and landing as lightly as he could. Aristide jerked, but settled quickly enough, and Brandon gathered the overlong reins, looping them around his wrist. He glanced back at Noonan, ready to tell him goodbye, but the old man had already managed to get himself onto the back of Aristide's twin, Apollo, with the grace of a man born to it, and Brandon remembered that Noonan was the best horseman he knew.

"Don't just stare at me, you fool boy! Time's a-wasting. We've got to rescue the maiden. No, not exactly a maiden," he added judiciously.

"If I weren't in such a damned hurry I'd plant you one for that," he warned, letting Aristide settle himself as he turned him toward the shadowed road ahead.

"I'd like to see you try. Stop jawing." Before he could even move, Noonan shot past him, Apollo taking his rider with grace and speed. Brandon dug in his heels and leaped after them, keeping his mind a merciful blank, concentrating only on the horse beneath him, the darkening road, and the absolute need for speed. If he thought about what Emma might be going through, what might have already happened to her, he'd go mad. All he could do was ride and throw caution to the winds.

EMMA FELL ASLEEP. She would have thought such a thing would be impossible, trapped in a fetid conveyance stinking of death and putrefaction, a madman for company, two murderers roaming outside, but exhaustion hit her. She knew full well the dangers of a head injury such as the one she might have incurred when she smacked down on the marble floor, and her nausea could have been a sign of concussion. Fortunately there were more probable causes. Her head ached, but not unbearably, and her masses of thick hair would have provided better protection than one of those padded helmets worn into battle. Even a charlatan like Fenrush would have noticed if her eyes were uneven, another sure sign, and the chance of being concussed was only a minor concern when faced with imminent death. She simply closed her mind to the noise Fenrush was making, closed her eyes to the sight of him, and slept.

"Where's he gone to now?" The hissed question came from Collins, and she opened her eyes to a darkness that was almost absolute. She was alone in the carriage—she could see just enough to ascertain that, and Collins was talking with his partner in crime just beyond the door of the closed carriage. She didn't move, observing what she could from her position tucked in the corner of the seat. The sky was inky black— no trace of a moon broke through, no stars provided any relief. The wind was rustling through the leaves, and the scent of a coming storm brought back her childhood in the country.

Her entire body ached from being held in constraints for so long. She jerked at her wrists, and the rope tightened painfully. Her instincts told her it was well before midnight, but she could smell burning coals, and she knew they would put their plan into action before long. She had limited time before they put their filthy hands on her and dragged her out, but in the meantime she had to do everything she could. No errant knight would save her, since the errant knight in her life had no idea where she'd gone. It was just as well—she would never want to risk his life. She'd never really expected much of a happy ending for herself—this was simply in keeping with the choices she had made.

She moved her fingers, trying to work on the rope that bound her wrists. It was covered in something both warm and wet, and she knew it was her own blood. She dragged the rough hemp over her wrists again and again, enough that the moisture was making the bonds ties slippery around her flesh. It hurt like hell, but the more blood she could summon the more chance she had of pulling her hands through the knots, and she kept at it, sawing at her wrists with ruthless efficiency, until one hand finally slid free.

She swallowed her gasp of relief, pausing for a moment, then tugged her other hand free. Her arms were still clamped to her side by the heavier rope, and the knot for that was in the back. She squirmed, trying to dislodge it, but it was useless. Whoever had bound her had done so with ruthless efficiency—she was already having trouble breathing. She was trapped and freeing her hands had done her absolutely no good whatsoever.

And then she saw Fenrush's abandoned surgical saw. It was on the seat opposite her—wedged into the back, and he probably hadn't even realized he'd lost it. Collins wouldn't know either, and she'd take any possible advantage she could get. She held very still, listening.

Neither of the men had taken any notice of her quiet exertions— they were too busy searching for Fenrush, who apparently had disappeared while she slept. If he was truly gone would they still follow his instructions, place her, untouched, inside the building, or would they do as they had wanted, rape and kill her and abandon her body by the side of the road? If she managed to gain possession of the saw it was, at least, something, but as a weapon it was hardly optimal. It could, however, cut through the ropes that bound her body.

She had to cross to the other seat without making a sound, a daunting prospect, but the longer she hesitated the harder it would be. She pushed herself up with her feet and tumbled across the narrow space, landing face first on the seat, her knees hitting the floor hard, noisily. She held still, listening, but her captors weren't rushing the carriage, and she had to assume they were out of earshot. She tried to push up, but her knees were weak, shaking, barely able to support her body as she tried to lever herself up onto the seat, and she wanted to weep in frustration.

She couldn't do it. Her cramped body couldn't hold her, and sounds were coming from the surrounding darkness, moving toward the carriage. With one last, desperate push she managed to trap the saw with her sleeve before tumbling back onto the floor.

A moment later the door swung open. "In a hurry, Mrs. Cadbury?"

Collins asked in a jovial tone. "Wouldn't want to keep a lady waiting." He hauled her out into the damp night air, the saw still shoved awkwardly up her sleeve. It split the fabric and cut into her skin, but there was already so much blood from her abraded wrists that it hardly mattered.

In the darkness, blood was black.

She was dropped on the ground, and she let out an involuntary cry of pain as the saw bit deeper into her arm. "Can't have that, can we, Beedle? You got something you could put in her mouth to keep her quiet."

The smaller man grasped the front of his trousers suggestively, grinning. "That I do."

"I wouldn't try it. She'll bite yer John Thomas clean off," Collins advised him, and Beedle squirmed.

She tried to scream, but Collins moved fast for such a big man, clamping a hand over her face, holding her jaw shut as she struggled, making strangled sounds of rage. He was too strong to fight, and he pushed some wadding into her mouth, almost choking her, before he hauled her up and over his massive shoulder.

"Bring the old man," he added, moving forward into the darkness, and Beedle nodded. From her ignominious position she could see Fenrush huddled on the ground, making snuffling noises that reminded her of a pig hunting for truffles, and then Collins swung away, and she had no choice but to try to retain her balance without him feeling the steel of the surgical tool against her skin.

She waited. They were an eerie procession in the moonless night, moving through the trees, the rustling of the wind covering any sound they might make. It had to be past midnight already, and if their plan was to burn the Dower House with Rockite kettles, then they would have to go back and secure the pots of coals they had planned to use, leaving her time to work her way out of her bonds and warn the women.

It was a vicious way to fight against the helpless. Rockite kettles had come from the farmer rebellion of the fictional Captain Rock against the greedy landlords, and when flung at a structure they burned with infernal intensity. If they managed to fling them at the Dower House the women would be trapped.

She couldn't let that happen. When Collins halted, sliding her down his body with revolting lasciviousness, she didn't dare wait any longer.

She tried to scream past the gag, she thrashed and struggled and made as much noise as she could manage, hoping it might wake the sleeping house, but she already knew it was too little to help. Collins's big fist came down, and the darkness caved in around her.

"NEXT TIME you want to rescue a damsel in distress, would ye at least plan it better?" Noonan demanded as they pulled their horses to a halt by the front gate of Starlings House. "I don't suppose we can get a dram of whiskey before we go haring off?"

"You can do what you want, as long you alert the household and send help to the Dower House," Brandon said grimly.

"I'll stay with ye." Noonan was long suffering but determined.

"No, you won't, you'll get help," Brandon snapped. "I don't know what they have planned, how many men are involved, but I can at least hold them off until help arrives."

"Lad, you don't even know if she's here."

"She is." Brandon stared into the darkness. He could just barely see the outlines of the Dower House, but his instincts, which had kept him alive in conflicts that had killed all those around him, told him he wasn't wrong. "Get moving!"

"One man against an army?" Noonan scoffed, but there was no missing the real concern in his voice.

She was here and she was still alive—he knew it in his bones, and suddenly all his fear vanished. There was time, he could save her, and relief and exultation filled him, wiping away his exhaustion. He would rip the heart out of anyone who had tried to harm her, he would take her to safety and never let her go again.

"No one's going to hurt her," he said, turning Aristide toward the winding road to the dower house. "I won't let them."

"Ye're daft," Noonan said, but he was already moving toward the main house, Apollo picking up speed.

Brandon started forward. He couldn't very well thunder up to the rescue—even if he had enough rage to destroy an army he was still only one man, and he needed the element of surprise. He nudged the poor, exhausted horse onto the grass to muffle the sounds of his hooves and moved forward into the inky blackness.

CHAPTER 29

Emma could smell fire. She slowly lifted her head, ignoring the pain, and looked around her in the darkness. She was in a room, not one she recognized, and she'd been secured to a chair, upright. There were windows—the patch of dark sky was still marginally lighter than the walls, and she tried to jerk her chair forward. The house was silent, but the scrape of the wood against the floor was too soft to rouse anyone. She squirmed, trying to see if she still retained possession of the small surgical saw, and a gratifying tear at her skin reassured her. She would end up covered with scars like a pirate, assuming she managed to survive this night, and she didn't care.

She must be in the Dower House, presumably in one of the attics. The house was still and silent—everyone would be asleep, and there was no terrifying crackle of flames licking at ancient timber.

But she could smell fire.

She jerked again in the chair, trying to make noise, making it thump against someone's ceiling, but she couldn't lever herself up enough for a satisfying sound. She tried it again, when a soft, eerie voice came to her out of the darkness.

"It's useless to fight it, Mrs. Cadbury. This is payment for your sins."

She froze, squinting through the shadows, and finally focused on Mr. Fenrush sitting placidly by the window, watching her out of glittering eyes. For a moment she was disoriented—what was he doing there? The fires had been set—she could smell the slow burning start of them—and he was still in the house.

She worked with her tongue, trying to dislodge the gag, but the piece of fabric was huge, and she was getting nowhere. She rocked in the chair again, hoping the repeated thumps might rouse someone, but she didn't hold out any great hope. She knew from experience that these women slept like the dead—too many nights of working had trained them to sleep well and deeply when afforded the chance, and it had always been absurdly difficult to rouse them for morning classes in London. No one would waken to a muffled thump.

She would have to be more creative. Fenrush hadn't moved, seeming relaxed and comfortable, and she tried to move her hand around to loosen the saw from sleeve.

She couldn't move. The new ropes that bound her to the chair had simply been added to the old ones, and all the squirming and twisting and fidgeting got her nowhere. She couldn't move her hand enough to reach the knife.

"You're wondering why I'm here, Mrs. Cadbury?" Fenrush said in that still eerily polite voice. "I wanted to see you burn. Collins thought it an excellent idea, though I expect I shall have to reprimand him when we return to London. He's become much too impertinent. I can't abide impertinent servants."

He might have been discussing the dismally crowded condition in the women's ward, as he often did. His solution was usually to set the women out on the streets to fend for themselves while he made room for male patients with such debilitating conditions as a mild case of gout, just as Emma had fought him tooth and nail. His current logic made no sense—he could hardly watch her burn without succumbing to the conflagration himself.

She jerked the chair again, but he didn't move, placidly watching her as he might observe a patient. "It's too late," he murmured. "The fires are set."

His voice was softly cheerful, but she ignored him, concentrating on reaching the saw. The smell was stronger now, and She knew it wouldn't be long before she heard the sounds of crackling flames, and by then it would be too late.

With sudden determination she flung her body onto the floor, making as much noise as she could, loud enough to wake the dead, she hoped, and the saw slid out of her sleeve, close enough to grasp. She rolled, banging the chair while she did so, kicking at the floor, and ended up with the saw clutched her fist.

Fenrush hadn't moved from his spot near the window. She'd seen dementia in late-stage syphilis cases, and he had clearly slid into that foggy world, but she didn't make the mistake of thinking him harmless. When madness hit, patients could be extremely violent.

She twisted her wrists, managing to reach the first layer of ropes imprisoning her, and she sawed through it with surprising ease. No wonder she seemed to be bleeding everywhere—the tool was razor sharp, and as it severed the second course of ropes it tore into her dress as well.

Once her arms were free, the pain of blood returning to her muscles almost made her pass out. It ripped through her, and she wanted to scream, needed to scream. She yanked the gag out of dry mouth and shrieked at the top of her lungs.

"Fire! Get out of the house. Get out, get out!" she shouted, reaching down to free her legs and ankles. At last she could hear movement down below—voices and cries, as the women awoke.

Fenrush was still watching her. "It won't do them any good," he said in a sweet, practical voice. "There are fires at each of the doors. There's no way out for them—I made sure of it. The whores must be destroyed by flame, so sayeth the Lord."

She tried to push herself up from the floor, using the overturned chair, but she fell back as blood came screaming into her muscles. "No, he doesn't," she snapped. "I had most of the Bible memorized by the time I was twelve, and nowhere does it say whores must be destroyed. Almost every time they're mentioned someone is saving them, and it's only the Great Whore of Babylon who gets eaten and burned, and she's not even a woman, she's a city."

Why in heaven's name was she arguing about church doctrine when she could hear the increasing noise of the flames, the cries of the women? There was now an orange glow in the window above Fenrush's body. She had to move, and now.

"Fornicator," Fenrush said, his voice rising. "*You* are the Whore of Babylon, filth and degradation and everything that is evil. . ."

"Like murdering men for profit?" She needed to shut her mouth, concentrate of getting out of there, helping the occasionally feather-headed women to get to safety, not enflame a madman.

It was too late. Fenrush stood up, a fluid movement for someone of such wasted corpulence, and moved toward her, madness in his eyes. She tried to rise one more time, only to collapse again as he fell on top of her. He was clawing at her, screaming at her, tearing at her skin, and she managed to pull her knees up, just enough, to lever him off her, as she shoved up with the saw and sliced open his throat.

It was quick and simple—she'd cut into flesh a hundred times with a blade such as this, and there was no squeamishness in her nature. He struggled, falling back to clutch at his slashed neck, but it was too late. He was still kicking the floor when she finally managed to stumble to her feet and find the door.

She heard the hysterical cries from down below. The fire had reached the Gaggle, and nothing mattered, not pain or weakness, as she threw herself down the narrow stairs, into the blazing heat, to get to them.

·

The Dower House was on fire, flames soaring up into the night sky, and Brandon's last bit of calm deserted him. Flinging himself from the horse, he started running toward the conflagration. Flames had engulfed the front entrance, and he could see women at the windows, trapped, desperate, and he knew Emma had to be among them, fighting for her life. He had to get to her, he had to get all of them out, he had to. . .

The cudgel smashed down out of nowhere, but he managed to jerk out of the way at the last minute, the blow that would have crushed his skull numbing his shoulder instead. It was the huge man he'd faced in the muddy field a few short days ago—he'd know those button-black eyes anywhere.

"Now, we can't have you interfering with our nice bonfire," the oaf said in a cajoling voice. "After all the trouble we've gone to. You messed with my work once—I can't have that again, can I, Beedle?"

The man with him, smaller, compact and hard looking, grinned. "That's right. He won't be no problem, though—the gentry don't know how to fight. I'll take him—you go ahead."

Brandon didn't move, a dangerous stillness that wiser men would have recognized. "Where is Mrs. Cadbury?" he said softly.

"Oh, she be dead by now," Beedle said. "We put her up in the attics with Mr. Fenrush, and if he hasn't killed her the smoke has. Unless he decided to take 'is pleasure with her, which is unfair, if you ask me, as he wouldn't let us touch the whore, and. . ."

He killed them both, without thinking, so fast neither could react, breaking Beedle's neck with one swift move, yanking the cocked pistol from the already dead man's hand and shooting the giant in the eye. He didn't even wait to see him fall. He knew how to kill like a savage – the horror of the Afghan war had taught him that much, and no one was a match for him in his desperation.

The flames had already begun to eat through the front of the house, blocking the entrance when he reached it, but the fires were smaller by the garden. He didn't hesitate, yanking the flaming brush away from the side, ignoring the fire that was scorching his hands, ignoring the heat that blistered his face. He had to get to Emma. If she was up in the attics then that was where he would go, and if they were trapped, so be it. He wouldn't live without her—it was that simple.

The door was on fire, with the women on the other side, screaming for help, and he had no choice. Reaching out, he caught the glowing door handle and yanked it open, and the women tumbled out, the gaggle of them, beating at flames as their skirts caught fire, helping each other, crying and howling and making such a racket that there was no way Emma could have heard his shouts.

He didn't hear that help had arrived, carriages racing down the drive, wagons and horses as well as the entire Starlings household. He caught one of the women, the big one from the kitchen, and stopped her. "Have you seen Emma?" he shouted over the noise.

The woman was dazed, uncomprehending for a moment, and then her eyes narrowed in her soot-covered face. "She's with Polly."

A shaft of relief speared through him—she wasn't dead. But he had to make sure she was safe, touch her, hold her.

"Where?"

To his horror, the woman jerked her head over her shoulder toward the burning doorway. "In there."

He didn't draw breath, but flung himself into the conflagration, smoke blinding him, fire licking at his heels. He screamed Emma's name, but his desperate voice was swallowed up in the roar of the fire.

He could still hear better than anyone, and the sound of the cough reached his ears as he was about to head up the stairs. He whirled around, peering through the smoke, searching through the rooms until he saw a huddled pile of skirts near a window. Emma.

And then he was on his knees beside her, trying to pull her into his arms, but she was holding the still body of a woman, so tightly, and he knew the girl was dead.

"Let her go, love," he said softly. "You can't help her anymore."

Emma looked up at him, and she was beautiful. Her face was scratched, bruised, and she was covered with blood, as if she'd taken a bath in the stuff, and he wanted so badly to snatch her to him, carry her out of there.

"I can't leave her." Her voice was so raw he knew she must have breathed in dangerous amounts of smoke. "She was afraid of fires."

The woman in her arms had the pale color of death, but she didn't appear to have suffered an injury. The flames were closing in on them, but he knew panic wouldn't move Emma.

"What happened?"

"She broke her neck," Emma said simply. "She was so terrified she fell on the stairs. I can't leave her here, Brandon."

"All right then, love, we'll take her with us." He rose, caught the nearest piece of furniture, and crashed it through the window. The flames burst into the room, fed by the air, but he'd had no other choice. "Let me have her."

For a moment Emma wouldn't release her, but there was no way he could carry them both. Finally she let go, and Brandon scooped the dead woman up into his arms.

He'd carried dead weight before, always a fellow soldier, and this woman seemed light as a feather. He moved toward the window, planning to drop her onto the surrounding grass as gently as he could, but people were already there, arms reaching out, and he placed the body into them, then turned to Emma.

She was still sitting on the floor, a bloody, smoky, stunned mess, and she'd never been more beautiful. "Shall we go?" he said gently.

She looked up at him, and then nodded, trying to rise to her feet. Her legs wouldn't hold her, but it didn't matter, he simply scooped her up, and there was no way he was ever letting go of her again. The men outside had brought a pump machine, and they were working on the front of the building, dowsing the flames, so he simply climbed through the empty window frame, dropping down, Emma still in his arms. He had her, and she was safe, and nothing else mattered.

CHAPTER 30

They had taken her away from him. Brandon would have hit any man who tried, but they were women—the Gaggle and his sister-in-law—and he had no choice but to release her into their loving arms, to turn back and join the men fighting the inferno.

It hadn't been just men. Those of the Gaggle who weren't tending to Emma, had joined the bucket brigade, along with his supposed fiancée and her companion. Frances Bonham's sleeves were rolled up, her hair mussed, she was looking efficient and determined, and for the first time he'd admired her. She and Miss Trimby would make an admirable couple, even if they had to hide themselves from the world.

But three days later, he still hadn't set eyes on Emma. He paced his room for the seventh time, his booted feet loud on the floor. Melisande had put him in the old bachelors' quarters, a wing of the building that some previous owner had added to keep young men from young women, and it was doing an admirable job of keeping him from Emma. He was in the furthest room from the main house, and for the first day he'd allowed others to constrain him, his hands clumsy from the bandages that covered them, his throat and chest aching from the smoke he'd swallowed. It suited his appearance admirably, the good side of his face now covered with bruises, burns . . . but then, Emma didn't think it was his good side, did she?

He stopped pacing abruptly, and Noonan looked up from his seat across the room where he was carving a piece of wood, dropping shavings all over the valuable Persian carpet. "What's on your mind, me boy? Mooning over your tart again?"

Brandon glowered at him. "If my hands weren't useless I'd give you the thrashing you deserve."

Noonan simply laughed. "You wouldn't hurt an old man, now, would you?"

"I thought better of you."

Noonan didn't have the grace to look abashed. "You really have a desperate case of it, don't you? You always jump to the bait like a starving trout. I don't hold the girl's past against her—women in her line of work are among the most honest I've ever known. I'm not as impressed with her since then, of course. I don't hold with 'good works' and surgeons are nothing but butchers. I'd be watching myself around her. She could slice off something vital if she got mad enough." He chuckled to himself.

Brandon shook his head, giving up. He knew what Noonan was doing—of course he did. It was exactly what he had done for the last three years—taunt him, goad him, insult him and everything he held dear in order to get him moving. It had always worked. But now he was strangely reluctant to break the stalemate. Emma would be safe as long as Melisande was looking after her, and Benedick had sworn to him that Emma's injuries, were healing rapidly. She should be ready to travel by the end of the week.

But travel where—that was the question. She loved him. They both knew it, and yet he still wasn't certain he'd won her. She'd run off that morning after they'd made love, clearly not intending to return, and even though she'd ended in his arms, the truth was he hadn't been able to rescue her. She'd had to do that herself. She'd fallen into his arms like a woman coming home, but still he wasn't convinced.

She must know his ridiculous engagement was ended—Frances had requested a visit with him, and with Miss Trimby an impassive observer she had quietly but firmly broken their short-lived engagement, saving him the necessity of doing it himself. But Emma had made no effort to see him, though Benedick said she was already up and about, and every time he inquired after her he was informed that she wasn't up to receiving visitors. He wasn't a visitor, God curse it, but he had no intention of making a scene, and that strange lassitude still had him in its grip. If he didn't force the issue there was still hope.

"So are you just going to stand there moping?" Noonan demanded, sounding exasperated. "Are you too much of a coward to risk an answer, or even ask the bloody question?"

Brandon looked at him without expression. The old man knew exactly what he'd done in the Afghan War, what he'd seen—cowardice had nothing to do with it. "What do you think?" he said, his voice even.

Noonan snorted. "Then do something about it! She's too good for the likes of you, but she seems to fancy you, so stop wasting time. I'm sick of this soft southern climate!"

Neither of them mentioned that an icy rain was falling, neither of them cared. "Screw my courage to the sticking post, is that it?" Brandon murmured, straightening his shoulders.

Noonan scoffed, no fan of Shakespeare. "That's about the only thing ye'll be screwin' if you don't get a move on."

Brandon laughed, hiding his uneasiness. "You're a pig, Noonan."

"Bog Irish and proud of it," Noonan replied, setting down his carving and rising. "Let's go win the fair lady."

Brandon raised an eyebrow. "You're coming with me?"

"Someone's got to speak for your good character, since you've made a piss-poor effort. Besides, everyone knows when a woman marries she marries the man's man as well."

"I think you might prove the sticking point," Brandon said.

The old man let out a wheezing chuckle. "We'll never know until you ask. You haven't yet, have you?"

"Not in so many words."

"Dunderhead," Noonan said.

"SHE LEFT THREE DAYS AGO." Melisande was glaring at him, his goddaughter snuggled against her ample breasts. Benedick said nothing, standing behind her, but Brandon didn't give a damn if he was feeling guilty.

"And you didn't see fit to inform me?" he demanded in a dangerous voice, bringing a swift frown to his brother's face.

"I'll remind you that's my wife you're addressing in such an uncivil manner," Benedick growled. "And I've always been able to pound you into the ground if need be."

Brandon wasted only a glance on him. "That was a long time ago. You forget—I was a soldier, you weren't."

Benedick's face darkened, but he said nothing—both of them knew he'd had no choice, and it was a low blow, one that shamed Brandon not one whit. He would fight dirty if he needed to. He turned back to Melisande. "Where did she go?" he barked.

Benedick stirred restlessly, but Melisande faced him with cool restraint. "There's no need asking—I won't tell you. I promised her I wouldn't. If she wanted to see you she wouldn't have run."

"Don't be an idiot," he snapped. "When it comes to me she does nothing but run, starting back when I was in hospital."

Her mouth thinned. "I gather you finally remembered, you spoiled dolt!"

"Jesus Christ, does everyone in this household know my business?" he cried in frustration.

"We know *Emma's* business," Melisande corrected. "She's one of our own, and you're nothing but an outsider."

"My dear. . ." Benedick began, his forehead creased, but Melisande was on a roll.

"You treated her like garbage," she snapped. "She loved you, and you didn't even have the grace to remember her, you stupid fool. She *loved* you."

He wasn't about to argue with another woman about this—it was Emma he had to convince. "Where did she go?" he ground out one more time.

"If she wants to be found then it will be up to her," Melisande said. "In the meantime why don't you get your sorry self to London? Your parents are returning from the Americas and could use your assistance."

Brandon didn't need to glance at Benedick to guess his reaction to such malarkey. "The day my father, or my mother, needs my assistance will be a cold day in hell," Brandon muttered. He whirled to face his brother. "Can't you make your wife tell me where she went?"

There was faint amusement in Benedick's eyes. "I couldn't if I tried," he said, "and I'm smart enough not to even attempt it. You're on your own with this one. Maybe our father will have some advice for you—I've got none."

PUNCHING a wall hadn't helped his burned hands, neither had riding to London wearing an old pair of gardener's gloves, the only thing that could fit around his bandages. He'd felt nothing but savage, impotent fury the entire way, and even Noonan had been hard pressed to keep up with him. It wasn't until he looked at his mother's clear, calm face that the rage left him, and he simply threw himself in her lap, shaking.

Charlotte Spenser Rohan stroked her youngest son's long hair and murmured soothing words, while the slightly disreputable Marquess looked on with sympathetic amusement, catching her eye over their son's bowed head.

"Love, my dear Charlotte, is a mean bitch," he murmured, looking down at his son.

"Yes, my dear," she said. "Do you not think it worth all the trouble?"

His eyes smiled into hers, glowing with a never-extinguished flame. "Allow me to answer that question when our little one goes to bed."

Brandon pulled himself away from his mother's gentle hands, glaring at both of them. "I don't wish to disturb your indecent advances to each other, but I'm the one with the problem here," he growled.

"So you are," Adrian, first Marquess of Taverstock, agreed. "Go away and fix it. Your mother and I wish to continue our . . . er . . . discussion without an obstreperous child interfering."

"Damn it!" he cried, pulling away to glare at his unrepentant father.

"Don't you understand? I've lost her!" Hopelessness washed over him. "I love her, and I've lost her."

"So Benedick informs me. You rather botched it this time, didn't you?" Adrian said smoothly. "Well, we all do stupid things on occasion, don't we love?" He addressed his wife.

Charlotte's mouth curled up in a cool, secretive smile. "A little patience will go a long way, Brandon. Give her time. She sounds like a sensible woman. If you're worthy of her she'll come back."

Brandon's eyes narrowed. "Exactly what do you know about her?"

"Everything," his father said cheerfully. "Your brother Charles will have a temper tantrum about it, which is recommendation enough to my mind. Much as I love him, I still can't fathom how we ever managed to produce such a pompous, judgmental prig." He glanced at Charlotte. "Are you certain you didn't have a mésalliance with a Quaker when I wasn't looking? Maybe one slipped into the Heavenly Host when we didn't realize it."

His mother laughed. Normally any mention of the Host would have aroused his attention, not because of his own involvement with them but for the long-shrouded details of his parents' courtship. He could no more picture his mother as part of that degenerate band than he could the Archbishop of Canterbury. His reprobate father was, of course, another matter.

But he didn't care. He had to find Emma before it was too late, before she was so lost he would never see her again.

"You have to help me find her."

"You'll find her," his father said, as sympathetic as a hedgehog. "If you deserve her."

"You'll find her," his mother said. "In time."

CHAPTER 31

Much to Noonan's disgust it was five weeks before Brandon finally returned to the Highlands. All hope had faded, and his father's wry remarks were less painful than his mother's warm sympathy. There had been no trace of Emma anywhere, not at the hospital that was quickly scrambling to replace two of their missing surgeons, not at her neat rooms in that wretched area by the docks, not at the newly restored Dovecote in Upper Rippington or the charities of London. She had disappeared completely, taking nothing with her but a few medical tomes, and he was beyond desperate. He was also getting nowhere.

Had she somehow managed to take ship for America, or someplace even more exotic? His parents had just returned from a tour of South America—if she'd headed there he might never find her. The east was also a possibility, and the thought that she might decide to head toward India or even Afghanistan filled him with horror. It would be just like her to volunteer as a medic for the army—the military couldn't afford to be too picky. His stomach roiled at the thought, but he wouldn't hesitate. He would find her, no matter where she had gone, he would find her and bring her back.

Fate wouldn't have interfered—not once but twice—if they weren't meant to be together, but winter was closing in. Like it or not, he had to settle a few things in the north before he went after her. He hired men to look for her before he left London, to comb the shipping manifests, with the hope that once he returned there'd be some word of her.

The trip north was endless. They could have gone by carriage, a slower but marginally more comfortable mode of transportation, but he didn't give a damn, and Noonan was impervious to trifles like the weather. The biting rain suited Brandon's mood perfectly, and his mare, Emma—damn, why had he named his horse after her? But of course he had—even in his drug-addled blankness he'd thought of her.

They mostly rode in silence, stopping at inns along the way just long enough to feed and rest the horses, and then they were moving again, over the endless, miserable roads. He barely noticed the changing landscape, as the fallow fields turned rockier, as the trees rose sturdier, the forests grew deeper, the coast wilder. He was in no mood to admire the world around him, he simply needed to get home, lick his wounds like Tammas, his old spaniel, and decide what he could do next. It would make no sense to take the next ship to America if she had set sail for India.

He knew what to do with the reckless anxiety, that wild impulse that drove him. He needed to go home, to the Highlands, where he could be calm and still and make some sense of it all.

It was in the darkest hours of night that they arrived back home, and the gamekeeper's cottage rose against the ebony sky, an unprepossessing building that had somehow managed to become safety to him. He should have had Noonan make arrangements for one of the village women to come in and tidy up—there would be rodent droppings on most surfaces, the fire would be cold and empty, the beds tumbled and the laundry scattered. Normally Noonan would see to things, but neither of them had been paying attention to details when they left, and they'd been gone far longer than Brandon had ever anticipated. There was a light breeze on the air, and he told himself he could almost smell the coming of spring, or what passed for it in this cold, unforgiving climate, and he felt some of the tightness that had been twisting his insides begin to loosen.

God, he loved it here, the wildness, the beauty, the fierce independence of the people in the small village. Unlike other landlords, the Rohans had never participated in the Highland Clearances, uprooting villagers and sending them to the cities to make room for grazing sheep. The Rohans had never had any passion for commerce, and small Glen Bally was self-sufficient if not profitable, and that suited Brandon. This had been the home of his great-grandfather who'd died on Culloden Moor, this was the home of his heart.

Except that his heart had gone wandering, and he had to bring her back.

"You want to start the fire and clean away some of the mess?" Noonan asked as he slid down from his horse with surprising spryness, "or do you fancy taking care of the horses?"

"House," he said.

"You can't cook."

"Neither can you," Brandon shot back, and Noonan chuckled.

"You're right about that, me boy. We'll find food tomorrow— tonight I just want to settle me bones on me own bed."

Brandon managed to laugh as he pushed open the heavy door to the cottage. It was pitch black, but the smell was surprisingly fresh— no stench of mouse piss or rising damp. He found his way to the tinder box and lit a candle, watching as it slowly pushed back the shadows, and he stared around him in surprise before taking the taper and lighting everything he could find to illuminate the place.

Some charitable soul had been there, and recently. There was no dust, no damp ashes but a fresh-laid fire, a spotless table with, good God, spring flowers in a crystal vase that had to have come from Ballykeep itself. The main house had been locked up for decades, but someone had clearly made free with the contents. He supposed he would have to do something about that, and he really didn't want to. He just wanted a few days of peace, for solitary hikes in the woods and long swims in the icy waters that ran through his lands. He had no interest in wasting time dealing with petty thieves.

He'd leave it up to Noonan. If they robbed him blind, so be it. He'd always thought, in some unspecified but rosy future, that he would be bringing his bride there. Then the war had happened, and nothing was the same.

Any right-minded woman would hate it here. It was cold and windy, it rained almost daily, the terrain was rocky and challenging. It was breathtakingly beautiful, but remote, and women liked company, didn't they? They liked society, and shopping, and even if he couldn't imagine Emma ever giving a damn about those things, she'd want a hospital, some place to use her talents and knowledge, and there weren't enough people here to justify one. The last sawbones had been old Dr. Letcher, but since he'd retired and moved south there was no one to see to the problems of the parish, no one he'd been able to bribe into moving there. It took a special person to thrive in the Highlands, and the doctors he knew were too delicate for this rough life.

Emma was far from delicate, but he'd go wherever she wanted him to go, as soon as he could find her. He would follow her if he couldn't go with her, and he would stay near her till the end of their lives.

Noonan had followed him into the front room, looking around him with an odd expression on his face. "Doesn't look half bad," he announced. "One of the local women must have come in and gotten it ready."

"How did they know we were coming?"

Noonan scowled. "How the hell should I know? I've been by your side the entire time we've been gone. Well, perhaps not the entire time, you randy dog, but enough so that I don't know any more than you do."

"At this point I really don't care." Brandon was bone weary—too many days in the saddle. His bad leg had seized up, his bum ached, and he wanted sleep more than life itself. "We'll find out in the morning. I'm for bed."

Noonan nodded, thoughtful. "You go ahead, me boy. It'll take me a while to settle down—you know how I get. I'll have a wee dram, maybe go for a walk. There's a bit of a moon tonight, and I'm feeling restless."

"Suit yourself. Just don't wake me when you go to bed."

"You sleep like a winter bear—nothing wakes you. Get on with you now, and I promise not to slam my door when I come in."

He was right about one thing, Brandon thought. He did sleep too heavily. If he didn't, Emma wouldn't have disappeared on him, twice now. Three times, if one counted the hospital. Every time he got too close she ran, and there was no way he could force her to stay. He was just going to have to hope he could change her mind.

He fell into his bed, his bones aching, his head pounding. It was better than sleeping on the ground, as he and Noonan had been doing the last few days, but only marginally so, and he remembered his own bed, back in London, and the woman who had lain beside him in it. Beneath him. He'd give decades off his life if he could have her in this narrow bed, in the cool damp air.

It wasn't going to happen.

He woke late. He didn't hear Noonan come in—for all he knew the man had been up past dawn, prowling around the estate, walking the hills, drinking whiskey in the cold night air, but he was up and stirring when Brandon wandered into the kitchen. "Where's Tammas?"

Noonan looked up from the food he was cooking, and Brandon could see the bright gold of real Scottish eggs. He'd missed them.

"That fool dog? I haven't seen him. Didn't you leave him with the crofters over by Thorsby?"

"I did. I just thought that since some good fairy seemed to know when we were returning then maybe Tammas would be around as well."

"Don't be worrying about the damned dog," Noonan said severely. "He'll be back sooner or later—you can't get rid of the things. Leave 'em in the forest and they'll beat you back home. Ridiculous creatures!"

Since Noonan was devoted to Tammas, as well as any other dog he happened across, Brandon didn't bother arguing. "Eggs," he said in a tone of satisfaction, heading for the table.

"Not for you, my boy. I only found three and I'm hungry. You might want to go check the big house—someone's been there, and that's a fact."

Brandon looked at the eggs longingly. "You're my man—you take care of it," he said, knowing what Noonan's reaction would be.

The bark of laughter verified it. "And you can go fart in the wind, *milord*."

"Coffee?" he asked plaintively. He *had* smelled it, he knew he had.

"Gone. Maybe you'll find some down at yer big fancy house."

Noonan was being odd, but Brandon didn't give a damn. The old man was crotchety, and argumentative, all fairly standard, but he seemed to be nursing a hidden amusement, and Brandon couldn't begin to fathom why.

He bypassed the chair to move to the open window. Scotland had defied predictions and offered a watery light at the beginning of the day, and he might as well take advantage of it. "It's not so big and fancy as all that, Noonan," he said. "It hasn't been opened in years, and moths and rodents have probably eaten into everything."

"Mebbe not. You ought to check anyway."

"It's waited this long—it can wait till I swim. I need something to wake me up, since there seems to be no coffee," he said pointedly.

"Suit yerself," Noonan said amiably.

If he hoped the small stream would have warmed in the sun he should have known better. Stripping off his clothes, he slid into the icy water, striking out towards the middle before he could think better of it. Tammas usually swam with him, a water dog to his very soul, and once more Brandon wondered where he was. He had the best nose in three counties—he would know that they'd returned. Where was he?

The water was cold enough to freeze his balls off, and he only wished that was a possibility. At least numb them for the next few months or however long it took him to find Emma. He dove under the water, trying to shut his brain off and came up with a sputter. He was already numb, every part of him except the area he didn't want to think about, and if he stayed in the burn's icy embrace much longer he wouldn't be worrying about a thing.

How demoralizing was that—to be found stark naked in a pool of water not much bigger than an ornamental pool on his sister's estate in the Lake District? If he was going to die he'd at least hope for some dignity in the process.

But he had no intention of dying. Pushing himself out of the water, he shook like a wet dog, and the early morning air felt like a warm blanket after the near frozen water.

His chilled body felt better after the long days of riding, reminding him why this was such a good place for him. Even after the icy numbness wore off his leg was much more responsive to his demands.

He would have to figure it out. Surprisingly, the sun was peeking out from behind the ever-present clouds, and he let the water bead up and dry on his skin before dressing in the clean, rough clothes he'd brought with him—breeches and a loose shirt, plus a long waistcoat to keep out the chill. It was a relief not to have to deal with all the fussiness of fashionable clothing—the cravats and tight-fitting coats, the fancy shoes and ridiculous trousers that would rip the moment he went into the woods. He'd learned to get used to them to them—after all, he'd spent most of his life in London and the family estates in the south. At eighteen he'd been a regular dandy.

He'd do whatever was needed. Whether he liked it or not, he wasn't going to spend any more time here than necessary. Noonan was infinitely capable of taking care of things, for all he liked to pretend he was a simple Irish peasant, and he was proving surprisingly amenable to the notion of staying behind. Brandon knew he could leave with a clear mind and conscience.

Noonan was older than he looked, and their breakneck pace of the last week must have taken its toll. Perhaps he was finally learning to accept the inevitable limitations age demanded.

"You're looking all bright and shiny," Noonan observed sourly. There was still no coffee, much to Brandon's sorrow, but there were bannocks on the kitchen dresser that looked fresh, and he picked one up, biting into it with pleasure.

"I'm going back," he announced. "Today."

"Are ye, now?"

He'd expected a more dramatic reaction from the old man, but Noonan continued as he was, puffing on an evil-looking meerschaum pipe.

"And you're staying behind. I need someone to keep an eye on things, make certain the tenants are doing well, check the land, see to Tammas if he ever returns. He's a good dog but he's too much of a burden for the Wallaces to take on."

"The dog's no burden—he earns his keep," Noonan said, mildly outraged. "And he'll turn up, I promise you. He's your devoted slave—

an Irish dog would be more discerning." Noonan was taking this all too casually—something was up.

Brandon narrowed his eyes. "You're not coming with me."

"So you said," Noonan replied, unruffled.

Was the man sick? Noonan never gave up without a fight. "It would be too much for you," Brandon added deliberately, waiting for the explosion.

"That it might be," Noonan said amiably.

Brandon slammed his fists on the table. "That's it—you're dying! Why didn't you tell me?".

Noonan's look of withering disdain was a small reassurance. "Don't be daft! What turned you into such a girl all of a sudden? Did that strumpet cut off your bollocks after all? She's got the skills." He glowered at Brandon. "Go on and hit me then. I can tell you want to, and I'm not some frail old man . . . oof."

Brandon pulled his punch, letting out just enough of his frustration to convince Noonan. "Call her one more name and I'll hold you down while she practices her cutting skills on you."

Noonan let out a rusty chuckle, a truly bizarre occurrence. Noonan never laughed. "Before you go off on your grand adventure you ought to hike down to the big house. Ballykeep's been lying empty for a long time, and if you're off to find your str. . . your true love," he corrected himself with a mock flourish, "then you'd best to see to your duties first."

"I leave that up to you."

Noonan snorted. "Happen I went for a walk last night while you were sleeping. Someone's definitely been in the house."

"See to it," Brandon said briefly. "You're my steward when I'm gone."

"You're not gone yet. Besides, I thought I saw yon Tammas down there. If you don't get him he'll go off looking for you and you'll never see him again."

Brandon hesitated. It was still early—he could reach Ayrshire if he left immediately.

But Ballykeep was more than a responsibility—he loved the old place, every mottled stone, every dirt-streaked window. Nor could he simply walk away from Tammas. When he'd first taken the tiny pup home with him he'd made a promise, not to the tenant farmer who'd bred him, but to the spaniel. He was no longer the man who ignored his responsibilities, he reminded himself. One day wasn't going to make any difference in how fast he was going to find Emma.

"I'll leave tomorrow." He reached for another bannock, then took two. "Where did these come from? They're certainly not from your miserable cooking."

Noonan didn't take offense. "Same place as the clean sheets and the flowers came from."

"And where would that be?" he demanded.

"Go find your damned dog."

The estate of Ballykeep had more than a thousand acres of well-kept tenant farms, for very little had been turned over to the sheep as had been on other estates in Scotland—a move that was profitable for the landowners and so devastating to the crofters and tenant farmers. For all their generations of notorious fecklessness, the Rohans had managed to amass a fairly staggering amount of land and capital, with large estates in Ireland, France, Italy and South America as well as the properties in Scotland and England. Ballykeep was neither the largest nor the most impressive, but he loved it, and his father had given it to him on his twenty-first birthday.

The road from the gamekeeper's cottage was a long, gently sloping drive that led to an impressive first view of the main house. He didn't need to see Ballykeep that way—he knew it in his heart, and instead he took the well-trodden path through the forest, calling for Tammas as he went. His frantic heart had calmed now that he had a plan. He would leave, and he would find her. It was that simple—no other outcome was imaginable. Leaving here again, so soon after he'd returned, would kill him, but he would do it for her. He'd do anything for her.

He crested the rise overlooking the house, and for a shocked moment he was dazzled. The sun, which had been playing a sullen game of hide and seek behind the clouds, had finally decided to change and do what it almost never did.

It was shining. The sun sparkled on the drops of water dripping off the leaves from the early morning mist, it shone from the vast array of windows that lined the front of the ancient house, the gloomy gray stones almost white in the sunlight.

It was shockingly beautiful, this home of his heart, and he was tempted to turn back, to keep that vision of Ballykeep secure, to remember on his travels.

But then the knowledge began to click in his brain. Filthy windows didn't glisten. The old gray stones didn't seem lighter in the sunshine—they actually were.

The massive front door of the house stood open, and he could see people moving around inside, including his blasted dog. Tammas had been sniffing around the freshly potted greenery by the front entrance, lifting his leg when he thought no one was looking, but then the sound of a piercing whistle made the dog lift his silken head and trot obediently into the house.

Brandon moved down the hill so quickly that he fell, twisting his bad leg. He rose again with a curse, ignoring the shaft of pain that sliced through him, and kept moving, not bothering to hide his damned limp. Maybe his mother had decided that opening the house would cheer him up, except that it was impossible that her orders could have arrived before he had.

The first person he saw when he reached the curving entrance was a maid, young, perhaps fifteen, with the bright red hair that was so prevalent in the Highlands.

She stopped dead still, staring at him like he was a ghost. His face, he assumed, but her sudden shy smile shot that theory to hell, and besides, young Scottish girls weren't nearly as squeamish as their English counterparts. It was a hard life up here, and pretty faces and smooth skin meant nothing without a strong back and a willingness to work.

"Mr. Rohan," she said breathlessly. "Welcome home. Everything is in order for you."

He was staring at her like a village idiot, and he quickly shut his mouth. "Ready?" he echoed lamely.

"Oh, dear, should I have called you 'Lord Brandon' then? My

mother said as I should, but the mistress told me not to, and I'm that confused. . ."

His damned mother! He should have known Charlotte Rohan would accomplish the impossible and arrive ahead of him. She hadn't wanted him to go haring off again, and she'd done everything she could to keep him here.

It wasn't enough. "Where's your *mistress?*" he demanded in a dangerous voice. "I have a few words for her."

"Last time I saw her she was in the kitchens. Cook is new, you see, and she was trying to explain simple country cooking. . ."

Brandon walked past her without another word, into the house that smelled of beeswax and honey and the earliest of spring flowers, straight into the kitchens that hadn't been used for more than twenty years. The kitchens that had provided him bannocks this morning, he realized.

It had never looked so good. The massive copper pots were shining, every surface was scrubbed, the ancient flag-stone floor was spotless, and there was only one woman in the vast room, and it wasn't his mother.

Tammas had been trailing at her skirts with abject adoration, but seeing his master was too great a temptation, and he bounded over to him, whining a happy little greeting, dancing around in joy.

And the woman turned around to face him.

She was beautiful, but there had never been a time when Emma Cadbury had been less than stunning, even battered and bruised and covered in mud. Her color was good—in fact, it almost looked like she was blushing. She'd added some healthy weight to her too-thin frame. Her thick dark hair was in some loose topknot, not the severe arrangement she usually favored, and the sun that speared through the windows seemed to capture bright crystalline wetness in her eyes. Emma didn't blush, Emma didn't cry. Emma didn't suddenly appear where she knew he'd come—she ran away.

But she was definitely here, and she was trying very hard not to cry, her smile a bit wobbly, her gray eyes almost panic-stricken.

The maid from the front of the house dashed in, coming to an abrupt halt when she saw him before turning to Emma.

"Beg pardon, mistress, but Mr. Ellis says I was to inform you that Mr. Rohan has arrived. Er . . . that is . . . Lord Brandon . . ."

"Mr. Rohan will do," Brandon said, never taking his eyes off Emma. She was trembling slightly, and he wondered what in the world she was afraid of.

He heard the girl scuttle away as they looked at each other. "Ellis," he said finally. "As in my sister's butler?"

She started to say something, choked, coughed, cleared her throat and began again. "He was tired of the Lake District," she said finally. "And tired of the Scorpion's ramshackle behavior. He wanted a more settled household."

Brandon had been moving closer, slowly stalking her, but she held her ground, when he knew damned well that part of her wanted to cut and run as she always did. For once she held still, her gray eyes huge and uneasy, as if she were a cornered hare. "Mistress?" he said, and Emma's flush disappeared.

"I know that's not appropriate," she said, eyeing him nervously now that he could almost reach her. "But I didn't want to be Mrs. Cadbury and a simple 'miss' would be more difficult to explain."

"You've never been a simple miss in your life. Mistress will do. Lovers. Bane of my existence. Harpy. Mrs. Rohan. Unless you prefer Lady Brandon. I'd think you'd hate that, but I'm game if you happen to want it."

There were tears in her huge gray eyes. The tears he had never seen before spilled over, sliding down her cheeks.

"Brandon, you can't marry me and you know it! The scandal would never go away. I'll stay with you as long as you want me, but I can't marry you. You've worked too hard to throw it all away on someone like me."

"You mean to tell me that you ran off and nearly got yourself killed because you were trying to protect me?" he said, astonished, amused and infuriated at the same time. "You darling idiot! I'm a Rohan. We thrive on scandal. We wouldn't have it any other way."

She backed away from him, coming up against a cupboard. "But I'm . . . I'm barren. I know I can't have children."

He felt only the tiniest hint of pain and dismissed it. "I'm sorry for that, but more for you than for me. My sister is busy populating the Lake District and Benedick is trying to catch up. We'll have enough little Rohans around to destroy the world, should they take it in their minds to do so."

"Brandon, think about what you're suggesting," she pleaded but he was done, crossing the last few inches between them and pulling her into his arms.

"I've had five endless weeks to think about it, you cruel woman, and if you ever run away like that again I'm going to beat you severely."

She looked up into his eyes, his beautiful wounded bird, no longer broken, no longer lost, and the wry quirk of her mouth told him just how seriously she took his ridiculous threat.

"And I'm not suggesting anything," he continued. "I'm telling you. You're marrying me and I'll build you a hospital wherever you damned well please. I'll go where you want to go, I'll do. . ."

"Um . . ." she said, breaking into his declaration of adoration with her usual practicality. "I've already made arrangements in Inverness. I'll go there twice a week for surgery and look after the local people the rest of the time. That is, if . . ."

He kissed her then, long and deep, cradling her head with his hands to keep her still, tasting, sucking, biting as she sank against him, and he felt the fight leave her body, leaving nothing but welcome.

Tammas had no sense of propriety and began leaping around them, making encouraging noises, but Brandon didn't let it distract him. He had no intention of stopping until he . . . he had no intention of stopping, ever. He'd kiss her in the kitchen, reach beneath her skirts and lift her up onto the work surface behind her, unfasten his breeches. . .

"I beg your pardon, Mr. Rohan," came Ellis's precise voice, and Brandon lifted his head to growl at the man, while Tammas did the same in an act of solidarity with his oddly-behaving master, but Emma reached up, grabbed his long hair in her fist, and yanked him back to her mouth, and he wondered what Ellis might do if his new employer came in his breeches.

"Go away, Ellis," he muttered when they both took a breath. "Or I'll fire you."

But Ellis wasn't going anywhere, curse the man. "I'm afraid I have a confession to make, Mr. Rohan. I have been working here under false pretenses. I am still attached to your sister's household—Lady Rochdale simply sent me here to ensure that everything was ready, but I do have the perfect candidate in mind for your permanent majordomo."

Brandon dropped his head down to claim Emma's mouth once more, but she put a hand against his lips, forestalling him. He ran his tongue over her fingers and began to suck one, well out of Ellis's sight, and her eyelids half closed in reaction.

"What do you mean, 'everything was ready'? Ready for what?" Her breathless voice held deep suspicion.

"Lady Rochdale and her family should be arriving in the next day or two, the Viscount and his wife a few days later, accompanied by his lordship's parents. I believe your father will be bringing a special license with him."

Emma appeared dumbfounded, a rare occurrence for his beautiful bride. "No," she said. "That is . . . I didn't say yes . . . I still think we should. . ."

Brandon took care of her protests in the most efficient way possible, and when she was too breathless to speak he glanced at Ellis. "Well, for the time being you're my butler, and you will leave and see that no one disturbs us for the next hour."

"Hour?" Emma said, sounding alarmed.

"Make that two." He focused all his attention on Emma. "And take the damned dog."

When they were finally alone he turned back to her, and she was wiping tears from her cheeks. "Damn these things," she muttered. "I only started crying five weeks ago and now I can't seem to stop."

"That's all right, Harpy," he murmured. "I'll always be here to dry them. Accept it—there's no way you can win against the assembled might of the Wicked Rohans. You'll marry me and live happily ever after."

"No one ever does," she said.

"You will," he said firmly. "I promise you."

EPILOGUE

The marriage ceremony was a wild affair, given that it was the Wild and Wicked Rohans. The special license proved entirely unnecessary with Scotland's appropriately random marriage laws, and Emma Rose Magdalene Cadbury and Brandon George Rohan were joined in holy matrimony by no other than a lapsed Catholic by the name of Noonan.

The bride continued her medical calling, despite her faulty diagnosis of her own fertility, and over time she presented her doting husband with four pledges of her affection.

And then, true to her husband's words, they lived happily ever after.

ABOUT THE AUTHOR

Anne Stuart has been writing since the Dawn of Time. She's been published by every major publisher, and made the *NYT, USA Today,* and *Publisher's Weekly* Bestseller lists. She's won numerous awards, including four RITAs, as well as RWA's Lifetime Achievement Award, and she's known for her dark heroes, black humor and hot sex.

Follow her on her website at Anne-Stuart.com and on the following social media sites:

Facebook: author.annestuart
Twitter: TheAnneStuart
Instagram: Annestuartwriter

DON'T LOOK BACK—THE MAGGIE BENNETT BOOKS

Escape Out of Darkness

Darkness before Dawn

At the Edge of the Sun

HISTORICAL ROMANCES

The Devil's Waltz

Hidden Honor

Lady Fortune

Prince of Magic

Lord of Danger

Prince of Swords

To Love a Dark Lord

Shadow Dance

A Rose at Midnight

The Houseparty

The Demon Count Novels

The Spinster and the Rake

Lord Satan's Bride

Angels Wings

Demonwood

Cameron's Landing

Barrett's Hill

WOMEN'S FICTION

When the Stars Fall Down

ROMANTiC SUSPENSE

Into the Fire

The Widow

Silver Falls

Still Lake

Shadows at Sunset

Shadow Lover

Ritual Sins

Moonrise

Nightfall

Now You See Him

Special Gifts

Break the Night

The Fall of Maggie Brown

Winter's Edge

Hand in Glove

Tangled Lies

The Catspaw Collection

Against the Wind

SUSPENSE

Seen and Not Heard

ANNE STUART'S GREATEST HITS

Cinderman

The Soldier, the Nun and the Baby

One More Valentine

Blue Sage

Night of the Phantom

CONTEMPORARY ROMANCE

The Right Man

A Dark and Stormy Night

Wild Thing

Rafe's Revenge

Heat Lightning

Chasing Trouble -

Lazarus Rising

Rancho Diablo

Crazy Like a Fox

Glass Houses

Cry for the Moon

Partners in Crime

Bewitching Hour

Rocky Road

Museum Piece

Heart's Ease

Chain of Love

Against the Wind

COLLABORATIONS

Dogs & Goddesses – with Jennifer Crusie and Lani Diane Rich

The Unfortunate Miss Fortunes with Jennifer Crusie and Lani Diane Rich

NOVELLAS

Blind Date from Hell

Night and Day

A Midnight Clear

Burning Bright

Dark Journey

Date with the Devil

MANGA

A Dark and Stormy Night
Night